DUSK AND EMBERS
BOOK 2

VISIONS OF FURY

K. V. MEADOWS

Content Warnings:

- Anxiety and anxiety attacks, PTSD, unmanaged mental illness, dissociation, suicidal ideation, mild self-harm (brief mention)
- Chronic pain and illness, seizures
- Disability prejudice, classicism, body shaming, misogyny, and sexism
- Domestic violence and implication of nonconsensual sex
- "Cult" trauma
- Violence
- Death and grief
- Fire and burns
- Profanity
- Vomit
- Blood, very mild gore
- Explicit sexual and sensual content
  - *Spice rack*: chapters 23, 42, and 59

Disclaimer

The signed language depicted in this book matches the grammatical rules of spoken English to make the dialogue more seamless to read. The language itself is specific to this fantasy world and is not intended to match a signed language in our world. I intend no offense or thoughtlessness through my portrayal. Durvla's story is uniquely hers and is not intended to represent the entire population of d/Deaf/HOH individuals.

For those whose power has been diminished by others:
it's time to reclaim it.

Erleya

Uldarvik

Moicriach

Diadun

Glinrew

Dubh Carrig

Barr na

Chapter 1

CARYS

WATER RUSHES from my lungs and sears up my throat like liquid fire. I retch onto the banks of the loch, ragged breaths following each bout of heaving as I fight to replace the water with air. Around me is an inferno, massive flames scorching the grass, the land, the bushes all around. Thick smoke fills the air, stinging my eyes and doing nothing to calm my respirations.

I'm on my hands and knees, my nails digging into the cracked soil beneath me as flames ripple through my hands. The heat in my body is unbearable, overwhelming my senses, scorching me from the inside out. Screams tear from my throat, and as much as I want to silence my cries, they come with the force of a tempest.

These flames are going to consume me.

"Please ..." I sob into the solemn night. My chest heaves with each intake of breath, forceful coughs following as my turbulent body fights to expel the smoke. Tremors rack my frame as I sit back on my heels and wrap my arms around my naked torso. My clothes ... Burned off, I suppose, somewhere between crawling out of the freezing cold depths of the loch and somehow setting the area on fire.

I stumble to my feet, intending to make my way back to the water. To hopefully sink like a rock and quell these ceaseless flames forever. As I turn, a voice calls to me.

"Princess?"

I whirl on my heel and a new wave of flames billows from my hands. A wiry man in flowing midnight blue robes stands before me. He lifts his hands, and a large onyx stone glints on one of his fingers. "I've been sent by Priestess Briony. Let me help you."

I step backward. He's out of his mind if he thinks I'll trust anyone. Not after Angharad, the guard who was supposedly helping me escape, shoved me off the fucking cliff in the first place.

"Princess, we don't have much time. The Zenith will be looking for you."

Images flash before my eyes. My advisor, Iywan, forcing me to translate the prophecy from the Ancient Tongue, the Skinchanger slicing into my flesh. Pain. So much pain.

So much bloody fear.

Ellynne, dead. Callum, dead.

Sobs overtake me, and in another blink, the wiry man stands before me. "There are limits to this magic," he says, holding up his hand with the ring. "We can only vanish away so much and so far. I swear on my own life and all the gods that I will get you to safety." He removes one layer of his robes and extends it to me. I take in his pale skin, fine lines at the corners of his thin lips, his eyes, and across his forehead. His somber brown eyes regard me with a certain patience. "Please," he says. "A lot of people are depending on your survival."

Who could possibly need me? What can I offer but destruction with this curse I bear?

But I take the robe in tremulous hands and slip my arms into the silken material. My legs buckle as the last of my strength begins to wane, the adrenaline abandoning me. I stare at my hands, turning my palms over. My usually pale skin is flushed bright red.

"Princess, we must go." The man's voice is laced with panic. He holds out his bony hand, and after brief hesitation, I slip mine into it.

The world around me disappears with an unsettling tug of my body. I'm in what feels like a freefall, weightless, my stomach left behind. When everything settles again, my head is spinning. My stomach has nothing left to give, but I hunch over and heave. It's as though my body is determined to expel my very soul.

The man gives me a few seconds, then wraps an arm around my shoulders and practically drags me toward a horse and carriage, the driver with the reins already in their hands. "In you go," he says.

My legs refuse to cooperate, yet somehow the fragile-looking man manages to haul me into the wagon where I slump down on the hard bench. I consider asking questions, but my head grows lighter, and I'm dragged into the merciful arms of oblivion.

There's nothing but darkness. Darkness, pain, despair, confusion ... So much confusion. I cannot wrap my mind around anything that's happening. My body feels wrapped in the heaviest of iron chains—my skin too tight, my bones too heavy.

Gods, everything feels so wrong. Like my head has been separated from my body. Nothing wants to function.

I force my eyes open and my vision swirls around me. No matter how forcibly I blink, my surroundings remain cloudy, like peering out from beneath water. My skin feels like it's on fire. I groan loudly.

"Briony, she's awake!" Angharad. "Your Highness?"

I squeeze my eyes shut and everything beneath me rocks again. I try to ask what's happening, but my lips don't part, and no words come out. My body doesn't obey me when I try to lift my hand, to wiggle my toes. Panic seizes my lungs.

"Why isn't she moving?" Angharad asks.

"Burnout. It's a wonder she's even alive," Briony says.

I wish I wasn't.

"Even an experienced Wielder would barely be able to handle such energy expenditure. Imagine an inexperienced Wielder who's had her powers dampened for over a decade." Briony's hand rests on my forehead, and a cool sensation trickles from my head, down to my chest, my legs, my toes. A comfortable warmth follows, flooding my body until blissful sleep submerges me again.

"Carys, can you hear me?"

"Hmm ..." I stir. My body feels as though it's been bashed into a wall hundreds of times. My eyelids must weigh a ton, but I manage to peel them open and blink. Slowly, my vision clears, and I see the outline of a narrow face and thin shoulders.

"Blink twice if you can hear me."

I can do that. I blink once. Twice.

"Good, good. Try to rest. Everything is alright."

I highly doubt that. I don't know where I am. Everyone I've loved is gone. I burned half the sentries in the castle. I burned the entire small council. The royal advisor. The land beneath the plateau of Paramount.

How is *anything* alright? How will anything ever *feel* alright? I lift my hand to my throbbing head and Briony places hers at my temple. A mixture of warmth and coolness wipes the ache away. With a few more blinks, I can see her sandy brown hair over her shoulders, her flowy grey dress, and her icy blue eyes wrought with concern.

"Where am I?" I mumble. My throat aches, my voice unrecognizable.

"Shh ..."

A brawny arm slips beneath my shoulder blades and inclines me so that I'm semi-upright. I glance to my right and into Angharad's mismatched eyes—one cloudy and scarred, one earnest brown. The large woman offers me a crooked smile and a metal ale mug. My arms refuse to cooperate with me, but Angharad holds the cup to my lips. I scowl at her. *You shoved me off a fucking cliff*, I want to say. But I restrain myself. Clearly, they're on my side.

"Try to drink slowly," says Briony.

The first sip feels even worse than my dry throat, but the liquid soothes the ache, leaving it bearable. Angharad lowers me again to a surface far from comfortable. The small room is all wood with a low ceiling. There are crates and barrels all around, and not much else save for this sorry excuse for a bed.

"We're sailing to Uldarvik," Briony says.

My brain is numb, and as much as I want to make a comment about Uldarvik, all I can think to ask is, "Who's ship are we on?"

"My brother's," says Angharad. "He's a scoundrel with a heart of gold. No loyalties to the Crown, nor to any particular cause, but he loves his family, and he wouldn't do anything to bring harm to me or my friends. We can trust him."

No loyalties to the Crown ... good enough. "How long have I been out of it?"

"Three days," they say at the same time.

My chest hurts from the deep breath I slowly pull into my weary lungs. "How much longer until ...?"

"If the gods are kind, four more days." Angharad tries to make this seem comforting, but she's a terrible liar; the smile on her face is nothing short of a grimace. And, clearly, the gods hate me. I have a bone to pick with bloody Agryna—she can take back her powers. Hells, she can take Enidwen's spirit while she's at it.

I sigh and nod before closing my eyes. "I'm tired."

"Princess," says Briony. "You should try to sip some broth. You expended a lot more energy than your body could handle. You need replenishment. Then you can get some more rest."

If I open my mouth to respond, I'll say I don't want replenishment. I never want to use those powers willingly or unwillingly again. By the gods, I never want to do or see much of anything ever again. What's the point?

But rather than voice what I know would be a shocking thought, I just nod.

Four days.

Four days to pull myself together.

Chapter 2

CARYS

THE SNOWY MOUNTAINS of Uldarvik loom ahead as the loud blast of a horn emanates from the shore. Gooseflesh breaks out along my arms as I take in the dozens of Uldaran warriors, armed and ready for battle. It's been one week since we set sail from Erleya. Since I was dragged, unconscious, from the only place I've ever known.

As we draw closer, my eyes lock on a warrior towering above the rest. His large hands are wrapped around the worn handle of a battle-axe, his broad chest puffed out.

"Princess, just give me the command ..." says the large soldier woman beside me.

I keep my gaze affixed to the warrior prince. "Very brave, Angharad, but if they attack, we're fucked."

She huffs out a nervous laugh as Briony comes to stand beside her.

Ashore, Odgar lowers his weapon, and the others follow suit. I release a breath, but a haze creeps into my awareness. I'm not sure how long it is before we disembark, but sapphire eyes with a sunburst of golden brown steadily regard me. A familiar man just shy of Odgar's height stands beside him. His name escapes me.

Dark ink peeks out from Odgar's trimmed beard and his sun-kissed curls are pulled back into four braids. The sides of his scalp are bare and proudly displaying numerous other tattoos. I resist the urge to press my hand to my face, to obscure my blemishes. My bruises are gone, but there are scars that Briony couldn't fully banish from my skin.

"Princess Carys," Odgar says in his deep, rumbling voice. "What a pleasant surprise." He gestures to the man beside him. "You remember Seth."

Seth bows. "Lovely to see you again, Your Highness."

"Likewise. And thank you," I say to both men. It's nearly summer solstice, yet patches of snow still cover the land behind Odgar. Many of the Uldarans gawk at me with varying expressions.

"Unfortunately, I have to take you to my brother," comes Odgar's voice again, cutting through the recurring mind fog. I pull my attention back to him. "But do not worry; he is a fair and just king."

I nod, schooling my features into courageous certainty, but the word *king* ricochets in the echo chamber of my mind. It sends my thoughts tumbling back to the Fortress on the Mount, to my father —the king—then my mother ... both gone when I still needed them ...

There's a subtle weight on my shoulder, and Briony's saccharine voice floods my senses. "Princess Carys." She sounds so far away as my hazy mind refocuses on the situation at hand. Icy blue eyes peer up at me with concern. "Are you alright?" she asks.

I shrug her hand from my shoulder, and the movement sends a ripple of pain through my still-healing body.

"Prince Odgar has given Angharad and the crew permission to replenish here before setting off again. She wishes you good fortune."

I turn my attention to Odgar who holds the reins of a dark grey horse. I don't recall him leaving at any point, but Angharad and Seth are nowhere in sight, and the worry etched between Briony's eyebrows is achingly familiar. She gives me an encouraging smile and turns to approach a sable horse beside the one whose reins Odgar holds. I blink away the grogginess and the frustration.

"Are you alright riding with me?" Odgar asks. "This strong fellow can handle us." He pats the horse's flank and is rewarded with a pleasant whinny.

I take a step toward the steed, but my legs are so unstable with disuse that I might as well be teetering on a narrow rampart. My stomach lurches as though I've toppled over an edge. I halt, standing still as the cold sensation of falling into icy water envelops me again.

Water in my lungs.

Fire all around me.

"Carys."

Odgar's deep voice tugs me from my reeling memories. My chest feels overstretched, my lungs reluctant to draw a full breath.

"You're safe," he tells me.

I clear my throat and lift my chin. "I'm in a new land. How can I be so sure?"

He arches a brow. "That is a very fair question, but you are with me. No harm will come to you." He steps aside. "Do you need help getting into the saddle? I'll sit behind you."

I swallow hard and nod.

Everything is a blur, as if we're riding through time—yet it feels simultaneously sluggish. My mind battles with the past and present as I fight to focus on my surroundings. There are mountains all around us and a fjord in the distance, the sun sparkling on the surface.

"Carys?" Odgar says my name in a way that hints it isn't the first time he's called me.

I don't glance back at him but stare ahead at the snow-specked dirt path instead. "Yes?"

"Is there anything I need to know before you meet the king?"

Everything within me tenses. Where do I even start? I suppress my torture-riddled memories and start with what's most important for him to know. "My mother, the queen, is dead. By now, the people of Erleya probably think I'm dead. I'm not sure what Lord Commander Rheon will tell them, but he intended to use me, not just to take over the throne but—" I pause to swallow. "In any case, all I know is that I don't have a place to go, nor a title anymore."

There's only the background noise of the villagers around us and the crunch of the layer of snow beneath the horse's hooves. After a while, Odgar says, "I'm sorry about your mother."

I wet my lips and stare straight ahead.

"In Uldarvik, the throne can be *won*—challenged, if you will. It's an entire ritualistic combat that most wouldn't dare to attempt, but you have nothing like that in Erleya, right?"

Numbly, I shake my head.

"So, the throne is rightfully yours no matter who sits on it now."

"I wish it were that easy."

He's quiet for a while longer, then he says, "Did you ever choose a suitor?"

A mixture of regret and anxiety settles deep in my chest. I try to make sense of the feelings, but my mind is a never-ending rope, all knotted up, and with no decipherable beginning. Nothing makes sense anymore. "Yes," I respond quietly. "I chose you."

If I'm not mistaken, he sighs with relief. I refrain from looking at Briony as she continues to ride silently beside us.

"Unfortunately, Iywan declined and insisted that I marry Rheon." A shudder rolls through me at the thought of being wed to a man who once publicly flogged dozens of people for the sake of *setting an example* to the masses.

"Did you end up marrying him or—"

"No, thank Rhianu. I fled before he could get his hands on me." It's a small lie by omission, but I can't bring myself to tell Odgar about the torture that came before. Not right now. Not when I need to keep my brave face on to meet the king.

"Alright, *revna*, what do I *need* to know?" Odgar asks.

My heart struggles against my ribs, fluttering wildly like a flag in a windstorm. I draw in a breath and swipe at the tear that slips down my cheek.

I try to think of where to start the narrative. Uncomfortable heat pulses in me, rushing down my arms and into the palms of my hands. I lift them from the saddle and ball them into fists, but the tiny flames are still evident. Fuck. Of course this would happen right now.

Odgar murmurs something in Uldaran and pulls the horse to a halt. Beside us, Briony does the same. Odgar's hands wrap around my fists and I start to tug away, but a cool sensation fills my palms. I stare down at his hand covering my fist—my skin is wraithlike against the coppery undertone of his light brown complexion. The tiniest ringlet of steam rises from our hands.

My eyes flare wide. "How did—?"

He releases his grip, water droplets dancing along his fingertips for a moment before he grabs the horse's reins again.

"Waterweaving," I whisper. I glance over my shoulder at him but can't crane my neck enough to see the expression on his face. "Is magic not outlawed in Uldarvik?"

"Outlawed, no. It's considered a rare gift from the gods."

I scoff. That's not quite how I'd describe my flamewielding.

Odgar nudges the horse into a walk, prompting Briony to do the same. She looks as surprised as I feel about Odgar's magic, but Briony is a woman of very few words most of the time.

"Do you trust me a little more now?" he asks, his tone gentle.

"No," I say.

The soft rumble of his laughter fills my ears. "We're almost at the castle. Tell me what you can about your situation."

I release a breath. "Iywan was part of a group called the Zenith. They want to tear open the Veil to the Otherworld ... Or, I'd say, technically the Underworld?"

"Why the fuck would they want to do that?"

"Ultimate power for Erleya." I can't bring myself to tell him about my connection to Enidwen. "They wanted to use me for it because my royal blood could sort of control whatever entity surfaces. That was their belief, at least. It's bullshit, if you ask me."

"I agree," says Odgar.

"But they were adamant. They insisted that I help them decode the prophecy—as it's in a language that I apparently can read. Don't ask. But refusing to help them cost me one of my most trusted guards." My voice catches. I'm unable to say Callum's name aloud. The memory of his face as he confessed his love to me triggers the sensation of Eefa slashing me with her dagger. My hand shakily goes to my face.

"Who did that to you?" Odgar asks quietly, one hand resting on mine atop the saddle.

"It doesn't matter. She's dead now. They all are."

"Well, she's left you with a mark of survival."

A scoff slips past my lips.

Our surroundings have changed by now as our horses follow the winding pathway that leads up to a stately building. It spans across the land, the exterior made of coarse, irregular stones, a tower on one side providing the only *height* in the otherwise flat architecture. "Is this your castle?" I ask Odgar.

"Yes, but believe it or not, my sister and I don't live here. We live in the Great Hall closer to the main village. It's a smaller castle, if you will."

How strange.

We continue toward the castle and Odgar makes a sound as if he intends to say something but stops. He tries again. "The Zenith ... I know they have this ridiculous plan, but what about your forces? Your guards? Army?"

My stomach twists. "Rheon isn't just the leader of the Zenith, he's the Lord Commander of the entire Royal Brigade. My guess is that he's taken the crown for himself."

"Well fuck," Odgar says quietly. "So, a ruthless sadist with delusions of opening a rift to another realm sits on the Erleyan throne."

"Yes, and I'm certain they all think I'm dead."

"Do you want to explain that or—"

"No."

I feel rather than hear his sigh. "Alright so ..." He pauses long enough that I almost prod him to speak again. "My brother will ask you this, forgive me. But what do you have to offer to Uldarvik with an alliance?"

I stare down at my hands again and then at his on the horse's reins. Briony is no longer staring straight ahead, but looking my way, curiosity on her face. "You said in Uldarvik, magic is considered a blessing from the gods, right?"

"Correct."

"So, if I'm blessed by the gods, I'd say that's fucking impressive enough to warrant an alliance. *Two* royals blessed by the gods?"

Odgar laughs, pulling the horse to a halt. We're close to the massive black door of the castle, a guard posted on each side. He dismounts and stands below me, peering up with a brilliant smile on his face. "I'm inclined to agree. *Now* you're thinking like a survivor."

Beside him, Briony dismounts. She looks at the castle, her hands folded demurely in front of her as Odgar helps me down from the horse. He offers me the crook of his arm, and I hesitantly link my elbow with his. "Let's go convince the king to let us be wed, then," he says.

Guilt churns in my gut, but I can't bring myself to tell him the full truth of everything. Not now. Not when it may very well scare him away, and not when simply talking about it may break me.

Guards open the castle doors for us to make our way inside. None of them are in uniform, but they're dressed similarly in black and grey with leather armor and furs.

Our boots echo on the tiled floors as we walk toward the throne where a slim man sits. A crown rests atop King Freyr's wavy blond hair, which falls to his lean shoulders. He casts a blue gaze down at us as Odgar announces our presence.

"Your Majesty, presenting Princess Carys Meredyth fa Rhodri, rightful heir to the throne and queen by succession of the Kingdom of Erleya. With her is High Priestess Briony."

Impressive introduction, but I've arrived with no crown, nor coin, nor worthy possessions. With a scarred body and bruised soul, my hair in shambles and a shadow of its former glory. I curtsy weakly and it feels absolutely unnatural. "Your Majesty," I say, lifting my chin a fraction and pushing back my shoulders. My body protests but I resist flinching. "My gratitude for the warm welcome to your beautiful land."

King Freyr raises a brow. "How odd," he says. "We just received word of your death, Princess Carys." His voice is not quite as deep as Odgar's, but it booms across the large space, nevertheless.

Even with my chin still lifted, my heart falters. "I—" My words run away. It's like I've forgotten how to speak. I clasp my hands before me, praying that no flames erupt. "I—" *Godsdammit, Carys.* I draw in a breath, but pressure quickly builds in my chest. I resist the urge to squeeze my eyes shut—to turn and run and never stop.

"As you can see, brother, she's very much alive." Odgar's voice is tight as he speaks.

"And you are certain this is the true heir of Erleya."

"Seeing as I danced with her at the Feast, yes." I stare at him wide-eyed; isn't he pushing it with the way he addresses the bloody *king* of his land? "I would like to ask for Princess Carys's hand in marriage." His voice is unwavering and wrought with certainty.

I turn my gaze back to King Freyr and his eyes meet mine. "You have been usurped. What do you possibly have to offer Uldarvik by way of marriage?"

I swallow thickly. "The Erleyan throne is rightfully mine, Your Majesty. My ancestors have worn the crown for centuries. My father's bloodline is descended from the sun goddess Agryna."

Holding out my hand, I focus, willing a tiny blaze to my palm. Instead, a massive flame ignites, sending Odgar, Briony, and a couple of the guards scattering to get away from the heat. I quickly clench my fists, but not before tiny embers jump from the flame and land on the carpet.

It doesn't ignite, however, and I notice Odgar's hand at his side flick subtly.

Thank you, I think.

"Someone else may sit on the throne presently, but it belongs to me, and with the help of Uldarvik, I can take it back."

The king is now sitting at the very edge of the throne, his face alight with anticipation. "You control fire," he says, ignoring all else.

Control … that's one way to put it. "Yes," I say.

"What are the odds?" He glances at Odgar.

"The flame to my water," Odgar says with a smirk.

If I'm not mistaken, the king returns his smirk. "You've made quite a journey, Princess Carys. Make yourself at home. Sumarvegr is upon us in a month's time. A marriage before that will not be accepted by the kingdom. I advise that you both court each other, according to our traditions, make the journey to the Hallowed Wood, and upon your return—provided that Princess Carys acclimates to our ways and is accepted by our people—we'll have a grand wedding immediately."

Odgar turns to me, waiting as if silently asking me for my thoughts.

"A *month*?" I ask, my voice shaky. My heart clenches. So much can happen in a month. Erleya could be destroyed. "Your Majesty—"

"Get some rest, Princess Carys," Freyr says coolly. "And Odgar, make sure that the princess is settled in and made comfortable at the Hall."

It's a clear dismissal, and who am I to argue when I have nothing? So, I put on a smile and exude as much gratitude as I can. With another curtsy that strips away what little pride I have left, I say, "Thank you, King Freyr. I will not disappoint you."

It's a promise I cannot possibly keep.

Chapter 3

THE VISIONS BEGAN as the cold grasp of death ensnared me. My splintered soul feebly cleaved itself from my listless, broken body. It fought my willpower, desperate to make its way to whatever lay beyond this realm, while my lifeblood pooled and congealed beneath me. While my body grew cold, violent tremors thundered in my bones.

I was as good as dead.

Until I wasn't.

It's been a year since that moment, and even now, I cannot get it out of my mind. It doesn't help that each night, pain comes flooding back into my body like clockwork if I don't take my elixir. Painting steadies my wayward mind; it gives me something other than the distress of this magical curse to focus on. Since my arranged marriage, however, these moments of peace have become rare.

With the paintbrush firmly clenched between my teeth, I admire the passionate red, gentle pink, energetic yellow, and sharp white on my canvas. A likeness to the sunset. Paint streaks my hands and the front of the apron I borrowed from the servants' wardrobe. I've had to stop myself from fidgeting with my hair or touching my face far too many times. The painting is one I can certainly be proud of, but it doesn't do the sunset justice. Brush in hand again, I dip the bristles into the black paint to begin working on the silhouette of a tree.

The door flies open with a *whoosh* and Gruffud barges in like a cyclone. It startles me so badly that I jab the brush against the canvas and bite back an expletive. My hands shoot out to steady the tipping easel.

The tall and slender man whose sleek, dark hair compliments his flawless tan complexion gapes at me. Grey eyes flecked with brown shift from the canvas to my face. "Your father has been injured," he says in his curt tenor.

My pulse scampers as I jump to my feet, dropping my paint-brush on the small tray table and closing the leather case that holds my paints.

"Your mother and sister await you outside."

I scrub my hands as best as I can on a damp linen cloth before shoving my gold bracelets onto my wrists and tearing my apron off. Flinging the apron onto my stool, I rush around my room and extinguish all the oil lamps. As my husband stands aside to let me through the door, I mutter a word of thanks. Shadows waver in the light of the sconces against the corridor walls, and my heels clack on the varnished dark wood floors. I hike up my skirt, careful not to trip as I take the lengthy, winding staircase to the ground floor.

The sun has long since departed, and I'm fairly certain that the ninth bell has tolled, but I've been so absorbed in my painting that I forgot to take my elixir.

Arionna is waiting at the door in a dazzling green dress fit for a ball. I make my way across the soft carpet of the sitting room, past indigo velvet chairs, and beneath a lyre-shaped chandelier with gilded bronze arms and glass prisms reflecting the candlelight. As I draw closer to my sister, I take in her full lips, painted mauve. Kohl subtly lines her dark eyes, giving them an even more sultry appearance than usual. The rouge on her cheeks brings out the reddish undertone in her sepia complexion—as if she needed any augmentation to her beauty.

"*Must* you take an eternity?" she snaps at me. Arionna is nearly a year widowed, and it's made her an odd combination of bitter and petty.

"Nice to see you too," I mumble. I'd hoped that moving out of my childhood home a few months ago, when I was married off to Gruffud, would've strengthened our relationship, but it seems to have only made things worse. Our family is renowned for owning the most successful book bindery and book trade in Erleya, so we're already held to a high standard. Having a father who is a revered Queen's Guard had only increased the number of eyes on our family. Naturally, Arionna gave in to the pressures of being the older daughter of Lord Eurig Davies, choosing to keep up appearances rather than be my confidante. She began reporting all my *misdeeds* to Mother, only exacerbating Mother's hostility for her younger wayward daughter.

After the tragic end to Arionna's marriage, I naturally became the next tribute, so to speak, through my marriage to Gruffud Pendry. For decades, the Pendrys have dominated the clock-making world, bringing customers from near and far, spearheading various trades, and burgeoning quite an eclectic collection. My arranged nuptials to Gruffud was to join our two eminent households—to secure power and influence that most would only dream of.

Except I was never one to dream of power. I only desire freedom.

Arionna's gaze snags on something over my shoulder, and I turn to find Gruffud standing against the sage green wall, between paintings in golden frames that match the details in the crown molding. His arms are folded tightly across his chest, his expression unreadable.

"Be safe," he says, clearly disinterested. He pushes himself off the wall and turns to walk away. I stifle a sigh and follow Arionna out of the grand house.

Summer will soon be upon us, but the cool air leaves me wishing I'd thrown on a cloak. The paved walkway is bracketed by manicured hedges and rose bushes. At the end, a carriage pulled by a beautiful horse with irregular brown and white patches and feathered heels awaits us. The footman holds his hand out and Arionna takes it to climb into the carriage. It's ridiculously graceful compared to the way I clutch the footman's hand and hoist my shorter body into the enclosure.

Dignified as always, my mother, Rhosyn, sits on the opposite bench to where I settle next to Arionna. Her caramel-colored eyes take in my appearance, and I self-consciously run my fingers through the indecisive waves and large spirals of hair resting against my shoulders.

"Good evening, Mother." I conjure a wavering smile, hoping it makes it to my eyes.

"You have paint on your face," she responds. Her words are impeccably enunciated, her tone flat.

Arionna shoves a handkerchief into my hand as I hide a wince. I grunt my thanks before wetting the tip of it with my tongue and aimlessly rubbing it over my face. Chewing on my lower lip, I dare to meet Mother's hard gaze again. She shrugs.

We are drastically different people, but looking at her is like looking into a mirror. We have the same ash brown hair and rich brown complexion. Her fuller upper lip protrudes in a way that gives her a perpetual near-pout—an inherited trait that has led me to receive many unwarranted *are you alright* inquiries. But while she is lithe, I am short with muscle definition that she constantly reminds me is too manly and requires covering up to protect the fragile male ego. I should be used to it, as there was never a moment in my life when she wasn't criticizing *something* about the core of my being.

I was too wild and free-spirited, too outspoken, too cheerful. I very quickly learned to shrink myself down into what I was expected to be as Rhosyn and Eurig's daughter—composed, quiet, and without an opinion of my own. I've bitten my tongue so many times that it's a wonder I can even speak at this point.

The carriage jostles us as it rushes over the cobblestones of the street, making my bones and joints ache. I hold on to my seat as we race through city roads illuminated by oil lampposts, toward Paramount. Across from me, my mother's face is stony as always, but she worries at her lower lip, her hands opening and closing in her lap as if she's trying to keep ahold of her façade.

"Mother," I say quietly.

My sister's dark eyes flick sidelong to me. She's a combination of our parents; her lighter complexion is closer to Father's, and her pitch-black hair is as tightly coiled as Mother's. Unlike either of our parents, however, Arionna's body is abundant with curves, and oh, how she loves to flaunt them with formfitting gowns and plunging necklines.

"How badly injured is Father? What happened?" Arionna asks.

At least I'm not the only ignorant one. I press my hand over the pocket of my dress, feeling the familiar shape of the pocket watch that Father once gifted me.

Mother levels us with a look, and we both shrink back slightly. "There was a colossal fire at Paramount last night. As far as I'm told, the Fortress on the Mount still stands, but ..." Her voice grows hollow and then fades completely.

"But?" Arionna prods.

Mother looks through the hazy window of the carriage, at the dark storefronts and few pedestrians. After hours in Barr na Cahar is my favorite time. Everyone around here retires to their homes early, save for those looking for trouble.

Or for a ticket to a different life.

"Most of those affected by the fire suffered fatal wounds," Mother says. She aims her words at the window, and shivers travel down my spine.

Fatal.

My mouth goes dry, my heart lurching. I lick my lips, trying to think of something to say. No words come.

The ride seems to last far longer than it should, but the closer we get to Paramount the more soldiers we see. Some are in brown livery and others in charcoal. Nagging aches thrum through my body, reminding me of my stupid lapse in memory. I should've paused to take the damn elixir. I stare at my hands, still stained, though faint, with a multitude of colors. I clench my fists and hide them in the skirts of my dress. Eventually, the carriage rolls alongside a loch toward the imposing iron gates that lead to the barracks and the brig below the plateau.

As we stop, there's a confrontation outside the carriage between our footman and a couple of soldiers. My mother pushes the carriage door open and steps out, shutting the door behind her as more muffled quarrels ensue. I rub my palm over the cool window, clearing the condensation, then press my forehead firmly against it. Mother faces two soldiers who look down at her, their postures rigid.

"What are they saying?" Arionna whispers.

"I don't know, Arionna. I can't read lips." I try to keep the frustration out of my voice; it's not her fault we don't know what's going on. I push the door open ever so slightly, allowing more sound to flood in, along with the acrid odor of smoke clinging to the air.

"We received an official summons to visit Sir Eurig of Barr na Cahar," Mother is saying. Her voice is steady, but from the way she's clasping her hands, she's certainly not calm.

"No one is permitted beyond the boundaries, Madam," a soldier responds.

"But it was an *official* summons." She rummages within her cloak, looking for said summons, but the soldier holds up a large hand.

"*Our* official orders are that no one goes beyond this gate." He gestures to the large gate of beautiful iron work, the royal insignia—a crown turned on its side, the sun eclipsing it—clear within the geometric design. "Turn back or I'll have to respond with force." The heart-dropping click of his crossbow resounds as he snaps the weapon into place.

I gasp. Could my magic steer the bolt away fast enough if the soldier acts on his threat? With haste, I push the carriage door open more. "Mother, we should go," I say, my voice quiet as to not make a bigger scene, yet firm enough that she hopefully gets the clue.

Mother's withering gaze snaps to me, but right now is not the time for stubbornness.

"We can try again tomorrow," I offer.

Turning back toward the soldier, Mother says, "Please, if you can get word to Eurig. Tell him that his wife and daughters came to visit." She unclasps a necklace, her locket, and holds it out to the soldier. "He gave me this as a lucky charm years ago. He needs it more than I do now." To my surprise, the soldier takes the necklace, looking at it before pocketing it. "May I write to him?" Mother's voice wavers, vulnerable in a way I don't ever remember hearing it.

"You may."

She nods firmly, then gathers her skirts. I sit back as our footman opens the door and offers a hand to help her climb in.

Suffocating silence fills the space as the carriage begins taking us back home. It isn't until we're on the cobblestoned streets of the city that Mother speaks up again, her voice like the crack of a whip. "You had no right to address me like that."

I blink. "The man was going to shoot you."

"He wouldn't have. I am highborn. Your father is a knighted Queen's Guard."

"That soldier was going to shoot you. In cold blood," I add. "He doesn't give a damn about your birthright." Beside me, Arionna's eyes widen, but ire fuels Mother's glower.

"I will pardon you tonight because I am certain you worry for your father. But don't ever speak to me that way again. Do you understand?"

"Yes, Mother."

The wagon creaks as it rocks with nauseating irregularity, the rumble of the wheels over the road filling the silence.

By the time the wagon pulls up in front of the Pendry manor, my eyes are stinging, and I'm sick with worry. What could've caused such a conflagration at Paramount last night? Why are there so many soldiers about? My mind goes to words I heard last year when I was shamefully a willing member of the Purists, a group with many contradictory ideologies. All of it is utter poppycock.

The fall of power shall herald the revival of the gods, but the Daughters of Agryna and Ehlach will prompt their permanent fall.

The Heirs of Dusk and Embers must be killed so that the gods can rise.

It was this philosophy that we'd been indoctrinated into with clever stealth. They believe the princess of Erleya is one of the Heirs. That she's an evildoer to be eradicated so balance can be restored and the blight concluded.

I highly doubt killing these so-called Heirs will stop the blight upon this land. A blight that most Mainlanders refuse to acknowledge. But what if one of the fanatics made it through Paramount's barriers to enact their wild mission of a mass Cleanse?

By infiltrating from the top down.

My pulse is erratic, sending a rush of dizziness to my head by the time I bid my sister and mother farewell. The dreaded, accursed ache settles into my bones, reminding me that the night is far from young —that I've been irresponsible with my elixir. I step out of the carriage and bite back a cry from the pang that shoots up my leg. Each step feels more agonizing than the last, the throb traveling up to my hip, lancing through my abdomen and causing me to double over as I step over the threshold and into the mansion.

The pain in my middle threatens to snap me in half. I clutch my forearm against my stomach and compel myself to remain upright. Half hobbling, half jogging, I retreat through the sitting room, the dark, empty kitchen, and finally out the back door to the garden.

A small network of hedges greets me, providing some privacy as I drop into a bed of limp shamrocks. I reach underneath a bush of wilting violets, my bracelets digging into my wrist, and press my hands into the cool soil. Through the dizziness of this ill-fated nightly relapse, I force my magic into the ground. My powers draw the chest hidden beneath the surface upward until the smooth stone meets my fingertips. The chest is far from ornate—a simple box with metal latches that flip open with the flick of my fingers.

Tiny vials of shimmery lilac liquid are organized in neat rows inside with a small satchel of rescue tea beside them. I hope I won't have to resort to drinking this tea. Made of wormwood, foxglove, and poppy with a pinch of zilla and valbane, it has less than half the potency of the elixirs. It lessens the pain enough for me to function, but in high doses or with frequent usage it's poisonous. Even with occasional use, the aftereffects are unpleasant. I snatch one of the vials from the box and relatch the vessel, sending it back into the earth far below with a firm press against the lid.

Only a few weeks left. Damn ...

I need to somehow find a way to get to Radika, my potion maker, before I run out. I watch the soil beneath the shrub knit itself seamlessly back together, and my hands shake as I uncork the vial. My back to the entrance to the house, I ingest the bitter liquid in one gulp.

I shove the empty vial and the cork into the pocket of my dress as I hear footsteps approaching. "Lady Gwyneth?" a voice calls.

"One moment," I grit out. I'm still on my hands and knees, fighting back a dry heave. Warmth and coolness spread through my body simultaneously. I shiver and swallow the excess saliva gathering in my mouth.

An airy voice speaks behind me. "Are you alright?"

I swallow again then sit back on my heels, suddenly aware of the moisture that's seeped into my knees. "I'm alright," I say. I drag in a breath, and the tremors slowly recede along with the nausea. "The news about my father wasn't great." I push myself to my feet, still mildly unsteady but improving. Thank the realms for magical potions.

The kindly servant, Sage, tucks her short brown hair behind her ear. Her cheeks are flushed pink as always, her eyes wide as saucers. "I am very sorry, Lady Gwyneth," she says.

"Thank you, Sage."

Her face grows even redder as she tugs on her apron, fisting her fingers in it. "Apologies, Lady Gwyneth, but Lord Gruffud awaits you in your chamber."

Nausea returns afresh, slicing across my stomach almost as intensely as it had before the elixir. "Thank you," I say. She curtsies and retreats into the house, leaving me standing in the garden amongst whispering bushes and swaying trees. For a heartbeat, I seriously consider walking away from the Pendry household, but instead, I walk right into the place I'm forced to call home.

Toward the man I'm forced to call *husband*.

Chapter 4

Two weeks later, the masses gather from across Mainland, cluttering the thoroughfares and wynds that pour into the city square. Statues of the sun goddess, Agryna, and stunning architecture surround us—the Llyrosta Guild, covered market, and Public House—and at the center is a wooden dais. The whipping post jutting from the platform draws wary attention; it's both an eyesore and a terrifying reminder of the horrors that occasionally occur even amid the beauty and merriment.

Bewildered chatter fills the square as traders, scholars, shop owners, highborns, and lowborns alike, cluster together. Everyone is aiming for a position close enough to the dais to hear the important announcement we've been told will take place today.

Royal Brigade soldiers in brown liveries and other soldiers in black uniforms I'm unfamiliar with are scattered through the square, their swords and crossbows at the ready. I have a feeling they won't hesitate to strike down any civilian that falls out of line. Crossing my arms over my stomach, I shrink back slightly.

On my left stands Gruffud and his parents, and on my right is my best friend, Neris. Her blond curls are pulled back into a ponytail and a lavender dress hangs off her average frame. It irks me that Mother still doesn't have her properly fitted with dresses tailored to her; instead, she gives Neris secondhand clothing, as though she's just another servant rather than the child she'd taken in years ago. As if we weren't raised alongside each other like sisters.

If Father was here, he would've never allowed Mother to treat Neris any differently than I was treated. He loved her as though she was his flesh and blood. The pocket watch weighs heavier within my dress—by the stars, I hope he's alright. It isn't abnormal not to hear much from him aside from the occasional letter or the exclusive events that take place at the Fortress on the Mount. Yet, knowing that he was injured and not having any more information has my stomach constantly twisted into knots.

Before becoming one of the Queen's Guards ten years ago, Father had been the glue that held this family together. We share the same love for pretty books, well-crafted pocket watches, jewelry, and fighting. While he taught me—in secret of course—how to wield a sword and dagger, my fists are my preferred weapons. Mother always saw the bruises on my knuckles and berated Father on how unlady-like, how unbecoming of a highborn it was. He'd simply respond with, "An elite lady deserves elite training, my darling."

It had always been enough to calm what Neris calls Mother's *highborn temper*. It probably helped that his visits after becoming a Queen's Guard were short and sweet—not much time for Mother to be cross with him.

The paradiddle of a drum cuts through the din of the crowd and a hush ensues. All eyes turn to the platform, and each wallop of the soldier's drumstick sends my heartrate higher. I reach into my pocket to run my thumb shakily over my watch as I squint and rise onto the balls of my feet. Seeing through the assortment of hats and hairstyles proves difficult.

Neris leans close, her emerald eyes alight with amusement. "Need me to hoist you up onto my shoulders?"

I scoff. "Neris, I'd break your bony shoulders. No offense."

Her hand flies dramatically to her heart. "Offense taken!" Neris isn't the healthiest nor the strongest, but she is abundant in sass and willpower.

Mother leans forward from beside Neris and cuts me a silencing look. Then by some sheer luck, the person in front of me shifts, and I get a view of the dais where a broad-shouldered man stands, wearing a gilded breastplate over dark blue livery. His thick, brown hair is streaked with grey, and his beard is neatly trimmed into an odd triangle. There are a multitude of emblems on his armor denoting different ranks and honors. He bears no crown, but he doesn't seem to need one to command the throng.

The hooded figure beside him is clad in a black tunic tapered at the waist and fitted trousers that cling to the full curvature of their hips. A hooded cloak of crimson is pulled over their head and a gold mask is visible above a black veil covering the lower half of their face.

"Greetings citizens of Erleya," a voice booms, drawing my eyes back to the man in the beautiful armor. I've seen him on more than one occasion, at formal events in the castle as a child. Lord Commander Rheon. "I come bringing grave news. Queen Morwenna Meredyth, the Good, is dead, and with her, Princess Carys Meredyth fa Rhodri, the heir to the throne."

I *knew* something was very wrong.

Panic rises up within the crowd and the soldiers raise their weapons.

A thin man in an azure suit steps through the crowd, toward the dais. "You killed them!" he shrieks. "Murderer!"

One moment, the man is pointing accusatorily at the commander, and the next, a bolt is protruding from his chest. He looks down at the shaft of the weapon, then drops to the ground as screams tear through the crowd.

Neris loops her arm through mine, squeezing hard as her olive skin blanches. To my surprise, Gruffud's hand flies to my shoulder and he doesn't even bother to mask his look of panic.

"Soldiers, hold your weapons!" Lord Commander Rheon orders.

With a collective stomp that sends a chill through me, all the soldiers salute, their weapons forgotten. The din gradually diminishes to a few murmured words of despair and soft sobs within the throng. Gruffud's hand slips from my shoulder, his gaze pinned on the platform.

"No harm will come to those who cooperate." The cold threat leaks into the commander's tranquil tone: anyone who dares to speak up will be met with the same fate as that foolish man.

"There is a dire need for change in the kingdom, for the betterment of this land we call home, and for Erleya's standing in the mortal realm. Together, we will reclaim Erleya's former glory, and more. Our kingdom shall rise above all others. Beginning today, I declare my reign as Sovereign of the Kingdom of Erleya and the Outer Isles."

Murmurs thread through the crowd, and again, the soldiers stomp to attention, weapons at the ready.

"Citizens, fear not. A time will come when we must act. Against evil, against corruption. But today, we mourn the loss of our good queen and our princess. A moment of silence for our beloved fallen leaders."

Gradually, silence falls over the square. An occasional cough or sniff taints the quietude. Neris glances over at me while our heads are bowed, worry in her eyes.

Sovereign Rheon speaks up again. "We also celebrate the rise of a new era."

A couple of guards clad in midnight blue at the front of the dais shout, "Long live the sovereign!"

Hesitantly at first, the crowd answers, "Long live the sovereign," then slowly, a chant builds, becoming more passionate, more sincere. I glance at Gruffud and his parents, then at my family. They all chant along, but Neris's lips are pressed firmly together, her eyes focused on the dais as if she's trying to look into the new sovereign's soul.

Sometimes I think *she* is the one with magic instead of me.

Chapter 5

DURVLA

Tiernan signs something as he jogs through the grassy pathway beside me. I'm too busy trying to suck in more air to make out a word of what he says. My ribs seem to tighten with each forceful breath. I hunch over with my hands on my knees, closing my eyes against the spots of white and red that tarnish my vision.

It's been two weeks since our arrival at the Verge. Two weeks since I declared that I wanted to join the rebellion. But where do I fit in? There are so many factions. There are the Verge Defenders: the ones trained in combat to guard the Verge should the wards be broken; the Seekers: those who step beyond the wards to find and report back information; the Safeguards: combatants beyond the wards who lead rescue missions; and then the Masterminds: the high-ranking rebels who set up safehouses, collaborate with the Seekers and Safeguards to arrange rescues, and to dispatch information where needed.

Where I would fit in is still debated, as I'm considered too unprepared for anything beyond the wards, but *too powerful* to remain behind them.

I've been running every evening with Tiernan, training my Wielding and learning runes with Oksana in the morning, and working on dagger throwing with Chiyo somewhere in between. I'm supposed to be sparring in the Skirmish Den with the other trainees, but Warden Ava, Alys's daughter who oversees the training, says I'm not ready.

I should've known from the start it was a delusional goal. I have no athleticism to my name. My shadow wielding would provide the perfect shield should we fall into danger, but not if I can't learn to control it consistently. And not if I can't run without immediately becoming winded.

I plop onto my bottom in the grass, and just as I'm about to lay flat on my back, a firm pressure pulls my attention to my knee. I look down, my vision still blurry, but I make out Tiernan's hand there. He gives my knee another squeeze, his voice filling my mind. "*Don't lie down. Put your arms atop your head and take deep breaths. Give your lungs space to expand.*"

My body, however, begs me to lie down. I could take a long nap right now. Reluctantly, I listen to his advice; I fold my arms atop my head and fight to breathe in deeply. My breath remains shallow for what feels like forever, until my pulse eventually slows down and my chest feels less crowded.

"Better?" Tiernan signs. His onyx eyes are filled with worry, light golden skin shining with perspiration.

I shake my head and sign, "I should have more stamina by now."

"Durvla, it's been only two weeks."

I lower my hands to my lap and blink away the tears that try to arise.

"You're pushing yourself too hard."

"I need to prove to Ava I can be an asset."

"Look," says Tiernan. "She might be the Warden, but Dayfyd ranks higher than her. If we go to him—"

"No," I interrupt a little too forcefully.

He sighs and places his hand on mine, his thumb stroking over the back of my palm. The tiniest flutters go through me despite my exhaustion and frustration. "It might not feel like it, but your stamina *has* improved. Perhaps it's not as quickly as you'd like, but take it from me: you're making progress. On top of that, it's hot as Lugda's balls tonight."

A snorting laugh slips out and I clasp my hand over my mouth and nose. There's a spark of amusement in Tiernan's eyes, but he looks equally perplexed.

"That sounds like something Carys would say," I explain.

The moment immediately sobers, guilt and sadness sinking into my gut. Carys ... who I've still not been able to dreamwalk to. Not since that moment I'd been guided by the goddess Sunlagh; not since I learned from the goddess that the veil between the dream realm and the Underworld is thin. A shudder runs through me, the hair standing on the back of my neck as I remember the goddess's ethereal voice, and the voices of Ellynne and Aneirin—Carys's closest friend and her brother—from beyond the land of the living.

The sun sinks lower on the horizon, grey clouds eclipsing the purple and orange streaks in the sky as a gentle breeze cools the sweat on my skin. *Now* the air decides to give us a reprieve. I inhale deeply, taking in the damp earth scent that clings to the air in the Verge. It always gives it a deceptively balmy feeling even in the coolest temperatures. Magelights come to life on the posts bordering the pathway. Tiernan tilts his head, both brows raised in a question. "Are you alright?" he asks.

I nod. "Sorry to be a killjoy."

Tiernan's lips curve in a gentle smile. He stands and extends his hand, pulling me to my feet.

"You aren't a *killjoy*," he says. "That role is already taken, remember?" He winks, and this time, I smile despite myself. His high cheekbones sharpen when he smiles, his dark eyes shimmery beneath the magelight shining from the lamppost. He nudges a few loose ringlets of hair from my sweaty face and smiles in a way that makes my stomach flip eagerly.

Since our arrival, we've been constantly pulled into various meetings and separate training sessions. I'm grateful for the occasional job of identifying and cataloging herbs, as it's given me something concrete to focus on, but with such a packed schedule most days, Tiernan and I haven't found much time to be alone or to discuss our relationship.

"Ready to go home?" Tiernan asks.

"Yes, I'm in desperate need of a bath."

We turn to head back down the pathway of smooth stone atop

the manicured wild grasses that cover the land. Lush forests, enchanted with strong wards to keep out any unwanted guests, surround the Verge. Swampy trees border the far east and thicker, fuller birch trees hedge the west.

At this time of the evening, the residential area of the sanctuary is calm. Sometimes there are bonfire celebrations in the square or larger dinners amongst families and friends. Everything is easily attainable in the Verge. Currency is not needed to buy anything. Instead, reasonable trades are arranged.

There's a forge, a community garden, the Skirmish Den where fight training occurs, the armory, a small library, and plenty of homes for all the families here. Right now, our house feels so far away, my body is exhausted from the day of training and the afternoon jog, and the dizziness setting in reminds me that I need to take a tonic once I'm back indoors.

A couple people cross our path, smiling politely. Tiernan and I smile back and continue walking.

Since coming to the Verge, I've been confronted with conflicting feelings of belonging and isolation. Back in Cluain Baile, I hid my ailment, my deafness, and the existence of my little brother. Here, none of those things matter, but my powers do.

People gawk at me sometimes when I'm out and about. The woman with dark magic. No one truly knows the extent of my powers. We've kept my dreamwalking a secret, but my shadows tend to show themselves when I'm *not* trying to summon them, so word spread quickly. This place may be accepting of everyone, but Basdu-unai were executed, even by other magic users once upon a time. Who's to say history won't repeat itself? Fear can drive even the kindest hearts to violence.

So, as far as people know, I'm just a botanist who happens to also be a Shadow Wielder.

The only Verge resident who knows of my dreamwalking is Dayfyd, Alys's husband and the second in command.

Tiernan's arm loops around my lower back, tugging me closer to his side as we continue walking. "*A shilling for your thoughts?*" he asks into my head.

"*Nothing important.*"

He stops walking right beneath the flood of light from a mage-lamp and gently turns me toward him. "That's a brave move—lying to a Mind Whisperer." There's the tiniest glint of amusement in his angular eyes.

"Unless my thoughts are just being loud again, I know that you don't read me."

"Oh? And you're certain of this?"

"I trust you." How could I not when he gave up his stability and status for me?

The playful smile on his face melts into something more pensive. "*I'm honored,*" he says into my mind. "*I would never do anything to betray your trust.*" His face inches closer and the bands that constantly squeeze my chest loosen as our lips meet in a gentle caress.

I catch the shadow of a figure moving past us as I close my eyes. Our lips part, but Tiernan's forehead rests against mine, one hand clenching slightly on my waist as if he's reluctant to release me. In my periphery, a couple more people walk by, followed by even more until we pull back from each other and glance around.

"Alright, what is going on?" I sign, watching a few children walk past, their adults not far behind.

Tiernan points behind me and I turn just as a figure speeds toward us, pulling a wagon behind her. Chiyo.

My stomach drops as I take in her frantic expression. Her chest heaves with effortful breaths, her fair skin flushed pink.

"What's happening?" Tiernan asks her.

She pulls a clip from her pocket and makes quick work of winding up her blue-dyed and brown hair into a bun. Within the wagon, Taig is beaming up at the magelamp above, his curls bouncing as he rocks side to side contentedly.

"The chief just called an urgent meeting in the courtyard," Chiyo signs. My stomach sinks.

If the chief has called everyone out of their homes at night, it must be serious. I swallow my fear and bend just enough to drop a kiss onto Taig's forehead. When eyes meet mine for the briefest moment, his smile widens. Then he goes back to staring at the magelamp.

Tiernan takes over pulling the wagon, his free hand wrapping around mine. We follow the Verge residents toward the courtyard where various logs, haybales, barrels, and other objects form makeshift seats. On the platform, Dayfyd stands a head above a stocky man with salt-and-pepper hair and tan leathery skin. Dayfyd is revered and renowned in the Verge; everyone greets him with sincere enthusiasm during the day. But he's also unassuming—one of the people. Chief Lyon Badeaux, however, is someone I've only heard about. He'd be considered the equivalent of royalty within this haven.

Chief Lyon's smile is warm, deep lines forming at the corners of his thin lips and small eyes. "Welcome," he says, leaning heavily on his ornate walking stick. A plump man to his left translates the word into signed language. My cheek twitches, but my smile is hindered by my fears about this announcement.

"I'm sure you're all wondering why you've been called here on such short notice. It is my displeasure to bring you news from Outside." He pauses, as if for dramatic effect.

As I stare at the translator's hands, everything seems to move as though we're suspended in honey. *The queen is dead, as is the heir to the throne.* The words sink into my heart, numbing my body. Beside me, Tiernan tenses, his hand suddenly holding mine, squeezing tremulously.

Panic erupts around us. Dayfyd and Chief Badeaux wave their arms, trying to capture the attention of the crowd while people stand and pelt the platform with questions. Taig begins flapping his arms, clearly distressed, but my limbs feel too heavy, and I find myself unable to move to comfort him. Chiyo reaches into the wagon to unstrap him as my vision blurs.

The words can't be true. I don't want to believe them.

Things can change at the drop of a coin, but …

I close my eyes against the rapidly building pressure in my head as a dull throbbing spreads from my temples to the rest of my face. My chest tightens before I hear Tiernan's voice in my head. "*Durvla?*"

I turn my gaze to him. I didn't even feel his hands on my face before, but now it pulls me back to the present where everyone is still in an uproar.

I replay the rest of the news in my head: *All of Erleya is under the duress of a military coup.*

My breathing grows shallow as I try to focus on our surroundings. That proves to be unhelpful; people seem to be shouting over each other, some clinging to their loved ones as though it could protect them from the truth.

Chief Badeaux's knuckles are white on the head of his cane. His face remains a mask of serenity as he methodically addresses one person at a time—as the uproar continues. I've never been so grateful that I can't hear.

Tiernan quickly motions, "Let's get back to the house."

I rise on unsteady feet, making eye contact with Chiyo who nods and passes Taig to Tiernan. Together, we maneuver our way through the panicking crowd.

By the time we get to the house, my head throbs in time with the hammering of my heart. My legs take me straight to the bedroom where I drink a small vial of tincture for my headache and sit on the mattress to gather my composure.

A military coup.

Carys, dead.

I close my eyes and clasp my shaky hands together. She can't be dead. Grounding myself in the present, I breathe in slowly through my nose and out through my mouth. In and out until my heart rate slows and my mind stops racing. I turn my thoughts to Carys, trying to find even the smallest thread of her presence. Some proof that she's somewhere in this realm.

She *has* to be.

I sit there until the throbbing in my head resurfaces despite the tincture, and my limbs start to fall asleep.

Nothing.

Absolutely nothing.

When I open my eyes, Tiernan is leaning against the closed bedroom door. He steps away from it, signing to me, "Anything?"

I shake my head, tears welling. "I was certain she would escape Paramount," I say. "So certain, I would've wagered my own life on it. That dream I had … the … goddess." I remember the song of Sunlagh that gave me the extra boost of willpower to daywalk to Carys. After swallowing a few times, I say, "It wasn't supposed to happen this way. I keep trying to daywalk to her but …" I slowly shake my head again.

Tiernan sits on the bed, facing me. His hands are clenched in his lap, his jaw so tight that a muscle twitches in his cheek. My eyes trail the silvery scar that goes from his collarbone up the side of his neck. The scar he's not wanted to discuss.

Back in Paramount, I'd dreamt of him bound in a dark room, a man looming over him. My blood chills at the memory of it—at the very tactile fear that exuded from Tiernan and the tormented look in his eyes. It's similar to the look in his eyes now. He's always trying to comfort me; always the calm presence when I need him to be. But what about when *he* needs comfort?

"Do you know anything about this new sovereign?" I ask. "Chief Badeaux said he's the commander of the Royal Brigade?"

His throat bobs before he nods. "Yes, I reported directly to him when I was still in the ranks," he signs. "He's someone who uses fear tactics to gain power."

The hair stands up on the back of my neck.

"Carys—" I begin, my throat immediately constricting. "Do you think he would've killed her to take the crown?"

The color rushes from Tiernan's face. I slide my hand into his surprisingly damp palm.

"I don't believe he would've killed her," Tiernan says after a few heartbeats. "I believe he'd want to use her." He releases my hand suddenly. "We should get Taig ready for bed."

I blink at him and nod as tears sting my eyes. He gets up without another word and stalks out of the room, leaving me behind to ruminate over the horrifying uncertainty of everything and the odd feeling that he's keeping something important from me.

Chapter 6

CARYS

DAUGHTER OF EMBERS. Why do you run from me?

A cold, black flame sputters in the back of my mind. I'm too cold and too warm all at once. My body is impossibly heavy, my lungs struggling to reinflate with each breath.

Don't be afraid. I am not your enemy, coos the voice of the enchantress.

Yet I'm paralyzed with fear as I remember the sensation of icy fingers raking against the recesses of my mind. Of her powers pouring into me and instigating a primal rage like I've never felt before. I remember my control slipping away from me along with my mind, and the insatiable thirst for vengeance taking over, demanding eternal sustenance.

Whether you accept me or not, the world will burn. It is foretold. Why fight against me when I only make you stronger?

How do you expect me to not be afraid when you say things like that? I ask her.

My question is met with taciturn silence. Then, in rapid flashes, images of the sun blacking out in the sky, of fire scorching the cracked earth fill my mind. Fear crashes over me before the heaviness in my limbs slowly recedes, leaving behind nauseating apprehension.

A more familiar presence enters my mind, then a voice gently pours over me like cool summer rain, eradicating the unbearable heat. *"Carys?"*

My pulse races, but this time it's not out of fear. "*Durvla?*"

My heart yearns for a glimpse of her gentle smile and ridiculously perfect curls—to know that she's truly there in my dreams and not just a figment of my desperate imagination. But at the same time, I don't want her to see me. Not like this.

"*Carys!*" There's relief and the tiniest hint of laughter in her voice. "*I can't see you, but I'm here. Are you alright? Are you alive?*"

"*Yes.*" But that's all I let her know before I fight against the urge to remain in her comforting presence. *Wake up,* I tell myself. *Wake up, wake up, wake up.*

I jolt awake, flames licking along my palms as my heart hammers. I press my hands together, and tiny embers leap off my skin and onto the furs on the large bed. "Shit," I mumble, patting out the embers just as they begin to grow.

Swinging my legs off the bed, I press my bare feet against the wooden floor beneath me and close my eyes. That cold presence, that voice in the very back of my mind whispers something incoherent, chilling me. Since leaving Erleya, the enchantress's voice has been muddled, as though the magical burnout I suffered back in Paramount has also weakened her.

For a few heartbeats, I inhale and exhale shakily, trying to slow my pulse, trying to keep that voice out of my awareness. Calling Alys's grounding techniques to mind, I focus on the feel of my feet against the floor and my arse against the soft bed. The room reeks of earth, leather, and lard. The sound of the crackling fire reaches my ears, and when I open my eyes again, I'm confronted with the dancing flames in the long firepit at the front corner of the room.

I draw in a breath and wave my hand toward the fire. It dies down to barely a flicker, and the room fades into darkness.

My heart pounds as my mind plummets back into that dark cell beneath Paramount. I can still feel the sting of Eefa's blade against my face and the agony of her betrayal. Of Iywan's betrayal.

My memories are painted crimson—Ellynne bleeding out from the dagger in her abdomen, Callum's throat slashed right in front of me. The sickening sensation of congealed blood on my hands, in my hair, and on my dress returns, and I press my hand over my mouth to suffocate a gag.

They're both dead by Eefa's hands.

But it might as well have been by mine.

I fling my hand toward the firepit again and flames roar back to life. The power of it blasts outwards and startles me out of bed. My body hits the wooden floor with a loud *thud*.

It takes but a moment before the hanging tapestry that functions like a makeshift door is thrown open and Odgar emerges. The deep rumble of his voice resonates in the space. "Are you—"

I lurch to my feet as I realize something that hangs nearby has caught on fire, the flames eating away at it. "Shit! Fuck! Sorry!"

Odgar just flicks the back of his hand toward the fabric, as if shooing a fly, and the flames are doused by his waterweaving. Small billows of grey smoke linger in the darkness.

I spear my fingers through my hair, having forgotten for a moment just how badly Eefa mangled it. And that was the *least* of her torture. All so that the Zenith could use me for this very power that I cannot control.

An entire *millennium* has passed since Enidwen's demise, and her spirit chose *me* of all people to manipulate.

That says a lot, doesn't it? I've always known that something was detrimentally wrong with me.

"Carys ...?" Odgar speaks as though I'm a wild horse in need of taming.

"Don't take that tone with me," I snap.

"Well, I'd rather not shout at you when everything in here is flammable. I'm fairly attached to the Great Hall."

I level him with a simmering glare, and he holds his large hands up.

"I was just checking on you." The depth of his voice—his singsong Uldaran accent—resounds like the gentlest ballad.

Yet I lash out at him like a provoked adder. "I don't need you checking in on me."

His brows disappear beneath bronze curls that glow red in the firelight.

I'm the one who came to Uldarvik for sanctuary. He doesn't deserve me snapping at him like a spoiled princess. "Apologies," I say, my voice tight. "I'm just exhausted. And I don't know how to control this." I hold my palms up toward the exposed beams of the ceiling. "The palace Healer taught me some general grounding techniques before I even knew I had magic, but whenever my emotions flare up, I forget it all."

My chest heaves even as I try to calm my breathing, as I once again turn from him. He steps into my line of sight, the glow from the flames dancing across his coppery skin.

"It happens to the best of us." When he straightens, I keep my eyes on him. He regards me silently, scratching his cropped beard and running his hand over the antler tattoo across his left cheek. As he lowers his hand and steps toward me, my entire body tenses, my lungs seizing.

Immediately, he steps back, putting more than enough distance between us. "Sometimes it helps to get outside in the cold. What do you say?"

My eyes widen. "Right now? In the middle of the night?"

He shrugs, muscles rippling obscenely beneath his tunic. "Why not?"

I sigh. "Alright."

It seems to take an eternity before the crisp air hits my face, feeling as soothing as the most delectable bath.

Gods, I miss my extravagant baths with rose petals and oils. Roses were my mother's favorite fragrance.

But my body is still holding on to more heat than it should, and I'm sweating beneath the hooded fur cloak Odgar found for me. I gulp and close my eyes, breathing in, then out slowly. When I peel my eyelids open again, my breath leaves my lips in visible wisps that hover in the air before vanishing. Odgar offers me his brawny arm, and I flinch instinctively.

A few lines carve the space between his thick brows, but he doesn't say anything about my skittishness, and he doesn't back down either. I link my arm with his, a comforting warmth radiating from him, and we begin to walk across the frosty terrain.

I remember leaving the castle as a child and traveling into Barr na Cahar—it's the closest I've gotten to seeing a village before now. Yet Barr na Cahar is vastly different from this village in Uldarvik. The city outside Paramount is filled with small shops, cobblestoned streets, and large manors for the elite. Here, wooden huts of different sizes appear more frequently on either side of us the farther we walk from the Great Hall. The mountains with their ice-capped peaks provide an ever-present backdrop. Slightly different from the green, rolling hills and black, rocky crags of Erleya.

"You don't have to talk about anything right now, but I want you to know that you can trust me. With anything."

I stop walking and turn my gaze from the frost on the low-hanging branches above us to Odgar. But no words come, and tangible awkwardness settles between us again.

I shift my hand to the spot where my amulet once settled against my chest. Its absence leaves my heart with an aching, sun-shaped hole.

"So, Sumarvegr," Odgar says suddenly. "It's approaching at the turn of the season." His words defuse the tension and call me back to the present.

"Suma—" I furrow my brows, then blink rapidly as frost drops from another low-hanging branch and onto my nose.

Odgar smirks and gently pulls the fur-lined hood of my cape over my head. "*Sumarvegr.*"

I try to commit the pronunciation to memory and *not* think about the tenderness in his actions.

"It's our yearly journey to the Hallowed Wood where the gods await."

Await ... No one knows when the Erleyan gods last walked among us, but perhaps it's different here. "Figuratively?"

"Or perhaps literally." He winks.

"That's ... cryptic."

A low chuckle rumbles in his chest, stirring a fleeting sensation that isn't unpleasant in my stomach. I resume walking and he follows.

"This ... journey. Is there any specific reason for it?"

"It differs for everyone. Some make the journey out of their devotion to the gods, or obligation, or a need for a renewal. An ancient Seer lives within the Hallowed Wood, and a lot of Uldarans visit during this journey."

"A Seer?"

"Yes, those who feel lost and need a bit of guidance navigating the emotions that come along with Sumarvegr visit the Seer. He answers the deepest, darkest questions of one's soul ... speaks about the hand of destiny ... cures the incurable. All with the help of the gods, of course."

My gaze shifts to a large cauldron hanging over a stony firepit in front of a hut. A small wooden horse on wheels lies on its side not far from the firepit. I replay Odgar's words in my mind. It's his culture, so I cannot say aloud that it seems absolutely ridiculous that one man can do so much.

Then again, Enidwen nearly destroyed the very existence of all Magekind. Maybe this Seer is just what I need to get rid of her bloody curse.

Chapter 7

DURVLA

HEART LURCHING, I spring upright in bed so quickly that I nearly roll off the mattress.

Tiernan's already standing at the other side of the bed. His hand hovers over his shoulder as though he intends to draw his sword. As if he's forgotten that we were both asleep a moment ago. The magelights brighten enough for me to register the panic widening Tiernan's eyes. Luckily, Taig hasn't moved, his breathing remains serene and even.

"I felt Carys's presence," I sign.

Brows lifted, Tiernan sinks back down onto the bed. "She's alive?"

Uneasiness threads through me. I'm not sure. "She feels ... different," I admit. "Wounded. I didn't see her, but I heard her. She *said* she's alive." Last time I'd dropped into her subconscious, she'd felt more solid, easier to hold on to; I'd been able to communicate with her, even touch her as though she was there in the flesh. This time, she sounded too far away and muddled. Like she was at the top of a mountain shouting down to me.

Despite dreamwalking to her, despite her saying that she's alive, I cannot ignore the knowledge that the veil between the dream realm and the realm of the dead is thin.

"Her voice sounded less clear than Ellynne's and Aneirin's had," I mention. "Theirs played in my mind like a memory—Carys's voice sounded distant. More like I just couldn't fully tap into the dreamscape."

The pensive look on Tiernan's face deepens along with the creases between his eyes. "Maybe it's her state of mind."

"Maybe we should keep this to ourselves then, until I'm more certain. I'll keep trying to reach her when I can."

Tiernan nods in agreement.

Sunlight begins to peek through the curtains. I groan, rubbing my face. The dark circles under Tiernan's eyes reflect how I feel. Neither of us speaks for a while, then Tiernan says, "I'll go make us some tea." He reaches across the bed to give my leg an affectionate squeeze before he hurries out of the room.

Sweat rolls down my neck as the walls covered in hanging herbs seem to close in on me. The announcement from last night still curdles my stomach every time I think about it. Military coup. Carys allegedly dead.

A tap on my shoulder startles me out of my thoughts, and I drop the meadowsweet herbs that I was supposed to be bundling with twine. My gaze shifts to the white-haired woman standing at the counter beside me. Deeper lines carve into her forehead and bracket her downturned lips.

"Focus," she chides. She has an accent that I've not had to lipread before, so I have to concentrate on her words more than usual.

"My apologies," I say as I wrap the twine around the stems of the herbs, careful not to destroy the fragile white flowers. The room is small enough to fit about four people and is used strictly for drying herbs that reduce inflammation.

Oksana takes the meadowsweet bunch from me and says, "Let's try shielding again." She sets the bundle on the wooden surface of the counter and waves her hand over it. Immediately, a small, shimmery dome encircles it. "You must focus your energy on your target.

Whether it be yourself, someone else, or an object." With another wave of her hand, she dismisses her power.

I frown. *Maybe my magic doesn't work the same way yours does*, I want to say. She's a Lightweaver and I'm a Shadow Wielder. Her magic is innately good and mine is ... not. An invisible hand squeezes my heart. Sometimes I wish I could go back to before I knew I had these powers. As much as I want to learn to wield them for good—to help bring other Undesirables to the Verge—learning to summon my shadows is difficult.

The older woman waves a pale hand corded with blueish veins. "Try again."

Incorporating today's lesson into this occasional job was Oksana's idea. Something to keep me from overthinking. So far, it doesn't seem to be working. I heave a sigh. Oksana has the patience of an immortal, which is appreciated. But it also means that she would be fine standing here until night falls if that's what it would take for me to summon even a fraction of my powers.

Her eyes narrow. "What is hindering you, child?"

What isn't? I run my finger under the hem of my right sleeve.

"Did you or did you not cast a shield over yourself and Tiernan Kilkenny when you were Outside?"

"I did."

"And what happened? What did you see?"

I swallow. "The attacker's sword bounced off my shadows when she tried to strike."

"And what did you feel at that moment?"

I close my eyes as the pungent odor of blood pierces my awareness. The image of Tiernan on the ground, a dagger hilt-deep in his abdomen, a gash in his thigh profusely bleeding fills my mind. It didn't matter to me in that moment that we had a Healer with us or that *he,* as a Mimic, could've healed himself. All I could fathom at the time was losing him.

I've lost enough. My parents. My best friend. I've even thought that Taig was dead.

"Fear," I say shakily as my lungs start to falter. My pulse kicks up. *Breathe.* I clutch my arm to my chest and count my breaths, completely missing what Oksana says.

She quirks her bushy white brows and repeats herself. "What did you feel the other times you cast shadows?" She stands so still that she could be a statue; meanwhile I can't stop picking at my sleeve. I clasp my hands together to stop fidgeting.

There was that moment I found out that Osheen had betrayed us. "Anger," I say after an uncomfortably long pause. "Hopelessness. Sadness ... Betrayal." Tears sting my eyes as a cool sensation runs down my arms and tingles my hands.

"Look," Oksana says. I turn my gaze away from her lips to my hands where tiny tendrils of black shadows dance on my fingertips.

I hold my hands up, watching the tendrils waver like ink in water. My heart hiccups as I bite back the unease. My hands start to tremble, and I clench them into fists, snuffing out the darkness.

The lines in Oksana's face deepen again. "Why did you restrain yourself?"

A tremor runs through me. "I grew up with stories of Dark Mages. I fear that if I continue to develop these powers, they'll corrupt me."

Her chest rises then deflates with a deep, resigned sigh. "The stories you grew up with were grossly misconstrued. A few Dark Mages ruined the reputation of all Wielders of the dark forces. Maybe it's time you showed people otherwise."

If only I could get a simple shield to work.

"In the past, Wielders used amplifiers, at least for training. Amplifiers strengthen powers—so you can imagine how dangerous that can become."

I think back to when my powers unleashed in the midst of my rage toward Osheen and imagine if that had been amplified. My clothes suddenly feel too tight. Does Oksana want me to use an amplifier?

"Clearly your powers are motivated by your emotions, so let's use that before we resort to an amplifier."

My shoulders sag with relief.

"You have so many fears and uncertainties bottled up. We just need you to learn to unleash them." Oksana shoves her hand into her pocket then slips a coin into my palm. The metal is cool against my skin. "Tell me ... if your younger brother was being attacked by Forayers—"

She doesn't need to say more. A cold sensation builds in my chest and trickles down my arms again. I close my eyes and focus on my hand, leaving whatever else Oksana says unknown as I try to summon a shield. When I open my eyes, the coin in my hand is obscured by a small, wavering dome of translucent black. It's not as beautiful as Oksana's light shield but, as she reaches out to touch the coin, it stops her hand from going any further, and she smiles.

"Well done, child. Now let's work on runes again."

The throbbing behind my eyes intensifies as I finally arrive at the house assigned to us. As I turn onto the flower-lined pathway, I spot a familiar face. Thick plaits hang down to her waist as she leans casually against the whitewashed stone wall. Her arms are crossed over her chest, her leather vest hanging open to reveal a loose tunic left unlaced at the neck. Her eyes lock on mine, and my stomach drops.

My steps waver. For being Alys and Dayfyd's daughter, Ava is nothing like them. While Alys is benevolent and nurturing, Ava is anger incarnate and all hard edges. Ava has the same golden brown complexion and hazel eyes as Dayfyd, her hair jet black like Alys's rather than Dayfyd's brown coils. She doesn't have even a breath of her parents' serenity. In every instance that I've been in her presence, she's glared at me as though she intends to banish me with just one look.

Disdain pinches her brows as she pushes off the wall of the house and signs with impressive fluency, "How goes your training with Oksana?"

Surprised by her proficiency with signing, I blink.

She waves her hand in front of my face. "Hello?"

"It's going fine," I motion quickly.

"Have you gotten command of your shadows?"

This time I hesitate. I *could* lie to her, but what good would that do?

"I'll take your silence as a *no*." She flicks a few of her long braids over her shoulder and props her fists on her hips.

"I managed to erect a small shadow shield around a coin this morning."

Her nose wrinkles in a scowl. For a moment, she just stares at me as though she's tasted something bitter, then she signs, "Show me."

Heart hammering, I lift my hand and focus on my palm. I try to think of all the moments I'd used my shadow wielding, just as Oksana had prompted me to not long ago. This time, however, my hands grow clammy, and my head pounds even more than it already had been.

"It's been two weeks of training, and you *still* cannot conjure shadows at will. Are you serious about joining the rebellion?"

"Yes, of course," I say, the words slipping from my lips before I can even sign. "I *can* conjure them. It just takes a mo—"

"Do you think that an attacker is going to give you a moment to get your shit together?" she asks. "You think they're going to excuse you because of—" She gestures vaguely to my body. "—whatever is going on?"

I clench my fists. My powers are spurred on by emotions, so I hold on to the annoyance and the offense and open my palms, letting the shadows fill them. The dark tendrils wrap around my wrists and snake up to my elbows while Ava stares at me, unimpressed. My shadows disappear.

"I need you to be able to do that immediately. Even our Seekers need to be able to defend themselves out there. If you're gathering information and you run into the wrong people—which is likely to happen—they won't hesitate to slit your throat. Out there, we already had the Forayers to deal with. We've already had to deter their efforts to corral Mages and Undesirables for a pretty coin from the Crown. And now the kingdom is under the rule of a man *known* for being a monster.

"The Purists are rising in power for whatever twisted reason, and on top of it all, we have the Zenith—no idea what in Lugda's hells is going on with those fucks. But I know it has to do with the prophecy, and I *know* you have a closer tie to the prophecy than anyone else here. You would be an asset in finding out more information, but not if you can't defend yourself. Not if you'll be a liability to a mission."

Tears sting my eyes, but I don't look away from her. I watch the angry motions of her hands and the contempt written on her face. I don't know what I've done to make her hate me as much as she does, but I know the fate of my role in the rebellion is in her hands. "I want to make a difference," I sign, far feebler than I intend to. "I'm willing to put the effort in."

A familiar presence prickles my awareness in a way I can't describe. I *feel* Tiernan before his figure comes into my field of vision. He stands beside me now, silvery strands of hair spilling out from his bun as he looks between me and Ava. "Is something the matter?" he signs.

"Just asking your precious Durvla if she's serious about joining the rebellion."

Tiernan presses his lips firmly together and looks my way. "*Is she bullying you?*" he asks into my mind.

I don't respond, but it's clear that he's picked up the streams of my negative emotions.

"She needs more training," Ava says to him. Then to me, "You are a Shadow Wielder. You have abilities beyond even your wildest imagination. If it were not for your shielding capabilities out there, your lover would've been killed." She jabs a thumb in Tiernan's direction, and my stomach turns over at the reminder. I'm too tense to be embarrassed by her loose usage of *lover*.

"I'm tired of keeping my mouth shut about this and everything else. It's up to you now. You either let everyone keep coddling you or take the reins and train more. Command your powers like they're *yours*."

Everyone keeps coddling me? She's tired of keeping her mouth shut? I'm about to ask her what she means when she steps away from the wall and turns so quickly that I barely dodge the braids that whip dangerously close to my face.

She storms off, leaving me standing in front of the door, not quite sure how to process everything. I turn to Tiernan and sign, "She said she knows that I have a tie to the prophecy. Do you think Alys told her?"

Tiernan shakes his head. "I'm not sure. I do know that Ava and Alys aren't exactly on friendly terms." He turns to the door, which is magically charmed to unlock as soon as any of our household members touches the knob. "I'm sorry I wasn't here when she pounced," says Tiernan. "What else did she say to you?"

I shake my head and follow him into the house, shutting the door behind me.

"Durvla—"

"You caught the gist of it."

He sighs with resignation. "If it makes you feel better, Ava is nasty to everyone."

"She's especially nasty to me."

"I can't deny that ... But I don't know why. I've even tried to get a read on her, but her mind is impenetrable—even to my Empath powers. I suppose, being the Warden, she would've been well trained with mental shielding."

"Does she have any powers?"

"Not that I can feel. But even Ordinaries can learn to shield. Not as well as someone with mind magic of any type but efficiently enough." He steps closer, resting one hand lightly on my shoulder and signing with the other, "Are you alright, though?"

I nod. "I'm fine. She's right. I need to train more. And not just with you and Chiyo."

"You're talking—"

"Skirmish Den, yes," I say.

I swear his eye twitches, but he nods.

"No coddling me," I tell him, and his lips curve up in a gentle smile.

"I wouldn't dream of it, beautiful." His fingers slide down my arm and send my stomach into a giddy little summersault. He takes my hand and kisses my knuckles, then the center of my palm. I feel it tickle all the way up my arm, and I tug away, repressing a giggle. The smile spreads wider across Tiernan's face. "If you want to change and relax, I can make you your tea." He points to my head, which is still throbbing.

Gratitude floods me.

"Then I'll freshen up, and we can collect Taig from the Hatchling's Nest together later, if you'd like."

"I'd love that," I say.

"Perfect." He drops a quick kiss onto my forehead, and we go our separate ways.

In the bathing chamber, as I scrub the lingering residue of the herbs and sweat off my skin, I try not to look at my branding scar. The royal insignia burned into my flesh isn't as obvious as it once was, but the dark brown and slightly raised scar stands out against my tawny complexion. The sight of it always elicits the memory of Bronn pressing the branding stick into my flesh—of the fear-filled days that followed before I got to know everyone at Paramount better. And now ... two are dead, one is working with the enemy, Carys is a conundrum, and now apparently a monster sits on the throne.

As much as I dislike how Ava spoke to me, she's right. I need to train more. I need to prove myself more than ever.

Chapter 8

GWYNETH

ANOTHER WEEK FLIES by in a flourish of mundane happenings. I still cannot stop thinking about the sovereign's impassioned speech. About the new world—no traditional monarchy, and equal treatment for all.

Apparently equal treatment means treating everyone like riffraff. The streets that once felt like home now threaten potential danger thanks to Peacekeepers dressed suspiciously like Forayers.

Over the years, I've heard the servants speaking of the injustice in the Grounds. Where people are hanged for the use of magic or being suspected of having a Mage bloodline. Here in Mainland, those suspected of having a magical bloodline or owning magic contraband are banished to the Wastelands. Perhaps that sounds like a fate worse than death, but I'd like to think it provides an opportunity for escape.

Then there are Undesirables—people with lifelong ailments or complexities that make them different. Grounders who are Undesirable are banished to the Wastelands if they come forward rather than being exposed. In Mainland, mercy killings by family members and friends are commonplace, but many Mainland Undesirables also take their own lives. It is a great shame upon the family to be an Undesirable, so they're most likely to be victims of unwarranted violence.

It always leaves me riddled with anxiety to have Neris out of my sight for that reason. Three summers ago, we were fortunate that Neris collapsed right in front of Radika's workshop. We hadn't known Radika at the time, but she'd been a kind stranger willing to help. With the tonics from the potion maker, Neris doesn't have as many fits as she used to, but stress always makes her condition worse.

Life under the rule of Queen Morwenna, *the Good*, was bad enough. But I'm certain life with Sovereign Rheon Odhran will be far worse for Undesirables.

As we walk through town, Neris is a source of nonstop chatter. Most of what she says goes into one ear and out through the other. I'd awoken this morning to the memory of my father's smiling face, his hands raised in preparation for me to strike them. *Strike like you mean it*, he used to tell me. And I would fire my fist into his hands with gusto. My heart aches. Realms, I miss him. I hate that we never get to see him. And that Mother has never shown us any of his letters. I suppose they're personal to her, but he's our father.

As I spiral deeper into my thoughts of Father, of this slowly depreciating kingdom that feels less and less like home, a sharp jab in my side startles me. I wince, rubbing my side as I register that Neris has stopped walking. Her face is as white as a sheet.

"*What*?" I demand.

Voices carry from somewhere nearby as she points her rounded chin toward a group of people. All garbed in white robes, they're gathered up ahead of us on the right. My pulse scampers and I'm suddenly rooted to the spot, prickling cold spreading through my body. Phantom pains send tremors through me, and Neris wraps an arm around my shoulders.

She gives them a squeeze. "Keep your eyes down and keep walking," she says.

I nod, though the chills don't abate.

I hear my own screams in my head, see myself writhing on a cold cavern floor.

My legs are still moving, but I don't register my surroundings. Not until we're passing the group of Purists at a proximity too close for comfort. We take as wide a berth as we can from the throng while they shout to the masses about the evils of raw magic and Mages.

While they hand out propaganda on parchment in hopes of recruiting more souls for their twisted mission.

"Shut it, you daft dingbat!" a man shouts from across the cobblestone street. "There *is* no magic. Come off it!"

One of the women cloaked in white shifting her message from the dangers of magic to one about the return of the gods. "The gods shall walk amongst us again!" Her impassioned voice rises as I look away, focusing on a wider-than-usual gap on the cobblestone footpath.

"Are you ready for their return? You there!"

I freeze, as I'm *sure* Nimue is talking to me.

"Keep. Walking," Neris whispers, her fingers digging into my biceps. But there's a strange power that radiates from that woman. Even to someone like me who can't sense other people's magical powers.

I keep walking, my legs like lead. Then another woman steps in front of me, silvery hair slipping out from her hood with silvery eyes to match. Her weathered skin has seen better days, though I know she appears older than she really is. *Damn, Credia.* I'd hoped to never see her again. Or Nimue.

"Nice to see you thriving, Gwyn," Credia says with unwarranted familiarity.

Not here. Not now. Not ever again.

I sling one arm across my chest and set off running in these ridiculous shoes that are hardly meant for walking, the heels clacking loudly against the cobblestones. Buildings whiz past me in a blur until one of my heels snags on a crack between the stones. My ankle wrenches, the grinding pain temporarily stealing my eyesight as I stagger forward on the broken heel. I kick off my shoes and continue running despite the hot, throbbing ache.

I'm not repeating my mistake of fraternizing with or even talking to those fanatics. I've already shattered my soul once with their help. All because I was desperate to be rid of my terraforging.

It's not until I veer off the footpath and into a small open field with a ruined shrine that I stop running.

The more years that passed after my powers manifested, the stronger I became. I had to travel to the middle of the forest to let out the pent-up energy from my unused magic with increasing frequency. On the weeks with no use of my powers, I felt it crawling beneath my skin like a parasite, threatening to hollow me from the inside out. Threatening to consume me.

Yet the older I grew, the fewer opportunities there were for me to release that energy, and the more desperate I became to be rid of my magic.

A year ago, Neris and I were walking through the forest when we came upon two women with platinum hair visible beneath their white hooded capes. The first looked at me with knowing eyes. "Fear not," she said, her voice both commanding and soothing. "I sense great turmoil within you. I can help you."

Neris tugged me away from the woman. "Get away from us!" she shouted.

Yet the woman didn't balk in the slightest. "My name is Nimue," she said, lowering her hood. The other woman did the same, her face identical to Nimue's. "And this is my sister, Aine."

With a smile and a troublesome glint in her eyes, Aine nodded with practiced politeness.

"It's not every day we encounter a Terraforger," Nimue said, and my heart just about tumbled out of my chest. "You carry a dangerous secret, Gwyneth."

"How do you know my name and—?"

Neris squeezes my arm *hard* to shut me up.

"The gods told me. I know you long to be rid of that festering curse that threatens to destroy your life. Many other Terraforgers, especially, have before. We can help restore you to the person you were meant to be. Ordinary. With so much potential to do whatever you want. No hiding. No fear. No shame."

Neris's arm tightened on mine.

"How?" I asked, my voice a mere whisper.

"There's a Cleanse—with water from the sacred River Daehan of Siad Nahar. It will cleave the powers from your soul."

"How can we be sure you're not lying?" Neris asked.

"Come with us," Aine said. "There are many of us living in perfect peace just outside the city."

"I can't just leave."

"Speak to your mother about it," said Nimue. "A mother only ever wants what's best for her daughter. If you decide to take our offer to *cure* you, head southeast to the temple of Rhianu. There, you will find us. You can come as well, Reneris."

Neris's lips were an unmovable thin line.

"There will come a day when Erleya will truly be purified of magic. Don't you want to be free of it before it is destroyed, and your soul along with it? Think on it, Gwyneth."

Neris and I didn't say a thing to each other about the odd encounter for days. With harp and dance lessons, constant preening of my appearance by the servants and my mother, and history lessons, the time continued to press on without any opportunity for me to use my powers. And sure enough, when Arionna provoked me, my emotions were so fragile that my anger nearly brought down the whole house.

It was then, with tears streaming down my face, that I told Mother about Nimue and Aine. Naturally, she agreed, sending a note to Father who came right home to sit down and discuss things. We came up with a plan—to tell everyone that I was going off to study history with a master historian. And then we left, Neris and I, to find the temple of Rhianu.

As dilapidated as the circle of stones that surrounded the statue of the Mother goddess was, the building in the field behind it was even more run-down.

The place where I now stand appears eerily similar. My lungs are ready to burst as I collapse onto my knees near the sacred circle of broken stones half my height. A cool breeze rustles the overgrown grass and my sweat-soaked dress, sending a shiver through me. I breathe in the loamy scent as I press my hand against the soil. The damp earth turns malleable beneath my powers, my fingers sinking into it like it's water.

I try to forget the lies about my magic—that I'm tainted for possessing such powers and would be better off cleaving it from my being.

I was so foolish. So damned foolish.

"Winnie?" Neris's voice reaches my ears, and I can't be more relieved to hear a familiar, comforting voice.

My hand comes out clean when I pull it from the soil. I sit fully in the grass and look up at my best friend, tears staining my face.

"That was Credia, wasn't it?" Neris whispers.

Wiping the sleeve of my dress across my cheeks, I nod.

Neris heaves a sigh. "Alright, let's get you home," she says. "I think we've had enough adventuring for the day."

Chapter 9

MOTHER IS HOSTING dinner at my childhood home tonight. While I'm happy to have the opportunity to see Neris again and pretend that not much else has changed since my marriage, I dread it. Lady Mari Pendry, my mother-in-law, effervesces with overenthusiastic charisma as she exchanges polite air kisses with Mother. Her straight blond hair curls slightly at her temples, softening the sharp angles of her face and prominent point of her chin. Her gown is the color of a robin's egg, complementing her peachy complexion and bringing out the soft blue of her eyes.

Lord Aled Pendry is an older version of Gruffud with sleek dark hair and stormy eyes. He greets Mother next, kissing the back of her hand with practiced courtesy. I smile at Mother, though her caramel eyes regard me with little warmth. Her slender fingers grasp my shoulders and squeeze with surprising firmness as she lowers her head to press her cheek against mine. A greeting fit for an acquaintance rather than her own flesh and blood.

As I step back into line with my new family, I catch Neris making a swift escape up the staircase. She doesn't even look our way, which is so unlike her. My logic slips through my fingers as I step forward to go after her. Gruffud slings his arm across my lower back, his hand catching my hip. I stop, my eyes flicking to him, and his brow lifts in a question.

"Apologies," I say, my voice hushed. "May I be excused? I just need to ... powder my nose." I can keep up appearances as well as any daughter of Rhosyn, but lying is absolutely not my strength.

Still, Gruffud releases me. He drops a kiss on my temple, murmuring, "Don't take too long," and it feels like a threat more than anything.

I nod and excuse myself, ignoring Mother's questioning look. I'm on my way to the staircase when I spot Arionna in front of it. Intricate braids weave around her head, decorated with tiny golden beads. The corset beneath her sapphire dress has cinched her waist so tightly that her breasts are practically hoisted up to her chin. It's a wonder she can even breathe—*I* can hardly breathe in my corset, which is considerably looser. Arionna is absolutely stunning as always. Her confidence in her body is a constant source of envy for me, but she's lost her mind if she thinks Mother would approve of such inappropriate attire for a highborn daughter of Lord Eurig Davies.

A dull ache settles into my chest at the thought of Father.

"Little sister," Arionna says with a mischievous smirk.

"Hello, Arionna. You look lovely." I respond.

"Thank you, and you look ..." She reaches out to the neckline of my dress and tugs it down, exposing my cleavage.

"Arionna!" I hiss through my teeth as I tug my neckline back up.

She smirks and steps around me, moving to greet the Pendrys. I heave a sigh and hurry up the grand staircase. I make my way to what used to be my old bedroom—now Neris's new room—where a framed painting is nailed to the door. In the painting, a waterfall cascades over a mountain, flowing into a winding river with lustrous waters. A rainbow reflects through the beams of sunlight. A smile tugs my lips up as my fingertips settle over the familiar brushstrokes.

Mother had scoffed at this painting, declaring that it didn't portray reality. That such a sight couldn't truly exist in nature. But the idea for this particular painting had come to me in a dream. Many of them do.

I knock on the door beneath the ornately carved frame. "It's me, Winnie," I say.

No response comes from inside, but Neris's footsteps approach before the door swings open. I'm left staring at her retreating back. Odd.

"Neris?"

She glances over her shoulder at me. Loose blond coils are plastered to her face where beads of sweat have formed. Her hand is white knuckled around an ivory, wide-tooth comb.

"Are you alright?" I ask.

"Yes. I just—" She lets out a harsh breath. "One of the servants fell ill and there was no one else to fill in with the dinner preparations."

My lips tug down, and heat spreads across my chest. "Did Mother ask *you*—"

"Winnie, drop it," Neris interrupts. Her voice only has the slightest edge to it. "Lady Rhosyn is not my mother. We both know that my adoption was unofficial; your mother can summon me to do servants' work whenever she pleases. Besides, I do enjoy baking." The smile on her pretty face is almost believable. She drops onto the stool of her vanity and swivels to face the mirror. Setting down her comb, she lifts a silken handkerchief to blot her face.

My steps are quick as I make my way toward her. I run the comb through her hair, pinning it in places to keep the curls out of her eyes. Then I withdraw rouge from her drawer and brush some lightly over her forehead and the apples of her cheeks. Her eyes are uncharacteristically glossy. My stomach drops a bit.

"Neris? You're not feeling ... unwell, are you?" I envision her on the ground, shaking uncontrollably.

"I'm fine," she says, looking away. She blinks rapidly and exhales.

"I'm sorry Mother treats you this way."

"It isn't all the time."

"Still ... Father would've never allowed it."

She smiles shakily. "He certainly wouldn't. By the realms, I miss him."

I nod and press my hand against my heart as that ache resurfaces. I truly hope he's alright.

The dinner bell resounds, and my shoulders tense.

"Thank you for making me look acceptable," Neris says.

I roll my tight shoulders. "You don't just look acceptable." I admire her heart-shaped face and the glow in her cheeks thanks to the rouge. She isn't the healthiest, but she'd certainly make a few heads turn tonight. She's more stunning than any highborn. "One more thing though." I open the drawer and hold my hand out, summoning a gold necklace with a dainty circular diamond. It floats into the palm of my hand and Neris rolls her eyes.

"Show off," she says with a giggle.

I wouldn't dare to use my terraforging in front of anyone other than Neris. "Did you take your elixir?"

Neris turns to let me clasp the necklace at the back of her neck. "I did."

Eventually, we head downstairs to suffer through dinner.

A few others join—a couple of proprietors from right here in Barr na Cahar and a book collector from Darragh. Lord Murtagh, a longtime friend of Father's from the Outer Isles, is the last to join us just as we're migrating to the dining room. The lilt of his accent is jarring among the aristocratic pretense of the evening; I find it a welcome difference. In fact, I'm mesmerized by it.

From the corner of the dining room, a lone violinist plays a drab tune throughout our meal, but Lord Murtagh remains the most intriguing. I remember Neris and I watching him spar with Father when we were children. He'd offered me his sword once and was flabbergasted when I held up the weight without much effort. The memory makes me smile.

Tonight, he keeps everyone entertained with tales of occasional seafaring and trades with marauders from Uldarvik. It sounds so exciting that I want to follow him home when dinner is finished. I want to live *his* life instead of the one I've been born into. Only Mother seems disinterested in Murtagh's stories and *politely* redirects the conversation back to business discussions of material acquisition from Ballygort and Ballybaeg.

"What if you cut out the middleman and go straight to Cluain Baile for dyeing plants? It's not entirely difficult to create dyes. Just a wee bit more elbow grease."

Mother pins him with a death stare. "The middleman is not an issue, Lord Murtagh."

"I ken, but think of the adventures, and the attainable skills."

His cerulean eyes turn to me. "Do you still enjoy art, young Gwyneth?"

"Gwyneth has no time for art these days, Lord Murtagh," Mother interrupts, and I swallow the eager *yes* that was about to slip from my lips. "Between her studies and marriage—"

"Studies?" Murtagh's discernible gaze doesn't leave mine. "What are you studying?"

"Gwyneth is quite the astute historian already," says Mother, once more cutting me off just as I pull in a breath to respond.

"Does Gwyneth know how to speak for herself?"

All eyes snap to Murtagh, then to Mother. Anyone else would've probably apologized, or at least given me the chance to speak. But Mother lifts her dimpled chin, the face of stubborn courage, and says, "She certainly does, but she's too humble to brag."

Well played.

"I see." Lord Murtagh casts me a look that says he doesn't believe a word.

Not quite sure what to say, I shrug. From across the table, Neris gives me a look that says *speak*.

"I prefer to keep an air of mystery," I say, and Neris scrunches up her face at my terrible comeback. I want to kick her, but the table is too wide.

Murtagh's boisterous laughter cuts through the tension, and I release a slow breath. "You are more than welcome to visit my estate at any time, young Gwyneth," says Murtagh. "The views are breathtaking, and my daughters will be grateful to have another young woman around. If it's alright with your husband, of course."

I smile politely, refusing to look at Gruffud, afraid of what I'd find on his face. "Thank you, Lord Murtagh."

Mother gives me a look that says *we'll talk later*, and now I'm truly grateful that I took my elixir.

It's going to be a long night.

We finish our courses of roasted quail, lambchops, potatoes in a hearty brown gravy, and a smattering of vegetables. I idly contemplate how the staff managed to get so many vegetables when the vegetation growth this year has been increasingly appalling. The gathering eventually moves to the sitting room, where everyone's engaged in various conversations.

I sip a floral wine that tastes an awful lot like perfume and try to keep a pleasant smile on my face, contributing to any conversation only when spoken to. The evening seems to drag on, and Neris looks a little pale. I wonder if she's lied to me about taking her tonic for whatever reason. I'm momentarily distracted from Neris by Lady Mari's pretentious titter.

The amount of phoniness in this room is almost suffocating. I pull my pocket watch from the skirt of my dress and peer at the gold hands again. We're within the ninth evening hour. Already, I feel the dull ache settling into my joints, something not even the elixir can completely eradicate.

"Dessert is served!" a servant calls out from the kitchen door.

As everyone stands to file back into the dining room, I hang back to check on Neris. I lean close to her, but someone grasps my arm with unnecessary force. I fight the urge to shove them away.

"We need to talk," a harsh voice says.

I look up at my husband, at the eyes that bear no patience nor understanding.

He turns those eyes toward Neris, but she holds his gaze. "Run along now, orphan," he sneers.

Her fists clench as she takes a step toward him. My heart leaps. "Neris." Her name rushes past my lips, helplessly beseeching. "Please."

She glowers at Gruffud and takes a step back, then another. Briefly, her gaze flicks to my face, something unreadable in her eyes, before she storms away from me. I want so much to walk away from Gruffud as well, to chase after Neris, but I face him. "That was unkind and uncalled for."

"She needs to be put in her place. Just as *you* need to be put in your place, *wife*."

I clench my teeth and inhale, my dress tightening with the motion. But as my lip parts, his head edges closer to mine.

"She may be your friend, but she's lowborn. Furthermore, you are a married woman now, tied to *my* family. Get your fucking act together and stop acting like a homesick child. I expect you to be standing by my side, not cavorting with the help."

"She's not—"

My words are cut off as his hand encircles the spot just above my elbow. He squeezes, and the bracelets on my wrist rattle, as if the metal is eager to cleave his hand from me. I exhale slowly and hope with all my might that he didn't notice.

"If you continue to disrespect me ..." He lets the threat hang in the air as he starts to move toward the dining room again. He moves too quickly, his grip unrelenting, so I have no option but to keep up with his rapid pace.

In the dining room, the servants have set out fruit tartlets and a piece of chocolate in front of each place. I would eat a solid three meals of dessert throughout the day if I had the chance, but my appetite has completely fled. Gruffud releases my arm and pulls out a chair for me, pushing it in once I'm seated.

Everyone digs into the tartlet, but across the table from me, Neris's eyes are on me. Her hands are clasped on the table behind her plate.

There is no anger or even disappointment to be found on her face.

But there's pity.

Chapter 10

DURVLA

It's been one month since our arrival at the Verge. My days are filled with training, meetings, and occasional work with herbs at the apothecary, while my nights are dedicated to family time with Tiernan, Chiyo, Taig, and sometimes with Alys's family when they invite us over for supper.

Today, before my eyes is a flurry of fists and flying feet. A crowd is gathered around the massive grey mat in the Skirmish Den where the Verge Defenders train. Innumerable weapons line one of the exposed brick walls, several mats are proportionately spread out through the space, and magelights shine down from the metal beams across the high ceiling. The stench of sweat and the increasing balminess within the Skirmish Den would be unbearable if not for the most extravagant display of athleticism I've ever seen.

Chiyo and Isobel are locked in a fighting match of spectacular magnitude—backflips, twirls, and magical fanfare grace the mat, completely unnecessary, but so captivating. The pair is a beautiful, lethal force to be reckoned with. At twenty, Isobel is a year younger than Chiyo with a personality as bright as her fiery hair.

Across the mat from us, Isobel's older sibling, Sloan, watches with steady blue-grey eyes. Despite the ten years between them, the siblings could be twins. Sloan seems unperturbed, clearly not worried about their sister's match against Chiyo.

While Isobel possesses impressive Wielding abilities, Chiyo

matches those skills with her diverse weaponry expertise. At last, Chiyo manages to pin Isobel to the mat, and onlookers applaud.

That is until Ava steps onto the mat, jaw fixed, braids swinging, lean shoulders thrown back. She draws her sword from her belt and points it toward the winner—a clear challenge.

Terrifying.

Chiyo's face drains of color, but she nods and steps forward while Isobel rushes off to stand beside her sibling. Sloan rests an arm on Isobel's shoulder—their sleeve is rolled back, revealing a stump that stops just below the elbow. If anyone dared to undervalue Sloan for their limb difference, they'd be making a fatal mistake; Sloan is deadly *without* a weapon and terrifying with a sword, even single-handed. Just yesterday, they faced Tiernan, and though Tiernan won, Sloan gave him a heart-pounding challenge.

On the mat, Ava and Chiyo circle each other like rival predators. Ava holds her long sword at the ready, and suddenly a presence appears beside me. I nearly leap out of my skin until I'm met with obsidian eyes and a small smirk that warms me even more than this stuffy building does.

"Just in time," I say to Tiernan, nodding toward the mat.

Chiyo has a dagger in each hand now, flipping one, then the other as her angular gaze locks with Ava's. They rush at each other with such swiftness, blade for blade, dodge for dodge. I gasp when Chiyo leaps back as Ava's sword slices across her upper arm, cutting through her sleeve. Chiyo's grip loosens on one dagger—it drops, but a breath later, Chiyo flings the other dagger at Ava. It whizzes past Ava's head, uncomfortably close, and the Warden flinches. Her hand flies to the tip of her ear, her fingers coming away red as she bares her teeth at Chiyo.

Another weapon is in Chiyo's hand—a shuriken—but this time, Ava's too quick. She darts to the side and drops down to the mat, forward-rolling toward Chiyo. One of her long legs swings out in a wide arc, effectively sweeping Chiyo's feet out from under her. Chiyo's back hits the padding with a slight bounce, and Ava leaves no room for recovery. She immediately straddles Chiyo, hips pinning her to the mat. Her sword lies discarded behind her, but a large parrying knife is now pressed to

Chiyo's throat, her free hand braced on one side of Chiyo's body.

My heart lurches almost painfully—I *know* Ava won't kill her, but ... Alright, I'm not all that certain.

The fight evaporates from Chiyo's body as her gaze latches on to Ava's. Everything seems to slow to a standstill, the pair of them unmoving, tension growing and stretching between them like a living entity. A flush creeps into Chiyo's cheeks until, at last, her eyes flick away from Ava's. Looking equally flustered, Ava scrambles off her as though burned. She tucks her dagger somewhere inside her leather vest and holds her hand out to Chiyo. Stubborn as a Kilkenny, Chiyo rolls away, getting up on her own.

Tiernan observes them with a single raised brow, several expressions playing across his face at once. His focus shifts, and I follow his line of sight to a crimson-faced Chiyo reappearing beside us. Tiernan claps her on the shoulder, but she only gives him a wavering, awkward smile.

A second later, they both tense. Chiyo looks my way, though Tiernan's hard gaze remains on the platform. "Ava's challenged you," Chiyo says.

I turn to the platform where Ava stands, her braids now pulled back with a scarf, her eyes burning a hole in my skull. My heart begins to pound. I've trained against a few others—and lost every time—but I've never gone against Ava. She's obscenely far beyond my league. In fact, people here have nicknamed her *the Beast*.

Shakily, I step forward and convince my legs to keep moving. I climb the steps to the platform and approach Ava. We get into a fighting stance and Ava says without signing, "Prove yourself."

Then she strikes.

Pain erupts in my forearm as it takes the blow intended for my face. The next strike from Ava's eager fist catches me in the shoulder as I turn my body away from her. She's too fast, too strong. I duck, but as soon as I'm upright again, her fist flies at my face, far too close for comfort. I *barely* avoid a nasty blow as I duck again.

I shriek, holding both arms over my head as I hunker down.

Ava's foot comes out of nowhere, clipping my ankle and tugging my leg out from under me. I'm left with no choice but to throw my hands back to catch my fall, but pain still throbs through my tail-bone and up my arms as I take the defeat.

Ava signs but my vision swims so badly that I cannot make out what she says.

I blink and will my head to cooperate. Embarrassment crawls over my skin, flushing my face with a heat that's hard to ignore.

Ava waves both hands in front of my face. "Are you even paying attention?"

"Yes," I grit out. "Just give me a moment." I'm not sure if the words are even loud enough for her to hear.

She crouches comfortably, her arms propped on her knees. Infuriation fills her hazel eyes as she levels a glower at me. "Get up."

I said give me a moment, I want to blurt. I meet her gaze with as much stubbornness as I can muster. Tiernan moves into my peripheral vision, still on the sidelines, but I refuse to look at him.

"Get up." Ava's gestures are aggressive.

I push myself to stand and hold my ground, even as my vision spots and my head threatens to sink me right back down.

"Focus," Ava signs, standing too close for comfort. "Focus through whatever is going on in your body. Do not give your opponent a chance to best you. Everyone has a weakness. If you can spot it at the very beginning, good. If not, keep looking for it, and strike them where it hurts. Your opponent is limping on his right leg? Kick him in the right leg. Favoring one arm? Strike his arm. A blow to the face is always good. You're not fast, nor are you strong—"

Thanks.

"—but you're clever. Use it to your advantage."

I sigh and reluctantly get into a fighting stance again.

Ava doesn't reciprocate. Instead, her gaze sweeps from my head down to my toes. She scoffs and says, "You're done here." My heart sinks. If this was my chance to prove myself, I failed.

But then Ava says, "No cowering next time. See you tomorrow."

I let my hands fall, my shoulders following. My legs wobble as I watch her walk off the mat, only to be blocked by Tiernan. I stand there, watching the heated discussion unfurl between them. Ava crosses her arms over her chest and cocks a hip as if casually waiting for something. Whatever he says, she rebuts, and whatever she says, he does the same. Tiernan's eyes meet mine, as do Ava's, and I know for sure that they're talking about me. *Arguing* about me.

Face burning, I rush out of the den, desperate for fresh air. I'm mere steps from the exit when Tiernan appears, his palms held up to gently halt me. "Where are you going?" he asks.

"Why did you challenge her like that?"

His face falls, but he doesn't respond. "Are you alright?" he asks instead.

"*Tiernan.*" I emphasize his name aloud without signing.

He huffs out an annoyed breath. "Ava had no right to publicly humiliate you like that."

I follow the movement of his hand as his fingers idly trace the scar that crawls up his neck.

"She's in charge, so she has every right," I say.

"Abusing her authority is *not* her right! *No one* has the right to publicly humiliate their subordinates! That's how people like Rheon come to be. Because everyone allows it!"

His hands move with such hostility that I blink and step back. A glance from someone a small distance away tells me that he's speaking quite loudly. Tiernan must notice the tears welling in my eyes, because he immediately holds his hands up in apology. "I don't mean to shout," he motions quickly. "I'm just—"

"Stressed? Frustrated?" I swallow, fending off the tears.

"Yes, it doesn't mean I have to take it out on you. I'm sorry." He sighs and rubs the back of his neck, his gaze growing distant.

"Tiernan, talk to me. Please. Ever since we found out about Rheon—"

His forehead crinkles. "This isn't about me. This is about you."

"Is it?" I keep my tone calm and cross my arms over my chest, tilting my head at him. His eyes soften and the anger seems to melt away. But that bothered look—like he's trying to hold back—remains on his face. My heart aches for whatever demons he's fighting. Resigned, I sigh and say, "Alright, I'm supposed to have tea with Alys, so I'm heading home to wash up."

"Do you want me to walk you home or—"

"No, it's alright. Stay here and get your training in."

He nods and gives my hand a squeeze before we go our separate ways.

After freshening up, I head out to pay Alys a visit. I can't stop thinking about the way Tiernan confronted Ava after she challenged me. I understand he only wants to protect me, but I can't help but think that it only made me look even weaker.

Alys awaits me in her sitting room, and a smile stretches across her face as she adjusts the colorful silken scarf around the front of her hair. "Good to see you, sweetling," she says. "No Tiernan today?"

I shake my head, regretting the movement as it makes me dizzier. Sinking down into the armchair across from her, I respond, "I just needed a moment to myself."

Surprise colors her face. "Sounds like we need some tea," she says. "I'll be right back."

Moments later, she settles in the chair across from me again, her steady gaze on me. I gnaw on my lower lip, suddenly questioning my decision to have a casual afternoon cuppa rather than resume training.

"Anxious?" Alys asks me.

"Hmm?"

She leans forward and places her mug on the tea table before pointing toward me. I follow the direction of her finger, to where my knee bounces up and down. Immediately, I stop, signing my apology.

Alys leans in, concern creasing her forehead. "Do you need to talk?" she motions.

I shake my head. "No—I just ..." The words flutter right within my reach, teasing me. "I should be training. I should be running. I should be—"

She very gently holds up a hand and signs, "You are allowed to breathe for a moment."

Yet when I try to take a deep breath, it feels like a boulder is crushing my chest.

"I can feel the pounding in your head, sweetling; I'm not even sure how you can keep your eyes open with that pain."

"I'm accustomed to—" My brows dart up as realization sets in. Maybe I misread her words. "Did you say you can *feel* my headache? Has your healing returned?"

A smile adorns her plump face as she nods, and happy tears glisten in her eyes. It's been a mystery why her recovery has been so slow given her Healer blood. But since the poison had also drained her of her healing capabilities, she's theorized that it was no regular poison, but one targeting magical blood specifically. A poison that was magically made.

I beam at her. "That's incredible, Alys."

"Thank you, sweetling. With that said, I've prepared a stronger tincture for you. Since you're exerting more energy, you'll need a more concentrated dosage. I have a week's worth for you already and I'm working on more."

"Alys, I don't want you to overexert yourself. I've been fine with the tinctures from the apothecary."

"It isn't a problem. It's been nice to feel useful again." She smiles. "Now tell me what's bothering you."

I gnaw on my lip again, and my fingers find their way under my wrist cuff, running along the seam. I try to think of what's *not* bothering me. "I hate that I still can't control the dreamwalking very well. I'm terrible with sparring and dagger throwing—I don't even dare to pick up a sword. I want to prove to your daughter that I can defend myself Outside, but I'm not so sure myself."

"You've been able to defend yourself and Tiernan before. You just need the motivation. Healing didn't come all that natural to me, you know." The surprise must be all over my face because Alys chuckles and signs, "So that's proof there's hope. It took a lot of moments where I *had* to use my healing, or moments where I accidentally used it. What I did was keep track of what exactly happened in those moments. What I was feeling, doing, thinking ... Things like that. So that the next time I tried to intentionally tap into it, I was able to recall how I felt when I accidentally used it. Does that make sense?"

I nod. "It does. Thank you, Alys."

"And how are rune studies with Oksana going?"

"Not bad. We mostly focus on me breaking her light shields with them, and fortifying them as well. But she's given me a small book of symbols that I look over every day at home as well. It's useful to have a good memory, I guess."

"I'm glad you're recognizing your strengths."

I smile and take another sip of my tea. Alys does the same.

As I'm about to speak again, I catch sight of brown leather boots and trousers the color of moss appearing behind Alys through the wooden balusters of the staircase. Ava's face emerges from the walled portion, recognition sinking in as her gaze snags on me. She rolls her eyes and heaves a deep sigh. She retreats up the stairs just as Alys turns toward her.

Uncomfortable heat pools in my chest as Alys faces me again. Her expression seems uncertain, conflicted.

"Your daughter loathes me," I sign silently.

"No, she loathes *me*. Not you. She doesn't even talk to me unless she has to," Alys signs back, her lips unmoving. I don't get to question her before she hastily continues, "There are a lot of behind-the-scenes things with her father and the panel. A lot of debate about who should be on the team dispatched to the Outside and when it's going to happen. It's almost like Carys and the councilors all over again."

My heart drops into my stomach as sadness washes over Alys's face.

"Still nothing from her?" she asks, speaking again as she signs.

"The same. It's as though the connection has a crack in it." I'm uncertain how to better explain. "I just want to believe she's alive and well."

"Me too, sweetling. Me—"

Sunlight pours in through the door as Dayfyd enters. He seems to startle at the sight of me, but his momentary surprise melts into a softness that I cannot quite place. "Hello," he says with a gentle smile. "I didn't know you'd be here. Good timing. I have something for you." He walks closer to the seating area, and my brows rise, my curiosity piqued. "And hello to you too, my darling Elviera," he says to Alys. Fine lines appear at the corners of her eyes, her lips curving sweetly as Dayfyd drops a kiss onto the crown of her head.

It's hard to believe that these two have been separated for years and seem to have so easily picked up right where they left off.

As Dayfyd disappears up the stairs, I turn my curious gaze to Alys who simply smiles at me. I have an inkling that she knows exactly what Dayfyd has for me. Alys shifts, sliding her hands over the top layer of her colorful wrap skirt. It's nice to see her dressing in a way reflective of herself and her culture, rather than what's expected of an assimilated Erleyan. We've asked her if she would prefer that we call her *Elviera*, but she's made it clear that *Alys* is an important part of who she is.

She lifts the cup of tea to her lips again and takes a dainty sip. My curiosity is getting the better of me, and just as my lips part to ask if she knows what Dayfyd has for me, he reappears at the bottom of the steps.

In his hand, he clutches a colorful handkerchief. His shoulders are rigid, the smile on his lips pulled too tight. I slide closer to the edge of my seat as he closes the distance with long strides and briefly regards me with what looks like apprehension in his hazel eyes. "I believe this belongs to you," he signs one-handed.

Hesitantly, I hold my hand out and he places the kerchief in my palm. It's surprisingly weighty and thrums strangely, warming my skin through the fabric. I peel the kerchief open to reveal a smooth opal stone, pearly white beneath mesmerizing iridescence. With each gentle tilt of my hand, the colors shift—purple, green, blue, pearlescent white. "It's beautiful. What is it?" My eyes find Dayfyd's again.

"A moonstone," he says. "No one truly knows how it works, but Alys and I believe that it should be with a Dreamwalker. It's been sitting in my drawer for years."

We're quiet for a while as I admire the stone, sliding my fingers over the smooth surface. A moonstone. I want to ask him what it's been doing in his drawer and why it should belong to a Dreamwalker, but I feel too awkward. "Thank you, Dayfyd."

There's a semblance of sadness or something else behind his smile. Does he regret giving me the stone? I wrap it gently but keep it nestled between my hands.

"Right," Dayfyd signs. "I must get going again. Nice seeing you, Durvla." He passes by his wife, stealing a quick kiss before hurrying out of the house again.

Eventually, Alys and I shift into normal conversation. We talk about Taig, Alys's family, the community garden, which seems to be faring better than any plants Outside.

The clock on Alys's wall reminds me I need to get going, but she insists I take a tincture before leaving.

By the time I return to our house, there's no trace of my headache. There's still the mild dizziness that often clouds my vision, more so since I've started training, but I just deal with it. This morning, Chiyo volunteered to pick up Taig from school, so I have a moment to practice my daywalking.

I head into the backyard and set my bag down in the grass before sinking down beside it. Crossing my legs, I close my eyes and inhale deeply. Lately, it's been harder to empty my mind. The more I try to reach out to Carys, the more hopeless I become. I sit there, breathing in and out slowly, enjoying the feel of the occasional breeze caressing my face.

I force myself to stop thinking of my physical senses and retreat into myself. I tap into my powers to seek Carys's fiery essence, searching for the fragmented trail that leads to her subconscious. My body grows lighter, and I latch on to the tiniest flicker of her dark flames, casting my thoughts toward it.

Carys, I know you're out there. We'll figure this out. I promise.

For a moment, I swear that tiny flicker grows hotter. I envision a flame coming to life, blazing brighter, but then it's snuffed out, shoving me back into myself. A small throbbing in my temples supersedes the tincture I've just taken.

"*Mind if I join?*" a voice says across the barrier of my thoughts.

I open my eyes as Tiernan crouches down in front of me. An awkward smile twists his lips, but there's sadness in his countenance.

"I'm sorry," he signs. "I shouldn't have publicly gone up to Ava the way I did. I just ..." He signs and looks away.

"It's alright," I tell him.

"I hate seeing you hurt. But the last thing I want you to think is that I don't believe in you. Because I do."

I'm trying my hardest to believe he does as well.

He frowns at me, and I pull up my mental shields, securing them. A proud glimmer appears in his eyes, his cheekbones sharpening as a smile creeps onto his lips. "It's impressive that you can shield so well," he says.

"I get a lot of practice with my constantly loud thoughts, you know."

"The loudest," he teases.

I smirk at him. "Oh ... Dayfyd gave me something today. A moonstone, he called it. He said it should belong to a Dreamwalker."

I reach into my bag and pull out the handkerchief, handing it over to Tiernan. Carefully, he unwraps it and cradles it in his hand. He tilts it back and forth just as I had. "If it should belong to a Dreamwalker, why did *he* have it?" Tiernan signs one-handed as best as he can. "And what exactly is it?"

"I'm not sure," I admit. "I didn't ask."

"I know old magic utilized stones a lot. They're great for imbuing. Amplifiers. Dampeners like Carys's."

Amplifier. "Oksana did say something about an amplifier, but she also didn't want to resort to it yet."

Tiernan's eyes widen. He passes the stone back to me and says, "Does it make you feel stronger? If it's a moonstone, I wonder if it requires ... well, *moonlight*. Or if it can strengthen your connection to the dream realm?"

Holding it between my hands, I close my eyes and try to get a sense of it. Something feels different about it, but I'm not quite sure what. I don't feel any stronger or any weaker. Opening my eyes, I shrug again.

"Keep it on you, maybe," Tiernan suggests. "And perhaps you should ask Dayfyd."

I make a face, wrapping up the stone again. "He acts kind of strange when I'm around. I don't know what it is."

Tiernan signs and motions, "I can't get much of a read on him either. And I'm certain he has no powers. The apple doesn't fall far from the tree with Ava, I guess."

My stomach churns at the thought of Ava again. "I need to learn the no-spin throw," I blurt out. "I've been working on it with Chiyo, but it's so difficult."

He stands and pulls me to my feet as well. "Alright ..."

"I just need to prove to her—"

"Durvla." He places a hand gently on my cheek and strokes it with his thumb. My lips snap shut. "Ava is an angry person, and she takes it out on everyone. Don't let her continue to make you doubt yourself and trust me when I say you're improving. You *are* improving. When we first got here a month ago, you weren't able to jog the distance you do now. You couldn't even summon a small shield on command and now you can. I know you're frustrated with the dreamwalking, but you'll figure it out. You just need that *aha* moment—it happens to all of us. Trust me."

He steps back and pulls one dagger from his belt before pressing the hilt into my palm. "Your throwing has been more than decent. For this new throw, you just have to focus a little more than usual."

It's kind of hard to do that when his sleeves are rolled back, displaying the sword inked onto his muscular forearm. It ripples as he grips another dagger to demonstrate once more, but I'm busy staring and miss everything.

It isn't until I register the playful glimmer in his eyes that I realize I've missed something. "Distracted?" he asks.

"Admittedly, yes."

His eyes crinkle at the corners, narrowing in a way that is truly endearing. "To start, let's adjust your stance. It's just a little different from the stance you'd use for the spin throw, but the subtle differences matter." He stands in front of me, placing his hands on my hips, squaring them. "Relax your knees."

It's only then that I realize that my knees have been locked; they protest as I bend them slightly. Tiernan moves to stand behind me, once more adjusting my throwing stance.

"*Lower your shoulders,*" he says into my mind.

I exhale slowly and force my shoulders to relax. Tiernan's hand glides along my side and down over my waist, adjusting my hips once more. Tingling warmth blooms against my skin as his fingers trail up my arm. I grip the dagger tighter in my clammy palm, trying to keep my focus on the target rather than on the pleasant lurch in my stomach and eager quiver in my chest.

His body is so close to mine that I almost *feel* his teasing smirk. I certainly feel the tickle of his breath against my ear. I'm overtaken by the scent of him—of leather, citrus, and mint. I'm tempted to drop the dagger and lean back into his strong arms. I've done enough training today, haven't I?

"*Throw*," he says, snapping my attention back to the tree.

I fling my arm forward, following through after I release the hilt of the dagger. The blade spins haphazardly before bouncing right off the bark and plummeting to the grass below. Yet, Tiernan is all smiles when I face him, another dagger in his hand.

"Close," he says, pressing the hilt into my palm again.

I glance down at the dagger, then back up at the handsome man before me. It's hard to believe that mere months ago I would've wagered it was impossible for me to feel attraction, let alone such adoration for someone. Yet here we are.

Tiernan quirks a brow, waiting for me to say something, and a fresh wave of embarrassment comes over me. The weight of the dagger settles in my hand again. "That was supposed to be a no-spin throw," I say. "It absolutely spun."

He laughs. "So, it was a little overenthusiastic. You'll get it next time."

I'm focused on his lips when I realize that he's signing something, but I've already missed most of it. Heat crawls up my neck as amusement plays over his face. "Perhaps we should take a break," he says.

I hold the dagger out to him hilt first. "Excellent idea."

Sheathing the blade at his waist, he steps a little closer and dips his head down to mine, waiting. I lift my face to his with every intention of offering him a brief, chaste kiss, but the moment our lips touch, my stomach dissolves into reckless flutters.

The echoes of uncertainty are silenced by the sweep of Tiernan's tongue against the seal of my lips. I'm enraptured by the taste of him

—jasmine tea and mint, and a burst of sweet and tart ... passion? Lust? It flitters across my tongue, then skin, tactile as the breeze. The sensation takes me aback as my mind grapples between the desire to make sense of it and the longing to dive deeper.

I wind my arms around him, and my whole body tingles as his lips trail along my jaw and down to the side of my neck. I suck in a small breath as my stomach tightens with want. On instinct, I tilt my head to the side, allowing his lips to further explore my skin, each kiss igniting something greater within me. His hand slides down my arm, his fingers lacing with mine, and we rush inside.

The door barely closes before Tiernan presses me against the wooden surface, his lips on my neck again, butterflies dancing around my navel as aching heat builds in my core.

"Tiernan," I manage to whisper as his lips brush against my collarbone.

Immediately he stops and I inwardly curse myself for interrupting. I desperately want to find relief for the building ache, but— "We still need to talk." I clap my hand over the first two buttons of my blouse. When did he even unfasten them?

His eyes are filled with carnal promises as he looks down at me. He kisses my fingers gently. "Alright, let's talk."

We walk over to the couch and sit down. But, for the life of me, I cannot get rid of the flustered feeling, or the lingering heat from his lips on my neck. I refasten the top two buttons of my blouse and exhale slowly. "I ..." *Words, Durvla.* "Before you, I never kissed anyone."

He doesn't look surprised, only curious where I'm going with this conversation starter.

"I've also never ..." I gesture vaguely, moving my open palm back and forth between us. "I never had an *interest* either."

He smiles warmly, though concern seeps into his eyes. "I hope I'm not pressuring you."

"No, but ... I ... No." Gods, why is this so hard to say? "I don't know if I'm ready. I mean, my body tells me otherwise, but this thing between us ... I don't even know if it needs defining. Perhaps I'm being unreasonable."

"You're not being unreasonable." He rubs the back of his neck as he seems to mull over everything I've said. "What are your expectations?" he asks after a while.

I shrug. I haven't been romantically involved with anyone before. I know it's not the same for him, and I know the only other relationship I'm aware of ended in tragedy. Guilt and mild discomfort sink into me, clouding my mind. Maybe I should be asking *him* what *his* expectations are; what if I cannot live up to them? What if I fall short compared to the standard set by his past relationships?

His head tilts slightly, but I don't bother to raise my mental shields—I try my hardest not to shy away. "Am I thinking too loud again?" I sign, sliding my teeth across my lower lip.

"Loud and clear." His smile is gentle. "But this is about *us*. Maura was my past. You are my—present."

My brow lifts. He'd quickly changed the direction of the hand sign, but I'd caught the beginning of it anyway.

Future.

My heart nearly leaps out of my chest—I cannot decipher if it's from excitement or fear. He thinks I am his future?

He takes a moment to recover his bearings. "We don't have to do anything we're not prepared for. There's no pressure."

There is pressure, just not from him. "It's probably silly, but I always assumed marriage would come first," I admit.

His back straightens, and I'm uncertain how to interpret the look that crosses his handsome face. He quickly schools his features into neutrality, and I rush to explain myself.

"It's how things are generally done in Cluain Baile. Most maidens are married fairly young because it increases our chance of ... survival, you know? I'm an exception for obvious reasons. It was too risky. But I'd always assumed I'd marry out of obligation rather than—" I stop myself, carefully considering my next words. "Rather than ... whatever this is." If things had carried on as usual, I would've likely married Osheen out of convenience. That thought turns my stomach for far too many reasons.

Tiernan's posture loosens as a smile eclipses his neutral expression.

"Not that I'm saying we need to get married." I bite my lip to shut myself up, but more words fly out. "And now, I've probably scared you off."

His smile falters slightly, but he shakes his head. "I'm not that easily scared off."

He takes my hands and faces me squarely before releasing me to sign, "We don't have to rush into anything. I don't want you to feel pressured. No matter what, at any moment, you have every right to bring anything and everything to a halt. I will *always* stop if something makes you uncomfortable or you're not ready for it. All you have to do is say so."

I nod, warm giddiness blanketing the self-imposed pressure surrounding our relationship.

"And when you *don't* want me to stop, I'll obey your commands like the most eager devotee. No questions asked. Just try me."

A snort escapes and I cover my mouth, making a grin stretch across his face. "Try you?"

"Try me. Any request at all."

I don't know what frivolous sprite whacks me on the head, but I blurt, "Dance for me." I grin, unable to resist, knowing that there's no way that Tiernan Kilkenny would dance on command.

His eyes go wide, but then he pushes himself to his feet.

Is he really going to …? I stare up at him and my jaw drops as Tiernan does a tiny little jig, jumping lightly with a hilariously straight face. I try to hold back my laughter, but it rolls through me uncontrolled. Tiernan's lips twitch with his own failed attempt to keep from smiling.

Gods, what a view.

His gaze abruptly shifts, and he stops dancing as the room brightens. I follow his line of sight to the open door where Chiyo stands with Taig in her arms. "What in Lugda's hells did I just walk into?" she asks as she sets Taig down.

My heart lifts at the sight of Taig walking into the room. His steps are so much steadier lately. He looks at me and his eyes light up. But just as I make it close enough for a hug, he throws his arms out with excitement, then turns and walks the other way as if heading back outside.

"Wow, nice to see you too," I say with a chuckle.

Chiyo redirects him to me. "Give your sister a hug."

Taig wiggles and gives a wide-mouthed laugh as Chiyo pokes him in the side. I get down onto my knees and wrap my arms around him. When I stand again, I glance at Tiernan and smile. "Thank you for the talk and the dance," I silently sign.

He smiles and nods. "You're very welcome, beautiful."

Chapter 11

GWYNETH

THE SCENT of oiled leather and parchment neutralizes the stench of the binding glue. Wall-to-wall shelves, most of them packed to capacity with books and empty journals, provide an oddly soothing background.

Despite being a noble, my inheritance doesn't belong to me. It was handed over as a dowry and I need my husband's permission to use what little is left. Naturally, the rules of the land never cease to amaze me in the worst ways. Most shop-owner families hire employees from outside their households. But not mine. Mother's greed has left us doing all the work, keeping the earnings within the family. So, I hide away some for myself. I've earned it after all.

To be honest though, I quite like binding the books—there's something soothing in the repetitive, intricate routine. Being in the bindery in the cellar beneath my childhood home also makes me feel close to Father even in his absence. Just as the pocket watch I keep with me provides comfort. He loved books—from historical texts to epic adventures akin to children's fables, he could never get enough of them.

Sunlight streams in through the window and across my work-bench as I flick my finger toward the wooden book-binding block. Propelled by my terraforging, the bolts that keep the blocks in place unscrew, the slabs of wood loosening, allowing the pages within to expand again. I yank the freshly sewn book pages from between the slabs and unintentionally slam them onto the workbench with a loud *thwack*.

"Realms, Winnie!" Neris exclaims from her own workbench on the other side of the room. "Tell me how you *truly* feel!" She glances up, her paring knife poised over a cut of calfskin, her spectacles perched on the tip of her button nose.

"Apologies," I mumble.

"It's alright. It's been a *Gruff* day for you." She smirks at her own joke, and I groan.

"That was *terrible*, Neris."

"Ah, you love my Gruffud puns," she says, flicking her blond curls over her shoulder playfully. She giggles as she gets back to measuring, positioning the paring knife against the ruler to cut the excess from the calfskin cover.

We continue working in focused silence. I slide a fresh ream of pages into the book block and set it upright to begin making careful cuts along what will become the spine. As I lift the small handsaw from my workbench, Neris calls to me in an odd, faraway voice. I glance up just as she sets her blade aside. There's a recognizable dazed look on her face that makes my chest constrict. But before I can remind the stubborn woman to sit down, she staggers back and drops like a ragdoll out of sight.

"Shite," I whisper, running across the room.

On the floor behind her workbench, Neris's body is rigid as a corpse, her spectacles akilter on her face. Her limbs twitch in forewarning before the violent convulsions begin. My stomach flips as I drop to my knees, removing her spectacles and turning her onto her side. There's nothing to do but to wait for the spasms to end, for my friend to come back to me, to breathe again.

Thank the stars the fit ends as quickly as it began, the color slowly creeping back into her face, her body going limp. I shift her, cradling her head in my lap as she drags in a heavy breath and releases it in an awkward *whoosh* as if she's forgotten how to breathe.

"It's alright," I croon as I smooth back her silky curls again and again. "Can you take another breath?" It's hard to keep the plea out of my voice.

Her eyes are still closed, pale lashes fluttering against her bluish cheeks, but she inhales deeply again. I let out a sigh of relief, even as her saliva seeps into my dress, even as her head grows heavier in my lap. "Stay awake," I say gently. I feel like the worst person to force her to remain awake after her body just betrayed her.

With a small moan she lifts a shaky hand to the corner of her mouth and wipes frothy dribble away. "Your dress..." she whinges. "I'm sorry."

A small, humorless laugh escapes me. "Dammit, Neris, I don't care about my dress."

"It's disgusting," she mutters.

I stare at her in disbelief. At least she's already more like herself. After a few minutes, she sits up with effort and presses a shaky hand to her head. With a sigh she pushes her hair back from her sweaty forehead and licks her lips a few times. She still looks slightly dazed.

"I'll get you some water."

She nods. I stand and set her spectacles down on the workstation before heading over to the pitcher and crystal on a nearby table. Neris sips the water slowly once I return. I observe her closely—the unsteadiness in her hands, the exhausted slump of her shoulders— while anxiety continues to hammer in my chest.

"It's been a long time since that's happened while taking the tonics," I say.

She ignores me and continues sipping the water.

"Neris?" My lips tug down.

Her glass is clearly empty, but she continues to feign drinking.

"Neris!"

She jumps and lowers the drinking glass with shaky hands. "Alright, I stopped taking the tonics. Or rather, I started rationing it. To stretch it. I figured it was better than running out and being completely without."

I open my mouth to shout at her, but she interrupts.

"You're doing the exact same thing with your elixirs!"

My mouth snaps shut.

Things have changed a lot since the queen's death was announced. For months, Radika has been having a harder and harder time replenishing her potions, medicines, and any magical contraband. I used to get *at least* one month's worth of my elixir with each visit. Now, I'm lucky if I get enough to last me a week, and I end up having to find more time to sneak out to Radika's makeshift workshop on the outskirts of the city.

When I speak up again, my voice comes out flat as I try to remain calm. "You didn't say you were running low."

"You're still adjusting to this arranged marriage, your father's situation, the shortage of your own elixir ... I didn't want to add my own shit to that."

"Well, you should've."

She looks guilty but forces a smirk onto her face. "I'm running low?"

"Dammit, Reneris, now is not the time for jokes!"

She makes a face. "Ooh, you called me Reneris. You must be serious."

"I am serious! *This* is serious. The kingdom is a mess. Who's to say that Mainland isn't going to face the same Undesirable rules as the Grounders face. You've heard the servants' stories about raids. About people being hanged just for having an ailment."

"Alright, I'm sorry," she says. "It's just that you're already working your arse off to get through each day. I didn't want to further overwhelm you."

"Neris. You mean more to me than anything else. Please risk overwhelming me. You're more a sister to me than Arionna has ever been. I don't know what I'd do without you." I stand and take her hand, pulling her to her feet. "Now go take the damn medicine before you relapse again."

She salutes. "Yes, ma'am."

As she walks off, I pick up the crystal cup to return it to the table. I pour myself some water, and as I turn with the freshly filled glass, a tingling sensation glazes over my skin. A figure materializes before me, covered from head to toe in a grey, tattered cloak. I gasp and drop the glass, which shatters. I bump my hip into the table, causing the pitcher to fall over. Water spills, pooling on the table and overflowing onto the floor.

The figure holds a withered, almost greyish hand to blue lips, the only thing visible under the cloak. The book bindery dissolves around me, and a dark, misty forest appears with a gigantic tree stretching toward the sky.

That damn tree again!

This isn't the first time I've seen it. It's appeared in my dreams many times before, always accompanied by an inexplicable desire to travel northward, away from here.

A shattering sound fills my ears, and I wince, closing my eyes. When I open them again, I'm back in the bindery, and the figure is nowhere in sight.

My heart is in my throat, cutting off my air supply. It takes a while before I can catch my breath again. Where the figure stood, four symbols glow on the floor. A singular spiral, three whorls, a cross within a circle, and a triquetra. But in a blink, they're all gone.

Realms above, what on earth is happening to me?

I need sleep.

I've been taking half an elixir every day, and it only takes the edge off the pain. By dinner tonight, the daily ache was already starting to sink in. Now, as I lay in bed, the sheets drawn up to my chin as Gruffud snores loudly beside me, the pain infiltrates my senses until I can't ignore it anymore. I stumble out of bed and don my nightgown, then my silk housecoat. I cinch it tightly around my waist and grab the oil lantern to light my way.

As I step into the corridor, the flame casts eerie shadows in the hallway. My pulse spikes as my vision darkens and wanes at the edges. I grip the banister with my slick palm and pad down the staircase. I just need to make it outside, get the herbal mixture, and brew the tea Radika gave me.

Cold sweat breaks out on my skin as I step outside and make my way to where I keep my elixirs buried. I close my eyes, breathing slowly as I draw the stony box from the earth and pluck the satchel of herbs from inside. Burying the box again takes more effort than usual, but finally, I make my way back into the kitchen and force my bare feet to take me toward the kettle hanging in the woodburning oven.

Water sloshes inside the kettle when I jostle it, so I light the logs with the flint and tinder while sweat continues to dampen my night-gown. Bone deep pain in my thighs forces me to my knees moments before a searing sensation pours down my throat.

Stars spot my vision as pain ripples through my senses. The world disappears. Saliva floods my mouth, and I gag. When my arms fail to hold me upright any longer, the cold kitchen floor against my cheek shocks my senses, keeping me fully conscious and aware. The slash of agony across my abdomen is a sadistic reenactment of the initial effects of the Cleanse a year ago. I curl into myself, breathless and nauseated, dizzy, hot and cold.

I'm not sure how long I lie on the floor, shivering and biting back groans of distress, but a voice wavers in and out of my senses. "Lady Gwyneth?" Sage's airy voice has gone shrill. Too loud.

My eyes blink open, my sight bleary.

"Do you need me to get Gruffud? Call for a healer?"

I push myself up on wobbly arms as the kettle starts to scream. "No," I grind out. I pause to swallow the acrid vomit that rises into my throat. "I just need tea. It's from a healer."

Sage squats in front of me, her plump face shifting in and out of focus. Her eyes drop to the satchel that's fallen to the floor. She picks it up, holding the pouch before my face. "This?" she asks.

I nod, and the motion makes my head and neck ache.

"Alright, I'll make the tea and add tepid water to cool it down."

I must lose consciousness for a moment, because the next thing I know, there's a clammy hand on my face. I peel my eyelids back and force my eyes as wide as I can. Sage sets something down with a dull *clink* and hoists me up, pain skittering across my sensitive skin. She braces me upright somehow and holds a porcelain teacup to my lips.

"Sip slowly, Lady Gwyneth." Her voice is quiet and gentle for once. The liquid still scalds my tongue and the roof of my mouth, but I drink it anyway. Perspiration cools on my skin and the pain slowly begins to fade as exhaustion seeps in. "One more sip," Sage coaxes. I barely get the liquid in my mouth before someone shouts over the gentle crackle of the woodstove.

"What in hells is going on in here?"

Sage jumps to her feet and steps aside, making way for Gruffud. Shite ... His face is even more menacing than usual in the light of the oil lamp. He sets it down on the table within reach and bends to grab my arm. Pain flares through my still-sensitive body as he hauls me to my feet.

"What is wrong with you?" he demands, his grip unfaltering.

"I—" The words snag in my throat as his eyes roam my body, my face.

He turns to Sage. "Perhaps you have better sense than my imbecile wife here. What is going on?"

"Lady Gwyneth is feeling unwell, my lord. I am simply helping her. Digestive troubles." Her eyes dart to me apologetically, and I hope she knows I appreciate her attempt to cover for me.

"It isn't the first time you've been *unwell*." He grinds out the last word as though it disgusts him. I try not to whimper from his grip still on my arm. "Of course, I had to be stuck with damaged goods." He releases me with a shove, and as if my legs have turned to pudding, I drop to the floor with a small cry.

Gruffud marches out of the kitchen, leaving the door to swing behind him as I get to my knees and rub my throbbing tailbone. Sage's eyes brim with tears as she hurries to help me to my feet again. "Let me help you back to bed, Lady Gwyneth," she says. "Though, I can imagine you aren't in a rush."

To my surprise, wet laughter rushes from me. "I wouldn't mind sitting at the table for a moment to gather my bearings, thank you."

With Sage's silence to keep me company, I sit at the table until the pain ebbs and my senses begin to numb as though I've consumed too much fermented drink. Sage helps me to bed as I drift and stagger, depositing me beside a snoring Gruffud. I whisper my thanks, and before she's even out of the room, I drift off.

Chapter 12

CARYS

Since my arrival in Uldarvik, the month has gone by in chaotic, choppy segments. I find myself in places I don't remember walking to—somehow bathed and groomed, somehow fed. When I'm fully aware of everything happening around me, my appetite is usually absent.

A warm hand on my arm pulls me back to the present. Through squinted eyes, I make out Odgar. His smile is hesitant, worried. How can I blame him when I don't even know where I am.

Gathering my surroundings, I find that I'm seated at a table in the main room of the Great Hall. Sunlight streams in through multiple windows onto one of the two long wooden tables running parallel to each other, extended benches on either side of them. At the front of the room is a dais with a massive throne-like chair. On the other side is a crackling firepit and half a dozen casks of ale that I've secretly gotten into more than I care to admit. Black steel candelabras line the center of each table, and rustic chandeliers hang from the beams in the ceiling, molten wax dripping from them like stalactites.

Briony sits across from me, a deerskin map spread out atop the wooden surface. Briefly, her icy blue eyes flick up and she offers me a tentative smile before returning her attention to the map.

"Carys," Odgar's voice makes me jump so hard that my arse leaves the wooden bench. Pins and needles travel from my feet, up my legs and thighs. How long have I been sitting here? When did I even get here? My heart flails in my chest, my throat too tight all of a sudden.

"Carys?"

"Hmm?" I tear my focus away from Briony, who seems to be deliberately averting her gaze.

"This is my sister, Valdis," Odgar says. It takes me a moment to notice the tall woman standing right beside him. She's garbed in a dress of blue wool, with a series of leather belts looped around her waist. A leather pouch and a bulbous bottle are fastened against the accentuated curve of her hip.

Her sapphire eyes regard me as I glimpse the large, purplish-red patch against the fair skin on the right side of her face. Strands of her blond hair have escaped from an intricate labyrinth of braids to fall in loose waves. She props a fist on her hip, a leather satchel clutched in her fingers.

Fluent Uldaran tumbles from her lips before she seems to come to her senses. "Nice to meet you," she says.

This is the *princess* of Uldarvik. I scramble to stand, but Valdis's brows draw together, her lips tugging down in a way that makes the purplish patch on her face pull. "You don't have to get up. No fancy rules here, Princess." Her voice has a low, sensuous quality to it—authoritative and confident, yet I'd bet my arse that she could calm a wild bear with one spoken word.

"Then you can call me Carys," I say.

Odgar shifts on his feet, and I spot the bow in his hand and the quiver of arrows peeking over his shoulder on the opposite side from his battle-axe.

"Were you ... out hunting?" I ask.

The concern on his face is poorly masked by an attempted smile. "No, but I thought *we* could go hunting together."

I look at him as though he's lost his mind while a vision of me lying on the hard floor resurfaces in my mind.

Me ... lying on the floor? I blink, my hand shaking as it drifts up to my sweaty neck. I clutch the suffocating neckline of this ridiculous wool dress, tugging it away from my skin.

"I've seen your skills with a bow and arrow," Odgar says, speaking far louder than necessary.

I glare at him.

"How good are you at shooting a moving target?" His voice is an acceptable volume now. "The fresh air may do you well. Keep you present."

His grip on the bow looks so hard, I fear it'll snap in half. But his brows are cinched together, and his eyes are filled with worry.

Overflowing auroch horns of fermented drink fill my mind. Cheers. Dizzying kisses from ... not Odgar. I even remember the taste of a woman's lips—honeyed mead and apples. Gods. I hope kisses were as far as things got.

What have I done?

"Odgar," says Valdis. "Would you give me a moment with her?" She looks to me. "If that's alright with you. I have some better clothes and such. I can bring them to your room."

I hesitate more than I want to, but then I nod.

"I'll be right here," says Odgar, setting his bow aside and sliding onto the bench. "I'll chat with Briony."

The priestess glances up at him and offers a small smile.

I head to my room, tears prickling in my eyes for reasons I don't even know. Rather than a door, my room is separated from the rest of the Great Hall by a colorful tapestry. On the mattress is a large fur blanket—which I usually discard given my body's habit of over-heating in the middle of the night. The tapestry flap flies open as Valdis walks into my room. She holds up a dress and says, "I'll have to take in the waist and the bust, for sure. And I've brought some supplies for your hair ... if you don't mind?"

Remaining utterly still, I try not to move my hand to my hair. A tremor shudders through me as I clasp my hands together to keep them from shaking.

"I don't know what you went through to get here," says Valdis, "but I can see you're hurting. I promise you that I have no intention of causing further harm. And if anyone out there has anything to say about you being here, tell them to come answer to Valdis."

She says her name with a surety I could only dream of having. All I can do is nod.

The smile that spreads across her face is warm and genuine. "Let's get you into some proper Uldaran royalty clothing. How do you feel about the lack of corsets here? Seth has told me about the stuffy garments in your world. I'd rather die than be shoved into such a thing."

My lips curve softly.

"Now, come on, off with that gods-awful apron dress."

And I thought *I* was blunt. I remove the garment, and Valdis shoves an ecru shift over my head so I can slip my arms through the long sleeves. The shift is followed by a sleeveless purple dress in light-weight wool. Bronze beads embellish the neckline and bodice. She wraps a woven belt twice around my waist and secures it with a knot against my hip.

"There," she says. She taps her fingers against the large birthmark on her right cheek. "How attached are you to your hair?"

You have the hair of a princess, but the heart of a warrior. Ellynne's words open the wound in my heart again. "Very," I say breathlessly as my chest tightens.

"Alright. There are some parts I cannot salvage, but ... if I get rid of the damage, I think we can save the rest. It's very uneven, so cutting it a little shorter may do you well too." She looks at me with such kindness that my chest loosens.

Most of my hair still swings well below my arse, but the front and sides range from ear length to shoulder length. Ellynne is surely rolling in her grave.

Soon, I'm holding my breath as Valdis takes a knife to my hair, sawing far too close to my scalp for comfort. The fragrance of oil fills the room as she rubs it along my scalp and all the way to the ends. My mind wanders back to Paramount—to all the times Ellynne styled my hair. Valdis holds the same gentle manner as Ellynne had when she did my hair, but she's silent while Ellynne would've been talking my head off.

It feels like an eternity before Valdis steps back, and a slow smile softens her face. "I think that will do." She glances around, looking for something, before holding a finger up. "Wait right here."

Before I can question her, she's out of the room. I stand from the bed and run my hand over the dress. It's the softest wool I've ever felt, but so very different from the silk and linen I was used to wearing. I'm not able to dwell on how much I miss my Erleyan clothing before Valdis returns with a large, handheld mirror with an oval surface and a long, thick, carved handle.

She holds it out to me, but I step away, my heart in my throat. I stare down at the wooden floor. At the scuffs and nicks that no one has bothered to fix or polish.

Valdis sighs softly. "Change is scary," she says. "Being a part of something that is not your own is scary. I understand. Maybe you won't like how your hair looks, but remember this... it's hair. It'll grow back."

I nod.

"I'm going to hold the mirror up now," she says.

I nod again, but I slam my eyes shut as soon as she lifts it. I draw in a deep breath, then slowly breathe out. When I open my eyes, Valdis has stepped back enough that my entire face is reflected in the looking glass. The scar bisecting my face diagonally from my left brow down to the right side of my jaw is the first thing I catch. Another is vertical against my left cheek. Briony tried her best to heal them, but they're still pink against my ivory skin. The freckles across my nose and the apples of my cheeks stand out even more against my pallor, and my amber eyes are lighter than usual, almost golden, and too hollow, too big for my face.

My heart lurches, and I take the mirror, turning my head to get a look at Valdis's handywork. Two braids split the center of my head, adorned with small metal rings. The right side is cut close to my scalp, and the left, also cropped short, is braided intricately into four and joined to one of the center braids. It doesn't look terrible ... I just don't look like myself anymore.

I suppose it's fitting because I also don't *feel* like myself anymore.

This feels like an official goodbye to Carys, the princess of Erleya, and a hello to ... whoever in hells I am now. I turn my head side to side. More golden streaks are present now—especially toward the front where my hair had been mangled—even more startling against the jet-black majority.

"It'll grow back," Valdis promises me. "Also, if you let it down, it should hide the sides. I had to cut it shorter in the front so—"

"It's fine," I say, a little firmer than I mean to. "I mean ... it's different, but ... decent."

Her laughter is as carefree as Odgar's, and it catches me off guard. Everything back in my castle was always so restricted and orderly.

I find myself smiling faintly. "Thank you, Valdis."

She waves her hand dismissively. "Let's go show off your new look."

As we enter the main chamber, Odgar rises from the table where he was in conversation with Briony—and Seth, who must have joined while I was gone. Odgar approaches me with long strides, his face exuberant. "You look ..." His gaze moves to my hair, and I clench my fists, resisting the urge to press my hand to the nearly bald side. "Stunning," he says at last. "Formidable."

A scoff leaves my lips so quickly that I don't have time to bite it back.

Valdis bursts into laughter. "Brother, I think your complimenting skills need a bit of work." She pats him on the shoulder as she walks past, and he bats her hand away while those sunburst eyes take me in.

"Ready to go hunting?" he asks.

I nod, and his smile only grows wider.

The bow is much different from mine back in Erleya. The span is shorter and has no definitive handhold, but it's lighter and of a simpler design than my lucky bow back home. Odgar set up a shooting range of sorts, little patches of cloth mounted to different trees. It's perfect, considerate, sweet, above and beyond. We take turns shooting the targets for a while—Odgar has certainly improved —then set off on our hunt.

Odgar shows me how to track animal footprints and scat through the woods, until we come across a deer. There are so many fairytales about Otherworlders who appear as a doe or a stag to guide lost souls. It makes me a little hesitant to shoot the creature, but I eventually take it down with a single arrow and try not to focus on the mild guilt that settles over me.

"Well done, huntress," Odgar says with a smile.

Huntress ... I kind of like that.

My head feels clearer than it has in ages as we make our way back toward the village. The cool air has forced sobriety back into my body. Twigs snap and grasses rustle as we walk in quietude. The chatter of a creature followed by scurrying comes from the trees above.

A stream of memories gradually resurfaces as we walk. Odgar tucking me into bed after I had too much ale, holding my hair back when my stomach rejected the excess drink. I vaguely recall a few moments when he gently encouraged me to eat, to bathe, to get dressed—to *live*. A strange blend of shame and gratitude bleeds into my awareness.

"Do you have *any* fondness for me?" Odgar abruptly asks.

Startled, my head snaps to his towering figure. When we danced at the Feast, and even after, there were definite sparks. Now, however, everything feels frozen in place—a lake in winter.

"You're a lovely man, Odgar," I breathe out.

He halts, his jaw working as though he's fighting to control what tries to come out of his mouth. "Being a *lovely man* does not automatically earn your love."

I wince. "Love is a strong word."

He heaves a sigh, the leather across his chest straining. "It is," he says eventually. "Maybe too much to ask of you, but do you *like* me?"

"Of course I like you."

He nods toward the path out of the forest, and we continue walking. "Before I win your heart, I hope I can earn your trust."

I bite the inside of my cheek, unsure of what to say.

He smiles down at me. "Just so you know, I will not stop until I earn one or the other."

"And how are you so certain you're going to earn one or the other?"

"Oh, I will." His smile shifts into a little smirk.

I roll my eyes, but it's hard to be annoyed with a man who has been nothing but patient with me.

Too many nightmares haunt me, but each time, I force myself awake to keep Durvla from wandering into my subconscious. I'm not ready for her to see me this way. Tonight, sleep evades me completely, and I find myself stumbling beyond the tapestry and into the main room of the Great Hall. I ignite a small flame in the palm of my hand and pray to Agryna that I don't burn the entire building down.

I cannot stop the tremor in my hands nor the pang of my thunderous heart. Every time I close my eyes, I see Callum's throat split right in front of me, I hear his last words—*I will love you even in death*. I didn't deserve his love. I don't deserve anyone's love.

Even as I make my way across the room to a keg of ale, I can see the life fading from Ellynne's olive green eyes as she bleeds out.

I want to unsee it all. I want it to be me instead.

I sit on the floor in front of the keg and down a mug of ale. It's followed by another, then another, until my limbs grow heavy, until my thoughts slow and then cease to exist. I lay on my back in the dark, staring into nothingness while my body seems to sink into the wood beneath me.

When I finally drift off, no dreams haunt me.

I awake with a splitting headache and my tongue stuck to the roof of my mouth. My body aches, my side throbbing and numb as I shift onto my back. Someone jostles my shoulder. "Odgar go away," I slur.

"Princess, it's me." That sickeningly-sweet voice. My eyelids feel too heavy as I blink up at the priestess. "Come on," she whispers. "Let me help you."

"Please stop calling me that." The twinge that buds in my chest has me rolling onto my side again and automatically reaching out for the ale mug. Briony puts a hand on mine, halting me. A sob hitches in my throat and embarrassment burns in my face.

"Pri—Carys ... let me at least take away some of the nasty effects of the ale. May I?"

I nod, and she presses her hand to my forehead. Slowly, some of the heaviness leaves my body, and the headache retreats. But the haze that so often shrouds my mind remains firmly in place. "I want to stop feeling like this," I groan.

"I know," she says gently.

"Just make me unconscious again. Please."

"I—"

"You had no problem doing so repeatedly back in Paramount! You had no problem inflicting pain either!" The anger comes out of nowhere, boiling hot.

Briony winces slightly. "I will forever regret my actions. I am so very sorry. But putting you into a state of unconsciousness is not going to help you learn how to cope."

Weak, comes Enidwen's voice from the mist in my mind. *Weak. Undisciplined. Cowardly. Control your impulses!*

I flinch so hard that Briony also jumps. "What is it?"

You don't have to feel all this pain if you let me in more. Let me take it away.

A shiver rolls through me, growing in intensity until my hands are trembling and sparks bead on my palms like sweat.

Briony whispers almost conspiratorially, "The enchantress again?"

"I can't block her out." I rub my hands together as if I could rub the sparks back into my body. "I can't. She's too strong."

"Breathe in slowly and think happy thoughts. Riding through an open field. Archery. That beautiful view of the fjord and the mountains."

I inhale deeply, counting to five.

"Exhale and push away the negative thoughts. Envision building that wall between your mind and the enchantress's."

I sit there, breathing and trying to follow Briony's instructions.

You cannot block me forever, says Enidwen.

I would rather die trying than let you take over.

Her laughter is the last thing I hear before my body relaxes. Briony eventually convinces me to go back to bed, and as much as I try to keep myself awake, I lose to a dreamless sleep.

About a hundred people move through the forest, beginning the three-day trek toward the Hallowed Wood. We're at the front of the multitude, Briony on my left, Odgar on my right. Somewhere to his right are Valdis and Seth.

I refrain from glancing back at the others. In Erleya, I was used to being revered when I walked through the corridors or the concourse, but here, I'm gaped at like an outcast. Unless I'm making a fool of myself in the mead house. I push away thoughts of the mind-numbing ale and trudge onward.

Our first stop doesn't happen until night falls, and everyone settles in to find some much-needed sleep. Bedrolls are scattered around us within the woods. I lie on my bedroll beside Odgar, the sparse canopy of two trees overhead. Their trunks bow toward each other without touching, eerily reflective of me and Odgar.

Briony is farther from me, settling onto her own bedroll.

Despite the cold, I tug off my boots and massage my aching feet through my socks. What I'd give now for a long soak in a hot bath. To smell less like perspiration and more like myself.

"Here, let me," says Odgar.

I lift my head to find him sitting in front of me. He pats his lap, and when I frown at him questioningly, he reaches out and grasps my ankle. I bite back a yelp as he tugs my foot onto his lap, but as soon as his thumbs press into my instep, a tiny groan slips past my lips.

I close my eyes and lean back, my palms against the bedding behind me. Odgar continues the massage, and it hurts so good that another tiny moan escapes.

A quiet, deep chuckle reverberates in his chest. "If a massage can elicit such sounds from you, raven warrior, I wonder—"

"Don't you dare," I say, cutting him off.

But when I peek at him from beneath my half-closed eyelids, the sparkle in his eyes and his playful smirk coax a smile from me. His hand wraps around my other ankle, but this time, when he tugs on my leg, I'm yanked so close to him that my arse makes contact with his thigh. He lowers his face to mine, and I half expect him to kiss me. My heart kicks into double the speed, but from what, I'm uncertain.

"Tell me what you like," he says in a hushed voice.

"*Pardon me*?!" The words erupt from me, far louder than I intend. I keep my gaze on his face, on his eyes that appear dark blue under the cover of night. Around us are a few flickering torches that scream *fire hazard*, and in my periphery, Briony is sitting upright, her face angled my way as if she's ready to jump to my rescue.

"What kinds of things do you like?" Odgar asks calmly. "Favorite scents? Foods? Colors?"

The tension that I hadn't realized gripped my shoulders melts away. "Why in hells do you want to know that?"

"Why not?"

"Alright—then you tell me first. What are *your* favorite scent, food, and color?"

Another low rumble of laughter in his chest. "The earth after a fresh downpour of rain or snow. Unless it smells like damp horse-shit. Venison. Black, blue ..." He lifts my braid from over my shoulder and slides his thumb over the golden streaks. "Gold."

When he looks up at me again, my stomach does a somersault. I tug my leg away from him and slide backward, putting space between us. "I ... should try to get some sleep." I pull the thick socks up and retie the ribbon around the top to keep them in place beneath my knees. "I'm not used to so much on-foot travel," I admit.

Odgar smiles and nods. He doesn't seem phased by the very obvious distance I put between us, but I'm certain he notices. "Good night, raven warrior."

I'm no warrior, I want to say in return. "Good night, Odgar." I roll onto my side and try to find sleep but with no luck.

I shut my eyes and cling to the little mental strength I have so I can keep up a wall between the enchantress within me and my own thoughts; she has a habit of slipping into my mind when I'm off guard. I'm not sure which of our thoughts are more daunting at this point, but I focus on the sounds of an owl hooting in the distance and the occasional rustle of the leaves, hoping that sleep will soon come.

Chapter 13

CARYS

OUR TRAVELS COMMENCE the next day without a hitch. For a while, Odgar walks ahead with King Freyr, whose wavy blond hair shimmers in the sunlight. There's another man among them, stockier than any of them, his bald head covered in tattoos. I vaguely remember the mention of him being Freyr's advisor or right-hand man. Or both.

I hang back with Briony, who whispers to me, "How are you faring?"

I pull the fur-lined cape tighter around my neck and roll my shoulders. The farther we walk, the colder it gets. "Just fine," I respond at last.

Boisterous laughter sounds, followed by shouting and the clang of steel against steel. We all turn as the crowd parts, getting out of the way of two men circling each other. The sun glints off the larger man's sword as he holds it up, prepared to strike. My heart leaps into my throat and I stagger backward with the memory of Eefa's knife across my face.

A small cry escapes before I press my hand over my mouth, over my face, squeezing my eyes shut. Phantom pain sears across my skin, and my heart hammers in my ears. When I feel the rising heat of my own hands against my skin, I clench my fists and hide them behind my back. Several eyes are on me when I look at the crowd again. The fighting has subsided, and now I'm the one everyone is staring at.

A hand rests on my back, and an authoritative voice rises behind me. "Are we all going to just stand here, have a little tea party while we're at it? Or is Sumarvegr upon us?"

The crowd cheers, fists and weapons pumped into the air. I turn to find Valdis's blue eyes on me with calculating concern.

"You're burning your cape," she says calmly.

"I'm—" Looking down, to where my fists now hang at my side, the fur of my cape has, indeed, ignited. "Shit." I smother the flames with my palms.

"You have got to learn how to control that," says Valdis.

"You don't think I know that?" I snap.

She looks down her straight nose at me, then tucks some of the hair that's come loose from her braids behind her ear.

As we resume walking, conversations pick up around us again as if nothing unusual had occurred.

"Carys," Valdis begins again, quietly. "I'm no Seer—I don't know what fills your nightmares. But ... you're safe with us."

For someone with embers residing in her body, I am unbearably cold. I cannot stop shivering as we make our way up the snowy mountain path, lined with thick undergrowth and deep green ferns that seem to thrive within the frosty terrain. Odgar is an unyielding wall beside me, his arm brushing my shoulder as we walk.

"Snow or rain?" his voice rumbles.

I glance up at him. "Pardon?"

His eyes brighten as he smiles. "Do you prefer snow or rain?"

"Oh ..." I think about it. "There isn't much snow in Erleya, but ... maybe snow. At least it doesn't drench me like rain."

"You have yet to see an Uldaran blizzard; it may change your mind."

I feel my face crumple, my expression causing Odgar to chuckle.

We walk in silence a while longer before he speaks up again, "Kisses or caresses?"

My eyes dart back up to him, but he's staring straight ahead, the corner of his lips tilted upward. It's so much like Callum's playful smirk in the stolen moments of privacy. His touch, his last words—the fatal declaration of his love—the lake of red pooling beneath his body. Enidwen stirs within me, that jarring combination of icy and blistering swirling around the recesses of my mind. The sensation floats toward the forefront of my awareness, bright yellow eyes glaring through my own.

"Carys?" Odgar asks.

"Neither," I breathe out. I look away in fear that my eyes will reflect what I see and feel internally. I inhale deeply, pushing back the enchantress like Briony has taught me. The bizarre hot and cold melts away.

Touch sets me off with ease lately; I'm not sure I could kiss another person—at least while sober—as long as the image of Callum's lifeless eyes is seared into my memory.

Odgar's voice sounds tentative when he speaks again. "Embraces or words of comfort?"

Do not show weakness, the enchantress whispers, her voice far away as if carried by wind.

I shiver as crisp mountain air carrying the aroma of fresh pine fills my nose. As I fight away the tears that sting my eyes. "Neither."

Odgar looks down at me, puzzled. He seems to be taking me in, like he's trying to figure out what the appropriate response should be. "You need *something*."

Heat pulses behind my breastbone. *No weakness!* Enidwen's voice booms.

I flinch hard enough that Odgar's brows quirk up. "I need a fucking break," I mumble. To *her* and to Odgar. I walk ahead of him, falling into step beside Valdis, who eyes me questioningly. But the woman, gods bless her, turns back to Seth and continues whatever conversation they'd been having before.

On the third day, a thunderous cheer fills the air. My lungs are still adjusting to the high altitude, but my breathing is slowly improving. King Freyr announced our arrival not long ago, just as the sun began its steady trek westward. By the time red and orange streak angrily across the dark blue sky, there's revelry all around.

Drinking songs resonate along with laughter and storytelling with incoherently slurred Uldaran. The boom of drums echoes in my ears, thudding in my chest as the waver of torches casts shadows through the trees and dense shrubbery. I remain with my little circle —with Valdis, Seth, Odgar, and Briony. As usual, Briony is quiet, but the others fill us in, describing the festivities.

A scraggly man with furs falling off his shoulders walks by, balancing several overflowing mugs. Valdis reaches back and plucks one from him, lifting it in a silent cheer before taking a sip and passing the mug to Seth. I look at her curiously.

"It's a mixture of henbane and mead," she says. "I'd keep away unless you want to wake up in the morning with a cock inside of you. Or a woman's breasts in your hands. Whichever you prefer." She winks at me while Seth offers me an apologetic look.

I shrug. "Either."

Odgar does a doubletake and lets out a short burst of laughter.

My back straightens and a scowl leaps onto my face. "*What?*"

"Nothing, nothing," says Odgar. "Just ... Likewise." He bites off a chunk of dry meat, smirking around the mouthful and I lower my defenses, unable to resist smiling back.

Valdis whisks the cup from Seth and holds it up as if making a silent toast to us before taking another sip.

For a moment, I regard her, heaviness crushing my chest. I swallow thickly and clear my throat. "You remind me of a friend," I say quietly. Over the merriment around us, I'm not sure if she hears me. But she passes the mug back to Seth, her forehead furrowed.

"What was her name?"

Was. Past tense. Is it that obvious? "Ellynne." Speaking her name feels like reopening a wound. My throat squeezes even tighter. I let my gaze fall to the log I'm sitting on, suddenly focused on the texture. My hands run over the rough bark, the distraction I need from the pressure building behind my eyes.

"I remind you of her, hmm? Sounds like she was amazing."

I lift my head, my lips tugging up shakily. "Definitely like Ellynne," I say.

Valdis laughs, the boundless warmth of it not unlike Odgar's.

"Please don't give Valdis a bigger head than she already has. I'm not sure how she continues to walk upright," Odgar says.

Valdis slams her fist into Odgar's arm, but he laughs while she shakes her hand out. Seth seems unbothered, sipping from the mug of the forbidden drink.

"Well," Valdis says, her husky voice suddenly airy. She rises from the tree trunk beside her husband and dusts off her hands and the back of her cape. "Try to get some rest. We visit the gods tomorrow."

My stomach lurches at the prospect of visiting the Seer—of perhaps getting some sort of Uldaran-deity insight. We bid them farewell, and then Briony also rises. "I'll give you two some privacy," she says cheerily, bending to grab her rucksack.

"No need." My words fly out perhaps a little too hastily.

Odgar grins. "Afraid of being left alone with me?"

"... No." I silently curse myself for hesitating. "It's not that."

"Good night, Carys. Prince Odgar." Briony smiles and heads off to somewhere nearby.

I stand as well, shifting away from the logs to spread out my bedroll. I sit atop it, and Odgar joins with his legs folded. "Don't you have your own bedr—"

Quiet moans resonate around us, and as I glance around, my jaw practically unhinges.

My focus barrels back to Odgar. "Are you kidding me?"

Odgar laughs. "Welcome to Sumarvegr, raven. Where no one has their wits about them. Less logic and more arousal."

"Magdin's tits," I mumble. "You all just ... in plain sight?"

Odgar laughs even harder. "Not all of us."

I shift uncomfortably.

"Alright, what do you want to know about me?" he asks.

Trying to ignore the activity around me, I pull my knees into my chest. "How old are you?"

"Twenty-six."

A year younger than Tiernan. My arms tighten around my legs.

Eventually, the sounds shift to the background as my thoughts fixate on my friends in Erleya. On the hope of their safety.

"Why aren't you already betrothed to someone right here in Uldarvik?" I ask Odgar.

He shrugs. "Not interested."

I'm certain that incredulity seeps into my face. "No lovers?"

He shakes his head. "Not for a long time. How about you?"

I let out a breath and raise my chin proudly, despite the shame from Iywan's past insults. "I've had a few," I admit. I wait for his mood to sour, for him to be appalled or disappointed. I resist telling him there had been a few within the same span of time.

"Your guard back in Erleya," Odgar says gently. It's not a question, but there is a curiosity in his eyes. To my surprise, there's no judgment.

I nod, and the flush in my cheeks disappears, replaced with cold guilt. "Just couplings. It never meant anything." My lungs deflate as the words send a surprising pang through me.

"Yet you weep for him."

Confused, I touch my fingers to my cheek, and they come away wet. I scrub my hands down my face.

"It's alright," Odgar says, resting his hand over mine after I wipe away another tear. I tug my hand back, but he continues speaking as if I hadn't recoiled from him. "Sometimes it takes a loss for us to realize how much something, or someone, truly means to us."

"You say that as though you've experienced such a thing." I abhor the strain in my voice.

"Losing my father," he says. "But I had Valdis to share the grief with. I could be your listening ear."

I squeeze my legs against my chest again as I rest my chin atop my knees. My burdens are too much to put onto another person. I opened up to Alys, Tiernan, Durvla, and even Callum ... Where did that get me? Where did it get *them*? I deserve to carry my burdens on my own.

Chapter 14

DURVLA

I wake up to the lasting image of icicles dripping steadily onto cracked earth and the feeling of impending doom. By sheer luck, I manage to untangle myself from the sheets and slip out of bed without waking either Tiernan or Taig.

Except ... Tiernan is nowhere to be seen. The first rays of sunlight creep through the small space between the burgundy drapes over the windows. Shivers rack my sweat-slicked body, cold chattering my teeth as though I'm standing out in the snow in my nightgown. I close my eyes and summon shielding runes around the bed to keep Taig from falling out before heading to the bathing chamber.

It takes ages in the tub of hot water before my body finally feels warm again, and my racing heart slows down.

When I return to the bedroom, a towel wrapped around my body, Tiernan is there, sitting on the armchair beside the bed.

The quick sweep of his gaze over my form is not lost on me, but concern dominates his expression as he gets to his feet. "That dream again?" he signs.

I nod. This particular one has been bothering me since my arrival at the Verge. I want to reciprocate his question and ask whether he's had *his* recurring dream. He doesn't think I've noticed, but he's barely gotten any sleep lately. Several times a week, he's startled out of his slumber, which then wakes me when the bed jostles.

He averts his eyes while I change into a comfortable dress with three-quarter sleeves that leave my branding scar visible. For a moment, I consider swapping the dress for one with longer sleeves like I always do, or throwing a sweater over it.

I know it's a part of me; I know I should consider it a reminder of having *escaped* Paramount, but the sight of it always triggers a sinking feeling in my gut. Which then triggers more worries about Carys and the overall state of the entire kingdom.

I turn, half expecting Tiernan to be looking at me, but he's staring down at the floor, seemingly lost in thought.

"Are you alright?" I reach awkwardly over my shoulder to button the back of my dress.

Tiernan turns to me, an odd coldness in his eyes. "Of course." His signed words are curt, leaving no room for more questions. Yet the cold detachment vanishes from his face as he stands and walks toward me. "Here, let me help."

I turn away from him, and the brush of his fingers through the fabric of my dress sends the tiniest jolt through me. I close my eyes and inhale, catching a whiff of the citrusy scent of his soap. When he finishes buttoning my dress, he gently turns me toward him.

"Thank you," I say with a smile.

He smirks and shrugs a shoulder.

The moment I draw in a breath to say something, I'm hit with an aerial image of foliage withering and dying as though ink has spilled across the land. Of ice spiderwebbing over the ruin, and trees beginning to crumble, thick trunks splitting as the earth cracks beneath them. Pain lances through my head, and with a sharp inhale, I grab on to Tiernan.

For a moment, it feels as though I'm in a freefall. I fear I'm about to slip into a dreamscape, but I ground myself in the moment. I focus on the scent of Tiernan's soap, on his strong arms squeezing around me. Fear reverberates within me along with confusion and worry. I cling to the emotions, and Tiernan's arms tighten around me even more.

We're propelled into a dark chamber, Tiernan sitting in that chair with the horrible figure looming over him. This time, however, when he glances up at me, his face bloodied, torment in his eyes, the figure in front of him disappears, and the image of the blighted, frozen land spreads around us. Cold terror pierces me.

"*Durvla—*" comes Tiernan's voice.

Everything crumbles around us, and I find myself falling again. I shut my eyes as my body becomes weighty once more. My awareness of a solid surface beneath me grows.

"*Durvla!*"

My head hammers, but my eyes fly wide open. I force a breath down as my stomach threatens to release my supper from last night. Saliva gathers in my mouth, bitterness creeping up my throat while my surroundings rematerialize.

Strong hands grip my shoulders, turning me toward a face etched with bewilderment. I stare into Tiernan's dark eyes, fear, confusion, and worry radiating off him so strongly that I shudder. He releases his grip on me, and the feelings disappear. I suck in another breath and scoot away from him, my hands against the cool floor.

"What in hells just happened?" Tiernan asks. His hands are shaking so badly, he doesn't even try to sign.

"I don't know." I keep my own hands pressed firmly against the wood.

I watch a string of expletives leave his lips as he runs his fingers through his hair, tousling it. He looks toward the bed where Taig is still fast asleep. "Was that the dream you've been having?" he signs when he's collected himself enough to face me again.

I nod.

"And ... my dream," he adds. His throat bobs as he swallows. "They merged. Except, neither of us were asleep. You daywalked."

Again, I nod. *It would seem so.*

He pinches the bridge of his nose and closes his eyes before his shoulders sag.

"I could feel *your* emotions," I say.

Surprise plays over his features, but he smirks despite himself. "Empaths can sometimes inflict emotions upon others. In this case, I think it was more your powers merging with mine, giving you the ability to temporarily feel my emotions." Getting to his feet, he reaches down, and I take his hand to let him pull me upright. "Do you think you can project that dream onto me again?"

I stare at him, flabbergasted. "I don't know how!"

"Do what you did before?"

I huff with frustration. "The dream hit me out of nowhere. Like a vision. But I don't have visions."

"Don't you?" He raises a brow at me in that way that forces me to stifle an eyeroll. "You've had ominous feelings many times before. Like right before the attack outside of the Verge."

"I assumed it was a coincidence." I glance over at the bed to make sure that Taig is still fast asleep before looking to Tiernan again. "You're telling me my powers can just keep changing?"

"Not changing," he says. "Strengthening. Evolving. And that dream you keep having ..."

I wipe my clammy hands on my skirt and lick my lips as my mouth goes dry. "I don't want to think of that being anything other than a dream. Because it seems very ..."

"World ending?" he offers.

I nod.

"You can say no, but do you want to try intentionally projecting this time?"

My fingers snag on my messy curls as I run them through my hair. Idly, I begin to detangle the knots as I try to think of how to use these *evolved* powers with intention.

My mouth still tastes bitter, and I could use some water, but I sigh and say, "I think I need to touch you."

He quirks a brow, and I lightly whack the back of my hand against his chest, making him laugh. "Alright then, beautiful. Touch me." There's the tiniest spark of playfulness in his eyes as he holds his hands, palms up, toward me.

I suffocate another eyeroll, but a small smile twitches onto my lips. Until my eyes shift to his extended hands, taking in the lines on his palms. The idea of intentionally projecting visions into his mind is daunting. Breathing in slowly, I place my hands in his. I close my eyes and concentrate on the dream. On the land being sapped, the ice breaking across every surface. My body grows weightless again, sensations morphing and undulating, multiplying until my mind is not just my own, but *both* of ours.

When the vision snaps into Tiernan's mind, it's like seaming fabric together—I hold on to it, letting the dream run its course—letting the icicles drip and the dark skies linger overhead. When I can't stand watching the dream any longer, I release my mental grip, and my hands follow, the vision slipping away.

My knees buckle, but before I can fall, Tiernan grasps my elbows. I grab on to him again. Throbbing grows behind my eyes as I meet his gaze.

Slowly, a smile spreads across his lips, his golden undertone seeping back into his face. "You amaze me," he says.

I would laugh from the improbability of it all if I had the energy. "I need to sit," I mumble.

The bed is too far away for the way I feel right now, so I shakily sit on the floor. Tiernan sits beside me and wraps an arm around me, letting me rest my head against his shoulder. The floor shakes very slightly and Tiernan's body tenses. My head is heavy as I lift it from his shoulder.

"Chiyo," he signs a moment before the door opens.

There's urgency in her signs as Chiyo motions, "You're wanted in the Assembly Lodge."

I point to myself. "*Me?*"

Tiernan gets to his feet while I gawk at Chiyo. "Yes," she signs. "Alys's cousin came by to bring the news. It seems urgent."

My heart clenches. What urgent matter could possibly require *me* to be present at the Assembly Lodge?

"I'll get Taig to the Hatchling's Nest. You two go on."

I take a tincture, drink a couple glasses of water, and we head out as quickly as we can. It's not the easiest given my exhaustion from the dream projection, but we arrive at the Assembly Lodge near the other main buildings. Inside, it opens to a large room with a platform and rows of chairs.

The O'Hara family is on the platform, and there are guards scattered through the room. Ava looks bored, if anything, and Alys looks concerned and apologetic, as does her husband. I'd expected Chief Badeaux to be here, but instead, there are more guards on either side of the platform where a thin form in a flowy, white gown is slumped in a chair. Her platinum hair obstructs much of her face, falling over it like a veil.

Her hands are bound behind the chair, but she tosses her head to shake some of the hair out of her eyes. Her pale gaze locks onto mine in an eerily intimate way—as if she can see into my soul. My eyes drop down to her lips to focus on the words that tumble from them.

"A Basduun!" she shouts.

The word kicks my heart into double speed, and her next words throw it into an endless tumble.

"You are the one we've all been looking for. The lost Heir."

Confusion furrows my brows, but I find myself stepping a little closer. *What are you talking about*? I want to ask.

The woman's silvery-blue eyes seem ready to pop out of her skull. "She must be stopped! Together with ... she will ... the end. The sun and the moon will fall. The king ... She will kill our gods!"

I can't figure out half of what she says, but ice stabs into the pit of my stomach and radiates out to the rest of my body until my legs wobble.

The woman is inconsolable, spittle flying from her mouth as she continues to scream various things, most of which are lost to me. "No royal should be allowed to live," she says, suddenly calm, her eyes pinned on mine. She tilts her head, her nearly translucent cheeks bright red from all her shouting. "She must be killed along with her monster of a sister."

With a hasty command from Dayfyd, a guard steps forward and presses his fingers against the woman's neck. Immediately she slumps over, unmoving until a deep breath causes her chest to rise.

Her last words still hang in the air.

Both Alys and Dayfyd's faces have gone ashen.

Ava's arms are crossed even tighter over her chest while she levels a glower at her parents. "So ..." she begins, signing with precision— she wants to *make sure* I understand. "Are you going to finally tell Durvla the truth, or should we wake the fanatic?"

"Tell me what?" I'm sure my voice comes out odd, because it feels strained.

Dayfyd seems at a loss for words, but he lifts a fist to his heart and rubs over it. *Sorry*.

My brows dip. Why is he apologizing? Why is the fanatic, as Ava called her, categorizing me with the royals? All eyes are on me, making me long for the ground to open up and swallow me whole. My skin prickles with anxiety.

Dayfyd gives me another apologetic look, then says something to one of the guards. The fanatic is hoisted over a guard's shoulder, but Ava is the first to storm out of the building. As Dayfyd and Alys move toward us, I force myself to face them, to pay attention to Dayfyd's hands. "There's something we need to tell you. If you can, meet us at our home before the next bell. Just you."

Tiernan goes rigid beside me, but I nod.

Alys lifts a hand, but then seems to think better of it, offering me a tight smile before walking side by side with her husband toward the main door. Once they're gone, I loose a breath, but I hold tightly to the control I have. Now is not the time to break down.

"I'm going with you," Tiernan signs, stubbornness etching his face. "I don't care what Dayfyd says."

I nod, grateful for him sticking by my side.

Chapter 15

DURVLA

THE O'HARA HOUSE feels daunting as we stand at the door. I'm not sure how long we stay there, but Tiernan's hand on my upper back keeps my mind from spiraling to the worst-case scenarios. I heave a sigh and rap on the door a few times. Alys opens the door with a tentative smile on her lips.

As soon as we step into the warmth of the O'Hara's home, the scent of spices wraps around me. For once, it isn't quite so comforting. Neither Ava nor Dayfyd are in sight. "Make yourself at home," Alys signs.

At home is the last feeling I have right now, but I thank her and sit down on the couch opposite the seat Alys takes. Tiernan sits beside me.

There's unease in Alys's grey eyes as she regards me. "Sweetling ... There is a lot I should've told you, but I hope you'll understand I withheld information to protect you."

Already, heat sinks into my gut—the tiniest indicator of anger. More information was withheld from me. I thought we were past the secrets.

Alys continues. "When I first met you in the brig, I thought there was something familiar in your eyes, in your features. But I wasn't sure. The last time I saw you, you were but a fresh babe. I intended to appeal to Carys and Iywan—to have you released from the brig and your botany knowledge put to use in the royal infirmary. But Carys beat me to it when she recruited you as her dress-maker." She smiles.

What is she talking about?

I glance sidelong at Tiernan, who looks equally perplexed. Alys's lips part again, but I catch a glimpse of Dayfyd and Ava appearing in my periphery. A muscle feathers in Dayfyd's jaw, his eyes wary. Ava's lips are firmly pressed together, her hands in the pockets of her loose trousers. While Dayfyd sits on the arm of the chair beside his wife, Ava stands off to the side near the hearth and leans against the brick wall.

Alys continues speaking. "Back in Paramount, Tiernan came to me when he realized you had shadow magic. That was the first clue that my suspicions may have been more than a coincidence. But as we fled, so much was at stake, including the mystery of your developing powers.

"The combination of your dreamwalking, shadow wielding, and the hint of puppet mastery was the final piece of the puzzle. The glaringly obvious hint that you were, in fact, Basduun." She glances at Dayfyd then back to me. "I became more and more certain. But I wanted Dayfyd to meet you first. And when we arrived here, you were just settling in. I didn't want to flip your world upside down all over again. We wanted to wait for the right moment. We didn't even tell Ava out of fear she'd let it slip. But she figured it out."

I press my lips together to keep from asking her what on Lier-wen's earth she's talking about. My fingers bunch in my skirt just to give my hands something to do. I breathe out slowly. "Apologies," I say. "I'm not following."

Alys looks to Dayfyd, who puts his hand on her shoulder. He swallows a couple of times, as if his mouth has gone too dry to speak. "Before Morwenna was queen of Erleya, we were in love."

I blink at him.

"We were young and foolish, and with Morwenna betrothed to the newly appointed king and even expected to be a stepmother to Prince Aneirin, we should've been more responsible. But before we knew it, she was with child. She managed to hide the pregnancy until the last couple of months, which was when we journeyed to Bayenbar to stay with my family. The babe was born, healthy and so beautiful, with Morwenna's brown eyes. Still, Morwenna insisted that the infant looked just like me." He smiles but sadness clouds his features.

"With Morwenna's impending marriage to the king, we needed to get her back to Paramount. We knew the baby wouldn't be safe in the palace, especially with the possibility of inherited powers. We also knew that once Morwenna was coronated, we could no longer risk even being *seen* together. So, her closest friend volunteered to take the child and raise her as her own. Her friend was called Enya Griogair. Later known as Enya Garrick."

My body goes rigid. The realization hits me so hard that, for a moment, I forget how to breathe. I stare at Dayfyd. "What are you saying?" I ask, because there's no way that the conclusion I've drawn is correct.

Dayfyd swallows hard. "Durvla, you're my daughter. And the daughter of the late queen."

I burst out laughing, unsure of how else to react. Hendwr and Enya Garrick are the only parents I've ever known. Now this man is saying he's my true father, and the mother who raised me was not the woman who gave birth to me?

I glance at Ava, but her austere expression tells me this is not some joke. When I turn back to Dayfyd, I *truly* look at him for the first time. How have I never realized that we share the same straight nose and full lips, the same dark curly hair that appears black indoors but brown in the sunlight? His eyes may be a different color, but hold the same oval shape. I glance between him and Tiernan, who is clearly at a loss for words. Tiernan places a hand on my knee, giving it a squeeze.

I swallow the lump in my throat and shift my gaze from Tiernan's hand to Dayfyd's ashen face.

"I've kept Morwenna's secret from everyone except Elviera. Not only was Morwenna a Basduun, but her bloodline carries the curse of Enidwen."

"The what?" Tiernan and I ask at the same time.

Dayfyd looks to his wife, as if seeking her help.

Alys rubs the bridge of her nose and closes her eyes as if praying for patience. When she opens them again, she seems more composed. "When Enidwen summoned the Underling Prince centuries ago, the story didn't end with her being banished," she signs. "Her soul was preserved within one of the Heirs. Priests and scholars theorized that Enidwen's tainted spirit has been dormant in the bloodline for years, just waiting for the right heir to come into her power. The daughter of Agryna and Ehlach. What's fascinating is that the bloodline of Agryna is not tied to Morwenna, but to the late King Rhodri. Mor's powers were of Ehlach. Her dreamwalking, shadows, and foresight were stronger at night. And in moonlight. She's the reason why Dayfyd has had that moonstone."

"It was a parting gift," he said by some twisted way of explanation.

I rub my temples, my head starting to ache from the sheer enormity of this new knowledge. Heavy tension fills the room, and no one speaks for a while.

Alys adjusts the scarf tied around her pile of salt-and-pepper hair and nervously wrings her hands as she seems to mull over the right words to speak. "What are your thoughts?" she asks at last.

"My thoughts ..." I can *feel* my voice shaking. I shift my gaze between the man who looks like me and the woman who kept his secret. A prickling chill spreads through my limbs. I take a deep breath and lock away the shadows that threaten to burst from my hands. *I command them; they do not command me,* I tell myself. The tingling in my limbs subsides, but heat flushes through my body.

"Enya Garrick was my mother," I say, tears filling my eyes. "Not Morwenna. And Hendwr was my father. Not *you*." I launch the last word at Dayfyd then jump to my feet and run toward the door.

The cool air against my face is a shock, but not enough to loosen the tightness in my chest or stop the tears from escaping. Alys knew. All this time, she knew. Or she at least *suspected* it and never told me. As if the hurt of Osheen's betrayal wasn't enough.

I'm two houses down, when someone skids to a stop in front of me. I jump. For a moment, I would have expected it to be Tiernan, but it's Ava. I hold up my hand, intending to threaten her with a display of shadows, but nothing happens. There's an odd stillness in my body that strangely reminds me of when I put on my dampener again for the first time after weeks in the castle.

I step back from Ava, bewildered, and my back collides with a solid mass. Tiernan.

Unsure of what to say, I swipe the tears off my cheeks and put on my bravest expression. Even as I feel one breath away from crumbling.

"Keeping that information from you was wrong," Ava signs.

Tiernan stands off to the side between us. "Now's not the time, Ava," he says.

"Let *her* decide that." Ava's glower is cold.

"I want to know what she has to say," I sign. I don't bother opening my mouth to speak and let my hands do all the talking.

Ava nods and continues. "No one told me the truth about you. I figured it out on my own."

My brows lift. "Which part?"

"All of it. I remember overhearing my parents' conversations about the queen when I was just a child. I knew she was a Basduun —which is unheard of nowadays. So, when another Basduun showed up in the Verge, looking an awful lot like my father ..."

"How did you know I was Basduun? Did your parents tell you?"

She shrugs and the corner of her lips curve up in half a smile. "I can sense it. Just as the fanatic apparently can."

Still frowning, I turn to Tiernan. As a Mimic, he would've sensed if she had powers, wouldn't he? "*You knew*?" I ask.

He shakes his head. "I had a feeling she wasn't entirely Ordinary, but I assumed it was just dormant Mage blood running through her because of Alys's powers. Since ..." He quirks a brow. "I didn't sense any Wielding capabilities. What *are* your powers?"

Ava deadpans. "It's personal."

My temples throb even more. I start to walk again, but Ava sets herself firmly in my path.

"There are two groups searching for you. Which means that your presence here puts the Verge at risk."

"Ava!" Tiernan exclaims.

Ava pays him no mind. "The word from Outside is that the Purists are like bloodhounds. They *will* find you."

My stomach clenches.

"I'm not saying you need to flee the Verge just for the hells of it.

I'm saying that you should try to get information from the fanatic. If you want answers, that is. She might be barking mad, but she's not afraid to hurt your feelings. She wants you dead, and I'm certain she'd tell you why."

I flinch unwittingly.

"If you want answers, go talk to the Purist."

I draw in a breath to ask her exactly what she means, but she turns and walks back toward her home.

I don't realize I'm trembling until Tiernan places a hand on my back. I recoil, and he lets his hand drop. "I just wanted to ask you if you want to go home."

I wipe more tears from my eyes. "No," I say. "I want to talk to the Purist."

He looks taken aback, but he pulls in a deep breath, his chest expanding. "Do you feel ready to face that woman? If you're even allowed?"

My teeth worry at the corner of my lip for a moment. He's not wrong. Right now, I feel like throwing shadows at people, like screaming, like crying. Dayfyd is my father. The *queen* is—was—my mother. The fanatic called me the lost heir.

But I need to know more. "Tiernan, I have to talk to her. I can't ... not know the truth," I sign. "I've lingered in ignorance for too long."

He rubs the back of his neck and shifts on his feet, clearly uncomfortable with me facing the Purist. "Alright," he says. "Your choice. If you want to face her, I'll support you. But you've just been hit with a lot of shocking information. It might be best if you go in there with a clearer head. Allow yourself to process everything first. Sleep on it?"

My lips part to let another protest through, but Tiernan gently places a hand on my shoulder and signs one-handed for a couple of words.

"I know this is bothering you. I understand, truly. What if we go there first thing in the morning?"

I heave a sigh and nod. "Alright. *First thing* in the morning."

Chapter 16

WITH GRUFFUD FAST asleep beside me, I roll out of bed and quickly don my clothes again. This time, I take a pair of his trousers, rolling them several times at the waist and stuffing the excess of the legs into my boots. His tunic is next—I have to roll the cuffs and belt it around my waist. I'm certain I look ridiculous, but with the Pendry family strictly against women wearing trousers, it's the best I can do.

Gruffud is still snoring when I slip my pocket watch into the pocket of the trousers and sling my satchel across my body. The hinges of the door creak obnoxiously, making my heart thud, but Gruffud only rolls over with a grunt and continues sleeping.

Tiptoeing down the corridor leaves my chest tight, but I manage to slip out of the house undetected. There's still a chill in the air reminiscent of spring despite the shift into summertime. I clutch the strap of my satchel as I walk as quickly as I can. Everything aches already—I truly hope I can get more refills from Radika tonight. At this point, I've grown accustomed to aches and pains, but they feel more pestering than usual.

One woman crosses my path, a hat affixed with flowers adding an entire extra arm's length to her height. A few other overextravagant nobles stroll by, but for the most part, there aren't many about.

Neris is already waiting outside when I arrive at our childhood home. She greets me with a tight hug then asks, "All good, friend? You're not still cross with me, right?"

"No, Neris. How could I stay cross with you?"

She smiles. "You're right. How could you? I'm phenomenal."

Neris is probably one of the humblest people I know, so her statement is even funnier than it perhaps should be.

We manage to arrive unscathed at Radika's little makeshift workshop within an abandoned home on the outskirts of the city. As I enter, the stout older woman is walking with purpose around the dank space surrounded by flickering flames from innumerable candles and dilapidated shelves lined with jars, dried herbs, scrolls, and other magical contraband.

The potion maker peers up at me with weary eyes, her bronze face drawn. "Gwyneth, I wondered where you were," she says. She makes her way over to a small trunk and withdraws a couple of small canvas pouches.

"It's becoming harder to get away," I admit.

She smiles, deep lines furrowing the sides of her eyes and mouth. "But here you are." There's a subtle pride in her tone as she steps toward me.

I take the two small pouches she offers me, the vials inside clanging against each other. There are even fewer vials than usual in each. I gnaw on my lower lip, my chest tight. After a moment, I meet Radika's assessing gaze again. "You don't have more?"

"That's all I can muster this time, I'm sorry. Hopefully, I will have more for you in two weeks' time."

Fortunately, there's an entire month's supply for Neris—her tonic is easier to concoct since it doesn't require magic. Mine, however ... I thank her again regardless as I head for the door.

"I'm sorry, Winnie," Neris whispers as we step outside.

"It is what it is," I respond.

We start the trek back, speaking in hushed tones as we walk. Neris is in the middle of telling me about some scandal with one of the servants when several figures step onto the pathway ahead. Neris must spot them at the same time as I do, because she halts and grasps my arm. Peacekeepers.

Shite.

I glance down at my clothing. "Bugger," I mumble as the figures close in on us. The click of a bolt in a crossbow jolts my heart. The metal bracelets weigh on my wrist, a reminder that I at least have some weapon of defense if necessary. I fight against my terraforging that begs to unleash rocks on the men.

Suddenly, Neris slings an arm around me and goes limp as a rag doll. For a quick moment, she throws off my balance. "Tell them you're taking me to a healer. And try not to let your highborn's accent give us away," she whispers.

I nearly scoff at her statement. The four men are mere paces from us as Neris coughs meekly.

"You two! Who are you, and what are you doing out at this hour?" A crossbow is leveled at us. I close my eyes, pushing away the panic that threatens to draw my powers from me. *Stay calm, Winnie. Stay calm.*

"Good evening, sir," I force out, aiming for a Grounder accent like Sage's. "We're servants for the Baelfire house. I'm just trying to get my friend to a healer." I don't think there's any such house, but I hope they're gullible enough to believe there is.

"What's wrong with her?" The man jerks his head toward Neris, who has taken to wheezing.

"It may be the grippe or the plague, sir."

The Peacekeeper steps back and lowers his crossbow. Neris coughs as though she intends to expel her lungs then gags far too believably. Even *I* fear that she'll vomit all over me, and I know she's faking it.

The men step out of our way.

"Thank you, sir," I say. We continue on as I half carry, half drag Neris. Luckily, she isn't very heavy, but I wish she'd help a little.

"Let's get off the path," I suggest when we're far enough away from the men. We leave the cobblestones and get onto a grassy part between houses. I release Neris so suddenly that she almost falls to the ground. I steady her with a hand on her elbow.

"Well done," she says, beaming.

I roll my shoulders as I will my heart rate to slow down. Around us, the bushes are balding, the flowers drooping. By now, everything should be thriving, but the blight is only getting worse.

What I wouldn't give to get away from Barr na Cahar. Away from the Peacekeepers and the nobility. From the foolish rules that keep everyone imprisoned in fortified lies and deceit. To take down the Purists who mislead people desperate to fit in or those afraid of the powers they possess. I would love to meet other Wielders. Radika is the only Mage I've ever met. She's told me plenty of stories about places where Magekind live in harmony with Ordinaries. Where everyone is treated as *human beings*.

If only those who hold the power to enact change could see that.

People like Neris and I could be banished to the Wastelands—it's supposed to be this foreboding place, but what if it's just the solace we need?

Back in bed for the night, Gruffud snoring softly beside me, I stare up at the ceiling. I replay the events of the day, of the past month, of so many moments I wish to change. I drift off and dream of that tree I saw in the hallucination a week ago.

Two women stand on either side of the tree. The taller woman has fair skin and the other woman is shorter, with curly hair. The taller woman is reminiscent of the sun; the curly-haired woman, the moon.

Light and shadow.

It shouldn't make any sense, and yet it somehow does.

As I step toward the tree, the curly-haired woman looks my way. In a cloud of translucent shadows, she disappears, only to reappear one pace away from me. I shriek and stumble back, but there's no malice on her face. Her brown eyes are kind, her demeanor serene. If anything, she looks perplexed. "Who are you?" she asks. Her voice is like a lullaby, like lavender gently wavering in the warm breeze.

This must be a dream.

"It is," she says as though she's read my mind. "Who are you?"

"Winnie." Suddenly, I feel a tug on my body, and everything starts to crumble away.

"Wait!" the woman calls, but her voice is distant.

My stomach bottoms out as though I'm falling from a height and I can't help but scream.

"Gwyneth, what in the hells!" Gruffud exclaims.

I jump out of bed, searching around me as I suck in shallow bursts of air. There's no tree. No women. No shadows. It *was* a dream. I scrub my hands down my sweaty face and turn to Gruffud, who looks at me as though I've lost it.

"Apologies," I pant. "Bad dream." Except this feels nothing like a dream.

Perhaps I *have* lost it.

Chapter 17

CARYS

THERE'S surprising quietude and order as we make our way into the Hallowed Wood. The expansive clearing in the forest is speckled with unnerving statues of the Uldaran deities. Immaculately upkept, some are carved out of wood, others of stone. The Uldarans around us take turns approaching the different statues, speaking in soft voices to them and laying down flowers, foods, and small trinkets as offerings.

On my left, Briony is quiet and observant, and on my right, Odgar brims with reverent excitement. He lowers his head to me, pointing toward the stone statue that looms above all the rest. "That's Hofadr the Father of the gods. Then there's the Mother, Amodir." He points to the second largest statue. "Goddess of fertility, beauty, and love."

There's a woman standing in front of the statue, tears streaming down her face as she presses a hand to the stone and another to her own abdomen. I look away, feeling as though I'm intruding on a far too vulnerable, far too private moment.

I remember my mother pleading to Rhianu, our own Mother goddess, for more children. I, on the other hand, even before knowing about the curse of Enidwen, feared reproducing. The world doesn't need more broken royals.

Perhaps Enidwen's curse can end with me if there's no one to pass it on to.

A hiss reverberates from within me. I close my eyes, fighting to fortify the pitiful excuse for a barrier in my mind. If only I had a strong drink right now ...

"Are you still with me, raven?"

I turn my attention to Odgar and nod before letting my gaze survey the clearing again. I know the importance of children for royals—for the continuation of the bloodline. But if Odgar knew the truth, I'm certain he wouldn't want my children.

Hells, he wouldn't want *me*.

I rub my hands over my arms and cinch my cloak tighter around my neck to fend off the cold. Above us, gossamer clouds lazily drift by, mellowing the rays of the sun. I tip my head up to Odgar.

"Where is the Seer?" I ask him.

Odgar points toward a thick copse of trees beyond the clearing. "He lives in a hut deeper in the woods. Right through there. Are you ready to see him?"

My heart responds before I can, hammering erratically in my chest. "No," I breathe. "But the longer I procrastinate, the more daunting it'll be."

Odgar nods and extends his elbow to me. I link my arm through his, feeling his muscles undulate as he gently pulls me against his side.

"Is it alright if I come along?" Briony asks quietly.

"Of course, Briony," says Odgar. "If it's alright with Carys, that is."

I nod. "It's fine with me."

We make our way through the crowds and into the dense forest. The trees stretch even farther into the sky, and our surroundings grow darker. The more distance we put between us and the Hallowed Wood, the more the stillness grows. My skin prickles, and my palms begin to sweat. There's an odd density to the air by the time a small wooden hut with a thatched roof comes into view. A worn pathway between taller unkempt bushes leads the way to the door.

Odgar's arm tightens around mine, and Briony stands so straight that it looks unnatural and nearly painful.

"Gods," I mumble.

"So, you feel it too," Odgar whispers.

"I was going to say the same," Briony adds. Her arm brushes mine as she nervously shifts closer. "That's the Seer's home? I expected a queue of people here."

Odgar looks past me to Briony. "They'll spend much of today appeasing the gods first."

"Ah." Briony nods in understanding.

I keep my eyes on the door covered with moss and ivy as I take a step forward. But Odgar doesn't budge, his arm a vise grip around mine. "You can let go now," I tell him.

He releases his hold after a moment of hesitation. But as I step onto the pathway, he's right beside me again. He wraps his hand around mine, and all thoughts abandon me. I peer up at him as his brows draw together.

"Let me come with you," he says.

My lips part, then close again. If this Seer is truly as powerful as I've been told, he may divulge things I'm not ready to have Odgar know yet.

I shake my head. "I need to do this on my own."

Odgar sighs. "If at any time you feel unsafe, shout. And get out of there."

My blood chills. "Are you *trying* to scare me?"

He smirks, and I want to slap him, but those twinkling sapphire eyes of his diffuse my temper.

"Fine, I'll shout and run, if needed."

His hand squeezes mine gently before I pull it away. Briony gives me a small nod when I look over my shoulder at her. I exhale and walk down the pathway toward the hut. My fist is only just raised to the moss-grown door when a gravelly voice calls from within, "Enter, child."

My palms grow slicker as my pulse quickens. I'm not sure what to expect, but as the door creaks open and I step into the dark interior, the sensation of spiders walking down my spine renders me immobile. An unpleasantly earthy stench reaches my nose, the uncanny chill rivaling the frosty outdoors. A few candles have almost melted onto a low table in the middle of the dark room. Behind the table sits a figure, the hood of a tattered black cloak pulled low over his eyes and flowy sleeves concealing his hands.

"Come closer," he drawls in the Common Tongue. He lifts a white, ghostly hand and waves me closer.

With my heart pulsating rapidly in my throat, I step forward until I can make out a bundle of furs on the floor. "Thank you for having me." The words feel foolish on my lips as I sit atop the furs.

"You come in search of answers."

I hold back a shudder. "Yes."

"And a cure."

"Yes." Surely, it's a coincidence, right? How many people come to him in search of answers and cures? It's vague and a decent enough guess. I feel something stretch within me, like a cat waking from a nap.

"You doubt my authenticity," the Seer says.

My throat squeezes. "I suppose there's no point in lying to a Seer."

"Correct." His gravelly voice is flat, not a hint of amusement in it. "Before we begin, bring in the Priestess of Death."

I frown, staring silently at his cloak where his eyes are hidden. Then it hits me. "Briony?"

"The priestess has ties beyond this realm. You will need her."

I've never taken the time to think about it that way, nor have I had a conversation with Briony about her powers. But I nod and stand awkwardly, heading to the door. I poke my head out of the hut, grateful for fresh air. "Briony, the Seer wants you present." My voice shakes slightly.

Odgar bristles and glances down at Briony, who wrings her hands together and nods, her movements jerky. In silence, I return to the hut, back into the earthy stench and unease as Briony follows.

"Welcome, Priestess," the Seer drawls once we're seated.

Briony reverently lowers her head. "Thank you, Your Holiness."

He leans forward, his hood slipping back slightly to reveal intertwining keloidal scars across his cheeks and nose. His eyes are still covered, but his head is angled toward me. "Within you lives darkness."

My heart wrings in my chest as Enidwen grows restless.

"An ancient darkness with the power to destroy nations. You are chaos and light, embers and shadowfire. The beginning of the end. The end of the beginning. The embers to the dusk, the sun to the moon. Without one the other cannot thrive." He pauses, taking a rattling breath. "Your soul yearns for that which both complements and balances the tenebrosity within you. The first daughter of Morwenna Meredyth—the lost Heir—she carries the same darkness. She is bound to you by shadows and dreams. By blood."

My head reels, my thoughts tripping over each other as my heart bottoms out. My limbs grow numb, cold prickles leaving me paralyzed even as flames warm my fingertips.

"You must find her."

Find the daughter of Dusk again. Find your sister. The memory of Enidwen's voice in my head as I plunged into the loch returns to my mind.

Bound by shadows and dreams. *Dreams.*

"Durvla." The name escapes my lips in a loud whisper as tiny embers burn in my clenched fists.

The Seer nods slowly. "The prophecy you seek lies in the Serpent's Hollow."

My brows furrow, but beside me, Briony fidgets with her dress.

"There you will find answers. A cure lies beneath the surface of a spring. Be forewarned: balance requires sacrifice, but sacrifice unleashes chaos."

"Where is this Serpent's Hollow?" I ask.

"In Erleya," Briony quietly says beside me. She's trembling, and it's noticeable even in this horrifically dim lighting. "We call it Siad Nahar."

The enchantress's nails tap against my mind, but I hold firmly to my own thoughts.

An eerie smile pulls up one side of the Seer's scarred face, but he doesn't say anything else.

Briony speaks again, her gaze still glued to the Seer as if she's afraid to look away. "It's supposed to be near the northeast coast of Erleya. It's said that the land only welcomes those who belong. That there's a *call* for some, but no one knows how it works."

Enidwen's apparent unease bleeds into my senses and crawls over my skin. I fight the urge to itch or worse, to run.

"What exactly does that mean?" I ask, my voice just a whisper. "And what exactly is the cure? Is it an item? Does the spring have magical properties?"

"Dark times are coming," the Seer croaks, ignoring all my questions.

Annoyance and frustration fill me, encouraging the enchantress's attempt to force her way into the foreground of my mind.

"Endless winters," the Seer continues. "Destruction. Death. Find the Serpent's Hollow. Find the lost Heir. May the gods be with you." With that, his head drops, the hood almost fully covering his face now.

I sit up straighter. "Wait. When do I need to go back? Now? And how will I find Durvla? How does the cure work? And the call? You barely gave me any—"

Suddenly, Briony is up, tugging me along with her. "Come on," she whispers with urgency.

We get out of that hut so quickly my head spins. I snatch my arm away from Briony, anger bubbling in my veins. The Seer gave me so much information that I can hardly wrap my mind around it but at the same time so few answers.

Odgar rushes toward us as soon as we step into the cold air. He takes in Briony's fearful face and my irritation. "What happened?" he asks.

I only gnaw on my lip, afraid that I'll turn into a dragon and spew fire if I open my mouth right now.

"We have to return to Erleya," Briony says, starting to walk away from the hut as though she wants to put as much space between it and herself. Odgar and I follow as I force myself to calm down and breathe in the cool air.

We stop a distance away and Briony faces us again. She looks between me and Odgar before her eyes linger on me. As if silently asking permission to speak, she lifts her brows, but keeps her lips pressed together.

I stifle a groan and gesture sharply for her to speak. "Odgar will have to know sooner or later."

She nods, relief loosening her shoulders. "There's a prophecy, and it seems the answers lie within *our* hallowed grounds. Growing up in the temple, I heard stories of Siad Nahar—Serpent's Hollow. It's no coincidence the Seer mentioned it in addition to parts of the prophecy that involve you and ... the other Heir. Durvla."

Gods, Durvla is my *sister*. I don't even know how to process that. My body grows cold, then hot. My muscles start to quiver. What else did my mother keep from me? And how is it even possible? Durvla is twenty-three, two years older than me ...

Odgar's jaw is tight as we make our way back toward the Hallowed Wood, but he stops just within the thick copse of trees that separates the dense woods from the statues of the gods. I halt as well, looking up at him. My insides are all knotted up.

"Your country believes you're dead, and there's an organization out to end your life or wield you for their mission. We've not been able to form a proper plan to get you back on the throne. Without reinforcement, it'll be a death trap if you return there," Odgar says.

I force myself to swallow. He's not wrong.

"If you return to Erleya, you're at least returning with protection. I cannot promise you an army. Not even close. But I can come along. Maybe we can be wed on the first day of Amodir once we return home. Before we depart from Uldarvik."

Sweat beads at the base of my neck. I pull my coarse wool dress away from my throat and slowly exhale. "Odgar ..." I wet my lips. "About being wed."

He looks at me with his brows raised, his posture rigid. "Have you changed your mind?"

"No, but you might ..."

His shoulders relax, his arms loose at his side once more. "Me?" His lips curve with uncertainty. "What in Fyera's name would've given you that idea?"

"Because ..." I hesitate for a moment. "I don't want to have children."

His smile collapses.

Briony looks between us, stepping back as she wrings her hands together. "I'll ... let you two talk." She walks through the pathway made by the trees and disappears.

As much as I want to follow her and avoid this conversation, I lift my chin and face Odgar.

"Why don't you want children?" he asks.

I shrug, now averting my gaze. "I have my reasons."

Disapproval that isn't mine whirls within me.

"Do you care to share?"

"No," I say to a spruce tree on my right. A pine cone falls as a cold draft rushes through the branches. My warm cheeks cool, my body following. For a moment, I just stand there, inhaling the scents of fresh pines and soil.

"*Revna*."

My head snaps to Odgar, and the weight of his hand on my shoulder slowly registers in my awareness. I step back, air rushing into my lungs as if I'd forgotten how to breathe for a moment. Deep lines carve between Odgar's brows, his chest deflating gently with a sigh. He clenches his fists at his side but they release a moment later.

"Did you happen to hear anything I asked?" His tone is gentle.

I shake my head, ignoring the sting of tears filling my eyes.

His hands clench again, his throat bobbing. His lips part, then close, only for him to ask, "Do you trust me?"

I get the feeling that he said a lot more than that. I shake my head down at the forest floor. "Odgar, I don't trust anyone."

He doesn't argue, but after a few beats of silence he says, "As a royal, it is expected that I have children. Freyr may be king, but he will never father an heir of his own."

I look up, staring at his leather vest over his grey tunic instead of at his face. "Why not?"

"Freyr has no desire to ever lie with a woman. So, the continuation of the family line may come down to Valdis and Seth, and ... us."

I scoff, disbelieving laughter slipping past my lips.

"But—" He holds up his large hands and places them lightly on my shoulders. I resist the urge to shrug them off. "There is Valdis. So, if you are truly adamant about never having children, then alright ... but can you at least tell me why?"

I turn away and fold my arms over my chest, feigning defiance when all I feel is uneasiness and shame.

"I cannot force you to trust me," Odgar says. "But lend me your ears for a moment, will you?"

Lips pressed firmly together, I cast him a hard glare.

"From the moment I laid eyes on you, I felt drawn to you. I immediately wanted to learn what made you laugh, what made you cry, what made your heart skip a beat. The dance that we shared ... I thought I felt a connection. Then there was that spark in your eyes." He tilts his head slightly, sadness drifting into his gaze. "There is nothing about this betrothal that is superficial to me. I would gladly spend a lifetime figuring out what will bring that spark back to your eyes. This marriage may be a political thing, but I truly do care about you."

His words chisel into the thick ice encasing my heart. I press my hand to the vacant spot on my chest, and the image of Eefa yanking my amulet off my neck hits me. I step back, my breath shuddering, leaving small clouds in the air.

Odgar frowns, but he doesn't speak up.

I breathe out and close my eyes. "The Seer said that I'm the beginning of the end and the end of the beginning. That I'm chaos." I dare to look at him again. "How can you care for someone destined for disaster?"

He blinks for a moment as though he needs to process everything that I've said. Then a soft smile lifts his lips. "I quite enjoy chaos."

I turn away. He wouldn't say that if he truly knew ... My muscles are too tense, making my extremities feel numb and weak, so I shake my arms out and sigh. "I'm going to pay my respects to your gods." I don't give him a chance to respond before I walk off, convincing my legs to keep moving despite the tremors in my body.

I burst through the trees and back into the Hallowed Wood, where it's even more crowded than before. Still, it's relatively quiet, murmurs and whispers floating across the space. Tears cloud my eyes, but I head straight to the Mother goddess.

Many are there praying for their wombs to be opened—for more children.

Me, I face the goddess Amodir—a winged crown atop her flowing hair, a staff in hand. She looks more like a warrior than a mother.

With all my heart and soul, I look upon the stony statue and silently pray for my womb to be closed. Forever.

Chapter 18

DURVLA

A GASP SNAGS in my throat as my dream falls away and the dark room materializes around me again. For once, my heart isn't racing; I sense no danger, but an unfamiliar presence lingers in my mind. One as shattered as Carys's aura—filled with thunderous defiance and brittle submission. Not just shattered, but something I cannot quite put my finger on. It nudges my curiosity.

At first there was only Carys in the dream, but somehow, I couldn't interact with her. But I *could* interact with Winnie. Something was off about her, like a dropped stitch in a knitted scarf—barely noticeable unless closely scrutinized.

Until now, I've never been able to connect with someone other than Carys and Tiernan in a dreamscape.

Or maybe it was a dream with no magic at play. I once had regular dreams, didn't I? It's hard to remember.

With a steadying breath, I peer at Taig sprawled out on his back, limbs outstretched, mouth gaping wide. Tiernan's the opposite, collected even in his sleep, his hand tucked under his head as he lies on his side. I curl up on my side as well, trying to get comfortable. As much as thinking *it was just a dream* would make things simpler, it's never simple.

I'm not sure what to make of it, but I have other things to worry about. Like the news that I'm the daughter of Dayfyd O'Hara and the late Queen Morwenna. Ava is my half sister. As is Carys. As impossible as this seems, my uncanny connection to Carys suddenly makes sense. It's why, even with great distance between us, our dreams are still easily interconnected. We share some of the same blood, some of the same magic.

We share the same darkness.

My chest aches at the thought that the parents who raised me weren't my birth parents. I know family is more than just blood, but it feels like my life has been a lie. Between not even knowing I had magic, and only now finding out that the woman who gave birth to me was the *queen* of Erleya. My gods ...

There isn't much time to dwell on any of this. I'm in desperate need of answers from the Purist and don't want to delay any more than I already have. As I slip out of bed, Tiernan sits up, his hand immediately reaching for the sword that is, *again*, not on his back. He's becoming jumpier by the day.

"It's just me," I say, hoping to keep my voice quiet.

His body noticeably relaxes. He blinks sleep out of his eyes and then groggily looks at me. "You're awake early," he signs.

I walk backward to the wardrobe with measured steps. "I had a strange dream," I admit. "It felt like a dreamscape, but it wasn't Carys. At least not by herself."

Tiernan frowns.

"Yes, it confused me too." I turn and reach into the wardrobe, choosing a cream-colored tunic and a muted blue skirt. Facing Tiernan again, I drape the clothes over my forearm to sign, "I couldn't interact with Carys, but I could interact with the other woman. Winnie."

"That's interesting," says Tiernan, his forehead creased in thought. Agreeing, I nod.

He begins getting dressed as well, and I leave the room to wake up Chiyo so we can all head to the Hatchling's Nest early to drop Taig off.

Before the ninth morning bell, we make our way toward the training fields where Chiyo is sure that we'll run into Ava. The grass is so trampled, there's more dirt than greenery. On one side there are sparring busts and bullseyes, and on the other, there's wide-open space. Already, it's been overtaken by fighters training with magic and with weapons.

My heart thuds in time with my rapid steps as hundreds of clouds scatter across the sky, glowing pink and gold from the hidden rays of the sun. Ava is shouting at someone when we first spot her, but she halts the session as soon as we approach. Even knowing what I do now, her purposeful strides toward us, shoulders thrown back, arms swinging, makes me tense up. But today, despite her perpetually unimpressed face, there's a hint of compassion in her eyes that I haven't noticed before.

"What is it?" she asks impatiently. Her gaze falters on Chiyo momentarily, but she turns steely eyes back to me while Chiyo seems to struggle to contain a smile.

"I want to talk to the Purist," I say.

Ava flicks a few of her braids over her shoulder. "I didn't know you had it in you." A muscle in her left cheek twitches, the corner of her lips momentarily quirking up. "You fit right in with the O'Hara clan."

I'm not ready to consider myself an O'Hara, so I keep my mouth shut.

"The Purist is being kept at the Hold. I can walk you over there; just let me dismiss this session."

I nod, and she turns to walk away. I keep my eyes on the trodden blades of grass as I try to think of what I'd even say to the Purist. There was so much she shouted at me that I couldn't make out.

As soon as Ava returns, we head to the Hold in silence. The building stands on the other side of the infirmary, closest to the battlements at the invisible barricade formed by the wards. Stepping into the building, I expect to feel like I'm back in the brig again, but it feels nothing like that. There's a small desk staffed by a portly man with wispy blond hair. A couple of guards, ununiformed save for a copper pin on their chests, stand on either side of a door.

Ava faces the man, who looks up from a small stack of paperwork. "This is Durvla Garrick ... and friends," she says. "We've come to see the Purist."

The man looks uncertain, but he nods. Ava thanks him before

approaching the guards. They salute, then the taller of the two opens the door and steps aside.

I expect to see iron bars and multiple cells, but a small room with a solitary chair and a commode in the corner greets us instead. My eyes follow iron chains bolted into the ground, ending in a cuff around the Purist's ankle. Slumped in the chair, she lifts her head, wild silvery eyes peering out from her curtain of unkempt platinum hair. The whites of her eyes nearly swallow her irises as her gaze lands on me.

My pulse spikes. I glance at Tiernan and rapidly sign, "Can you translate for me if needed?"

"Of course," he motions back.

The woman's eyes go impossibly wide. "You're deaf," she says, seemingly befuddled.

"I am." I step closer, and she noticeably flinches. "And you're afraid of me."

"Why wouldn't I be afraid of a Basduun?"

My heart constricts. Why not, indeed? Taking a breath, I try not to let her words get to me. "How do you know I'm a Basduun?"

"I've been blessed by the same goddess who cursed your bloodline," she spits. "The gods have blessed us with various gifts. The power to imbue talismans to track down evildoers. The power of discernment—to sense the magic that lies within the tainted many."

Tiernan quickly translates for me, and I run the words through my mind. "Who are the tainted many?" I ask.

"Those cursed with elemental Wielding, with dark magic. Those who abuse the gifts of the gods."

She's trembling like a leaf in the wind—out of anger or fear, I cannot tell.

"What makes the magic of others different from yours?"

"No mortal should be allowed such unlimited power. To summon flames, water, wind, to manipulate the earth, the skies. It's an abomination. My people utilize our imbuing powers for good. The few of us that were once tainted have Cleansed our blood of that undeserved power. We will Cleanse all of Erleya. And then the gods will rise again and walk among us."

The hairs on the back of my neck stand on end. "The gods? Walk among us?"

Her eyes grow distant. She begins to recite her words as if she's practiced them for years. "The fall of the gods will begin with the rebirth of the Enchantress Queen. The daughter of Agryna and Ehlach—bearer of the curse of the enchantress—shall unleash chaos on the kingdom. Unless the ultimate sacrifice is made to Caiolair."

My skin crawls from her words. "Who is Caiolair? And what sacrifice?"

"Caiolair is the god of balance. The sacrifice he requires is a life for a life."

Lierwen and Rhianu are the father and mother of the gods—they hold the pantheon in balance. Or *did*.

The same confusion that I'm sure is on my face twists Chiyo's. She crosses her arms, and Ava steps forward, a domineering presence. "A life for a life?" she asks. "Whose life?"

The woman turns sharply to Ava. Tiernan translates her spoken words for me: "The lives of the Heirs of Dusk and Embers. Of the one touched by fire and of the lost Heir with the corrupted powers of Ehlach—of the abhorrent Basduunai. They both must be destroyed."

My stomach twists.

"And your people seek to ... terminate the Heirs?" Ava asks.

A grin splits the woman's face. "For the greater good."

Ava rolls her eyes not so subtly. "Where did you get your information from?"

"Our high priestess, Nimue, the greatest oracle of our time. Has spoken the truth about the doom upon Erleya. The Heirs must be destroyed, and the Zenith must be stopped as they seek to bring Erleya back to its corrupt magical existence."

"How many of you are out there? And where do you reside?" Ava asks.

"We are countless, and we are everywhere. We won't give up until we rid the land of all aberrations." She blows hair from her face and focuses her hateful eyes on me. "I'm not the only one in search of you, Basduun. My kin will find you. And when they do, they'll end the Basduunai bloodline once and for all."

I don't notice I'm shaking until Ava, Chiyo, and Tiernan's attention is fully on me. I wrap my arms around myself, feeling the quake from deep within my body, my chest growing tighter until it pains me. I back away and rush out of the room, refusing to stop until I'm outside. Doubled over, I fight to regulate my harsh breathing.

A moment later, the lightest touch on my back causes me to jump so hard that I nearly fall over. "Just me," Chiyo quickly signs. "Just me."

I nod and put my hands atop my head, still trying to breathe. The world around me blurs and wavers. I close my eyes and force more breaths down. An entire group of people wants to kill me. Countless members. Everywhere.

The ground beneath me seems to shift and warp. A burning presence taps against my mind. Just as it starts to flitter out of my reach, I grab on to it, commanding it to stay. Commanding *her* to stay.

"*Carys*," I mentally grind out.

Her safe place is always on a ship, always in the sunlight. I bring the images to mind, grounding myself in it. I feel the floor of the ship materialize beneath my boots, the waves rocking the vessel. I will the sun to shine, the wind to whip. Desperately trying to lure her to this place, I send my thoughts out toward Carys. With all my might, I fight to reach her.

"Carys, find me." My words are swept out into the ocean air, but I call to her once more. "Carys, please."

"Durvla?"

I turn, the wind whipping through my curls, and there she is.

But rather than the radiant Carys that I last saw, there's a sickly thin woman, her skin paler than ever, her once lively amber eyes like rusted gold.

"Durvla!" She lifts her foot as if to step forward, but seems to change her mind and steps backward instead. I feel my own legs gravitate toward her.

But when I touch her, it's like touching air. Not like before. Her internal flame seems to flicker—to barely be there. Everything feels wrong about her. Like a bird with its wings clipped, longing to soar.

Tears stain her sallow face, as well as something that faintly resembles a scar.

"What's happening?" she asks, staring at her own hands as the image pulses. "This feels different."

"Maybe because we're both different. What happened?"

She shakes her head firmly, and everything wavers as though the dreamscape is threatening to disintegrate.

"Alright, alright, you don't have to tell me!" I shout over the wind as it howls. "It's alright, Carys. I'm just happy you're alive. You *are* alive right?"

"Yes. I'm in Uldarvik."

Relief weakens my knees. "Uldarvik?"

She nods. "Yes, but I've been told that I must return to Erleya. To a place called the Serpent's Hollow or Siad Nahar. It holds the answers about the prophecy. The same prophecy that the bloody Zenith is trying to find."

My heart trips. "Do you know where it is? Siad Nahar?"

"Northeastern Erleya. As far as you can go. But apparently it only welcomes a few chosen. Don't ask what that means; Briony is cryptic. But we're the ones the prophecy speaks of, so ..."

I grimace, my head starting to pound. I press the heel of my hand against my temple as our surroundings wane. This time, I know it's me causing it. I've created this place out of nothing, and it's taxing on my body. "I have to let go now," I say. "I'm not sure I can hold this dreamscape much longer. But I will see you again. Somehow. I promise."

Does she know I'm her sister? Should I mention it now?

"Durvla ..."

But my vision dims, and my limbs tremble.

Everything goes black.

When I wake, I'm in a soft bed, the scent of medicinal herbs filling my nostrils so strongly that I sneeze. *Everything* aches, my head especially. I peel my eyes open, but even the dim magelight hurts, so I shut them again.

The next time I try to open my eyes, a face hovers above mine. "*There you are,*" says a familiar, baritone voice, mind to mind.

Immediately, I feel calmer and cast my thoughts toward Tiernan. "*Where am I?*"

"*Alys's place. We figured you wouldn't want to wake up in the infirmary, and our house was much farther. We weren't sure how much we should jostle you. You gave us quite a scare.*"

At last, I manage to keep my eyes open. Tiernan's dark gaze is wrought with concern. My muscles strain as I lift my hands to say something, so I lower them again. "I think I intentionally daywalked ... to Carys." It feels absurd to say it aloud. "Full dreamscape."

My head pounds painfully with every beat of my heart. Tiernan reaches out to my head, then pauses, "May I?"

I nod, and he places his fingers lightly on my temple. Coolness followed by a comforting warm sensation flows through my head, dulling the ache. Alys must be in the house somewhere.

My body feels as though it'll sink right through the bed, but I gingerly push myself up to a sitting position and lean back against the headboard. The room we're in has a couple of swords on the wall, dark curtains, and dark sheets, and there's a coat rack in one corner where colorful scarves like Alys's are on display, but ... "This isn't Alys's room."

"Ava's," Tiernan says, and my brows shoot up. "I know. I was surprised too, but Alys had been resting in hers."

The odd conversation with the Purist comes flooding back to me, making the room seem smaller. And smaller. And smaller.

Tiernan is at my side in no time, putting an arm around me. "Deep breaths," he signs.

For a moment, I just sit there, breathing.

"So, without a doubt, Carys is alive?" Tiernan asks.

"Yes. And she's been told she needs to go to Siad Nahar. For answers about the prophecy and for a cure. I suppose she's speaking of that curse of Enidwen." I shudder at the thought, though I don't fully understand it. "Have you ever heard of Siad Nahar?"

He shakes his head.

I let out a sigh as the door slowly opens. Wavy salt-and-pepper hair swings into view before Alys's round face appears.

I sit up straighter as I take in the concern on her face, and I'm struck with warring hurt and relief. On one hand, Alys is someone I've come to trust, but on the other hand, she's been lying to me. She knew—or at least suspected it—all along. Perhaps her motives behind it were valid, but it still aches.

"I understand if you are angry with me," she motions. "I didn't know how to bring up such a thing. There seemed to have been no good way."

"Perhaps there wasn't," I admit. Glancing to Tiernan and then back to Alys, I sign, "Is Dayfyd here?"

Curiosity lifts Alys's brows. "He is. Do you want to speak with him?"

"Yes." I shift to get off the bed, but the movement is dizzying. Tiernan offers me an arm to lean on, and I hold on to him for support.

We relocate downstairs to the kitchen, where Dayfyd looks up from a book on the table. He gets to his feet so quickly that his legs bump the table. As I sit, he slowly takes his own seat again. Alys and Tiernan stand aside, moving out of the way.

Dayfyd's eyes are wide. His lips part as if he intends to say something, but he just closes them again. He lifts his hands ... only to do the same thing.

"May I ask you some questions?" I ask. "About Morwenna and my bloodline?"

Dayfyd nods, his movements hurried. "Yes, of course."

I try to keep my leg from bouncing beneath the table and take to fidgeting with my sleeve instead. It doesn't help. "Did you say Morwenna had foresight?"

Dayfyd nods again. "She was plagued by prophetic dreams. Of the world ending. Of the doom of ... her own children."

My chest tightens, forcing the air out of my lungs. My leg continues bouncing up and down.

"Are you having prophetic dreams?"

I swallow, my gaze wandering over to Alys as she leans against the counter, Tiernan next to her, looking like the guard he used to be. "I think so," I tell Dayfyd. "How did Morwenna know for sure?"

He exhales heavily. "Sometimes she didn't. But often her recurrent dreams were. Sometimes they came to her in song or poetry." He smiles as if struck with a pleasant memory in the midst of his words. With slow precision, he closes the book he'd been reading and slides it across the table. *Dreams and Symbolism.* "Oracles and Dreamwalkers aren't the same, and this book is heavily geared toward Oracles. But perhaps it can be of some use to you."

I smooth my hand over the leather cover. "Thank you."

"Again, I'm sorry for lying to you. I hope you'll forgive me."

I don't know how to feel about it, so I only nod. I bid him and Alys farewell before leaving with Tiernan.

As we walk away from the O'Hara household, Tiernan turns to me and signs, "So, it seems you have a mission proposal for Ava."

"It seems so," I reply. "Now I just need to get more information about Siad Nahar."

"Indeed," he says. "Where do you want to start?"

Chapter 19

DURVLA

To my dismay, the library doesn't have any information about Siad Nahar, and neither does Dayfyd nor Alys. The librarian mentions that Siad Nahar is a myth—which is far from comforting —but my gut tells me otherwise. Perhaps the Purist isn't entirely in her right mind, but I don't believe she's lying about this.

After the library, I head straight to training with Oksana. As I dismiss a small wall of shadows from in front of me, Oksana beams and applauds. "Well done, Durvla," she tells me.

I smile and take a few breaths. "Thank you." We've been practicing in her garden for a while now. It's filled with flourishing plants and small fruit trees. "Oksana, do you know anything about Siad Nahar?" I ask.

The broad smile falls from her face.

She gestures to a wooden bench not far from where we stand and we sit beneath the shade of a tree. "I do," she responds once seated. "When I was just a child, many Mages spoke of seeking the truth through Siad Nahar. Once upon a time, it was almost like a spiritual retreat—a place to replenish one's soul and therefore one's magic. Some people believe magic is tied to the soul, while others believe it comes from a more external source such as"—she waves her arms around—"nature, for example."

I'd never thought of it that way. I hold my hand up, watching faint swirls of shadows gather in my palm. "I feel like I draw my shadows from within rather than from around me—perhaps that's why people consider it from the soul?"

I look up at Oksana again, and she says, "Perhaps, but more importantly, might I congratulate you on such excellent control. You've come a long way."

"Thank you." I smile at her. "I was afraid I'd never be able to control them well enough to go Outside."

"You youngsters put far too much pressure on the showy displays." She scoffs. "Control and strength are about more than being able to do things on a large scale. Sometimes it takes more control to summon a tiny shield than it does a larger one. *Smaller* takes precision and patience. The elements are hard enough to control, but shadow and light are a different beast. Too often, Mages are forced to learn skills quickly, which sadly causes a lot of people to skip over learning control. You know what too much magical expenditure leads to?"

I nod. "Burnout."

"And burnout leads to death."

My chest tightens.

"That's why I advise you to take some time to *rest*. It's equally as important as training. Study the runic symbols in case you need them when you go Outside—and remember what I've said about visualizing them in your mind. As for Siad Nahar, only a few are ever able to see it. There's something mysterious about the place. Some say it calls to certain individuals."

I sigh. "What if I'm not one of those certain individuals?"

"Then you'll figure it out. You're an intelligent young woman."

"Thank you, Oksana," I say with a smile. "For everything."

Rising, I follow the pathway toward our house. Everyone is busy at this time of the day, and a few people cross my path. After the training session, I just need a moment to breathe before meeting with Chiyo—everything feels more overwhelming than it should.

For hours yesterday, I pored over the book from Dayfyd. It's filled with songs and stories about the moon and dream deities, and it speaks of the symbolism of dreams. Death doesn't always mean death, and life doesn't always mean life. It's all open for interpretation. The problem is that, as Dayfyd said, it's geared toward Oracles, not toward Basduunai who dreamwalk and face very concrete, very *real* circumstances in dreams. Mine aren't generally symbolic ... except perhaps that one dream in which I met Winnie.

I still have no answers for that.

But today, Chiyo arranged for us to meet with Ava at midday while Tiernan trains with various elemental Wielders. As much as I hate to miss him strengthening his Mimic powers, it's important to show Ava that I can be proactive and that I don't need anyone coddling me.

In the afternoon, as scheduled, I don't even get to knock on the O'Haras' door before it swings open. Ava leans against the door-frame, looking me up and down. Beside me, Chiyo seems to tense, but color rises subtly in her cheeks. I force my focus back to Ava.

"Sorry to bother you," I automatically say.

Ava's eyes roll. "I *agreed* to meet with you. Don't apologize for unnecessary shit." She turns and heads inside. Beside me, Chiyo's face contorts. With a sigh, she holds her arm out, gesturing for me to enter before her.

Ava moves through the sitting room, past the kitchen, and toward a small study. A large map is plastered against the wall, topo-graphical elements drawn in muted reds and greens, location names labeled with copper engraving, and various route lines in black ink. It's a rather impressive map of not just Erleya, but our neighboring countries: Caldeon, Ardall, and Uldarvik. Where Carys is.

"Alright, what did you want to meet with me about?" Ava asks as she leans against the massive desk and crosses one ankle over the other.

"I'd like to go in search of Siad Nahar," I sign.

"You'd *like* to?" Her brows cinch together.

"I need to," I say with far less confidence than I'd like. "I know it sounds unwise given that there are people out there who want to kill me, but we need answers to the prophecy. It could help us figure out how to handle the Zenith as well, since they're also trying to follow it."

Ava stands upright and walks around the desk. She rummages somewhere behind it and clears a space in the center to roll out a large, yellowed parchment. The edges try to curl in, but Chiyo plucks two daggers from somewhere on her person and lays them flat on either side of the map to anchor it to the desk. It closely resembles the map on the wall, but it's more detailed and focuses solely on Erleya.

"We are here," Ava signs before pointing to a swampy area across the northern coast of Erleya.

"Carys said that Siad Nahar is all the way to the northeast," I tell her.

Ava moves her finger to the east where bogland abruptly ends, replaced by forest. There's a winding river nestled between forests and mountains near the coast. A winding river that looks like a serpent. "This region is unlabeled," Ava motions. "Do you think ...?"

There's a strange certainty that comes over me as I stare at the winding river. I gently trace it with the tip of my finger. There seems to be nothing around it but forests and mountains. "I think so," I reply. I look at Ava again whose lips are twisted in thought.

Chiyo's eyes go wide. "Does that mean we can go straight through the Verge and right into Siad Nahar?" she signs.

Frowning, Ava shakes her head firmly. "The bogland at the edge of the Verge is ... let's say, poisonous. There is no land—only water, and it's essentially acid and cannot be touched by magic. Myth has it that it was a protective measure erected by the gods. If you believe that kind of thing. But I suppose if it's right at the edge of Siad Nahar, perhaps there's something to it."

A chill trickles down the back of my neck. I squint at the map, trying to follow the path from the Verge. "We'll have to go through the mountains, it looks like?" My eyes flick up to Ava.

"Correct," she says. "Through Diadun, and that may be the only village we cross. The rest is wildlands, it seems."

Another chill cuts through me.

"I haven't called a meeting for this yet, but we've gotten more information from Aine. The fanatic. The Zenith seems to be working with Mages. While the Purists want you and your sister dearest dead, the Zenith wants you alive. In fact, they *need* you alive."

My gut roils aggressively. I press my hand to my stomach, swallowing back the nausea. Ava doesn't speak for a while, her lips pressed together, her hands against the desk.

"What are you thinking, Durvla?" she finally asks.

I don't respond. Living in the Grounds with an ailment and the inability to hear the dangers around me was so difficult. Hiding Taig only added to my vulnerability. I never cared to fight for justice. Not when I had to cower beneath the injustice to simply stay alive.

But now with Carys off the throne, and the kingdom and all its inhabitants in danger, if I can do even the smallest thing to help, it would be worth the risk.

Ava slams her hand against the desk, disturbing the map. "Speak up!"

I blink at her and draw in a breath. "I spent my whole life hiding," I tell her. I tug back the sleeve of my tunic to show her my branding scar. "And it got me this."

Faint surprise flickers on her face.

"I buried my head in the sand and minded my business. I protected Taig from the world, and he still ended up in danger, and I still ended up being arrested. Hiding here in the Verge feels pointless when there's *something* that I may be able to do. It's terrifying. I'm terrified, for sure, but I'd be terrified just sitting here waiting for the world to end as well." I tug my sleeve back down. "I have a connection to Carys. That *has* to be important. She's the one who's supposed to be on the throne. If we can get her back there—even if it takes learning all we can about the prophecy—then I'm willing to do it."

Ava nods, clearly sobered. Chiyo gives my shoulder an encouraging squeeze.

"What will we need for this mission, then?" Ava asks.

Suddenly unsure of how to respond, my hands falter. I rub them on my skirt before signing, "Preserved food, fresh clothing, hygiene supplies, and a group of rebels willing to help. But not too many that it'll draw attention."

If I'm not mistaken, that's a mildly impressed look on Ava's face. A poorly hidden smile twitches on Chiyo's lips.

"Specifically, what do you need of these rebels? Any particular skill sets?"

"I …"

"Stop hesitating," Ava berates.

"We'll need a Healer!" I blurt. "A powerful one who can handle an entire group and … well, me." It takes a lot of effort not to fidget. "I can travel with tinctures, but they only last so long and are only so strong. Your mother would—"

Ava's eyeroll cuts me off. "No," she signs firmly. "There's another Healer. Wain. He's the one who's been working on *her* recovery. In addition to his Mage healing, he's a Waterweaver."

I lick my lips and stand straighter. "But Alys knows how to keep my symptoms best handled, and she's a stronger Healer than Wain."

An angry muscle twitches in Ava's cheek before she makes a *go on with it* gesture. "Healer aside, what else?"

"Fighters. They don't have to be Mages, but Mages would be helpful in a small group."

Ava pulls out another parchment and slaps it down on the desk, grabbing a quill and inkwell. She sits, quietly scribbling for a while before putting her supplies away. When she stands again, she hands me the parchment. It lists names and related skills. "I believe Sloan and Isobel in particular will be great for your mission."

My mission.

She plucks the daggers off the map and hands them to Chiyo. I focus on Ava's lips as she rolls the map back up.

"Sloan is level-headed, and Isobel has been waiting for a mission —plus she's an incredible fighter, loyal, and brave. As you know— you've sparred with her after all—they're both Galemakers. Chiyo, do you—"

"Hells yes!" Chiyo says.

Ava nods firmly, though something I can't quite figure out sparks in her eyes. "So, Durvla, you also have an incredibly strong weapon master."

Now Chiyo's face goes bright red as she tries and fails to hold back a smile.

Ava continues as if she hasn't noticed. "I'm sure your lover won't let his precious partner out of his sight. And then you have me. Leader and Obstructor."

Obstructor?

I'm certain Chiyo echoes the words, but Ava doesn't explain. She holds the map out to me. "Keep this," she says. "Study it. Let's aim to leave in one week. Get all the information you can find. And get your ass in better shape."

"Thank you," I say. She sits down behind the desk and makes a shooing motion with her hands.

As soon as we step out of the office, Chiyo dissolves into a fit of giggles. "For what it's worth, you have a great ass," she says.

I press my hand over my mouth to cover my laughter as we put some distance between us and the office.

"Looks like we have a quest," Chiyo says. "And *you're* the key player."

She drapes one arm around my shoulders and squeezes. For a petite young woman, *gods* is she strong.

Key player. One week. There's a lot of work to be done.

Chapter 20

A LOUD *BAM* startles me out of my thoughts. Since that vivid illusion of the tree, I've been unable to focus on much. Gruffud is sitting on the armchair across from me, simmering, his hand resting on the tea table he'd no doubt just slammed his palm against.

"For the gods' sake, woman. Get your damn head out of the clouds."

"Apologies." My voice comes out breathless and my heart is racing. I try to suppress the thoughts of that bizarre dream I had of the two women, but my mind keeps wandering to it.

"I must get to that meeting."

What meeting?

Gruffud sets his teacup down on the table and stands, stepping toward me. I turn my face up to him, and he drops a kiss onto my forehead. His fingers slide through my hair, tugging slightly. "Why don't you have curls like your sister and mother?" he asks.

My brows scrunch. That's a new one. I'm used to criticisms about my body, not my hair. "My father's hair is on the straighter side, I suppose?" Am I really explaining my appearance to this man?

His gaze drops down to the full swell of my breasts, his knuckles following, grazing over my cleavage. My shudder is not so subtle. He pulls his hand away and clenches his jaw, as if cutting off the flow of a nasty comment.

The more time that passes, the faster my tolerance for Gruffud dwindles. The stubble that once gave him an attractive, rugged look now clashes with his otherwise polished appearance. His voice is too harsh, his speech often gallingly like an encyclopedia. He's stopped opening doors for me, pulling out chairs. Courtesy was the only affable trait he had, and even that is gone.

He straightens to walk to the door as Sage rushes to fetch his cloak from the coat rack. "No need to wait for me tonight," Gruffud tosses over his shoulder.

I nod foolishly, unsure of what to say. Long after he leaves, I remain sitting there, staring at my own teacup until Sage takes it away. The sound of the clinking porcelain grows more distant, and I'm left alone with my thoughts overwhelming the silence.

I hate it here. With all my heart, I hate it. Even more than I'd hated residing with my own family.

Sage rushes past me again, this time heading to the door. My brows lift as she yanks the door open, and Neris steps in. I hadn't even heard a knock.

Neris looks me up and down, her curly ponytail bouncing. "Realms, Winnie, you look—" She tilts her head. "Like you need some fresh air."

I nod and get to my feet. It isn't a bad idea. Without another word, we head through the kitchen and out into the cool air. I'm a tangle of nerves and negativity—in desperate need of literal grounding. I kneel to remove my shoes and my stockings, unhooking them from the garters beneath my dress. Standing with my bare feet in the grass, the soil underneath brings my body to the most comforting stillness.

I close my eyes and breathe in the crisp air, reveling in the *life* beneath my feet. I can feel animals burrowing under the surface, minerals and precious stones thrumming with their own heartbeat. I can feel strength, power, and possibility.

But the earth feels bruised. The plants cry out for help, struggling to grow against a strange force that seems to be sapping energy from the land. I've been feeling it for a while, as sure as I feel whatever force still lies within me, sapping me with equal fervor.

I crouch and press my hands against the grass, whispering to it in my mind. *I hear you. I'm sorry.* It feels like a slow-moving poison. A shattering.

Like a cleaved soul.

Does the earth have a soul?

"What does it feel like?" Neris's whisper startles me.

My eyes blink open to the curiosity marking her face. "It feels like freedom. But also, the blight ... it doesn't seem like it'll end soon"

She sighs heavily. "I'm jealous of your abilities. They seem amazing. Minus feeling impending doom."

I smile wryly. "My powers weren't so amazing when they first manifested."

"I remember." She makes a face. "But I've said it many times before and I'll say it again: if you want to leave, I'll come with you. Barr na Cahar is boring anyway. You speak of freedom; why not take a leap of faith?"

"Neris, I'm *married* now," I remind her. "Also, Barr na Cahar isn't so boring anymore." I gesture vaguely over the house, to the streets beyond, where Peacekeepers patrol.

Neris deadpans, "That's not the kind of excitement I'm looking for, Winnie. I'd prefer the kind that doesn't get me shot with a bolt if I so much as make the wrong face. I'd love to wander the forests, gaze upon the beauty of the ocean." She beams. "I've been saving up my earnings."

"Likewise." I plop down into the grass and sprawl out on my back.

Neris spreads out beside me. "It's no secret Gruffud is a prick, but he doesn't ... hit you, does he?"

My throat tightens.

"And if he does, will you tell me?"

I keep my face pointed toward the sky where clouds race across the sun. We're bathed in shadows repeatedly, but golden rays surround the pillows of white. My fingers itch with the desire to grab a paintbrush. This would make a beautiful painting.

If Gruffud didn't become so surly whenever I took the time to put brush to canvas.

We sit in silence within our privileged prison. Neris doesn't push the topic further, and for that, I'm grateful. Gruffud's weapons of choice are words sharper than any knife, but I would not put it past him to hone those insults into something more physical. Just as I wouldn't put it past Neris to act on impulse if that ever did happen. It would only put *her* in danger, and I cannot have that on my conscience. So, if he ever lays a hand on me, Neris will never know.

In the morning, as I'm pressing letters into one of many leather book covers lined up before me, I feel the weight of Neris's steady gaze. I gently lay a strip of goldleaf over the book cover and grab the metal embossing stamp. Painstakingly, I roll the embosser over the goldleaf, then clear the excess away to reveal the golden letters indented into the leather cover. *The Life of Caoimhe Brogan*. Perfect.

"Winnie, are you alright?" Neris asks. "You're quiet today."

I sigh. "I just wish I could stay here. Not *here* in the workshop, per se, but I suppose I miss the comfort of not having to—" I pause, wondering what the apt thing is to say.

"—go home to your husband?"

My gaze is drawn up to her expression of understanding before I refocus on the books. "I thought I would've become accustomed by now. That I'd learn to ... enjoy things." I lift an untitled book and spot a remnant of goldleaf stuck to my dark skin.

"You just miss me," Neris quips as I remove the shimmery material from the back of my hand. "Admit it."

I set a new book in front of me and stick my tongue out at Neris. She laughs, but my own amusement is interrupted by a wintry breeze sweeping over me.

A symbol glows on the ground as if lit by some kind of internal flame. My hackles rise, but I don't make a peep. I set down the embosser I'd just picked up and walk toward the symbol just as it disappears.

A moment later, another appears a short distance away, but when I reach it, that one also disappears. Two more times, two more symbols, and the shelves upon which we keep our books draw nearer.

"What in hells are you doing?" Neris asks.

The whoosh of a tattered grey cloak catches my attention as it disappears around a corner of the shelves, heading farther into our storage area. I take off running across the room in pursuit, my hand against my chest for stability, my corset threatening to tear under the sudden act of athleticism. I probably should run in the opposite direction, but I go against my instinct and move toward the oddity.

"Alright," Neris says, suddenly behind me. I jump so hard that I nearly collide with the nearby shelves. "Now I really think you've lost your marbles."

When I look back, there are no symbols and no figures.

Neris sighs through her nostrils, her lips forming a thin line. "Have I told you lately that you need more sleep?"

For the first time in quite a while, I feel a familiar tug from within me. The one telling me to get out of Barr na Cahar, to head northeast. The same sensation I get when I envision that damn tree. They're the ideas of a madwoman, and I promised to be done with fanatical ideals. But it doesn't hurt to dream about it, does it?

The sounds of rustling paper, clanging metal, and occasional hammering soon fill the space again. I take comfort in the tedium of it all, knowing that I'll need to return to my husband before long, and wondering if a moment like today will happen again.

In the darkness, the tree stretches to the sky like hands trying to grasp something out of reach. It resonates deeply in my soul. I, too, am constantly grasping for something I can't reach. For something unknown to me.

A figure moves across my plane of vision, spiking my pulse. I lock my knees and stand my ground. The figure turns to me, eyes like embers, an axe dragging on the ground. They lift a hand, a finger pointed toward me before they vanish.

I suck in a breath as another figure appears. Familiar curly hair and a gentle presence extinguish the flames and dread. In another swirl of shadows, she's right before me, brown eyes large and pleading. "Try to stay with me," she says in a gentle, soothing voice that I could listen to all day.

"How?" I ask.

A smile spreads across her lovely face. "Fair question. You ... fight the urge to wake up or run."

"Is this really happening?"

"It is. I'm a Dreamwalker."

I squint at her. "How can I be sure that you're trustworthy?"

"What does your instinct tell you?"

"My instinct is not the best," I admit.

She's quiet for a while. It's an odd stillness, though it's comforting somehow. I don't want to leave this place, but it wavers around me, and a shiver crawls up my back as a voice prods at my senses. There's a warm feeling against my neck—a kiss, a caress. My stomach turns.

"Where are you in Erleya?" the woman asks.

"Barr na Cahar."

"I'm uncertain how or why we've found each other in this dreamscape." Even her voice starts to fade. She's speaking faster now as I become more aware of my body, of Gruffud waking me with immediate demands. "But there is a reason. Something bigger than both of us. All of us. So, whatever you're enduring, I'm so very sorry, but try to hang in there. I can feel your strength. Don't give anyone the power to deplete your strength."

Over a year ago, I awoke with a gemstone clutched in my fist, the sensation of rocky shards in my lungs and scalding liquid in my blood. My entire existence was pain, but my pleas for release into oblivion fell upon the merciless ears of the gods I'd sworn my life to. The gods I would've given anything to bring back from the in-between where they'd been losing power for centuries.

At least that's what the Purists told me.

It started with the moment Neris and I walked up the crumbly stone steps of the temple of Rhianu—the place where Nimue had told us to go, should I change my mind about the Cleanse. At that point, I'd been so tired of hiding, of being afraid to lose control of my magic and be discovered, of never truly earning my mother's love, that I was desperate to be Ordinary.

As we entered the temple, we were welcomed by several people all clad in white, as well as the overwhelming aroma of food. They all seemed ... happy. At the very least, they were immeasurably forthcoming.

We remained with them for a week, learning their ways, listening to their teachings of the prophecies, believing Magekind was tainted but there was hope in the Cleanse. The elder Purists took us under their wings—Credia in particular, with her steady silvery eyes and leathery skin from years laboring in the sun. She tutored me on what to expect from the Cleansing ritual.

I looked forward to the ritual. I imagined being able to do whatever the hells I wanted without fearing that my terraforging would lash out and ruin everything. Meanwhile, Neris enjoyed this newfound freedom and camaraderie. She liked spending countless hours out in the garden, looking at the stars, teaching the younger members to make her favorite baked goods, and ogling the young men her age.

Meanwhile, I prepared for my Cleansing ritual. Only the ones to be Cleansed were allowed at the final site, but we all traveled together.

For days, we trekked along the woodsy coast, up toward a cave nestled high in a small mountain. The other Purist members remained at camp while Nimue took me and two others to the purifying cave. There was nothing extraordinary about the cave, but it felt heavy with something that I couldn't quite describe.

The three of us stood in line, each of us with our elders—Credia smiling, confident that I was ready. A lamb was sacrificed, the blood spilled from its neck used to create markings across each of our foreheads. Then the Cleanse potion was divided into golden goblets inlaid with iridescent stones. Nimue spoke a strange language over the goblets, and I remember feeling something ominous in the air, but I pinned it on being nervous.

I stood there, my fingers trembling around the goblet. But when Nimue said "drink," I tipped my head back and poured the liquid into my mouth. Beside me, the other two initiates coughed, then one of them vomited and was promptly pulled from the cave while the other ran screaming.

At first, there was a swell of nausea; I feared that I'd also be sick, but the agony hit with such force, I was brought down not only to my knees but flat onto my face. The pain was beyond all reckoning. Once I started screaming, I didn't stop—not even as my voice abandoned me. Not even as *everyone* abandoned me. I lay in the empty cave with my cries echoing all around me. Pain cleaved through me like a chisel carving into my bones, down to my marrow. My blood seemed to turn to scalding lava.

I pleaded with the gods to take me. Pleaded with any entity to take me.

My only thought was to slam my head into the cave floor.

But even that pain was nothing in comparison. My vision went white and then red from the blood flowing into and from my eyes.

A voice spoke to me in that strange language, hands roaming over my body while I shrieked, warmth and cold warring with the pain—warring with the insanity threatening to tarnish my spirit forever.

"Kill me," I tried to say, but my voice was gone. I mouthed the words over and over again while the woman spoke to me with uncanny calm.

"You will be well again. You have a greater destiny than this. Even with a fractured soul, you have a purpose."

Then she was gone. I lay there, my body continuing to heal amid flares of pain that ripped more silent screams from my raw throat. Blood congealed around me, and I couldn't stop shivering as death's icy fingers taunted me but refused to take me.

I denounced the gods right there.

To hells with Lugda, who refused to pluck me from this bloody mortal body.

To hells with the Protector and the Mother, who didn't give a damn about my pain.

To hells with them all.

I screamed all my rage in silence until my heart stopped threatening to burst and my skull stopped splitting. Until I heard Neris's sobbing voice whispering in my ear.

"Oh, Winnie. What have they done to you? We have to get you out of here. Come on." She started to pull me upright, but I screamed hoarsely.

Neris swore through her tears. She lay beside me on her stomach, her cheek pressed against the bloodied cave floor, her emerald gaze staring into my bleary eyes. "I cannot even fathom how much you hurt right now, but don't let these fucking fanatics win. Let's get the hells out of here and get you back home. You can do this, my friend. I believe in you."

And so, we began the excruciating trek back home.

To a place that never quite felt like home again.

To a soul that never healed.

It had been a week since my disappearance, but thankfully I didn't need to come up with an excuse—one had already been forged for me. An excuse that had to be backed by my parents, eventually forcing me to study history with a mentor. A cover-up that became a truth. I hoped that the new life I'd been allotted would be uneventful.

Back at home, I tried countless times to get rid of the milky green and white stone that I'd found clutched in my fist when I first awoke in the cave. Yet each time I attempted to throw away the odd gem, I couldn't bring myself to do it. It felt like losing a part of myself. Another thing left unexplained, much like the images that had begun plaguing my mind. Black skies and endless winters.

That damn tree.

I would often find myself walking along the streets of the city one moment, and in the fields of someplace otherworldly the next. Meadows of flowers more vibrant than any I'd seen before would stretch out before me. Then, as though siphoned by dark magic, the flowers would begin to wither, a trail of black traveling across the expanse of the field, the sun darkening and swallowing up all visibility.

When the visions first began, I was certain that the Cleanse had taken my wits. That I was rapidly descending into madness. But the intensity of the visions gradually began to wane, and their frequency as well. Now they mostly appear to me when I'm painting or asleep.

I have yet to understand them, but I'm not sure I really want to.

In all the time I've been afflicted with this inconvenience, never has one of the figures in my dreams spoken to me. Not like the curly-haired woman who'd asked for my name. And I've certainly never experienced anyone appearing to me while I was wide awake—like the cloaked figures.

With the queen and her heir dead, I sense that something terrible is coming, and though I feel like I'm supposed to do something about it, I fear I don't have the means.

All I know is that there's a constant tug within me, calling me away from Barr na Cahar, away from Mainland. Calling me to a life unknown.

Sometimes I feel like I'm walking a tightrope between life and death.

Perhaps it's my subconscious desperate to get away from my suffocating circumstances, but unfortunately for me, I'm too afraid of the abyss to take a step into the unknown. Neris is completely on board with running away to something better—to freedom.

But I'm trapped here by my own cowardice.

Taking a deep breath, I steady myself. *Don't give anyone the power to deplete your strength*, the Dreamwalker said. I slip out of bed, leaving Gruffud spent and fast asleep, and hurry to the connected bath chamber to wash up.

I've let others diminish my strength before—in the most embarrassingly literal way. I've allowed my soul to be shattered. That's something I will never stop paying for.

But I'll be damned if I let Gruffud annihilate what's left of me. I just need time to earn his trust.

I light the mounted oil lamp sconce and snatch a washcloth from a hook on the wall. Cool water sloshes out over the sides and dribbles down the bathroom vanity as I plunge my hand into the wash basin.

I stare at my shaded reflection in the looking glass. Even my eyes have lost their luster. My chest aches and I hold back tears as I start to clean any evidence of my husband from my body.

When I'm scrubbed until my skin feels raw, I gawk at my reflection again, tucking a large ash brown ringlet away from my face. I press my palms against the vanity and inhale deeply, steeling myself.

It's time to plan an escape.

Chapter 21

CARYS

THE JOURNEY to the Hallowed Wood and back took nine days. It's been only a month and a half since I landed on Uldaran shores, but it feels like I've been here far longer. Last night, we rested upon returning to the Great Hall, but today, we're determined to figure out the next steps regarding Siad Nahar.

A deerskin map is rolled out on one of the long tables, all of us gathered around it. Seth taps the outline of Uldarvik and drags his finger across the ocean to the southern coast of Erleya. "The castle is about here, correct?" he asks.

My skin feels too tight for my body, and sweat breaks out along the back of my neck at the mere thought of being near the Fortress on the Mount. "Correct," I respond.

Briony glances up at me, an unspoken apology in her eyes. I avert my gaze, but it lands on Odgar. He stares at me as if he's reading my mind.

I refocus on the map and ask, "So where's this magical land supposed to be?"

Briony stares at the map for a while before her slender finger rests on a heavily wooded area somewhere in the east of Erleya. "Somewhere here," she says. "I have no definitive location, unfortunately. But this has been widely agreed upon as the vicinity. It's not easy to get to, however. You cannot just *walk in*. The land only welcomes those who belong."

"What the fuck does that mean?" I ask.

Briony shrugs. "I'm not certain, but I suppose we'll find out."

Odgar scratches his beard, lips pursed as he stares at the map. "It would be too risky to travel across the kingdom. I imagine we'd draw too much attention. Sailing northbound puts us in Ardallan waters —those shits are always far too eager to instigate battle. No offense, Seth." Seth shrugs with a *none taken* look. "We've not been in active war for years, but they're bullies in the waterways." Odgar looks at his sister. "Valdis have you found anyone willing?"

"You know I have my loyal crew," she says with a wink. "They're ready whenever. Have you spoken to Freyr?"

Odgar sighs but says nothing else.

"*Odgar.*" Valdis starts to argue with him in rapid Uldaran. As they go back and forth, I stare at the map. At the neatly drawn rivers and trees. Returning to Erleya feels like walking into a death trap. What if I'm caught again?

My throat constricts, my lungs seizing up.

Silence falls around me and a firm weight settles on my back. "*Revna?*" Odgar questions.

I drag my gaze up to his concerned face, my breath haggard. "If I'm caught in Erleya, take me out," I whisper. "Whatever you have to do. Throw an axe, knife, shoot an arrow. I don't care. Just don't let me live if I'm captured."

Odgar blinks; clearly it was not what he expected me to say. "It'll be hard for them to capture you with their heads cleaved from their necks," he says evenly.

Valdis nods in fervent agreement.

A tear slips down my cheek, but I swipe it away and refocus on the map. "The Outer Isles has a port," I force myself to say. "It's Erleyan territory but notoriously more lenient than either Mainland or the Grounds. There isn't a large presence of the Royal Brigade or even Forayers there, so it's our safest bet. We could perhaps go further North to avoid much time on foot, but we'll risk guarded forces along the coast. Entry may be more difficult."

"We can aim for the Outer Isles and recalibrate if needed," says Seth. "Valdis's crew are esteemed warriors. A small bunch but mighty."

I nod. That's good to know.

"So now, we just need Odgar to speak to Freyr, and we need the two of you to be wed. Let's get this alliance officially set in place," says Valdis.

"Does that sound good to you, *revna*?" Odgar asks.

Enidwen's annoyance has a hold on my mind; she's always in utter disagreement of this marriage—specifically of any feelings, mild or otherwise, toward this man. But when I glance up again, Odgar's warm smile obliterates her irritation. My own smile twitches on my lips, but it's smothered by a sinking feeling in my gut. The reality of marrying him is growing, and I can't help but feel like it's unfair to him.

For so many reasons.

Chapter 22

DURVLA

TAIG IS six years old today. Where has the time gone? Ma and Da would be so happy to see him thriving. His exuberant grin as he's showered with love by everyone is a soothing balm over my grief. The O'Haras are here, as are Alys's cousin, Jali, and her family. Alys brings out a cake of rich chocolate and warm spices with a delicious strawberry filling in the center. Fresh berries adorn the top of the molten chocolate finish. Taig devours his piece, even eating the berries, much to my surprise.

As night draws near, I lounge on the couch with Taig on my lap, watching Chiyo and one of Jali's children take turns telling fables and sharing songs. It's incredible celebrating Taig with a group of people that care so much about him—no need to hide him or pretend he doesn't exist. I gently caress his curls as he starts to doze off against my chest. Tiernan smiles at me, tenderness in his eyes.

"Ready to send everyone home?" he asks with gentle signs.

As much as I wish to remain in this loving atmosphere, I nod. Taig is half asleep and we have training in the morning.

Hugs are exchanged, final birthday wishes uttered, but I call to Dayfyd as he's about to step out of the house. He faces me, a mixture of anticipation and remorse in his expression. "Alys told me once that you were a talented tattooist," I say.

The remorse melts away, a smile taking over his handsome features. "I am," he says, not haughtily.

I pull back the sleeve of my dress to show him my branding scar. "Would you be able to cover this?"

He gently takes my arm in his hands, getting a good look at the scar.

"Every morning when I get dressed, I see this, and I remember feeling so completely powerless and *terrified*. Covering it with something that would be more pleasant to look at would be so lovely. Besides, it would probably be safer not to have the royal insignia clearly branded into my arm."

When Dayfyd looks at me, there are tears in his eyes as he nods. "I can certainly help you with that. Do you have anything in mind?"

I smile at him and nod.

"Perfect. Then come by when you have some free time."

Over the next few days, I train longer than usual. I still make it a habit to pick up Taig early from the Hatchling's Nest so I can spend as much time as I can with him. We walk through the community garden, cuddle on the couch before the hearth, and every night I watch him sleep.

I memorize the dimples in his cheeks when he smiles and the way his hair coils in perfect corkscrews over his ears. I hoard the images of his little puckered lips, his small frame, the wild flapping of his hands, and goofy, crooked smiles.

Gods, I'm going to miss him.

My heart feels ready to cleave in two. I'm almost certain that when we ride away from here, I'll be leaving behind a part of myself. It brings back the memories of the Forayers barging into my home nearly four months ago, of being branded, of living in constant fear of being discovered as an Undesirable.

This time, I'm leaving willingly. I'm leaving knowing that my heart won't, in fact, cleave in two—that his will remain intact.

I'm leaving because everyone's lives may depend on it.

Still, it doesn't make things easier.

Tears brim in my eyes. I stare down at my forearm while Dayfyd meticulously works over it with a delicate bone needle. Gone are the obvious discolored ridges in my skin, the unsightly remnants of my branding scar from back in Paramount. The sun and eclipsed crown turned on its side are no longer visible.

With each sting of the bone needle, the design I'd asked Dayfyd to ink slowly emerges. My right hand grips the cushion beneath me as I sit on the floor with my arm propped on the tea table. Dayfyd kneels on the other side with ink, a handkerchief, and a replacement bone needle within his reach.

He glances up at me, concern etched into features that I foolishly never realized looked so much like my own. "Am I hurting you too much?" he asks. "We could take a break."

I watch the words form on his lips and shake my head. Dayfyd nods, compassion in his eyes. He gently blots a dribble of blood from my arm with a handkerchief before resuming the inking process. I grit my teeth against the bite of the needle. It's nothing compared to a decade of headaches, nausea, and dizziness, but it's still unpleasant.

Dayfyd looks up at me again and I catch his remorseful expression. "I know I don't deserve forgiveness," he says. "But I am truly sorry for not speaking to you earlier. Alys feels awful about it as well."

"You did what you thought was right," I say.

"No, I did it out of fear."

I cock an eyebrow at him. "What were you afraid of?"

"I was afraid of the prophecy. Morwenna frequently dreamt about it. I suppose I feared that once you knew the truth about your bloodline, it would all come to fruition. I was also afraid to chase you away when I'd dreamt of meeting you again for so long."

My heart tugs as I look away. When I turn back to say something, he's refocused on my forearm, putting the final touches on the tattoo.

"There," he says after a few moments. He takes a cloth and dabs away the blood. "It's going to look a little swollen and red for a couple days, but afterward it should be fine. A Healer could also speed up the process."

A smile blooms on my face as I take in the artwork in the middle of my inner forearm: an image of the moon phases inline, nestled within a branch of flowers and foliage. It's symbolic of the only person I thought I could be before arriving at Paramount, and my hope of embracing who I truly am—dreamwalking included.

Tiernan appears from the kitchen where he'd been chatting with Alys—as if my thoughts have summoned him. He looks down at the tattoo, then at Dayfyd. "Beautiful work," he signs.

Dayfyd's smile is humble and sweet.

"I agree," I say. "Thank you, Dayfyd."

"It was my honor," he replies. As he gathers his supplies, Tiernan takes my right hand to pull me to my feet. My body is a little stiff from sitting on that small cushion on the floor for too long, but it was worth it. I peer at the complete tattoo and begin smiling anew.

"I think it's perfect for you," Tiernan says as Dayfyd heads into the kitchen. "Do you like it?"

"I certainly do." The skin is swollen and sore, but the ink is perfect.

"I can heal your skin before we head home if you'd like."

"Please do." I place my arm atop his, and his other hand floats above my skin. Healing light soothes the soreness from the bone needle. A sigh of relief leaves me.

Now I feel even more like a rebel.

Chapter 23

DURVLA

TIERNAN HAS BEEN TAKING a lot of time to train, even when we're home. Perhaps I need to remind *him* about burnout, but I'm certain he's keeping himself occupied so he doesn't have to face whatever is running through his mind. He's become more withdrawn, quieter. I feel like I'm losing a lot of the Tiernan I've come to know since and coming face-to-face with Major Kilkenny of Paramount again. It's evident something is bothering him, but he won't speak to me about it, and I fear that continuing to press him will only make him pull away more.

My shadows have been more willing to obey my commands, and I've been working on daywalking every day. Chiyo has volunteered a few times to be my subject to practice on, and that has been particularly helpful. I haven't had many more sessions with Oksana, but I've continued to memorize the runes in the book and practice putting up sound and protective barriers, as well as taking them down. I also spar with other Mages to work on my offensive shadow wielding. I lose every spar, of course, but I try not to let my anxieties about it get the best of me.

With just a couple days left, I've chosen to take a break, to breathe and enjoy the last moments of normalcy before we leave the safety of the Verge.

I'm not sure how long I stand there, staring at Taig fast asleep. He'd dozed off while playing, and Chiyo had tucked him into her bed while she gave me a chance to meditate and pack for our mission. A newfound determination stirs inside me at the realization that I *must* survive this journey in order to return to him. My stomach is all twisted up with the thought.

Chiyo places her hand on my shoulder, pulling me out of my worries.

"Apologies." I say. "I'll take him now. Thanks for looking after him while I packed and such."

"No thanks needed." She smiles and drops her hand from my shoulder. "You ... can leave him here a while longer if you aren't going to bed yet. I'm not going anywhere. Just drying my hair." The damp strands, freshly dyed blue from indigo plant paste, hang limply against her shoulders. "I wanted to freshen this up before we set off and it immediately turns fully silver. I can't go looking haggard *and* like an old woman, you know."

I laugh softly. "Again, you do *not* look like an old woman, even with the silver hair, Chiyo."

She grins and shrugs before steering me out of the room. "Now go ... do something relaxing for a while. We'll be here."

The door shuts before I can say anything. I make my way carefully down the stairs. I'll miss this place. As I step into the sitting room, I expect to see Tiernan, but he isn't there, nor is he in the kitchen or the bathing chamber.

I step out of the house in my lightweight summer dress and inhale sharply through my teeth when my bare feet touch the cold grass. Wrapping my arms around my torso, I brave the cold and hurry toward the backyard. A single magelight lamp illuminates very little, though it gives a clear view of Tiernan hurling daggers into a poor tree.

I barely register him turning, another throwing knife in hand, but I manage to fling up a shadow shield as the weapon flies toward me. My heart is in my throat as the blade bounces off my shield and drops to the ground.

In the magelight, Tiernan's eyes blow wide. "Fuck!" he exclaims, running toward me.

I drop my arms and dismiss the shadows as Tiernan grabs my shoulders.

"Durvla!" With frantic movements, his hands run along the length of my arms. "You startled me. I'm so sorry." After a moment, he steps back and bends to pick up the knife.

My hands are shaking even as I assure him I'm fine. "I'm the one who snuck up on you."

His eyes remain wide, frantic. He still seems spooked. Disturbed, even.

"Let's get inside, hmm?" I sign gently. "My feet are freezing."

His gaze drops to my feet, and amusement overshadows the haunted look in his eyes as he sweeps me up into his arms. My hand flies up to cover the shriek of surprise that nearly escapes me. Brief laughter vibrates through his chest as he carries me toward the house. My feet hit the floor mat inside, and I hurry toward the hearth where I sit in front of the roaring fire.

I motion for Tiernan to join me. He closes the door before coming to sit beside me on the floor. I wave my hand a few times, calling a silencing ward. No shadows show, but it feels no different from casting a shadow wall.

Tiernan nods and says, "Clever. It doesn't keep prying eyes from seeing us though." He winks.

I try to smile, truly, but my lips don't cooperate. "I want you to talk to me. You once told me that I should share my woes with you. Yet you're shouldering all the burdens."

He produces a smile that might have been believable to someone else, but after months of seeing him every single day, I know better. He takes my hand and kisses my knuckles. "I'm just spooked by the thought of going back out there with so many after us. After you, especially."

Of course, he's shifted right back to me again, but I don't argue.

"That's all." Something in his gaze has me thinking he knows he hasn't convinced me, but he continues. "Once we're out there," he signs. "I want you always by my side. Riding with me. Sleeping with—"

His abrupt halt forces giggles from me. *Very mature, Durvla.*

"You know what I mean," he says with a sheepish smile.

"Yes. It's a different sign anyway. It's rather innocent the way you just signed it."

"Oh?" He raises a brow, and I demonstrate the sign for *sex*, ignoring the flush that spreads across my chest. I pray it doesn't spread to my cheeks, especially as Tiernan repeats the sign back to me, both brows raised, his head tilted.

It's the sweetest expression from him, which makes me giggle even more, until he's suddenly staring at me in that intense way that makes me want to run my fingers through his hair, over his shoulders, his back, everywhere.

"You are endearing, you know that?" he asks.

I gawk at him, uncertain of how to respond or how to stop the thoughts of my hands roaming over his body like he's clay to be modeled.

What is happening to me?

Thank goodness, he abruptly stands and extends his hand to me. "We'd better try to get some sleep," he says. "A couple more days then who knows when next we'll find a bed."

I groan. "Don't remind me." As I place my hand into his palm, he not only pulls me to my feet but straight into an embrace. His lips claim mine, and I react with a slight startle. But then I allow myself to melt into him, to savor the sensations that temporarily shove aside the fears of the unknown.

We have limited time to enjoy a bed, indeed? What will happen out there, outside of our bubble of safety?

His hands slide over my back, down to the swell of my behind. He pulls my hips flush against him, his arousal evident in the hard bulge pressing into my thigh.

My coyness is absorbed by the heat that spreads through the depths of my belly. My fingers bunch in his tunic, my lips parting from his. I gently pull back, my eyes searching his face, finding his dark gaze heavy with lust. Dropping my eyes to his lips, I watch the words form: "We should get—"

"—to our room, yes." The words leave my lips with breathy urgency. It's almost dizzying how much I long to feel more of his hands ... *everywhere*. "But I need to bathe," I sign.

"What a coincidence. So do I!"

A witty comeback is at the tip of my tongue just as he sweeps me off my feet for the second time tonight. Laughter tumbles from me as I cling to him. "Tiernan, I can walk!"

"I know." His smirk and the sparkle in his eyes leave my body tingling with delight. He barely sets me down inside the bathing chamber before his lips are on mine again, his fingers loosening the strings of my bodice. He steps away to crank the lever of the tub and get the warm water flowing.

"I'm going to miss warm baths," I say as the water begins to fill the tub.

"Gods, same." He slips his tunic off over his head and casts it aside.

My eyes roam his chest, his muscles and scars, the dark hair that trails from his navel down to—

I jerk my focus back up to his face as he starts to loosen the strings of his trousers. He grins as if seeing me flustered is topmost amusement.

I can't help but smile as I remove my dress so I'm standing in my breeches and the band of fabric wound around my breasts. The flustered look on *his* face makes me giggle. "Payback," I say.

Half of his mouth curves up, his gaze flicking down then immediately back to my eyes. "Are you *folding* your dirty clothing?" he signs.

I glance down at my hands, which have evidently folded my dress. Stepping toward the counter, I set the folded garment down. "Apparently, I was," I say with an awkward chuckle. "Is that odd?"

His smile could melt ice. "It's *you*, Durvla. Never change." He steps toward me, his eyes roaming my face. His thumb strokes lightly over my cheek. "Looks like you freckle when you're out in the sun a lot."

My hand flies to my own face. "*Do* I?"

He chuckles, nodding as his thumb slides from my face, down along the side of my neck. "I like it."

My stomach tightens. His fingers lightly trace along the bottom of the fabric around my breasts. "May I remove this?"

I nod, my breath hitching.

"*Yes*?" He signs, his brow quirked.

I lift my hand, shaky from a mixture of nervousness and excitement. "Yes."

His teeth sink into his lower lip as he finds the end piece of the fabric and untucks it before pulling it down. The fabric slips free, pooling around my middle. I tug on it, fully unfurling it so that it drops down from my hips and onto the floor. My heart is hammering so hard that I'm almost certain it's visible. I'm all soft curves and no muscle while Tiernan looks like a god. He's already seen me in a complete state of undress before; gods, he's helped me *bathe* before. But this feels so different. What if he dislikes my body?

"You are breathtaking," he signs. My ribs stop strangling my heart, but my pulse still pounds in my throat. I stare at the hard length of him straining within the breeches that now hang off his hips.

My mouth goes dry. "Should I ... help you out of that?"

He nods.

With a cheeky grin, I lift my hand, replicating his early insistence on speaking rather than nodding. "*Yes*?" I sign with flamboyant emphasis.

He smirks and says aloud, "Yes, beautiful. Please help me out of these."

With my mental shields firmly in place, I tug his breeches down. I hope he doesn't notice the shake in my hands. My heart pounds with a dizzying mixture of desire and anxiety. I fear my inexperience will shine through and magnify all my flaws, but everything he says and does makes my body hum with growing anticipation.

Both our undergarments soon lie on the floor while we take our time exploring each other's bodies. Steam fills the room, but it isn't until I'm pressed against the counter, lost in a haze of kisses and caresses that I feel something warm and wet at my feet.

Tiernan's mental voice is nearly a purr as his knuckles lightly slide over the side of my breast. "*Tell me if you need me to slow down at any point.*"

I'm definitely standing in something wet.

"Uhm ... Tiernan?" I whisper as his lips caress mine again.

He breaks away from me and looks down at the floor, where water is rapidly spreading around our feet from the overflowing tub.

"Shit," he says, releasing me and running to stop the flow of the water while I try my hardest not to laugh.

I grab towels from the cabinet and lay them on the floor to soak up the flooding. Tiernan retrieves the plug from the tub, letting some water drain before replacing the stopper.

"You'd think that a magical system would know when to cease, right?"

I laugh. "Even magic has its limits."

We get into the tub, indulging in soft caresses and kisses, lathering each other with soap, and signing sweet nothings above the water. Eventually, we leave the bathing chamber, restraining our giggles as we lightly pad past Chiyo's chamber with our towels clutched to our bodies.

Ambient magelight greets us as we shut the door behind us, and it dims even more as we crawl into bed. Tiernan tugs me to him, my towel falling away as my back meets his torso. Thighs bracketing mine, his hand slides over my soft curves, teasing, caressing, making my breath hitch and my eyes flutter closed.

My head falls back against his shoulder, and I feel him smile into my neck. Tiny tingles dance along my skin and throughout my body.

"*Just tell me when you want me to stop.*" Even his mental voice is laden with such longing that I nearly turn molten in his arms

His hand trails up my thigh, pausing.

Every part of my body is abuzz, longing for more, but the faintest hint of hesitation buds in my chest. I have no doubt by now that he's attracted to me. I see it in his eyes; I feel it in his touch. I even feel it in the flitter of his Empath powers across my skin.

Yet something still hinders me—a warring within myself. As much as I think I want this man, I wonder how much I truly know him.

But then his fingers find a spot at the apex of my thighs, stroking in tight circles until my thoughts are consumed and my hips develop a mind of their own. He repositions, his arm supporting my back, the other hand still moving against that sweet spot.

"I wanted to see your beautiful face," he says. His fingers still tease and stroke, causing my breath to grow shallower. I grip the bedding beneath me and try to keep myself from squirming. Cool vapors begin to flood my hands, my powers eager to unleash.

My shadows respond to my emotions; what if I lose control and unwittingly hurt him? The thought makes my heart hammer and my body cool.

I bite back a moan that threatens to break free as I fight to regain control of my body.

What if the sounds I make are awkward or off-putting? What if my inexperience ruins everything?

I clutch my arms to my naked torso as a band of shadows wraps around my wrist. My thighs lock up, my chest caving in at once as panic fills my mind and my heart pounds with enough intensity to break through my chest.

I can't do this. I can't let go ... I can't—

"*Durvla?*" Tiernan says into my mind. "*Do you want me to stop?*"

Do I? *No,* I think. I shake my head, but my body feels as tight as a bowstring in more ways than one.

"*Durvla ...*"

"I don't know," I say aloud.

He immediately withdraws his hand, and a shudder rolls through me. Tears fill my eyes, the pleasure morphing into embarrassment and confusion, cold seeping into warmth. Just as I felt on the brink, I'm left shockingly bereft, my body desperate for more while my mind berates me for allowing the indulgence. I squeeze my thighs together, the throbbing between them pitifully ebbing away, and I take a shuddery breath.

To my dismay, the tears flow hot and fast down my cheeks. I pull my legs to my chest and wrap my arms around them, dropping my face into my knees. Tiernan doesn't waste a moment before pulling me to him, my face now buried against the downy hair on his chest. He fumbles for something then soft fabric covers my body.

How did my mind convince me to stop enjoying that moment? Why is it that, even when I'm shrouded in pleasure, the doubts drop in so forcefully? I ruined the moment. Epically.

"I'm sorry." I swipe away tears.

"Don't be. It's alright."

"I think ..." My cheeks burn. "I guess I'm not as ready as I thought I was." I shut my eyes and immediately feel his hands on my face. My eyes open tentatively to find him smiling with such affection that it's hard to hold on to the shame and annoyance.

"You never have to apologize for something like this." He kisses my nose. "We'll take our time."

"We're leaving in two days."

"And?" He winks at me. "We'll find moments." He slides his fingers through my hair, and I wince as they catch in my curls. He pries his hand free with a sheepish grin that makes me smile.

"Tiernan ... do you think you would be able to deflect my shadows well enough if ..." I'm not sure how to word it without my entire face turning red. "If I—"

"If you lose control when we're intimate?"

I grimace. "Yes, that."

He smiles with understanding. "Yes, but also I don't believe you'll hurt me."

I sigh, starting to climb out of bed, but he gently presses a hand against my shoulder to stop me.

"If it makes you feel better, it's normal for your magic to slip and respond differently in times like this. I know mine does. *You* know mine does. My Empath powers don't stand a chance when your body is against mine. It's always too late when I realize I've cast all my feelings onto you."

I don't know whether to blush or laugh. "I should get dressed and get Taig," I sign.

"Well ..." A look of focus comes over his face—his magic likely reaching out to them. "They're both fast asleep."

Tiernan rolls onto his side facing me and I sidle up to him, tugging the covers up to our waists. For a while, we study each other's faces in silence, his hands idly caressing my sides and hips. All the while, I wish things were different outside the Verge—I wish we had more moments to simply explore each other—not just physically.

I'm not ready to leave. Not at all. But we have a mission to fulfill, and the fate of the entire kingdom may depend on us finding out more about the prophecy.

Chapter 24

DURVLA

"ALRIGHT, I'm not a fan of repeating things, so listen up," says Ava. She's now every bit a commander as she stands at the head of the table in one of the small rooms of the Assembly Lodge. Aside from the round table large enough for ten and the map against the wall, there's not much else to the room.

"There's no exact protocol for this mission," Ava continues. "Magic never follows protocol, after all. Siad Nahar is where we'll get answers. We just need to figure out how to get there, and we *need* Durvla to get there for this prophecy shit."

A cool sensation rushes down my spine. No pressure. I shudder and my head throbs as I turn Ava's words over in my mind. Tiernan places his hand on my knee, his fingers lightly caressing me in a way that stops the feeling of impending doom from spreading through my body.

"Her safety comes first. Is that understood?" Ava's hand is on the hilt of the sword at her hip as her calculating gaze shifts to look at each person.

Around me, lips move, and heads swivel my way. Isobel steps forward. "It's my honor to be entrusted with this mission, Warden Ava. I will do everything in my power to help deliver Durvla to Siad Nahar. It sounds very exciting!" She beams at me, her eyes sparkling with sincerity.

My stomach knots, even as I try to focus on Tiernan's grounding caresses rather than my fear.

I stand, smoothing out my dress, and step forward. I look to Alys and Dayfyd, then to Chiyo, Isobel, and Sloan. "I appreciate everyone's determination to protect me, but this mission isn't about *me*. It's about all of us and the fate of the kingdom." I swallow, feeling my voice waver. "Please don't sacrifice someone else's safety for my sake."

"That is very noble of you, Durvla," says Ava. "But if sacrifice is what it takes to get you to Siad Nahar, then so be it."

I take my seat again, and Tiernan gives my knee another squeeze. I swear I can feel his pride, warm against my skin. My shoulders roll forward and I release a breath.

"If there are no further questions, assembly adjourned."

"He just rolled his eyes at me again. Did you see that?" I ask, squinting at Ghendor. The black stallion nickers and spittle lands on my face, forcing me to step back. I stumble, almost tripping over Taig and knocking him over instead.

He lands on his bottom with a panicked look in his eyes, and I immediately lurch to pull him to his feet. "I'm so sorry, Taig!" I sign as my vision swirls and my head pounds from the sudden movement. He beams and wildly shakes his head back and forth with excitement, his curls flying everywhere.

I glance over at Tiernan, who's watching the mild chaos as he runs a brush through Mirren's cream-colored mane. He's already groomed Ffion, and the brown mare looks on with curiosity while Mirren is groomed.

"What were you saying about Ghendor before your newborn foal legs took over?" Tiernan asks.

I groan through my laughter. "Not that again. I have improved considerably, thank you very much." Running daily and training have improved not only my stamina but my balance too. It's something that will never be great or even typical compared to others, but the improvement is appreciated.

Tiernan glances over at the stall where Ghendor stands, the horse staring at me with neutrality now. "I think you're being paranoid," Tiernan says, smirking at me.

"I'm not. Ghendor just *tolerates* me. Don't you, boy?" I reach out to rub the stallion's snout, and he lets me.

The stable is dimly lit with magelights, like all buildings in the Verge. A few other horses look on with curiosity while others are asleep or too preoccupied nibbling hay. There are a couple other riders there as well, checking in on their horses. Taig teeters down the row of stalls, then turns and walks back our way, again and again without seeming to get bored.

I wish we were so easily appeased in life as adults.

"I cannot believe we have to travel again," I say. I don't really want to see Tiernan's response, so I keep my focus on Ghendor. With a sigh, I pull an apple from the pocket of my dress and offer it to him. "You're stuck with us again," I tell him as he lips at the apple. "My sincerest apologies. Hopefully it won't be for very long. And this time, we'll have a better saddle."

Ghendor takes his apple and presents his rump to me, sauntering off with clear dismissal. Tiernan has set the brush aside and is walking my way. As Taig starts to hobble past him, Tiernan hoists him onto his hip and reaches out to take my hand.

"See you later, Ghendor, Mirren, Ffion," I call over my shoulder as we walk toward the entrance to the large stables.

We take our time walking across the grounds, letting Taig get a chance to walk and trailing him when he wanders.

The community garden lures us in one last time and we oblige, stepping into flourishing bushes of tomatoes, peppers, and spinach. It's so very different from the blight we witnessed Outside. How much worse has it gotten in the two months we've been here? We pick some produce to leave behind for Alys's cousin. A token of my gratitude for their willingness to look after Taig in my absence.

By the time we return to the house, I'm holding back tears to the best of my ability, but I eventually escape to the bath chamber to have a good cry. I need to get it out of my system before we set off, because once we're on the road, there will be no time for tears.

Saying goodbye to Taig the next morning proves to be even more difficult than I imagined. He presses his little head against my collarbone as I kneel in front of him, and I wrap my arms around his lithe frame. His chestnut curls get in my mouth, and I cannot help but think, with sheer absurdity, that I'll miss having his hair in my face. I press my hands to his dimpled cheeks, and he grunts, his narrow shoulders jutting upward. I stare into his big, brown eyes, and for the briefest moment, he returns my gaze.

"Be good, alright?" I sign, choking out the words as best as I can.

I search his face for any sign of understanding before he teeters away from me and toward the family who will be looking after him. If we're somehow never reunited after today, would he remember me? Would he understand that I'm not walking away from him because I don't want him, but because I want to help make a better world *for* him?

Perhaps he's better off existing in his bubble of blissful ignorance, but I selfishly want him to understand how much I'll miss him.

Alys's cousin, Jali, approaches me, steady grey eyes filled with compassion. "We'll take care of him like he's our own," she signs. I peer over her shoulder at Taig hobbling toward the youngest of Jali's children, and then to her older daughter who sweeps him into her arms.

"I trust you," I tell Jali, and I'm relieved by my own sincerity.

Still, it feels unnatural to walk away from my little brother, not knowing when I'll see him again. To realize that he doesn't need me, and that perhaps I've always been the one who's needed him more.

The seven of us stand at the invisible wards with the ramparts behind us and Verge guards overseeing our transition through the barrier. Oksana and another Wielder I don't know stand on either side of our group as we mount our horses. The air is charged, and Ghendor's uneasy as Tiernan takes the reins, his thighs on either side of me. Perhaps it isn't *necessary* that I ride tandem with him, since I seem to have more control of my daywalking now, but a part of me is grateful. This time, we even have a saddle made for tandem riding.

"*How are you feeling?*" Tiernan asks as my eyes are trained on the Wielders.

"*Anxious. But what's new?*" I smile despite myself and Tiernan's chest ripples with subtle laughter behind me.

"*We can do this,*" Tiernan says. "*One step and one day at a time.*"

I nod. "*I hope so.*"

The uncomfortable buzzing subsides. There's the slightest shimmer where the wards are, then it disappears. Oksana gives me an encouraging look and smiles. I wave to her and sign *thank you,* and she returns a slow nod.

Our travel party stares out at the rolling green hills and the plethora of sheep and goats wandering about. Ava looks toward us, signing, "Ready?"

We all nod in agreement and set off on our mission.

Chapter 25

DURVLA

WIDE PASTURES FALL behind us as the afternoon brings scattered trees and trodden pathways through the grassy knolls. We're somewhere outside of Moicriach, the village where we discovered that Osheen had betrayed us all. My heart pounds as we ride on. I focus as best as I can on the path ahead, not on the climb of our horses over these hills or the painful reminder of the fallout to end all fallouts with my former best friend.

We travel past patches of grass that look almost as if the earth has been scorched. Past withered flowers and browning bushes. Briefly, we pause at a river to replenish our resources and wash up before we continue onward until we're just outside of a small village when night falls.

We find a place where the trees are slightly more condensed— just enough to offer us some coverage. My whole body is already sore, and my head aches. Hopefully it's something that rest can help remediate. As we dismount and everyone begins to set up their bedrolls, I turn to Tiernan as he lights a mage lantern and hangs it off Ghendor's pommel. "Are you alright?" he gestures.

Everything hurts—especially my back—but I don't want to worry him. "Yes. Just tired," I sign.

He begins to unstrap our packs from Ghendor while his gaze is still locked on me. There's that knowing look in his eyes I've come to recognize too well. "How's your back?" he asks.

I squint at him. "That's unfair."

He grins as he slings the pack over his shoulder and grabs the lantern. The movement of shadows around us reminds me, quite painfully, that we're not alone. I've gotten far too used to the moments of quiet and privacy back in the Verge. Oh, how I miss those moments already, and oh, how I miss Taig. I hope he's doing well—I'm sure he is.

We roll out our sleep sacks beside Chiyo's, and Sloan lays theirs out on our other side. We exchange a few brief pleasantries before Sloan mentions they're going to take the first watch with Ava.

"How are you feeling?" Chiyo signs to me, her words hard to see in the dim lantern light.

"So far so good," I reply. "You?"

"Same. I hope we can get some rest out here."

I squint at her hands and then nod, smiling.

"Good night, Durvla."

"Good night."

I watch as she rolls onto her side, facing away from me. Immediately, I feel the familiar presence of Tiernan's mind reaching out to mine. "*I can take care of that for you, if you'd like,*" he says.

I turn back to him, a question in my expression.

"*Your back.*" He holds up his hands, the faintest glow on his fingertips. "*Am I using this as an excuse to get my hands on you? Maybe.*"

I nearly choke on my stifled laughter as my cheeks and stomach fill with heat. I know I shouldn't be embarrassed, but this man so often makes me feel like I could lose control. It's not a sensation I'm used to. Especially after years of practiced restraint and concealment. I have a habit of suppressing what I feel and how I truly want to react to a situation.

Tiernan's brows are raised, a quizzical look on his face. "*Gods, woman, you really need to give your mind a rest sometimes.*"

My cheeks twitch as I try to resist smiling, but I lose the battle.

"*Just a massage. If you'd be so kind as to lie down on your front.*"

I glance around at the others. "*Wouldn't that be awkward?*"

"*What on earth do you think I have in mind?*"

I nearly laugh again, but I can't bring myself to be massaged in front of everyone.

Tiernan huffs a sigh and grabs a lantern. "Let's get away from prying eyes then," he motions with his free hand.

My confusion leaves me speechless as he helps me to my feet and leads me away from the group. He holds the lantern out in front of him, his fingers laced with mine as we maneuver through the trees until we get a very small distance away, behind some thick bushes. I turn to him with a lifted brow. "Alright," Tiernan signs one-handed, holding up the lantern. He hooks it over a low-hanging branch. "Hold on to that tree."

"What?" I glance at the thick trunk of the tree.

He grins. "You truly make it difficult for a man to give a simple healing session."

I turn and press my hands against the rough bark. Tiernan steps closer behind me and immediately, my heart hammers ... from anticipation?

"*I haven't even touched you yet,*" Tiernan says into my mind, amusement in his inner voice. I'm about to retort when he lifts the hem of my tunic and cool air kisses my skin. Goose bumps rise along my flesh until his hands warm me. His fingers encircle my waist, thumbs pressing into my lower back.

There's the slightest twinge of my sore muscles before more warmth flows into them, calming the ache and dragging out some sound that vibrates in my chest. I close my eyes and relax, my forearms now against the tree trunk, my forehead against my arms.

"*Didn't I tell you I was very skilled with my hands?*" Tiernan asks.

I chuckle. "*Yes, ironically it was also while you healed me last time. After you forced me to throw daggers and caused me to cut my hand in the first place.*"

His groan fills my headspace and causes my stomach to clench pleasantly. "*You sure know how to ruin a moment,*" he says with amusement.

"*Oh, were you trying to create a moment?*" I glance over my shoulder at him, smirking.

Simultaneously, we shift—Tiernan lifts his hands and I turn, pressing my back against the tree. He steps close enough for us to share a breath, his nose brushing mine. "*How's your back?*"

My pulse quickens. "*As if you don't already know the answer.*"

His eyes crinkle. "*I do. I was just stalling.*"

"*Stalling for what?*"

He gently tips my chin up so our lips meet. His hands cradle my face, and I'm hyperaware of every place where his body meets mine. Our lips part, but our foreheads linger against each other. Overwhelming longing weakens my knees, stealing my breath.

"*Sorry,*" Tiernan says. "*Projecting again. If we keep going like this, I may never want to stop.*" As I'm about to protest, he adds, "*And we really ought to take advantage of this time to have a solid rest before we're back to traveling.*"

I give a dramatic sigh, and he lifts his head, chuckling as he caresses my face. I drop the theatrics to admire the light in his eyes. Gone is that haunted look he's had lately. Right now, there's only admiration and joviality, and I wish it would last forever.

"*Durvla, the way you're looking at me—*" He steps back.

"How am I looking at you?" I sign.

The cheer is ghosted over by something I can't quite pinpoint. "Like I'm worthy of such admiration."

"What do you—"

He takes my hand, lacing our fingers together and effectively quieting me. "Bed," he enunciates without signing. As much as I want to press him further—as much as I wouldn't mind remaining here longer, lost in his kisses—I let him lead me back to my bedroll. As soon as my body hits the material, I drift off into a dreamless sleep.

An overwhelming chill yanks me from my slumber. I sit up, my heart racing, my head throbbing, and glance over at Tiernan. The faintest stream of sunlight filters through the trees and onto Tiernan's body. His legs are tangled in his bedroll, pain and fear twisting his features as his head whips back and forth. I scamper over on my knees and palm his face. An image leaps into my mind—a bloodied dagger and a vicious grin—bringing along a searing pain that cuts down my neck to my collarbone. My chest collapses in on itself, my heart squeezing. I pull my hand away from Tiernan to clutch my own throat.

He continues to thrash, but I clasp my hands together to keep from reaching out again. "*Tiernan, wake up!*" I shout in my mind, hoping he'll hear me. When that doesn't work, I give his shoulders a firm shake.

His chest heaves, wide eyes frantic as he jolts from his sleep and grapples for the swords beside his sleep sack. I fall on my behind, my hands out and ready to unleash a shield should I have to, but recognition quickly fills his eyes.

"It's alright," I say, hopefully soft enough that it doesn't wake everyone. "It was just a nightmare."

Sweat coats his skin, plastering his hair to his forehead. His throat bobs as he swallows, and slowly he realizes there's no real danger here. He slides his fingers along his scar then over his forehead, pushing his hair from his face.

After some hesitation, I finally sign, "Do you want to talk about it?"

He rolls his shoulders and untangles his legs from the bedroll before replying with a curt, "No, I'm fine."

Before long, we all set off again. Tiernan doesn't mention the nightmare, and I know better than to bring it up.

We remain amongst the trees outside the main route of the nearby village for as long as we can. Sunlight kisses my skin every now and then as we walk through open areas in the canopy. The leaves aren't as full as they should be after summer solstice, the warmth of the sun holding very little power.

Chiyo and Ava walk alongside each other, seemingly engaged in a pleasant conversation. Isobel is chatty with everyone now that we're temporarily off horseback, giving our steeds a bit of a reprieve.

I fight to keep my mind from mourning what I've left behind or worrying about the uncertainty of where we're going. Instead, I focus on the sweet honey scent of the woodbine that twines up the sides of the trees. The vines are a lighter green, the ordinarily brick-red flowers limp and muted in color. Tall stems of fairy thimbles fill the spaces between the trees, their fuchsia flowers also less vibrant than usual.

We pause every now and then, watering the horses and taking a moment to stretch our limbs and munch on blackberries from the brambles around us. We mount our horses again to get a bit farther before settling down for the night.

By dusk, my body feels heavy, my mind groggy. One of Tiernan's arms wraps around my middle, pulling me against him, but I sit up straighter, opening my eyes as wide as they can go. Fighting the headache and the sleepiness trying to tug me under proves difficult.

"*Try to relax*," comes Tiernan's voice. "*Take a nap. I've got you.*"

"*Tiernan, no. That's not fair. No one else can just take a nap on their horses.*"

He sighs. "*Stubborn woman.*" It doesn't come across as an insult, but as a compliment. I find myself smiling through the sleepy haze before my head starts to droop again.

Tiernan tugs Ghendor to an abrupt halt. My head jerks up. Ava also stops and holds her hand up, commanding everyone else to pause. The smell of burning wood reaches my nose, the faintest glow of a fire somewhere up ahead. Ava leaps off her horse, her sword already drawn. Moments later, Tiernan does the same.

My heart thunders, all sleepiness forgotten. "What's happening?" I ask as Ghendor's ears flatten against his head in irritation.

A few figures rush toward us, and Ava deflects one of their swords with her own while Chiyo slips down from her horse. Sloan and Isobel join in the fight while Alys steers her horse out of the way. The attackers are dressed in dark colors, but they have no insignia to identify them.

Tiernan shouts something toward our group and Chiyo looks back at him, eyes wide. Tiernan reaches up to grip my knee. "*Get as far away as you can,*" he says, and my heart all but falls out of my chest.

"What? I'm not leaving without you."

Chiyo pulls her dagger from one of the attacker's chests and wipes it on her pants before practically taking a running leap onto her horse. Everything moves too quickly, my head swimming with the confusion of it all.

"You'll have Sloan, Alys, and Chiyo. Stay between them. We'll take care of these people." He clasps my hand as I'm about to argue. *"I will find you. I promise. Our journey doesn't end here."*

I swallow, but he releases my hand and taps Ghendor's rump. The stallion takes off at a gallop, shoving my body backward. I grip the reins in my slippery palms and steady myself as best as I can. Immediately, I'm flanked by Chiyo and Alys with Sloan riding behind.

Something flies past me, too close, sending a sharp sting through the tip of my ear. My pulse triples and I immediately lift a hand, prepared to form a shield. A figure in white appears directly in my path, and Ghendor skids to a stop. Startled, the horse rears up on his hind legs, hooves flailing. My heart lurches, my stomach bottoming out as I'm propelled backward.

With a shriek, I throw out a shadow shield just in time to break my fall, but I still land hard on my hip. Ghendor rears back again, and I roll away from him into the thick brush at the edge of this tiny clearing where he's stopped. Lights and shadows waver through the clearing as Sloan and Chiyo dismount and get in front of me. They fend off more attackers as Alys crouches among the bushes beside me and I try to regain my bearings.

Our horses rush off the pathway, retreating into the woods. Chiyo and Sloan manage to get the attackers away from Alys and me, but a man in white *materializes* in front of me. A bright white orb in his hand sends light flooding all around us. In contrast, a black stone stands out on his finger.

I blink through my wavering vision while my head pounds. I stare up at the man as he towers over me, his limp black hair hanging out from beneath his white hood. He tugs a wicked, curved blade from his belt, but a second later, his eyes go wide as an arrowhead protrudes from his neck. I scramble to my feet as red seeps into the collar of his garb, more blood bubbling out of his mouth when he coughs.

He falls forward onto his face, and my eyes lock on to another man in white, an arrow nocked and ready to fly. I take in his ruddy face beneath a thick auburn beard. A bruise darkens the left side of his face, and his broad shoulders rise as his body tenses. Bright blue eyes meet mine, and my mouth suddenly goes paper dry.

Chiyo jumps in front of me, a dagger in her hand, but I shout at her to stop. She goes still, though she doesn't look back at me. Osheen drops his bow and arrow, hands held up in surrender. Chiyo lowers her arm and steps to my side just as Sloan appears behind Osheen. The sleeve of their missing limb is unrolled, tattered and muddy as it hangs at their side, but the sword that appears against Osheen's throat is held by a steady and sure hand.

"Sloan, no! Don't kill him" I shout.

Sloan's face contorts with confusion. Nausea rolls through me as too many emotions flood my body at once. I step back, but my leg gives out and I go down hard on my knee. Chiyo crouches beside me, her hand on my back.

Sloan asks something I can't make out.

Beside me, Chiyo lifts her hand from my back and hesitates before signing as she verbally responds to Sloan. "Yes. His name is Osheen."

Chapter 26

DURVLA

My STOMACH SQUIRMS as Sloan lowers their sword from Osheen's neck.

He's alive.

He's here. I shouldn't feel relief—I don't *want* to feel relief. But I feel a tightening in my chest and pain in my throat.

Osheen's body relaxes, but Chiyo says, "Don't let him out of your sight."

Sloan nods and sheathes their sword as they grab Osheen's arm and tug him away.

A warm presence blankets my mind before a familiar voice infiltrates. *"Almost there, beautiful. Thank the gods for your loud mind. Are you alright?"*

"Just shaken up."

Chiyo and Sloan draw their weapons again.

"Wait!" I exclaim, frantically waving my arms. Ava's brown stallion rides into the clearing first, followed by an ivory horse with Tiernan and Isobel atop. Isobel's red hair sways as she peeks around him, the grin on her face radiant in the lantern she carries.

I'm running before I even realize it. Tiernan's feet barely touch the ground before I have him in a crushing embrace. My heart wants to leap for joy, but it's tacked down again, squeezing almost painfully as the full extent of everything that's happened hits me. Tears well in my eyes as I glance around, taking silent inventory of everyone.

Tiernan holds me at arm's length, giving me a once-over. "What in hells happened?" he asks. There's a small cut on his cheek, but aside from looking exhausted, he seems uninjured.

Chiyo rushes to Ava, tugging her aside to catch her up, I suppose. Tiernan's gaze has gone cold, fixed somewhere past me.

Osheen.

"Tiernan," I start to say, but his steps are quick and sharp as he storms across the clearing.

Sloan barely gets out of the way before Tiernan's fist meets Osheen's face. The second strike sends Osheen sprawling on the ground. Part of me feels satisfyingly avenged while the other part feels guilty. I *shouldn't* feel guilty, yet I do.

Hands over his cheeks and nose, Osheen stares up at Tiernan. His fists are still clenched as Tiernan says something to Sloan, who nods and drags Osheen to his feet again.

More dizziness rushes in, but there's nothing for me to steady myself on, so I sink down to the ground on my hands and knees. I squeeze my eyes shut until someone's hand brushes over my back. Their hand slides up over my neck, then lightly over the back of my head.

I'd recognize Tiernan's touch anywhere.

The dizziness subsides enough for the ground to stop shifting. I open my eyes and sit back on my ankles, meeting Tiernan's concerned gaze.

Looking past him, I notice that Osheen now sits near a tree, his wrists bound with rope while Ava crouches in front of him with a lantern.

Chiyo and Isobel are nowhere in sight, and panic returns swiftly as I glance around.

"They went off to find the horses," Tiernan signs.

I have so many questions. So, so many questions. I close my eyes and massage my temples for a while before looking at Tiernan again. "Who were those people?" I ask.

"Back there—" he points to where we'd ridden from, "Either bounty hunters or Forayers. There were Purists in the area too, as you can see. A lot of them took each other out, which made things easier for us. What in hells happened here? Where did

193

that son of a bitch come from?" He jerks his head toward Osheen.

"These attackers were dressed in white. Purists, I'm guessing? The man who attacked me had ..." I look around again, but the white orb is gone. "Something like a ball of magelight. He was about to kill me but Osheen ..." My throat tightens. I let my eyes wander to him and say aloud, "Osheen saved me."

Something sharpens in Tiernan's eyes. He clenches his jaw and heaves a sigh. "Saved you?" he motions.

"He shot that arrow." I nod my head toward the dead Purist several paces away, who Sloan is currently inspecting. Sloan lifts the Purist's hand and slides the large black stone off it. My stomach churns, forcing me to look away from the dead body.

"We should get going again," Tiernan says as Sloan moves on to investigate another white-garbed body. "To put as much distance between ourselves and all of this while we still have the cover of night. Then we debrief and rest in the morning."

I nod numbly as Isobel and Chiyo return with the other horses. We're at least all accounted for now. Thank the gods.

The first light of dawn begins the next time we stop and dismount our horses. Ava drags Osheen to the trunk of a fallen tree and shoves him onto it. As we gather around, Osheen's eyes focus on me and no one else, even as Ava hovers over him menacingly. "I'm sorry," he signs awkwardly with his wrists bound.

Ava squints at him, her focus shifting to me and back to Osheen. "I don't care about whatever history is here, but if there's something I need to know—"

"He betrayed me. He betrayed all of us," I respond.

"Please hear me out!" Osheen's eyes are pinned on me. His face is horribly bruised, dried blood mingling in his beard and across his cheeks.

It's so strange reading his lips—for the longest time, he was the only person in my life who communicated with me by signing.

Having to read his lips now feels like salt in a wound. I blink, embarrassed about the tears prodding at the backs of my eyes, but I don't look away from him.

"Why are you dressed like a Purist?" Chiyo asks.

"Because I've been traveling with them. *For information!*" He adds the last bit as Ava's fist clenches as though she's about to strike him. "Just for information. I'm willing to share it all if you'll give me the chance."

"And how are we supposed to trust you?" Chiyo motions.

I turn to Tiernan who drags his eyes from Osheen to look at me. "Can you get a read on him as he speaks?" I ask. "Tell us if he's lying?"

Tiernan's arms are crossed over his chest in a way that makes the muscles in his upper arms flex menacingly. He nods and Ava's brows rise.

"Excellent," she says. She crouches and glares at Osheen. "Speak."

Alys moves to the other side of Osheen, and as he speaks, she translates his words into signs.

"After you all left the inn, I continued working there," Osheen begins. "They offered me food and lodging in exchange. But I did leave occasionally for fresh air and to get to know the village better. While walking in the woods, I got caught in a pitfall—some sort of animal trap. Aine Slan found me. She's the sister of the Purists' leader. She'd been with a group of followers. I'd overheard them talking about prophecies and lost Heirs, so when Aine invited me to dinner and, ultimately, to join their cause, I played the part of the grateful new follower."

His story sounds like something out of a book, but Tiernan nods almost imperceptibly. *True.*

"I stayed with them for a few weeks, got to know Aine, and I learned a lot about the Purists and their mission. They wanted to kill Princess Carys, and now that she's gone, they're looking for the lost Heir. The last of that bloodline."

My throat tightens.

"But it's not just that. They *want* the Veil between our world and the Otherworld torn. Their mission requires sacrificing the

Daughters of Agryna and Ehlach to wake the gods. They'll stop at nothing to find the lost Heir. Just like the princess was, this Heir is considered the ultimate evil. In fact, most with magic in their blood are considered evil—a threat to the power of the gods and to the balance of the realms. Balance requires sacrifice, and all of that."

The contents of my stomach churn, prepared to make a reappearance. I swallow thickly. *I* am the lost Heir ... Rhianu, help me. Chiyo, Tiernan, and Ava glance at me as if wondering whether I'll volunteer this information to Osheen. But I keep my lips pressed into a firm line.

"So, what else do you know about these people?" Ava asks Osheen.

"I know their way of life, and that they have an entire sector on the outskirts of Barr na Cahar," he says.

"How did Aine get to the Verge?"

Osheen's eyes go wide and his lips part, but he only snaps them closed again. "I didn't know she got to the Verge."

"You knew how to get there," says Chiyo. "Did you tell her? You said you were traveling with her."

"I didn't tell her anything."

Tiernan nods again. *True.*

"The group split, some heading westward, the rest of us heading ... well, here."

I sigh and rub my temple.

"What else do you know?" Ava asks him, and I look to Alys for the next translation.

"They're enacting a new Purge. This time by gathering willing followers and offering Mages a supposed cure called the Cleanse. The Purists promise them they can live without the risk of being discovered and hanged. Soldiers called Peacekeepers have begun making rounds—like the raids, but they're not scheduled, and they're far less controlled. The Peacekeepers are even worse than the Forayers. They're merciless. I've heard they're even attacking Mainlanders, and so more Mages are inclined to take the Cleanse."

Fear grips my stomach and heart as I blow out a slow breath.

A million thoughts eclipse Osheen's face before he speaks again.

"All my life ... we all thought the gods abandoned us. Or lost their power. To hear people speaking of their fall and their rise, it feels—"

"Farfetched," I say. "But I suppose, even if none of it's true, people believe it is. And that danger is very real."

We all nod in somber agreement. The question is: what *is* the truth?

"Anything else?" Ava asks him.

Osheen looks at me again, his eyes pleading in the magelight. "Durvla, I truly am sorry for everything. I understand if you won't forgive me, but please believe that I would never do anything to intentionally hurt you or Taig. I will spend the rest of my life trying to find a way to make it up to you."

My hands shake, but from anger or the effort it's taking to keep my tears at bay, I'm not sure. I look to Tiernan, who nods—*truth*—but he still seems incredulous.

"He has valuable information we can use," says Sloan.

Ava nods in agreement, though she doesn't seem happy about it. Her lips press into a firm line for a moment, then she looks at me almost apologetically. Turning to Sloan, she asks, "Can he ride with you?"

Sloan nods, and my chest lurches. I turn on my heel and hurry away from everyone. I keep walking until I'm as far away as I can be while still keeping them in sight. Then I turn my back on them, letting the tears fall. I give myself a few moments to feel this reopened wound before I draw in a few deep breaths, steel my resolve, and return to the group to continue on our journey. This time with Osheen—our prisoner, so to speak—in tow.

Chapter 27

I STARE ACROSS THE TABLE, repulsed by my own husband as he noisily eats a slice of crusty bread with honey and butter. Butter mingles with his stubble, and each smacking sound of his lips raises my gorge more. Was he always this disgusting?

He glances up from his food, his eyes questioning. Grabbing a napkin to wipe his mouth, he asks, "Is breakfast not to your liking, wife?"

"It is." A closed-mouthed smile follows my hasty bite. I'm certain there's nothing wrong with the food, but the honey tastes bitter and the butter like grease. I force myself to chew and swallow before immediately drinking my entire glass of milk.

I pull my pocket watch from my dress and peer at the time. "I should get going," I say, pushing my chair back to stand. My shift in the bindery doesn't begin for another hour or so, but he doesn't know my schedule.

As I walk past Gruffud, he grasps my wrist, tugging me to him. "No kiss for your husband?"

Swallowing, I turn and lean down to press my lips to his. His fingers tangle in my hair as he holds me captive for annoyingly longer than necessary before letting me go.

I grab my satchel from the bedchamber and head downstairs to ask Sage to call for a carriage. My heart warms at the thought of seeing Neris again while being wrapped in the familiarity of working among the books.

Ten minutes later, the carriage barely pulls up in front of Mother's house before Neris runs out. She crushes me in a hug, and when she steps back, her eyes are assessing as they sweep from my head to my toes. Tears well in my eyes, my throat aching from the fight to keep them at bay.

"Oh Winnie," she says tenderly. "Let's get inside. There are books that require painting. Your favorite, right?"

I nod though she doesn't need the answer. Sometimes I think she knows me better than I know myself.

She links her elbow with mine, and we hurry down the walkway together. But as soon as I step into the house, I'm flocked by Mother and Arionna.

"My daughter," says Mother in a strangely airy tone. She places her hands on my shoulders as Neris had. "How are you faring? Are you treating him well? Keeping him satisfied? Are you getting enough nourishment? You look a little pallid." She puts her hands on my cheeks a tad too roughly.

I step out from her grasp. "I'm eating just fine. Everything is wonderful. I have to get to work."

The entrance to the mudroom feels too far away as I rush to it with Neris right behind me. Yet by the time I'm downstairs, greeted by the scent of leather in the bindery, Neris is nowhere to be seen. She arrives several moments later with a porcelain plate balanced on her palm. There's an assortment of pastries on it, and for once, the sweet smell does nothing to tempt me. "Your mother says to bring these for you."

I arch my brows.

"She's overjoyed with the possibility of getting a grandchild."

"A grand—" My words are cut off by the realization. "No." I hold my hand to my stomach. "She's mistaken."

Neris sets the plate aside. "How are you certain? Are you doing anything to prevent it?"

I sigh and approach the workstation where my paints are waiting along with a stack of books. "I've been taking a fertility suppressant."

Surprise ghosts over her face as she sets her spectacles on her nose.

"I didn't tell you because I hadn't quite decided on using it yet, but I am." I pick up a sleeve of parchment with a list of names written on it.

A smirk on her lips, Neris moves toward her workstation. "Good on you, Winnie."

For a while there's silence while I read through the list of designs required for each book and Neris begins checking books for imperfections before stacking them into a crate. When she speaks again, it startles me for multiple reasons.

"Arionna is fucking someone."

I cough to dislodge the gasp that gets stuck in my throat. "Neris!"

"What?" Her smile is cherubic, false innocence shining in her emerald eyes.

I set the book down and select my thinnest paintbrush, looking closely at the bristles to check for splits. It seems intact. "Perhaps a different word choice?" I dip my paintbrush into the green paint. "Making love? Lying with? Doing the horizontal dance?"

She guffaws just as I'm about to begin painting foliage on the border of the leather book cover. "We don't know the extent of the relationship to infer something as meaningful as *making love*. And I've *lain* with you plenty of times."

"Ner—"

"—in your bed! Don't be crass."

I roll my eyes.

"And *horizontal dance*? Winnie, please." She winks at me, then pauses to focus on the engraving. "Fine. Arionna has been *bedding* someone. Since shortly before your wedding."

"Why do you say that?"

"I was covering for one of the servants and discovered your sister's stash of fertility suppressant tea while I was cleaning." She shrugs.

"Interesting. I'm sure it's some affluent nobleperson. But imagine if it's a lowborn. Or worse, a *Grounder*."

Neris laughs. "Realms, I'd love to see that."

We laugh and come up with even more farfetched scenarios—per my family's beliefs—before silence settles in the room again for a while.

As I paint tiny leaves around the book, it brings a sort of stillness within me, temporarily making me forget about everything else. When there are five books drying in a line on the workstation, I step away to stretch my stiff back and fingers. It feels good to get lost in such a creative outlet. I dread returning to the Pendrys.

"Winnie, are you happy?" Neris asks.

I don't want to lie to her, so I simply keep my mouth shut and step up to my workstation again. "It's mealtime." I finish putting my jars of paint into a wooden chest. "I'll see you upstairs."

"Winnie ..." She calls after me, but I keep walking, knowing that she still has a lot to put away before she can follow. It'll at least give me the chance to pretend that I am, indeed, happy.

As I step into my childhood home the next morning, Arionna rushes down the steps with a cape draped over her arm and a frazzled look on her face. She spots me and reels back, pressing a hand over her heart before smoothing her hands over her ebony coils.

"Gwyn," she says breathlessly. "You're early." A headpiece comprised of three strands of silver and gold beads wraps around her head—her tight curls are otherwise loose. Light kohl lines her lashes today, making them look even longer and thicker than usual.

"I'm ... on time." My eyes dart to the clock on the wall and back to her.

She continues walking toward me, now swinging her cloak over her wine-colored gown and fastening it with a golden broach. There's an odd look in her eyes, an awkward smile on her lips that doesn't seem to fit in with the rest of her face.

"Where are *you* off to so early?" I ask.

Her plump lips tug down. "Sterling's manor. His brother is

selling the estate, but he wants me to help him sort through some of Sterling's possessions. You know, since I spent more time with him than anyone else in his final days. He wants to ensure his more prized items be handled with sensitivity."

It's not often Arionna speaks of her late husband. I try to keep the surprise from my face and out of my voice. "That sounds very considerate. It's kind of you to agree. Will you be alright going there by yourself?"

Again, that odd smile. "Hamish is coming along."

The footman is hardly company. Aside from driving the carriage, I'm not sure what support he can offer Arionna. Especially when it comes to this already emotionally stunted family of mine. "What about Mother?" I ask.

Arionna laughs—and rightfully so—as she steps past me. She pats me on the shoulder as if I'm Erleya's most naive child, then sweeps out of the house without another word.

Bizarre. But when is Arionna anything but? Even when we were children, she was always up to *something*, always in a hurry, always secretive. Rolling my shoulders to dissolve the tension from simply being in my sister's presence, I make my way to the book bindery.

To the last haven I have in this miserable life.

Dry grass rustles beneath our feet as we trod through a dense copse of trees within the dark forest. The night air is cool, the moon-light soothing. Though I use small bits of my magic daily, it's been a while since I've unleashed it enough to feel settled in my own skin.

"I kind of miss this," Neris says beside me.

"My magic bullying me?" I ask.

She chuckles. "In a way, yes."

I nudge her hard with my elbow, and she yelps through her laughter.

"No, just heading to the forest with you. It gives me a chance to pretend that we're getting out of here."

"Neris, don't start."

Small wisps of smoke billow into the air up ahead, and the alluring aroma of savory spices that drift toward us almost has me salivating. "Smells like a feast," Neris says, reflecting my own thoughts.

"It does." I inhale deeply, wishing that dinners at home smelled this delectable.

Scattered beams of moonlight shine down through the trees to illuminate our way. Soon, the flicker of orange in the darkness catches my attention. What if it's Peacekeepers or some other faction of soldiers?

"We should turn—"

I don't get to finish my sentence before a heavyset man leaps out from the bushes as we're about to approach. I hold up my fists, ready to call my terraforging when Neris shouts, "We're unarmed!"

The man lowers what looks like a butcher's knife, and I find myself unable to exhale fully. "Sorry," he says. "It's hard to trust anyone these days." He tucks his butcher knife into the back of his pants while my heart hammers. "We're just traveling through here. Do you …" He gestures in the direction he'd just come from. "Want to join us for dinner?"

"Yes!" Neris exclaims at the same time as I say "no." She tugs me into the clearing after the man. "Then you'll have some fuel for your terraforging," she whispers to me.

Before long, Neris and I are sitting around the fire, shoveling savory brown broth from the mutton stew into our mouths as the travelers take turns telling stories. I can't help but think what we're doing is foolish, but as I'm about to try convincing Neris to leave, an emaciated lad stands in front of the roaring fire and begins a tale in a surprisingly deep voice.

"In the days before the release of the Underling Prince, the Enchantress Queen, Enidwen, gathered followers from far and wide. One by one, Dreamwalkers, Healers, Sorcerers, and Wielders—especially the Flame and Shadow Wielders—signed their souls away to Enidwen. Days later, the enchantress would unwittingly relinquish her own soul to the Underling Prince. When chaos bled into Enidwen's being, so too were her followers tainted.

"Darkness encroached on the followers, and they found themselves bound to and by the shadows. Few embraced their newfound powers, honing them, learning to hide within the same darkness that threatened to pull them under. The shadows emanated from within them, slithering along their skin, blackening their veins, as though wiping away their humanity. They flirted with death and manipulated mankind; they bent reality and brought terror upon the realm. Feared and revered, they became known as the Basduunai. Death bringers.

"Even after Enidwen was vanquished by the Heirs, the Basduunai continued their reign of terror. Some say they still walk among us, stalking us in our shadows, hiding within the umbrella of the full moon. Some say they haunt our dreams, waiting for a moment of weakness to take over our minds, to bring madness upon us, to compel us with puppet mastery. They lie in wait, patiently, to rise from the darkness and revive Enidwen's mission. Some say they seek to awaken chaos—"

A high-pitched whistling sound followed by a nauseating *squelch* fills the air as a bolt lodges itself in the young man's stomach. Screams resound and everyone tries to flee ... in vain. My eyes fixate on the storyteller, his lifeblood seeping into the earth below.

A cold shiver runs through me, and I swear I see that damn tattered, grey cloak again.

There's an echo of laughter, and my head whips toward it—toward a pair of red eyes glowing between the trees and the sensation of heat kissing my face. The scene before me disappears, replaced by a form cloaked in black, wielding a flaming axe.

She strolls through the blood-soaked forest. Past Neris, face-down. Dead. All the travelers. The Peacekeepers.

Call to me and spare your friends this fate, a voice says. *Choose the Forge. Choose Fury. Fight with me and I will smite the Purists that dared to shatter your soul.*

A blast of heat hits me until another voice speaks from elsewhere, sending ice skittering across my skin. Her voice rattles like bones in a bag. *Resist. Run.*

"Winnie, *get up*, dammit! What is wrong with you?" Neris shouts over the commotion as Peacekeepers apprehend several of the travelers. I'm back in the forest, a blur of black militia uniforms attacking the civilians.

No voices. No signs of red eyes or cloaked figures. My entire body shakes, my legs leaden. But Neris tugs me away from the horrifying sight, from the screams of fear. From death.

Why am I always running from death?

Why do these visions choose the worst possible times to plague me?

Our feet pound against the forest ground as we run.

Another high-pitched whistle sounds behind us only to end with a dull *thud*. My heart leaps, but neither of us has been hit.

There's a flash of white ahead as someone steps out from behind a tree and into our path. My foot catches on a branch, and my ankle twists for the second time in recent months. I bite back a whimper of pain and manage to keep to my feet, hopping on one foot as I back away from the stranger. Grey hair peeks out from beneath their hood, sending my heart into triple time. A hand reaches out to me with a black stone set in a silver ring.

"Hurry," the figure urges. She shakes her hand for emphasis.

I step back and wince, and Neris grabs my arm as I regain my balance. "What makes you think we'll trust you, old hag?" she asks.

"It's either that or meet your untimely death at the hands of Peacekeepers. The gods are at play here tonight too, it seems."

Another chill runs through me. The gods? Right ...

I grab Neris's hand, holding it in a vise-like grip as she tries to pull away. "Winnie, you can't be—"

But before she can finish her sentence, I grasp the woman's waiting hand, and we're immediately sucked into a void. We're weightless, being tugged and pushed, hurtled through the shadows. Once our feet hit solid ground again, I close my eyes and focus on steadying my breath. Neris retches, and my own stomach twists, but the old woman looks unfazed.

We're inside what appears to be a workshop of sorts with rickety shelves of jars, dried herbs, and colorful bottles that seem luminescent in the dark interior.

I know this place.

My gaze flicks back to the woman in white. "Radika?" I exclaim.

She holds a finger to her lips.

"Since when are you a Purist?"

She lowers her white hood and smooths her weathered hands over her hair. "That is neither here nor there. Now let me see your foot." She plops herself onto a tall stool and pats her lap.

"My foot?"

Radika mutters something in another tongue and snaps her fingers. By some invisible force, my foot is tugged up onto her lap. I struggle to maintain my balance, but Neris steadies me, her eyes wide. As Radika unlaces my boot, I wince from the sharp pain. Before I can ask her what she's about to do, my boot thuds to the ground, and her hands envelop my throbbing ankle. Lilac light surrounds her hand, sending tingles into my ankle before the pain dies down.

"You're—"

"Some say Sorceress, I say Healer." She smiles and pats my leg. I lower it and collect my boot from the floor. Radika silently regards me as I stand again, my boot relaced.

At last, she speaks up, "You will, someday soon, cross paths with the daughter of Dusk. Whether indirectly, or directly, the gods weren't clear."

My lips part to object.

"Yes, yes, you lost faith in the gods after the Cleanse, but that doesn't change your part in all of this. You will have a choice. It won't be easy."

"A choice?"

"You already faced one tonight. Didn't you?" She gives me a knowing look, and I visibly shudder as I think of glowing red eyes and flaming axes, and then of the other presence like winter in the middle of summer.

"Things are never as they seem at first, Gwyneth," says Radika. "But you're intelligent." She gets up and rushes off to the leather chest on her table, where she pulls out a few satchels that clink as she moves. "No more acting out of fear." She lifts two of the satchels and holds them out to me. Then to Neris, she holds out the third. "And you, no acting out of impulse. You're equally important. Equally unique and powerful."

Neris huffs. "I wish," she says.

"It doesn't take magic to make a person powerful." She inhales deeply, her chest expanding. With a huge sigh, her shoulders droop. "Love and friendship are just as strong."

Neris and I exchange confused looks.

"Listen, children, I have to disappear for a while, but those vials should hold you over for now."

The pouch in my hand does feel a little heavier than usual.

Radika absentmindedly spins the ring on her finger as she stares down at the floor.

None of this makes sense. How can Radika be a Purist *and* a practicing Sorceress? All Purists of higher stations wear vanishing rings, like the one Radika fiddles with. They justify this particular use of magic by saying that the stones are of natural origin—mined from an enchanted cavern.

The Purists are against magic except for when it suits them. Some are Oracles, others are Healers, some even possess mind magic, but never sorcery. Sorcerers can potentially Wield elements depending on their skills and use of spells; it's too close to elemental Wielders like me, who are an abomination in their eyes.

"It's not just Purists who own vanishing rings," Radika says as though she's heard my thoughts.

I meet her dark gaze. "Then which group do you identify with?"

"None, dear girl." She grabs my shoulder, then Neris's, steering us toward the door. "Things will get worse before they get better, but have faith. That *calling* you feel, you'll eventually have to follow it."

"Calling?" My forehead scrunches.

"You will know when the time comes." With those last words, she shoves us out of her workshop and slams the door shut.

I spin back around, knocking on the door. "Radika, wait!" When she doesn't respond, I turn the knob and, to my surprise, the door opens. But inside, the workshop is *empty*. No shelves, no potions, not even that odd light that often flickers in the ceiling. It's as if none of it has ever existed.

"Let's get home before more Peacekeepers come around or

something even stranger happens," says Neris, wide eyes on the empty room.

I nod and slip my hand into my pocket, wrapping my palm around my pocket watch. My head spins from everything that's happened tonight. The visions, the travelers dead or dying. Radika, a living, breathing Sorceress.

I have a choice to make? A *calling*?

What I'd really like is an *answer*.

Chapter 28

CARYS

BETWEEN CONSTANTLY FIGHTING against the enchantress and my own insomnia, the next two weeks are severely distorted. I'm pulled and pushed by an internal force from one extreme mood to another. Sometimes it happens just beyond the reach of my awareness, and other times I'm simply unable to stop the geyser of rage or tears. I'm either shouting at Odgar or lying curled up in the darkness, wishing that the prison of my mind would release me.

I've come into my awareness only to find someone's horrified expression staring back at me too many times. I vaguely recall Valdis fitting me with a wedding dress, Briony helping me with mind shielding. I remember snatching a knife from Seth's waist and threatening Odgar with it for gods know what. When I turned the blade on my own throat, Odgar easily plucked it from my hand.

At the memory, I clutch my neck, panicked breaths following as I remember how Odgar hugged me until I found myself again. I don't know how to make these moments stop. I hold on to the hope that once we find Siad Nahar, this cure will release me from the bounds of my brokenness.

Tired of being cooped up and avoiding everyone in the Great Hall, I slip away while the main room is empty and make my way across the village.

Dead grass rustles beneath my boots on the trodden path as I make my way toward the mead house. Despite it being late afternoon, the village's center is bustling with activity—running children, bartering vendors, and others just going about their usual routine just before the sun begins to set. The stench of piss, fish, and henbane fills my nostrils as someone clasps their hand over my mouth and yanks me back against their hard body.

"Where do you think you're going?" a man growls in my ear, his words heavily accented. His hand tightens around my mouth, but I bite down as hard as I can.

He yelps and yanks his hand away from my face. "Erleyan bitch!" he shouts, tugging on my hair so my head whips back, my neck straining. He flings me against the wooden wall of the mead house, and a burst of pain flares in my face, staining my vision with blurry flecks.

"Why are you *really* here?" the man demands.

I spin toward him, slumped against the wall as my toes grip through my shoes to keep me upright. A familiar, ruddy face sneers at me. This man has filled many an auroch horn in my time here. He works at the mead house and has never shown me any contempt until now.

"Well?" he asks.

As he leans close, I spit in his face. He snarls and grabs my wrists, pinning me to the wall. I scream and thrash against him, and my knee connects with flesh. Uldaran curses spew from his mouth as he releases me for a moment. But before I can run, he grapples for my arms again, and a glint of something shiny catches my eyes.

"You don't belong here. You have no right to claim Uldaran royalty. Your children will be bastards." Cold metal presses against my cheek, sending my heart into an erratic rhythm. Instead of the man's brown eyes, I see the wild look in Eefa's vibrant green ones before she slashed her blade across my face. My scars seem to pulse and burn.

This isn't happening. I *can't* let this happen again. I can't ...

Enidwen's nails rake against the barrier of my consciousness as she hisses, *Let me out*.

I grit my teeth, unwilling to relinquish my control. Afraid to lose myself.

You'll lose yourself, regardless. Her tone is brusque, impatient. *Let go or this man will further mar you.*

I growl and let the barrier fall away. Heat floods my senses, pain searing up my arms and burning my eyes. As my palms ignite, the man gasps and steps back. Odgar's fist slams into his nose with a *crunch*.

When the fuck did he get here?

My body trembles as I stare at the miscreant.

Destroy him! Enidwen shouts. Overwhelming heat pulses through me. It threatens to shatter me if I don't release it.

My first blast of fire erupts at the man's chest. His nasal screams fill the air as blood pours from his nose and fire eats through his tunic. The flames are immediately doused, smoke rising off his charred clothing. With a wave of my hand, black flames coil up his body. His screams are shriller, laced with unbearable pain.

What a beautiful sound, hmm?

A grin stretches across my face as Odgar and Valdis put space between themselves and my attacker. I strut toward the man, mesmerized by the shadowfire that neither burns nor blisters. His screams are endless—maybe he'll scream himself to death. How long would that take?

Minutes?

Hours?

Days?

"Carys!" Odgar shouts, but I ignore him and all the people now gawking at us. Enidwen's cackle reverberates in my head.

I narrow my eyes on the man as he sinks to his knees, hugging himself through the black blaze.

"Payback's a bitch, isn't it?" I ask him in a low tone.

"Carys ... release him. Please," Odgar says. "We'll handle this."

"No." My voice comes out in a snarl.

"Carys ..."

My head snaps to him and Valdis. Her eyes are wide, but she doesn't dare to speak.

Odgar steps toward me. "You're safe now. He won't do you any more harm. Killing this man will only lead to a trial and *your* death."

"He attacked me."

I swear there's a blaze in his eyes as well. "I know," he shouts over the man's shrieks. "And I want to drive a sword up through his cock and into his heart, but there are laws. He deserves to pay, but not at the risk of forfeiting your life."

I only increase the shadowfire, orange embers beginning to spark through the black flames holding the man in agonizing captivity.

Until ice cold water splatters against my face.

I gasp, my muscles seizing up and cutting off the shadowfire. Shock whitens my vision, and my knees buckle. Sharp pain jolts through them as they hit the ground.

Odgar's at my side in an instant, an arm around me. "I'm sorry," he whispers.

The growl that comes flying out of my mouth sounds awfully animalistic. More raging fire builds up inside of me.

I want to throttle Odgar. To burn my attacker. I want Uldarvik up in flames. Then Erleya. Then the world.

Tears sting my eyes as the thoughts swirl through my mind, parrying logic strike for strike. My limbs quiver with the mental battle.

"Look at me," Odgar gently says as he pulls my cape around me, trapping my arms.

Everything around me is a blur, and even Odgar's voice sounds so far away. But my attention is drawn to my hand peeking out from the cape. Thick, black veins crawl up my fingers and beyond my wrist. I shove my hand fully beneath the cape, my breaths coming in shallow, panicked puffs.

Go away, I say to Enidwen.

Heat only flares hotter within me. I flinch and clench my fists, trying to subdue the enchantress.

I said: Go. Away! I shout within my mind.

With one last snarl, Enidwen sinks back into the shadows of my psyche.

Odgar calls to Valdis and rattles off something in rapid Uldaran. She responds affirmatively as Odgar wraps his arms tighter around me.

"I'm going to lift you now," he says. "Close your eyes. I've got you." He scoops me into his arms, and I do as he says.

An odd, rocking movement churns my stomach when my eyes fly open again. Heavy awareness falls on me, fatigue sinking into my flesh. We're in the middle of a fjord, mountains and land blanketed in white all around us. What appears to be a strip of land is a small distance ahead of us.

"Don't panic," Odgar says as I glance down and realize that we're in a small rowboat. My back is against Odgar's chest, his legs stretched out on either side of my body.

I lurch upright, my knuckles white on the edges of the vessel as I hang on for my life.

"I said *don't* panic, huntress. Deep breaths."

The first breath feels like inhaling through a straw. But slowly, my respirations stop coming in short bursts. "Where are we going?" My voice comes out hoarse and fractured. My eyes feel feverish. Slowly, I shift so that I'm facing him.

"A short way from here," he says. Every now and then his hands move as if pushing back some invisible force. There are no oars in sight, but the boat is propelled forward without stopping.

By Odgar's waterweaving.

It's fascinating, but I find great difficulty in meeting his steady gaze. Unspoken questions expand between us until we're near a small inland isle and Odgar steps out of the boat. He pulls it ashore and anchors it with rope tied to a wooden post. I slip my hand into his as he reaches for me, and he tugs me onto the land. My legs wobble as though I'm still on the boat.

My body feels both heavy and light at once, everything fading away until Odgar's distant voice pulls me back to the present. The whisper of the wind along with the occasional crunch of Odgar's boots in the frozen grass are the only sounds as he walks away. I watch his broad back, the battle-axe strapped to it glinting orange as the sun sets. My hands no longer bear the telltale black veins of Enidwen's curse, but they shake with such fervor that I have to clasp them together.

Enidwen's voice in my head is quiet, but that dark flame within my core continues to waver.

Waiting.

My stomach sinks. My lower lip quivers, but I clamp my jaw until my teeth ache. I will not cry.

"Are you coming?" Odgar tosses over his shoulder. His voice sounds warped and far away, but I cling to it.

I don't respond, though I hurry to catch up with his long strides. The island is dense with shrubbery but sparse on trees. A small, rocky hollow lies ahead, the clearing in front of it glowing red as the sun continues to sink.

"I used to run away a lot as a child," Odgar says quietly. "Never felt like I belonged. I had this ability to bend water—something that people claimed was a blessing. The weight on my shoulders was so heavy sometimes. Either I was expected to be a savior or someone's worst nightmare. Often it was the latter, thanks to the role my father gave me." His pause is heavy.

"My illegitimacy is obvious." He lifts his hand, displaying the back of his palm and pointing out his coppery brown complexion. "I don't have the same mother as Freyr and Valdis, obviously. My mother was a foreigner—outcasted by most Uldarans, naturally. Thank the gods my powers made people too afraid to challenge me. Especially given my reputation and my role I was forced to take on. Especially when my father so publicly declared me his son. When he died, my brother took the throne with a public declaration that I was still the legitimate heir. After Valdis, of course. He relieved me of the role I hated. A life I never wanted. He gave me a fresh start."

His words flow over me, so different yet so oddly familiar to my own plights.

"To never feel like you belong in your own homeland is hard. To feel estranged in your own body must be harder."

I gaze up into his eyes, realizing that he's talking about me. I swallow as my heart cracks, only to immediately fuse. I've been broken enough times; it won't happen again.

"I've felt like that even before the—" I pause, hesitating. But what am I afraid of? He's seen me overcome with Enidwen's vengeful spirit. "Before the curse awoke within me."

Deep lines form on his forehead, but he doesn't step back from me at the mention of the curse.

From above, white flecks float down through the air. The first speck lands on my face, chilling me. We both glance up at the dark sky as snow begins to fall. "Welcome to summer in Uldarvik," he says with a smile. He extends his hand to me, an encouraging look on his face.

He leads me a few steps forward, and we duck our heads to enter the dark, rocky hollow, the vivid moon providing just enough light. It's just large enough to fit both of us. I sit and pull my legs to my chest, tucking my feet underneath my dress. Odgar sidles close to me and loops his arm around my back.

"Tell me about the curse."

When my body tenses, he gives me a comforting squeeze. I close my eyes and try to focus on everything else outside of my fears. "About a millennia ago, a Dark Mage named Enidwen tore open the Veil and unleashed the Underling Prince. His spirit was too strong and overtook hers. Unfortunately for them, her soul and the prince's soul were said to be banished from our realm. The truth is that while *his* was banished, hers latched on to one of my ancestors. Since then, her spirit has been reborn through the generations, remaining dormant until ... me."

Odgar sucks in a breath, then blows it out on a slow, descending whistle.

Gnawing on my inner cheek, I let the words settle around us. I keep my face forward, not wanting to see his reaction.

"How does it feel to bear the curse?" he asks after a while.

That question makes me face him. There's an uncanny gentleness in his eyes as he leans in slightly, his lips parted with curiosity.

My throat constricts, making my voice sound hoarse as I respond. "Like I could lose my mind at any moment. Or lose control." I blink through my tears. "I ... can hear her voice. I can *feel* her emotions at times. When I give in to my anger in particular, she sort of—"

"Takes over?"

I nod. "So when the Seer said I'm chaos, it wasn't just some casual statement.."

I expect fear or at least concern in his eyes, but instead there's something that looks oddly like understanding. Like acceptance. Pensive, he folds his lips in while my tears flow unchecked down my cheeks. The cool air immediately dries them on my skin while the snow falls outside our little shelter.

Realization widens Odgar's eyes. "Is this why you don't want children?"

I nod somberly.

"While you may have this Enidwen living inside you, you're still Carys," he says.

Taking a deep breath, I finally tell him everything about the conversation with the Seer—about the cure for the curse and Serpent's Hollow—Siad Nahar. "I feel less and less like myself," I admit. "I need that cure."

He sighs. "Alright." Staring into the distance for a while, he seems to come to some sort of conclusion. He turns back to me and says with determination, "We'll leave Uldarvik and find the Serpent's Hollow. We'll get you that cure. When the sun disappears, Valdis, Seth, Briony, and the crew will be here."

"How—"

"We've talked about it. And the moment I saw what you could do to that man who attacked you, I told Valdis to gather everyone and meet us here. If we stay, you'll have to go through a trial, and even though we're betrothed, you're an outsider here. I can't risk that. I'd rather leave."

"But this is your homeland! You can't ... We've not even been wed. You have no obligation to look after me."

"Carys, I'd sail to the ends of the earth if it would bring you ease. I'd bury my axe in the heart of anyone who dares to lay a finger on you." His hand clenches momentarily in his lap as he exhales loudly. "You need to get back to Erleya, and I happen to have a ship and a crew. I will be right by your side. Even if you hate me, even if you don't trust me yet."

Gods, there's my heart cracking again. "I don't hate you," I say softly. Willpower is etched into his face, curls spilling from the braids over his shoulder. He looks ...

"Are you alright?" he asks. He lifts his hand hesitantly before placing it on my cheek, his callused thumb stroking across my skin with such gentleness.

When we danced at the Feast, it felt so simple. The pressures from Iywan and the Council had ceased to exist. I remember the feeling of his hand against my exposed lower back. His playful—albeit cocky—comments. All at once, flutters fill my stomach—a feeling I can't remember having.

At least, not in this way.

Part of me wants to reject the feelings—to shove them deep down, back to wherever they've been hiding. But the mixture of meekness and strength in Odgar's eyes pierces my hardened heart.

My gaze drifts down to his full lips, and I find myself reaching out to him for once. My fingertips trace over the antler tattoo on his cheek, partially hidden by the soft hair of his beard. He places his hand over mine, and I lean in before I can lose my tenacity.

Salty tears mingle with the taste of something sweet as his lips move against mine. My eyes drift closed, his hand slips behind my head. The kiss is tender and bottomless, filling me with pleasant warmth. I'm breathless and dizzied by the sudden shift from perpetual agony to gratification.

Until something bright infiltrates my eyelids, drawing them open to light wavering through the hollow. Fear grabs ahold of me as I expect an ambush. But no ...

The most vibrant purples and greens dance through the dark sky, billowing and oscillating. Stealing my breath. Odgar wraps his arm around my shoulders, a blanket against the frigid air. My cheeks ache before I realize I'm smiling at the incredible view.

"One of my favorite sights," Odgar murmurs as I rest my head on his shoulder.

I hum in agreement, my eyes still on the beautiful choreography of the aurora.

It takes a moment before his words fully sink in. I lift my head, turning to look at him. "*One* of your favorite sights?" I ask. "What's your favorite?"

His gaze meets mine, the lights reflecting in his eyes as his lips curve upward. "Your smile."

Chapter 29

GWYNETH

It's my birthday today—but no one says a word about it. I stand as motionless as possible while the heavy-handed dressmaker pins a shimmery black material around my waist. Beneath it, I wear a thin summer chemise that doesn't leave much to the imagination. It makes me wish that Lady Mari—or *Mum,* as she insists I call her—wasn't lounging in an armchair, mere paces from me.

Delicately holding a cup of tea in one hand and a saucer in the other, she watches the dressmaking process with intense curiosity. I thought being under Mother's very loudly opinionated scrutiny was bad, but Lady Mari's silent observation feels weightier. I'm suddenly self-conscious. All the criticisms I've heard about my body swirl in my head. Too muscular, too short, too—

"Dearest, has anyone told you that for one of such petite stature, you have quite ... ample ... attributes?" Lady Mari's gentle voice pulls me from my thoughts.

I quirk a brow, but the demure look on her face makes me want to laugh. *Ample attributes*?

"No one has quite put it that way," I say, still holding back laughter. "Have you seen Arionna? She makes *ample* an understatement."

Her face pulls tight, but it's amusement that glimmers in her eyes and crinkles at the corners. I press my hand over my mouth to stifle the sound as laughter slips free. It earns me a sharp pinprick in my side. I suck in a quick breath and jerk away involuntarily.

The dressmaker winces. "Apologies," she says, and Lady Mari's dainty giggles flitter across the room. She has a certain tenderness to her that makes me wonder how she could've raised a man like Gruffud.

Sobering again, Lady Mari tilts her head as she regards me. "The muscle definition in your arms and legs is uncanny."

I meet her gaze, trying to figure out if it's an insult or a compliment. It seems to be the latter, so I tentatively thank her.

"My father used to train me," I admit, sadness knotting my throat. "He tried to convince me to love sword fighting as much as hand-to-hand, but he wasn't very successful."

Lady Mari presses a hand over her heart. "Oh dear. Hand-to-hand? As in ... fisticuffs?"

I smile and nod.

"That's awfully odd for a woman of high standing."

Everything is *awfully odd* for a woman of high standing. I shrug. "He wanted me to be able to defend myself." *Against pricks like your son.* And yet I don't do a thing about it ...

Lady Mari sets her teacup and saucer on the accent table and runs her fingers through her blond hair, which has been steadily turning silver over the past year. It reminds me of another platinum-haired woman from my past. *Nimue.* Fear suddenly has me in a chokehold. I close my eyes to repress the memories of lies and pain. I push away the thoughts only to land on last night's attack. The scent of blood returns to my senses. The Peacekeepers shot down innocent travelers ... who were simply having dinner.

"Are you well, dear?"

I open my eyes to look at Lady Mari again, forcing my lips to curve into a smile. "I am." The dressmaker begins pinning fabric around the large swell of my bust, so I hold my arms out and remain still.

For a while, there's silence save for the rustle of fabric and occasional clink of Lady Mari's teacup. The dressmaker unpins all the fabric from me and jots down a few notes on parchment with a quill and ink.

Moments later, I head downstairs to brew a cup of tea, hoping to take it up to my room for some much-needed quietude. Instead, I run into Sage, who beams at me as soon as I enter the kitchen. "Lady Gwyneth," she says enthusiastically. "I have something for you. From Neris."

My interest piqued, I step closer. "From Neris?"

"Yes." She marches toward the counter and lifts a small package of sorts. With quick steps she returns to me, holding out something in beeswax paper. Slowly, I unwrap the paper as the servant continues to speak. "Catriona delivered it a moment ago. She said Neris wishes you a very happy twentieth birthday and owes you a big hug. Neris hopes this satisfies the craving for her hugs for now."

I catch the buttery sweet aroma of caramel before I even finish unwrapping the confection. A smile splits my face at the sight of the flakey squares of shortbread biscuits layered with caramel and topped with chocolate.

"She also says she owes you a cake."

I chuckle. What I'd give for one of Neris's cakes, but the caramel-chocolate biscuits are more than enough. "Thank you. Would you like one?" I extend the parcel, but she shakes her head.

"Oh no, I couldn't impose."

"Please, you're not imposing. I'm offering. I cannot eat all of these by myself. Or rather ... I shouldn't."

She smiles and nods before delicately plucking one of the biscuits from the wax paper. "You are very kind, Lady Gwyneth. I hope that never changes."

I smile.

"Oh, and Neris said to give you this." She pulls out a folded sheet of paper from her pocket and hands it to me. Bobbing a small curtsy, Sage strides away with her treat.

I set my birthday treat on the counter and open the letter of Neris's almost-illegible scrawl.

My dearest sister-friend,
I love you, and I hope you have a great birth-

*day. Don't forget that you're <u>called</u> to great things
and don't forget who you are.*

Neris

The familiar feel of the paintbrush as it glides across the canvas quiets the unease I've felt for a while now. My thoughts are stilled, my body settled. As I'm mixing colors to get the perfect shade for the stag's antlers, loud footsteps echo behind me. I set my paintbrush down quickly and turn in my chair as Gruffud storms into the parlor.

"What in hells are you doing?" he asks.

"Painting ...?"

He steps closer, something flaring in his eyes that presses my desire to run.

"I thought it would be nice to paint something as a gift of gratitude to your wonderful family for welcoming me. Your mother does like collecting art, doesn't she?"

The harshness in his eyes slowly dissolves, but his body remains tense. He rubs his hands down his face and fixes a smile onto his lips. "Come with me into town," he says.

A frown pulls at my lips. "Right now?"

"Yes. There is a new building that has just been evacuated. The Peacekeepers arrested the owners."

Hesitant to take my eyes off Gruffud, I turn to put my paints away. I glance back at him several times, but he remains standing in place. "Do you know why they were arrested?" I ask. "Who were they? Do we know them?"

"That is none of your concern," he snaps.

"Apologies. What was I thinking?"

"Of frivolity." He jerks his head toward my canvas, and I fight to keep a neutral expression on my face.

In silence, I finish putting my paints away and swish my paintbrush in a jar of water, watching the colors bleed and trying not to think of making Gruffud do the same.

Notices are nailed to trees and lamp posts throughout the town center. As much as I want to stop to get a better look, I trek onward with Gruffud. He's a man on a mission. His elbow is linked through mine, a smile plastered onto his face, but his grip is so hard that my arm is growing numb.

Gruffud's gaze sweeps over the various buildings as we walk. More storefronts appear empty, but they're clearly not *the* storefront that Gruffud is in search of.

As we approach a larger red brick building with a wide expanse of windows, Gruffud releases my arm and rushes toward it. Left behind, I take the opportunity to rip a notice off a nearby lamppost and stuff it into the pocket of my cloak. I'm back at Gruffud's side in no time. "This is the place. Look how large it is." He beams at the door. "What a shame for Lord Myron. He was our biggest competitor with his bloody miniature clock towers."

My hand moves to my dress pocket automatically, my fingers sliding over the warm brass of my pocket watch. Sometimes I fear that Gruffud would take it away from me. For no reason other than to remind me that he owns me now.

The door swings open just as Gruffud reaches for it, and out steps a broad man with grey hair and a warm smile. Gruffud startles, scrambling back. If I weren't equally startled, I would've laughed.

I stare up at the man, at the fine lines at the corners of his cerulean eyes. "Lord Murtagh," I say with surprise, while Gruffud clutches his chest.

Realms, if only his heart would truly give out. I shake the thought away, cringing at the immorality of it.

Lord Murtagh's smile widens. "Nice to see you again, Lady Gwyneth. Lord Gruffud. How goes it with you two newlyweds?"

My stomach curdles, and I swear that Murtagh's brows rise as if he's sensed my reaction. "Swimmingly," I say, my voice cracking slightly. I clear my throat.

Gruffud laces his fingers with mine and gives it a bone cracking squeeze. I wince, though I try to keep a well-trained smile on my face.

"What brings you here, Lord Murtagh?" Gruffud's tone is clipped, but he manages to look pleasant.

"I'm considering relocating to Barr na Cahar. My daughters are excellent jewelry makers. What better a place for them to set up shop than in the greatest city in Erleya?"

I swear Gruffud's eye twitches. "For *them* to set up shop?"

Lord Murtagh smiles. "Absolutely. My daughters dinna just excel in artistry, but in enterprise as well."

An uplifting warmth fills my chest at this prospect. Women running a business in Barr na Cahar? Half the city would riot—the rest of us would gladly throw coin at them.

"Kenna, my eldest, would like to have painting classes for the wee littles. I've told her all about you, Lady Gwyneth, and she is just dying to meet you." His gaze moves to Gruffud as he adds with exuberant charm, "If you could bear to spare your talented wife every so often, young lord."

To my absolute delight, Gruffud trips over his words, then draws in a harsh breath and gives a tight-lipped "Of course."

I'm beaming now, but something in my husband's eyes tells me that I'm going to get an earful once we're home. I want so much to tell Lord Murtagh what an unpleasant person Gruffud is. That he's a brash man with a horrid temper. A narcissist at best.

But instead, I loop my arm through Gruffud's and say, "Well, Lord Murtagh. It was a pleasure running into you again. Best of luck in your family's endeavors."

"Until next time," he responds.

By some miracle, I steer Gruffud away from the building without another word. We barely get two shops away from Murtagh's new business when Gruffud grasps my arm with such a vise-like grip that I can't help but cry out softly. He backs me against a wall, the rough brick snagging my cloak as his stony eyes glare daggers down at me. His face fills my field of vision, and my terraforging threatens to unleash. I hold back, my body trembling with the effort to contain my powers—a reaction that can easily be mistaken for distress.

"Do not ever embarrass me like that again," he growls.

"I did no such thing," I snap back recklessly. "If anything, you embarrassed *yourself*."

His upper lip curls, his hand rising, when a smooth, baritone voice interrupts.

"Good afternoon."

Gruffud whirls on the stranger, and I peer around him at the older gentleman. Concern etches the man's peachy face, brown eyes regarding me rather than my brute of a husband. The man is dressed in a plain grey tunic and linen trousers. Leather peeks out from his collar and I sense some kind of metal weapon somewhere on his person. Perhaps more than one.

"Can I help you?" Gruffud asks, his tone sharp.

The man tucks the short strands of his salt-and-pepper hair casually behind his ear as Gruffud looks him up and down. "I was rather wondering if this young lady was in need of help," the man says with a smile that relaxes the hard cut of his jawline. Neris would swoon over this stranger, even though he must be in his late fifties.

"State your name, old man," Gruffud snaps.

My eyes roll, and I'm certain that amusement twinkles in the stranger's eye. He stands even taller, facing Gruffud without fear. "Niall Kilkenny. I am nobody to you, Lord ..." His voice trails off, his brow lifting in question.

"Pendry."

Niall repeats the name then looks at me. "Is all in order, Lady Pendry?"

I nod, though part of me wants to scream that all is certainly not in order.

"Well, if either of you are in need of any forging ... metalwork is my favorite. I also enjoy getting my hands in the dirt, moving the earth around a bit. I find gardening and landscaping soothing." He withdraws a small piece of parchment from within his summer coat, but Gruffud doesn't reach to take it.

My heart hammers as I mull over his words. *Forge*. Move *earth*. My gaze meets his, and the knowing look in his eyes chills me. But before I can figure out how to address the hints that are clearly being directed at me, Gruffud wraps his hand around my upper arm and tugs me away.

He grumbles about filthy Grounders infiltrating the city. We've always had traveling merchants and the like from across the bridge, but this man seems different. As I glance back at him, he winks and pats his pocket almost as if pantomiming. I cannot figure out the gesture, but I don't get a chance to try as I'm hauled back into the carriage parked a few buildings away.

Once we arrive back home, Gruffud rushes off to complain to Lady Mari about the unfairness of his encounters, and I retreat to the bathing chamber, still wearing my cloak. I pull the notice from my pocket, and another smaller parchment falls to the floor. It looks just like the one Niall tried to offer to Gruffud. I unfold it and regard the messy handwriting in bold letters:

Do not fear the rebellion. We are not the enemy. We are the hope of Erleya.

Safehouses: Cluain Baile, Dubh Carrig, Darragh, Wastelands, Verge.

As I read, the words fade until the parchment is as blank as if it never held any writing at all. I shake my head, dismissing the thoughts. It's just poppycock from a stranger who likely means well. Completely irrelevant. But clearly a Mage … Curiouser.

I sigh and smooth out the notice I'd taken from the lamppost.

Mages and Elemental Wielders needed.
Lay down your fears, give up your seclusion.
Join the Zenith at the Fortress on the Mount with this notice.

You and your family will be given immunity and rewarded generously in exchange for your service to Erleya and the Outer Isles.

By the decree of His Excellency, Rheon Odhran, Sovereign of the Kingdom of Erleya and the Outer Isles.

My blood freezes in my veins. I must be seeing things, because there's no way this new sovereign could be offering immunity for having magic. This must be some kind of trap—if anyone falls for this, they're either foolish or desperate.

As I read the notice again and again, a horrifying realization dawns on me.

I may be both foolish *and* desperate.

"I won't be home from tomorrow night," Gruffud murmurs as I rub obnoxiously fragranced oil into my skin.

I glance up at him from the vanity as I seal the jar and set it on the table. "Where are you going?"

"Darragh."

Lips puckered in thought, I run my fingers through my wavy hair, dispersing any leftover oils from my palms. Carefully, I begin braiding the wavy strands. When Gruffud still doesn't volunteer more information, I dare to request it. "Business deal?"

"Yes. Since damn Murtagh snatched the building I had my eyes on right from my grasp."

That's ... not how that occurred, but alright. "What will you gain from this business deal in Darragh?"

He climbs into bed and pulls the covers up over his legs. "Don't worry your pretty head about it, wife."

I bite my lip to keep more questions from spilling out, even though they gnaw at me. Gruffud leans over to his side table and turns off his oil lamp. He rolls onto his side, facing away from me.

For a few heartbeats, I stare at his back, certain that I'm imagining things. Since we've gotten married, there's rarely a night when he's simply fallen asleep. But the last couple nights, he's left me alone.

Maybe the gods *are* alive because this is the best birthday present I could've asked for.

Chapter 30

DURVLA

FOR DAYS, we don't see many others on our route. Every so often, a tradesperson crosses our path with a wagon of goods. The sun is sinking in the sky as we trek through Diadun. A woman with a knotted mess of chocolate brown hair runs out of a nearby house, waving her arms frantically above her head.

Ava looks back at us and says something. Tiernan relays the words into my mind. *"She's asking us to help her ill child."*

There's hesitation within our group; an unscheduled stop is risky. But what is the point of having the ability to help if we don't use it?

What if the rebels hadn't gone out of their way to rescue Taig?

We all seem to come to the same conclusion—that we cannot just walk away and leave someone in need. Especially a child.

We dismount in the small front garden among limp flowers and bushes, a wheelbarrow, and a toy pull wagon made of wood. Sloan, Isobel, Osheen, and Chiyo stand watch while the rest of us trail the frantic mother into her home. On a bed of quilts in the center of the modest room, a child lies shivering. She looks to be no older than twelve. A lean young man with unruly dark brown hair and a square jaw stands from where he'd been perched beside the child.

"You've come to help ...?" I don't quite make out the name he uses for the child or Ava's response to him. I miss being able to easily communicate and understand what's happening around me.

I feel Tiernan's magic nudge against my mind, and I let my walls sink. "*The child's name is Nuala. She's eleven years old. The lad is Cahel, and his mother is Jacinta.*"

"*Thank you,*" I mentally respond as Cahel leaves the room.

"She's been feverish for days," Jacinta says as we step closer. Numerous candles burn around the room, leaving a greasy scent in the air and making it harder to read Jacinta's lips. I find myself having to focus intently on her words.

"I've tried giving her teas and herbs. I've even—" She stops speaking abruptly.

Tiernan's gaze is on the child, his shoulders tense. I glance at him, a question lifting my brows.

"*What is it?*" I throw my words toward his mind.

"*She's a Wielder ... Waterweaver.*"

"*Oh!*"

Alys is already walking toward Nuala. Ava stands nearby, her arms folded over her lean torso as she stares at the woman she's been avoiding speaking with. Alys kneels beside Nuala and places her hand on her shoulder. A heartbeat later, she flinches back and looks to Jacinta, then us. She signs as she speaks, "I sense dark magic."

My heart jolts—partially because of Alys's words, partially because of the delivery of them. Signing publicly is dangerous, but I suppose since the child is a Waterweaver, they're in the same boat.

Jacinta's eyes widen. She shakes her head sharply, sending her wild brown hair flying every which way. "I haven't used any magic! Certainly not dark magic. I swear by all the gods!"

Ava steps in, calm as ever. "No one is accusing *you* of using magic. At least not willingly."

Jacinta waves her hands around, uttering too much at once for me to catch. Tears stream down her face as she looks back and forth between Nuala and Ava. With a gentle hand on the woman's shoulder, Ava leads her out of the room. It gives Alys a chance to work without the extra distraction.

I'm entranced by her healing light and the serene, focused look on her face. It's fascinating. Slowly, Nuala stops trembling.

When Alys's gaze settles on us, I sign, "Will she be alright? What dark magic do you sense?"

"I'm not sure, but the child has magic of her own."

"Waterweaving," Tiernan says.

"Ah." Alys glances briefly at Nuala. "It will be extremely difficult to heal her of whatever dark magic is inflicting her body. I'm not certain if it's even possible to fully cure her. Especially in so little time. It feels very similar to the poison I battled."

"What if this is the work of Purists?" I silently motion. "Osheen may know something. Unfortunately."

Tiernan swears, likely under his breath.

I volunteer to collect Osheen rather than risk Tiernan giving in to his harsh feelings toward the betrayer. As I step out of the cozy house and into the blustery night air, I gain everyone's attention. Osheen's blue gaze focuses on me, sadness and regret aging him. Without a word, I wave him over, and though he seems surprised, he doesn't question me.

When he's standing close, I fight the urge to step away. The coolness of my shadows prickles my fingertips, but I control myself as well as the urge to shake him. "You're needed inside," I say.

Without another word, I open the door and step inside. Alys is still crouched, watching the rise and fall of the blankets over Nuala's chest.

"What exactly do you know about that cure against magic you mentioned?" I ask Osheen. "The Poison? Can you tell Alys a bit more about it?"

He frowns in confusion. "The Cleanse?"

I shrug my shoulder and gesture to Alys, perhaps a little sharper than I mean to. My muscles are tense, as if merely being in Osheen's presence is changing my body's harmony.

Tiernan's arm wraps around my upper back, his hand squeezing my shoulder. I will my muscles to unclench as I watch the fluent words on Osheen's hands. "It's been given to Wielders mainly, I believe. But that's only for those who want to get rid of their magic. They have a poison that targets magical blood. It's more potent—a few rare herbs imbued with what sounds like old dark magic. Like from that book of fairytales Durvla used to love so much." He glances sidelong at me before his eyes shift back to Alys.

He's heard me read that book to Taig countless times. He used to playfully tease me for my love of those stories. It's difficult to believe so much of it turned out to be true. A despairing laugh almost leaves my lips. Tiernan squeezes my shoulder again, his warmth keeping me from bursting into tears.

"It's not the first time this has been attempted," Alys motions. "Widespread poison was the first attempt at the Purge, before the violent massacres began. Too many survived the poison, so they started to use more … aggressive methods."

Osheen flinches, as do I.

"They're planning to fully weaponize the poison, but they're mostly focused on the Cleanse. I've heard it's gruesome. Those who take it rarely survive, but they don't care about the casualties."

Gods …

"It could be the weaponized poison, but I'm not sure how they've been testing it."

As much as I hate to admit it, Osheen's knowledge on this journey is indeed useful.

Alys glances at Nuala then runs her hand over her salt-and-pepper hair. "Thank you, Osheen. The poison seems likely. I sense magic within her, but it's tainted."

Tiernan releases me to sign. "If I help with the healing, can we reverse the effects so that she's at least stable long enough for a rescue? We can send word to the Verge now and, in the meantime, heal her as best as we can. Maybe we can leave them with a few tonics to keep the fever down and the pain at bay."

Alys nods in agreement. "We can try."

Tiernan turns to Osheen before signing a tad too forcefully. "Have one of the others send word to Dayfyd. Sloan has done rescue missions before; they know what to do."

Osheen nods and gets out of the house quickly. The door hardly has time to close before the child's mother steps into the room, a tray of teacups in her hand. Ava walks behind her with a steaming kettle.

"Durvla, would you mind catching them up while Alys and I get started?" Tiernan asks.

I nod, and he gives me a tense smile before he and Alys take their places beside the child. Jacinta is wide-eyed and haggard as she places the tray down on the small, low table, and Ava places the kettle on a thin stone slab beside it. I catch them up with all that was discussed, including Alys and Tiernan's healing and the rescue attempt.

For a couple hours more, we remain in the house, taking turns refreshing ourselves, munching on stale bread and bland broth. I stand guard with Ava for a while as the others head inside. Cahel waters and grooms our horses before leaving them to get some rest.

I lean against the house, my head pounding and my legs growing weaker. When Chiyo steps back outside, she's washed the kohl away and pulled her hair back into a simple ponytail. "Your beau is sleeping off the healing sessions. We leave in under an hour. Perhaps you should get some rest too?"

I shake my head and white spots dance in the darkness, a ghost of nausea lightly nudging me. What I need to do is take a tincture before I faint or vomit. Or both.

"*Rest*," Chiyo says with a firm gesture. She holds my gaze for so long that I feel like I'll fall asleep where I stand.

"Fine," I concede.

When I get inside, Alys and Tiernan are asleep in each of the raggedy armchairs. Jacinta smiles crookedly at me from where she sits on the floor beside Nuala. As she refocuses on the girl, I cautiously squeeze in beside Tiernan. His shoulder makes the perfect pillow for my head, his chest a welcome place to drape my arm. To my surprise, his hand slides over my back, but he doesn't stir beyond that.

I wish I could get a better idea of what happened to Nuala. Beyond the inferences that were made based on Alys's healing senses and Osheen's knowledge, that is.

Then again ... *can't I?*

Taking a steady breath, I close my eyes and focus on Nuala, lowering my shields tentatively until I feel her presence. There's an innocence to it—something that feels like a gentle summer breeze. My body seems to drift, a vivid image of a garden materializing in my mind.

A small, fair hand plucks a lily from the garden and tucks it into a bouquet of wildflowers. They droop, but the child seems unbothered. Her blond hair is like spun gold in the sunlight. I remain a small distance from her, observing silently until her honey brown eyes find me. She hardly startles, a toothy smile lighting up her face.

"*Hello there!*" she chirps. "*Who are you?*"

"*Hi.*" I step closer to her. "*My name is Durvla.*"

She tilts her head at me, her lower lip bitten in thought. "*Your voice sounds familiar. Like I've heard you before. A moment ago. But ...*" Her eyes wander, and the beautiful garden wavers around us, the dreamscape threatening to collapse.

"*My friends have been working hard trying to make you feel better.*"

Her lips tug down. "*I was fine until I found an arrow in the stable. I wanted to bring it home to Cahel because he has a bow, but it cut my hand.*" Her gaze wanders to the distance.

My heart contracts. Poison indeed. Perhaps exactly the kind that had struck Alys.

"*For you,*" she says, her eyes on me again. She extends the flowers to me, but as I reach for them, I tumble back into my body, awake again.

I flinch so hard that Tiernan's arm tightens around me. I feel the slightest nudge of his magic against my mental barrier, but I don't let him in. He needs to rest. I reposition myself, my bottom wedged between the arm of the chair and his body, my legs draped over his lap. I lower my head to his chest and his arm relaxes, his breathing deepening again.

I must doze off for a moment, because the next thing I know, I'm being shaken. I startle, sitting up. It takes quite a bit of blinking before my vision clears well enough for me to make out Chiyo's face. "Cahel says he spotted Forayers riding this way," she signs. "We have to go!"

She runs off to wake Alys and I jostle Tiernan's shoulder before stumbling off his lap. "Forayers are coming," I tell him. His obsidian gaze is bleary, but he's on his feet, his swords in his hands in no time.

He sheathes the swords on his back and tightens the straps across his chest. We race outside, and as my eyes meet Osheen's, I'm reminded of the many times we've had to hide Taig during an impending raid. I'm even reminded of when we all fled Dubh Carrig during the Festival of Damarlach, leaving the entire village in flames.

Tiernan helps me onto Ghendor as Cahel and Jacinta rush out of the house. They hand us satchels of food for the road, thanking us for the potions and for helping Nuala. Then we're off, riding into the night ... again.

I hope that Nuala will make it. That she can be rescued.

That by some divine intervention, we can stop running all the time.

Chapter 31

CARYS

WE SET sail in a stolen tradesman ship without a banner, headed around the southern border toward the east of Erleya. It seems the safest, given that there would only be one territory—Erleya—to deal with rather than Caldeon and Ardall in the north. I rest my forearms on the handrail and lean my weight against them, peering out at the orange and pink waves beneath the rising sun.

There are so many questions I have that will remain forever unanswered. How is Durvla my sister? Who was my mother with before my father? Did my mother know the extent of the turmoil within Erleya, or was she as ignorant as I was? For all the secrets that she apparently kept, it hurts to think it's possible she was very much aware. That she concealed it to keep herself safe. To keep *me* safe.

Morwenna, the *Good*. Yet based on what she condoned, she might as well have killed all those Mages with her own hands.

My body starts to feel weightless, a fog misting over my mind, until someone rests a hand on my forearm. I flinch so hard that all my muscles twinge. I lift my gaze to Odgar's, forcing myself to breathe in steadily, forcing my pulse to settle. Odgar's hand gently squeezes my arm, and I hang on to the sensation, to the focus etched into his rugged face.

"Stay with me," he says.

I frown in confusion. Where does he expect me to go?

"Tell me what you're afraid of."

Myself. The word is on the tip of my tongue, but I clench my jaw to keep it from flying out. "Being imprisoned again," I say instead.

He tucks his lips in for a moment before releasing them. "I won't let that happen."

I turn my face to the brightening horizon. The world around me feels hazy and intangible. My legs start to feel numb.

A large hand suddenly appears in my view. I startle again before seeking Odgar's face. His lips are a straight line for a moment, though there's a softness in his eyes that irritates and draws me in at the same time. The tightness in my chest is uncomfortable. I press my hand against it and somehow it *still* surprises me to find my amulet absent.

Odgar continues to offer his hand.

My eyes dart between his palm and his face as a soft smile curves his lips.

"*What?*" I snap.

His smile grows wider. "Dance with me."

I stare at him as though he's lost his mind. "There's no music, Odgar."

"Then we'll make our own music." His grin is so bloody contagious. I want to direct my anger toward him. It would be easier than confronting the warmth slowly spreading through me.

I roll my eyes at him. "Our own music," I echo incredulously.

He takes my hand and steps back, tugging me so that I'm practically catapulted into his burly frame. His other hand splays across my back and the knot in my chest loosens slightly. Keeping me close, he begins to sway. He vocalizes an entrancing tune that summons gooseflesh to my skin and silences my cynicism. Awed, I sway along with him, soaking up the melody, lowering my head against the muscles just below his collarbone. The knot completely dissipates, the world around me feeling more substantial than it has in a while.

His vocalizations lure me like a merrow whose song I would gladly drown in if I could feel at peace like this forever.

My feet move naturally, in sync with his. We twirl and sashay across the swaying boat as though we're alone in a grand ballroom. I'm reminded of that night when I thought my whole world would fall apart—when the weight of a decision rested heavily on my shoulders.

When he made things feel less daunting, and I already knew that I wanted him. At least for the betterment of Erleya, but also ... maybe more.

Do I still want him?

My uncertainty diminishes the effects of Odgar's soothing song. I tug away from him, flabbergasted by my own actions as my heart trips over itself. Odgar's confusion reflects my own as his lips open, close, and open again.

"Did I offend you?" he asks at last.

"I—"

He reaches out to me, but I take a large step back, and he immediately holds his hands up.

Do I still want him? The question resurfaces in my mind. Somewhere deep within me, I know the answer, but I try to lock it away just as I lock away Enidwen.

Odgar is devastatingly handsome and gentle. He deserves a woman that doesn't need him simply for political gain. One who would give him the same level of caring he so willingly shows.

One who isn't broken.

Without another word, I turn and rush off, nearly running into Valdis as I make it to the narrow steps. Tears are welling in my eyes, so I hurry past her and down below deck, shutting myself in the small cabin.

As if the space isn't tiny enough, the walls seem to press in on me. The beginnings of embers heat in my palms. I squeeze my hands into fists, but the flames erupt nonetheless.

Enidwen's voice rises from the shadows in my mind. *Keep repressing and you'll never be able to learn control.*

"Shut. Up!" I say through clenched teeth. "Shut up, shut up, shut up!"

A click sounds behind me. I whirl to find Odgar hunched in front of the door, his head nearly touching the ceiling. He points to himself, eyebrows lifted nearly to his curly hairline. "Me?"

"No, you giant oaf. I'm talking to the bloody voice in my head that chooses the most random times to talk to me." Gods, do I sound unstable or what?

Odgar smirks, and I want to clout him in his infuriatingly perfect nose. "Giant oaf, eh? What a sweet term of endearment."

I growl at him. *Growl*. And as embarrassment blooms on my face, Odgar's low laughter rumbles through the cabin. My stomach tightens. With anger? Longing? I don't want to find out.

"Leave!" I shout, shoving against his chest.

He doesn't budge. Not even by a hair.

"Get out of here! Go!" Another shove that goes absolutely nowhere.

When I shove him again, he catches my hands and takes a step forward, forcing me back. I try to pull away, but with another step, I'm forced backward again. And again, until he sends me toppling onto a semi-soft surface. My heart lurches as the surface gives slightly. The cot.

The cabin suddenly feels far smaller than it already is. Odgar presses a hand against the wall to the side of the bed, leaning over me. "You're free to strike me," he says. "But you're going to damage your delicate princess hands if you keep striking my armor."

I'm not sure what comes over me, but with a grunt, I kick out at him. He catches my ankle, and tugs me so that I somehow end up flat on my back.

"I think you were in Uldarvik for too long, *revna*. But alright, you want to hit me?"

I stare at Odgar, wide-eyed as he casts his battle-axe casually aside and begins unfastening buckles and laces on his leather armor. They hit the floor with a series of *thunks* and *clangs*. I sit up, swiveling to face him, my back against the wall. The rest of his hidden weapons are next. My breath hitches as he rolls up his sleeves, corded muscles tensing beneath the symbols permanently inked into his coppery skin.

"Well?" He pulls his bronzed curls up into a messy top bun. "What are you waiting for? Have at it."

The fight in me has been doused, but I hold my chin high, not wanting to give him the satisfaction of knowing he effectively distracted me. I stand and take one step toward him, but as I raise my hand to strike him, my traitorous body acts on its own volition.

His tunic is bunched in my hand, and I yank his head down toward me, crushing my lips against his. I'm sick and tired of feeling out of control all the time, of giving in to unwanted emotions. I charge him backwards until his back loudly rattles the door. He flinches before stepping forward to put some space between his back and the wood. I shove him against the door again, staring up into eyes likened to sunlight bleeding into the depths of the ocean. Gods, they're so beautiful, I would gladly drown in them too.

This time, it's Odgar who crushes his lips to mine. In a feverish squall of impatience and passion, his tunic goes flying as does my overdress. Hurried, frenzied kisses fill the moments when we're not tearing clothing off each other. Lifted atop the narrow bureau anchored to the wall, I tip my head back as Odgar steps between my thighs. His tongue and lips explore my neck. His hand slides above my knee, pushing up my underdress. I hook my fingers into the waistband of his trousers as a loud pounding sound jars my senses.

"Odgar! Carys!" More loud knocking against the door emphasizes the urgency in Valdis's voice. My heart nearly leaps out of my chest, but it's Odgar who growls this time.

His eyes are glazed over as he lifts his head, but he doesn't look away from me. "Go away, Valdis!"

"Get your horny asses out here," Valdis shouts back. "We're under attack!"

My stomach plummets, all pleasure along with it. "Shit," I mumble. *Under attack.* We've only been on the sea for three days.

My heart races as Odgar lifts me off the bureau before gathering his own tunic and tossing my overdress at me. I swear there's the smallest hint of embarrassment on his rugged face.

"I left armor at the door for Carys," Valdis says over a rising tide of distant shouts and clanging weapons.

I get dressed in record time before Odgar haphazardly cinches the leather armor onto me and shoves my bow into my hands. The armor feels odd and bulky, but I don't have time to fuss over it.

We resurface on deck to a skirmish of thrice as many people than just our crew. Alongside us is a full-rigged ship similar to ours, but with four masts instead of three. Beneath yellowed sails, a red flag with a winged lion flaps in the wind, denoting that they're from Ardall like Seth—not exactly a political enemy but hostile nonetheless.

As the realization hits, I lock eyes on Seth. He fights back-to-back with Valdis, his movements fluid and effortless. Valdis's attacks are sharp and precise. Her intertwined braids and flowing blond hair whip around her as she ducks the slash of her opponent's sword and drives her spear through his back. The man drops to his knees as Valdis tugs her spear free and moves on to the next attacker with equal fervor.

My body starts to drift, as if I'm watching everything unfold from a distance. As if my mind is retreating into itself.

"Stay close," Odgar shouts. I jump, my mind snapping back fully. My hands have gone slick on the bow, blood racing through my veins in a way that makes my limbs feel sluggish and my breath go shallow. Odgar shoves me behind him as a large Ardallan comes at me. I yank an arrow from the quiver on my back and nock it, but in such close combat, it's not the best choice of weapon.

Tiernan was right; I should've learned to wield a dagger. Dammit!

I take a deep breath and summon flames to my hand as I step out from behind Odgar. My fire blast goes straight into the man's face. He goes down screaming as his skin blisters and chars. I throw out a fresh conflagration at two more men who charge at me. One of them, his clothes in flames, still slashes wildly with a broadsword. Odgar flings his battle-axe into the man's chest, and he drops dead.

I look away as Odgar wrenches his weapon from the body, but his voice urges me on. "Can you shoot fire arrows at their ship?"

Brilliant. "Yes, I think so."

"Alright, I've got you covered. You shoot, I'll ward off these shit sacks."

Energy buzzes through me as I grab the arrow again and nock it. I focus on setting the arrow tip on fire, but it doesn't come willingly.

"Any time now, *revna*," Odgar says in a singsong voice. The sound of squelching flesh follows.

Ignoring the churn in my stomach, I will my flames to life again.

This time, I let the embers shoot up along the shaft of the arrow to the tip, then loose. It soars toward the other boat and into the chest of one of the Ardallans.

I shoot another, then another, alternating between aiming for parts of the boat and the attackers.

The fight seems to go on forever. My entire body is quaking, and I'm not sure I can summon any more fire. When I'm certain I have nothing left, the surviving Ardallans jump from our ship and swim for theirs.

A small cheer rises up around me. Odgar douses any remaining flames, his water sweeping across the floor of our boat and overboard.

My knees buckle, but by the time I realize I'm falling, I'm already on the hard deck. I force breaths into my raw throat, my skin feeling as much on fire as the other boat desperately steering away from us.

Odgar drops down beside me. "Are you alright?" he asks, sounding breathless.

I can barely lift my arms, but I nod, meeting his gaze.

"Thank Brenjor," he says, invoking the Uldaran protector and god of thunder. He lets his head sag for a moment.

Someone pats me on the shoulder, but it's not Odgar. I glance up at Valdis, and her blue eyes regard me with respect. "Well done," she says, wiping blood from her spear with a stained cloth.

I turn away from her and retch my guts up all over myself and the deck.

Chapter 32

DURVLA

Days transpire, and my entire body feels on the brink of rebellion. My head throbs endlessly, even with the tinctures and Alys's healing. The dizzy spells come more frequently, and my back and bum twinge incessantly. Even dismounted, everything hurts— my thighs scream at me as we trek up a mountain. I focus as best as I can on the path ahead and not on the crumbly edge of the mountain where death taunts us.

Tiernan has been teetering between simmering silence and tenderness almost constantly. It seems that the farther east we travel, the more tense he becomes, and the less he seems to sleep. Often, when I wake in the mornings, he's no longer on the bedroll beside me. He's always quick to bring me a tincture or even to heal me so Alys doesn't need to exert more energy than she already does, but he becomes more and more withdrawn. Every day I ask him if he's doing alright, and every day he says he's fine. But there's a look in his eyes I cannot quite figure out, and the more I remind him that he can tell me anything, the less he seems willing.

I try not to let the frustration get to me as we hike up the mountain at the start of the late afternoon. I mull over my ancestry, wishing I had time to talk to Alys privately about my birth parents and her history with them. It still stings knowing that the only parents who'd ever been part of my life weren't related to me by blood. That Taig isn't even related to me by blood. Part of me is angry that Alys didn't tell me the truth sooner—that she had these suspicions about me and chose to keep them to herself—but had I been in the same position, perhaps I would've done the same thing. Still, it feels like another betrayal of sorts, and with Osheen traveling with us as well, Ava not speaking to her mother, and Tiernan being unbearably secretive, there's enough tension in our group to cut with a knife.

Isobel is always a tension breaker. I'm not sure I've *ever* seen her in a bad mood. She seems to have endless energy and chatters almost nonstop. She's been trying to learn more signs, but she often forgets that she needs to sign for me to understand. Still, I find it endearing, and I find myself wishing I had her enthusiasm for everything. Her sibling is the opposite—much like Ava, they always seem unimpressed. They're one of very few words, but never malevolent and always helpful.

We're trudging through a grassy forest of tall trees packed close together when the sun begins its descent. Ava calls for a stop. We're all dragging our feet—all in desperate need of a good night's sleep.

Isobel and Sloan make a fire, and Chiyo approaches me as the others patrol to ensure the coast is clear. "This place reminds me of Dubh Carrig," she says.

I glance around and smile. "I can see why. Do you miss it there?"

"I do. I wish I could exchange letters with my mam more frequently, but ... I don't want to waste all our enchanted parchment, of course."

"Of course. It wouldn't hurt to use *one* though."

She chuckles. "Look who's embracing her rebel identity!"

I laugh, and my back protests, but it's worth it. Tiernan returns, a smile on his face. "There's a private spot near the river. Perfect for bathing," he reports.

"Great," says Chiyo. "Ladies first." She slings her arm around me as a look of disappointment, if I'm not mistaken, crosses Tiernan's face. I raise a brow at him, but he seems to remember to school his features into a carefree expression.

I cast out my thoughts to him. "*Unless you want time to talk or something?*"

Tiernan shakes his head. "*Go ahead. Chiyo's excited.*" Even as he mind speaks, Chiyo releases me, seemingly calling to the other ladies. Ava and Isobel look our way, but Alys smiles and politely declines.

I look to Tiernan again, but I'm barely able to even think clearly before he says, "*Next time. You and me.*"

I pull up my mental shields firmly as I think, *I'll believe it when I see it.*

Chiyo runs off to gather my pack and a couple of lanterns. Then the four of us set off through the forest again, heading in the direction Tiernan mentioned. Isobel is practically skipping ahead as we walk while I can't decide whether to distribute my weight onto the balls or the heels of my feet. No matter how I step, it aches, and I fight not to hobble. I am not made for constant traveling. The trees clear slightly, giving way to a grassy mound. Flat, moss-speckled rocks form steps down to a small body of water surrounded by shrubs and stony walls.

As uncomfortable as it is to disrobe in front of the others, everyone is respectful, and we get into the river with limited awkwardness. Despite the overwhelming cold, my body craves the comfort of the water. Silence falls between us all as we take in this rare comfort. I lift my gaze from the water and stare across at Ava, who regards me with a stern expression.

I hold my breath and submerge myself, getting my hair saturated before beginning to unravel my braid. I wince again and again as I untangle the mess of curls. Never have I been so tempted to chop it all off. Ava looks similarly aggrieved—her hair is more tightly curled, thicker, and far longer than mine. It's beautiful, but I don't envy her after trekking halfway across the kingdom.

Chiyo swims toward the rock and grabs soap to lather her skin while Isobel waves her arms suddenly. "Let's play a game!" she says.

The three of us narrow our gazes on her. Sometimes she is just so … young. I nearly laugh at the thought. I'm only twenty-three, yet I feel like I've aged so much in the past four months since leaving Cluain Baile that a twenty-year-old seems juvenile.

"Never have I ever," says Isobel. "Come on. We could use some fun."

"What's so fun in—" Ava starts, but Chiyo interrupts her with a look.

"Alright, who's going first?" Isobel asks.

Chiyo lifts her hand to tamp down Isobel's enthusiasm. "Isn't ale required for this game?"

Isobel's face falls, and I feel guilty to be relieved in the face of her disappointment. She heaves a visible sigh, and Chiyo takes pity on her.

"Alright, alright, fine. But let's make it interesting. How about ..." Chiyo purses her lips in concentration, her dark eyes focused. "Whoever loses does all the menial tasks—horse grooming and such —for a day?"

Ava flicks her eyes skyward with annoyance and tips her head back.

Chiyo and Isobel look at me expectantly. I make a face, but before I can say anything, Isobel raises her hand, beaming as she waves it in the air, and I find myself unable to ruin her excitement.

"Alright ..." Chiyo translates for me as best as she can after asking the question. "Have you ever kissed anyone?"

Isobel makes a thoughtful face. "Does Sloan count?"

Chiyo raises her brows.

"On the cheek!"

Chiyo bursts out laughing, as does Isobel, and I cannot help but chuckle lightly. I grab my own bar of soap and rub through my hair, massaging my scalp with my fingers and once again trying to get through what feels like hundreds of tangles.

Chiyo's face scrunches in thought. She looks at me, swatting her hand as if shooing a fly. "We all know who *you've* kissed most recently, Durvla. What about before that?"

I shake my head, slightly embarrassed.

Her face softens, as if she's spotted a puppy. "That's so very sweet," she says.

I slide down further into the water, my ears feeling hot.

Chiyo turns to Ava who raises her brows at her. "What are you looking at me for?"

"Have you kissed anyone?"

Ava smirks. "Have *you*?"

Chiyo's face turns red all the way up to the silvery roots of her hair. Ava's lips flatten, but her attempt to keep from laughing fails, and she claps her hand over her mouth, which only makes Chiyo start laughing too.

At last, Chiyo says, "My neighbor, Claude. Your turn."

Ava rolls her eyes. "I didn't ask to be part of this ridiculous game."

Chiyo splashes her, and to my surprise, Ava splashes her right back. Isobel shrieks, ducking for cover before moving away and dissolving into giggles. I remain at a safe distance, unable to resist smiling.

When the splashing settles down, Ava says, "I have, but it was meaningless."

Chiyo's cheeks pinken again. "That's how I felt about Claude," she says, her signs coming a heartbeat later.

She and Ava exchange lingering gazes, as if Isobel and I have ceased to exist.

Isobel lifts her limp hair, the red hue darkened from the water. "I'll be detangling this bird's nest for a thousand years still after we get out of this water," she says.

I sigh. "Same."

Ava returns to painstakingly unbraiding one of her long, thick plaits. "Don't even get me started."

We finish washing up and get out of the river, discreetly drying ourselves and getting dressed. As I sit on a large boulder, rolling on my socks, I feel someone watching me. Isobel's looking my way.

She blushes and lowers her head for a moment before facing me again. "Apologies, I was admiring your tattoo," she says.

I roll the sleeve of my tunic back farther so she can see the tattoo better. "Thank you. Never in my wildest dreams did I imagine I would permanently put ink on my skin."

She reciprocates my smile. "Why did you?"

Chiyo and Ava look on once they're dressed. Ava finger-combs through her thick, curly tresses that fall to her waist.

"A fresh start, I suppose," I say. "In the early spring, I'd been apprehended by Forayers. When I arrived in Paramount, one of the soldiers branded me." I slide my thumb over the inked floral moon phases on my left inner forearm. Though the burn is no longer easily visible, I can still feel the raised skin. "I hated the reminder of the moment they tried to destroy my life, so I chose to have it transformed into something beautiful. I know many people have scars—but every time I looked at this one, it felt like a physical blow. It's probably a trivial thing."

Isobel smiles, but for once it isn't just glee or excitement in her grey-blue eyes, but something deeper I cannot quite place. "It isn't," she says. "I did the same." She hesitates for a moment before tugging down the shoulders of her tunic and turning her lightly freckled back for me to see. She pulls her hair over to the front of her body, revealing a tattoo of what looks like butterfly wings between her narrow shoulder blades. I have to squint to make out the scar where the wings join. When she turns back to me, she says, "I think scars are beautiful in their own right, but I also hated how mine made me feel. So ... unwanted."

For a moment, she doesn't say anything else. She only tugs her tunic on again and sits on the ground with her shoulders slumped over. "My mother took it upon herself to put me out of my misery once my galemaking fully manifested. It was a poor attempt at execution." She smirks darkly and I nearly fall off the boulder.

My heart sputters, suddenly heavier in my chest. Even Ava's eyes are wide, and Chiyo's jaw is practically on the floor.

"*Execution*?" Chiyo asks.

"Not an official one or anything. Left me with a blade in my back." Isobel wrings her hands awkwardly, before looking back up so I can read her lips. "I was in the kitchen preparing a snack when my mother came up behind me. I could hear the tears in her voice as she told me she was sorry and it was for my own good. I'd just started to turn to ask what she meant when she struck."

I'm certain I look as shocked as Ava and Chiyo do. Ava swears and rubs her temples as if Isobel's story has given her an instant headache.

"Isobel, I—" Chiyo's lost for words, as are we all. "How old were you?"

Isobel inhales deeply. "Thirteen. I'd like to think it was for the best. They'd always treated Sloan badly. Sloan was their great shame, their Undesirable, deformed child. Our parents kept them hidden as much as they could. Sloan somehow managed to hide their stump for a while, but by the time people found out, no one truly cared. Except for our parents. It was my injury that gave Sloan the push to drag me away from that place."

She pauses and exhales. "We sailed from the Outer Isles while I healed from the wound in my back. It was the worst pain I've ever felt, and I was sure I wouldn't survive it. We met a kind man in Bayenbar where we stayed for a while. Niall Kilkenny."

My heart leaps at the name, and I blink at Isobel. *Niall Kilkenny.*

She nods, then looks at Chiyo with a smile. "The apple doesn't fall far from the tree."

Chiyo returns her smile.

"I saw him only for a moment before he put us under the care of a man named Murtagh. Eventually, we made our way to the Verge. That was five years ago."

"Did you join the rebels right away?" Chiyo asks.

"I didn't. I needed safety and consistency more than I needed to be a savior. But now ... I only hope to return the favor of the rebels and help this kingdom in any way I can. I cannot let people like my parents continue to win and continue to spread hatred."

A heaviness hangs in the air until Chiyo gets up and walks over to Isobel. She crouches to embrace her, hugging her so tightly, I'm afraid she'll snap her in half. When she finally releases Isobel, she says, "The fact that you kept going after your own mother literally stabbed you in the back means they've already lost."

Ava and I nod in agreement, and Isobel laughs through tears. "Now, an important question: who won never have I ever?"

Her question surprises laughter out of us all.

When we return to the campsite, Tiernan kisses me on the cheek and mentions that he and the others are off to wash up. I settle in near the campfire beside Alys, who smiles at me with such warmth. Traveling with a bigger group this time makes bonding with one particular person so much harder, but I make sure to smile back at her.

"I'm so glad you made a recovery from that arrow," I say.

"Me too, sweetling. I'm grateful I get to travel with you all again."

"It must not be the easiest to leave your husband behind again," I sign.

"No, but ..." Her gaze wanders to Ava, who's chatting with Chiyo a small distance away.

I smile and nod with understanding. There's division between them for sure, but I don't know why. I already spend so much time trying to pry information from Tiernan that I feel bad doing the same to Alys.

"So, you were friends with Morwenna?" I ask Alys.

"I was. Since she was about Carys's age."

My chest tightens. It's been so long since I've heard from Carys also. "What was she like?"

"Full of life." Alys's smile grows distant, as if she's remembering Morwenna in vivid detail. "She loved the outdoors—she could spend hours just frolicking in pastures. She also loved roses. She took pride in planting and tending to them even when her mother told her it was lowborn work." Alys chuckles. "As much as she was a free spirit, she was also a tormented soul. Like Dayfyd said: plagued by nightmares."

I blow out a breath. "I understand what that's like." As does Tiernan.

I'm about to ask her how Dayfyd ended up with Morwenna when I glimpse a light to my left. I turn as Tiernan approaches with a mage lantern. He smiles, glancing from Alys to me. "I don't mean to interrupt—"

"It's alright," Alys says.

"Do you mind if I borrow her?" He looks to me, a smile that's almost reminiscent of the Tiernan I saw at the Verge before Rheon was announced as the sovereign. It warms my heart, giving me the smallest bit of hope.

"Not at all," Alys signs.

I smile and face her. "To be continued?" I ask.

She nods. "To be continued."

Tiernan tugs me to my feet and motions, "I selfishly just want a moment to talk to you alone. Is that alright?"

More hope fills me. I nod. "Of course."

He takes my hand, and we walk away from the group, onto the

pathway that leads to the river where I'd been with the girls earlier. As we reach somewhere between the river and our camp, Tiernan stops and turns to me.

"We're nearing where Siad Nahar is supposed to be. How are you feeling?"

I try to hide the puzzlement from my face and turn inward to make sure I'm not leaving my shields down for him to read me easily. Why did I think he wanted to talk about what's has been bothering him? "I'm alright," I respond, clearing my throat. "I wish I could hear more from Carys, and I still wonder about that other woman, Winnie. Sometimes I fear things are too calm and that the other shoe may drop soon, but I'm trying to remain positive."

"I understand that feeling though. Too calm is almost like tempting fate."

I laugh. "Well, I didn't say *that*!"

It's a relief to see that crinkling at the corner of his eyes again, that endearing sharpening of his cheekbones and that overall light in his features. How long since he's smiled this genuinely? What makes tonight any different? Is it because we're nearing our destination? In any case, I'm relieved by the sincerity in his smile tonight.

"You're looking at me that way again," Tiernan signs.

"*Tiernan* ... I can't help the way I look at you."

His smile falters, but he sets the lantern down beside a tree and sits down.

"What are you—"

He snags my wrist, tugging me onto him so abruptly that I can't help the yelp of surprise that slips out. "Shh," he says, his smile wide as he presses a finger to his lips.

"Then don't surprise me like that!" I say through my giggles.

His grin only grows wider. One hand splays across my back while the other slides up into my freshly washed and braided hair. My breath catches, my heart thumping so hard I'm almost certain he feels it through my back. "I thought we were here to talk?"

"*We will*," he says into my mind as he presses me to him.

I'm still holding back giggles when his lips find mine, but instantly the heat of it silences me. I press my hand against the prickly stubble of his cheek as he draws me deeper into the kiss. His hand shifts from my back, gripping my waist as if he's afraid I'll let go.

An aching, wanting need clenches deep in my gut, spreading down through my thighs until my breath grows shorter. I close my eyes, trying to find my composure. We're bare to the elements and not very far from the rest of the group. But this feels like a relief from everything—something mind-numbing against all the fear and uncertainty of this mission.

My knees end up on either side of him, my arms over his shoulders, brushing against the tree as I wonder if he's only doing this to distract himself from everything. My lips part to ask him to talk to me—for the umpteenth time.

When he kisses me again, I'm overcome with images of darkness, of a sword slashing through the air. I see throats slit, blood flowing, manacles snapped onto wrists. There are uniforms, a familiar sneering face, lines upon lines of soldiers saluting. I smell blood and taste fear and regret. It's pungent and leaves my stomach churning and my heart pounding as though I've just run across an entire village.

I pull back from Tiernan, but his fingers dig into me.

His eyes fly open, his face draining of all color as he releases me and presses his back into the tree.

I practically jump off his lap as he tugs his hands through his damp hair. "Tiernan," I whisper, my hands shaking as I try to make sense of the images I'd caught. His fear radiates from him, so strong that I'm forced to step back, my hands flying to my temples.

Tiernan's hands shake as he pushes them against the ground before getting to his feet. "What did you see?" he asks. All the light is gone from his eyes.

"I don't know," I say.

"Durvla, *what* did you see?" He steps closer, panic lacing his features so strongly that I take another step back.

"Tiernan, I told you I don't know! What is going on with you?"

He rakes his fingers through his hair, his chest rising and falling with panicked breaths. I've never seen him this way. It crushes me. I step closer, reaching out to him, but he recoils.

His reaction is like a mortal wound. Bitterness and fury seethe in my chest and crawl out of my throat before I can stop them. "Why don't you trust me?" I don't even bother to sign. I try to tamp down my words, but more fly out. "I've set my heart before you on a golden platter while you hide yours away like a dragon's hoard."

"You won't understand," he signs.

"How do you know that without even *trying* to explain?"

His jaw clenches, his words locked away.

I feel like a kettle bubbling over, and I fear that I'll say something regrettable. I turn to walk away, but he grabs my arm.

My gaze snaps to his. "Let go of me."

He releases me like a hot stone but follows infuriatingly close the whole trek back to the camp. I need some time alone to gather my composure.

With a glance back at Tiernan, I sharply sign, "Don't follow me," then I rush right past everyone.

I eventually stop and lean against a tree trunk to catch my breath when I spot a glowing light moving toward me. As I snatch my dagger from my waist, ready to throw it, Chiyo emerges from the shadows.

She holds her arms up, the lantern dangling from her fingers. "Just me," she signs after a moment. With a rushed exhalation, I slip my dagger back into its sheath and sink down against the rough bark of the tree to the forest ground.

Chiyo crouches in front of me, holding the lantern up beside her face. She doesn't say anything, and at first, I'm grateful. Until my mind replays everything—the avoidance, the kiss, the inexplicable images. The fact that, for the first time, I'm *truly* angry at Tiernan Kilkenny, and I'm not even sure if it's warranted. I feel like I know so much about him and, at the same time, so little.

"I'm not a Mind Whisperer," Chiyo says. "So, you'll have to spell it out for me. What happened? Do I need to slap Tiernan again?" She holds up her hand, the rings shimmering on her fingers. "I'll do it, you know."

I prop my chin on my knees, wrapping my arms around my lower legs. "I don't know what to say," I admit.

She makes a thoughtful face. "What happened between you two? The appropriate version, if possible."

I snort a humorless laugh and shrug. After a stretch of time, I say, "I wish he'd trust me more."

"He does trust you. He's just bullheaded. Perhaps more so than I."

"Impossible," I say with a small smirk.

She laughs, her eyes growing endearingly small the way her brother's do. I wrap my arms tighter around myself. "I know there's something that's been bothering him, but I want him to offer it willingly. If that makes sense?"

She nods. "I'm not saying he's right," she begins. "But this is how Tiernan copes. He keeps secrets. Don't forget that he didn't even write home for *ten years*. I still have no idea what happened in that time. So, it's not you, Durvla. He ... needs to work through things, I guess."

I sigh. Perhaps she's right, but we all have things to work through. He expects me to share my feelings, and yet he continuously pulls away from me. My heart aches.

"We should really get some rest," Chiyo tells me. She jabs her thumb over her shoulder. "Shall we head back? I can throw a shuriken Tiernan's way to keep him back if you'd like. I promise I'll only nick him a little."

It pulls a wavering smile from me, but I simply shake my head and get to my feet again.

My anxiety returns as we start the walk toward the camp; I'll have to face Tiernan.

Once we get back, my eyes wander past Osheen, Alys, and Sloan chatting, to Tiernan sitting alone. He's focused on the flames as if he expects to find answers in them. When he glances up, he holds my gaze. But, unable to see the pain in his dark eyes and still not know why it's there, I look away.

If he wants to be secretive, then I have nothing to say to him.

Chapter 33

DURVLA

AVOIDING Tiernan is impossible when I'm stuck riding with him. As frustrated as I am with how things are between us, I don't want to draw attention to the situation more than we already have. We're nearly three weeks into our travels, and based on the map, we're supposed to be near Siad Nahar by now. Yet we seem to be walking to no avail, and things are stressed enough for everyone without the petty issues between Tiernan and me worsening things.

The mountains are like a labyrinth. Somehow, the path we drew on the map doesn't align with the path we're taking. We stop more often than usual to calibrate and figure things out, but where we'd hoped to find a trail into what should be Siad Nahar, there are mountains too tall to scale.

We camp again. Ava, Chiyo, and Tiernan pore over the maps while Sloan and Isobel engage in a weapons-only spar—as declared by Ava—beside the campfire.

Chiyo and Ava chat with comfortable familiarity, Chiyo placing a hand on Ava's knee as she says something. To my surprise, Ava smiles with warmth I didn't even know she was capable of, then addresses whatever Tiernan says. It tugs a smile from me as well, as I peel pieces from a twig just to keep my hands busy.

I miss the everyday life at the Verge. At Cluain Baile. I miss Taig so much it hurts. With that thought, my gaze roams past Alys, who's brewing tea at the campfire, to Osheen sitting by himself.

He looks so forlorn. He's not given us another reason to mistrust him, but I'm still sore about what he did. I understand he'd been trying to save his family; Iywan's threat to hang them if Osheen didn't do his bidding must have been horrifying. Still, I cannot shake the thought that he would've allowed the Verge to be infiltrated.

Osheen's auburn hair appears bright red in the sun as he meets my gaze from across the campsite. For once, I don't turn away from him. His face remains earnest for a moment before he offers me a tentative smile. I don't reciprocate.

Isobel and Sloan stop sparring at last. Sloan puts their sword away and rubs their stub as if it's gotten sore, and Isobel claps them on the back. Then Ava steps up, leaving Chiyo and Tiernan behind. She points to Sloan, challenging them, and they smile briefly. Pulling their sword from the scabbard at their hip again, Sloan gets into a fighting stance. Ava mirrors and immediately lunges.

Both warriors are *quick*, their swords catching sunbeams with each swing. The pair seem equally matched, but Sloan strikes with wilder swings, countering Ava's precise, deadly attacks. The point of Ava's sword ends up against Sloan's chest. Sloan seems unsurprised but nevertheless impressed. With a satisfied smirk, Ava steps back and lowers her sword as Sloan gives her a small bow and steps aside.

Sheathing her sword, Ava glances around, then points at me. When I continue to gawk at her, she waves me toward her, aggression in the gesture. Having gained everyone's attention, my pulse quickens. I carefully get to my feet, brushing my hands over the seat of my trousers.

Tiernan moves closer as I approach Ava. He seems ready to object, but refrains.

I don't even have the time to get fight-ready before Ava swings at me with such force that wind rushes over my head as I duck. When I stand upright again, I step and punch, but she simply leans to the side, avoiding it with such ease that my next punch is strictly out of annoyance. Her perpetual look of boredom grows substantially.

After a while of me punching and her dodging with embarrassing composure, I'm tired, frustrated, and nearly ready to call it quits. Then, instead of blocking yet again, she throws a punch, and I summon a wall of darkness that stops her strike.

With a mild grimace of pain, she shakes out her hand and I lower the shadows. "*Now* you're using your head," she signs.

"I— I'm sorry, *what*?" Confusion furrows my brows. "I thought there was a no magic rule?"

Ava rolls her eyes. "There are no rules in warfare. Except: save your ass. I said weapons only. Your powers *are* your weapons." Her leg comes flying at me, and I throw up another shadow shield, though this one causes me to fall onto my bottom. The shield dissipates, and Ava lunges at me, but I immediately push my palm out toward her, releasing dark vines of vapors that coil around her arms. Clenching my fists, I tug at the vines and they tighten, anchoring her arms to her body as she struggles.

A child's voice resounds in my head. *Mama, please don't go.*

Sweetling, I have to. But I promise I'll return soon. Alys's voice.

Large hazel eyes in a familiar face, far younger than the one before me right now, fills my mind. Pain, sorrow, and anger move through me. I release the hold of my shadows, and the images fall away. When the present surroundings rebuild around me, Ava is on the ground, her chest heaving as though the wind has been knocked out of her. Chiyo is at her side.

A deep tremor runs through my body, energy seeming to drain from me even though I'm still seated on the ground. An eerily familiar pressure builds in my head, squeezing my throat ... It's almost suffocating. I force down a deep breath.

Tiernan kneels beside me. "Are you alright?"

I nod and refocus on Ava as the woman shoves Chiyo's arm away and unsteadily gets to her feet. Her eyes are wide, homed in on me. I shrink beneath her gaze, but then her eyes soften, and she says, "Whatever you just did. Don't forget it." She rubs at her arm, her sternum, a faraway look in her eyes.

"What *did* you do?" Tiernan signs.

"I—I'm not sure. I saw ..." I glance at Ava, who looks more vulnerable than I've ever seen her. She rolls some of her braids into a pile atop her head, securing it with a gossamer black scarf as her gaze sears me. I'll keep what I saw to myself; it isn't my place to share her trauma with others.

"I saw a memory. And I suppose ... I wielded it?" I say.

Chiyo's jaw drops. "Shit, Durvla. Just when I thought I couldn't love you any more than I do."

I ... don't know how to react.

Ava sighs. "Had we known you could do this before ..." A muscle feathers in her cheek. She tucks another braid into the scarf and jerks her chin toward Tiernan. "Practice on your man."

I glance at Tiernan, who pales, and my heart sinks. I can't do that to him—we're hardly even on speaking terms at the moment.

Chiyo waves to catch my attention and says, "What about on me? Or Isobel? Or Sloan?" Bless her for trying to spare me the awkwardness of this.

Ava shakes her head. "No. Tiernan is the Mind Whisperer and the Empath. They're a match made for this twisted situation. Tiernan, you know how mind magics work ... use it."

I press my hands over my cheeks as if it could stop the heat from infiltrating. I half expect Tiernan to look away, but he doesn't. Our gazes align, and there are so many emotions in his face, in the tension of his posture ... I can't handle it with everyone looking at us.

I turn to walk away, but Tiernan's hand lands lightly on my shoulder. I face him, though the movement is a little too quick for my head. But I don't allow him to see the dizziness that immediately sets my vision wavering.

Until he signs something, and I miss what he says. I close my eyes and his hand envelops mine, giving it a little squeeze. His expression is drawn with worry when I look at him again. "What do you need?"

I tug my hand away. "Nothing." I've tried so hard to connect with him, while he's hardly told me anything about himself. Yes, I know about Maura, but that's the extent of things.

He steps a little closer. "Can we talk? Privately? Or do you need me to drop to my knees right here in front of everyone and beg your forgiveness? I will, you know."

His eyes crinkle at the corners, but I avert my gaze. I sense a shift in my peripheral vision. Then ... Oh gods, he's not really—

"Tiernan, no," I say, grabbing his arms as he's about to take a knee.

He pauses mid-kneel and straightens up again. Though he maintains a straight face, his lips twitch, dark eyes twinkling. I scowl at him to keep from laughing at his restrained amusement.

"We can talk. Just, please don't draw any more unnecessary attention to us."

My hands are still gripping his biceps, and he's standing so close, his head inclined to mine. I want to kiss him and tell him everything's fine.

I release him. I can't keep sweeping the unpleasant moments under the rug. Without another word, we walk off together, stepping away from the others and behind scraggly bushes that barely provide any privacy.

Tiernan draws in a deep breath and runs his hand down his face before sitting in the gravelly dirt and patches of grass. I sit in front of him when prompted.

"I never wanted to shut you out," he signs gently. "I just ..." He hesitates, his hand moving to the side of his neck where the scar mars his otherwise smooth, fair skin. "You accidentally walked into my dream back in Paramount, and other times since," he motions. "I'd like to willingly let you in. To show you my past."

I try not to look surprised, but my brows lift of their own volition. "Are you certain? I'm not even sure if I can—"

He takes my hand and kisses my fingers before pressing my palm against the scar vining up his neck. His eyes close, and I allow myself a brief moment to admire the contours of his face, the stubbly line of his jaw. There are more silver streaks in his hair now than when I'd first met him.

With a deep breath, I close my eyes and lower my shields, letting his magic flow through me as surely as I let mine flow through him. Our powers twine around each other, his warm aura mingling with my shadows and stars, and slowly I tumble into his past, into the Fortress on the Mount.

Tiernan is dressed in the brown livery of the Royal Brigade, his hair cut short, only the beginnings of silver at his temple. There's a smile on his face and warmth in his eyes. His fingers lace with those of a tan-skinned woman, her hair like the darkest copper tied back with black ribbon. Maura, like Tiernan, wears the Royal Brigade uniform with a sword strapped securely to her hip. Her regalia lacks the badges displayed on Tiernan's chest, but her body language shows no hint of subordination. They chat with Alys, whose hair is more pepper than salt but her face is otherwise unchanged from the Alys I know.

Tiernan places a hand on Maura's flat abdomen as they share the good news. Anxiety and excitement mingle with tender warmth—shared emotions from the happy duo—hang in the air. Alys grins, congratulating them both.

Something shifts in the atmosphere as a younger Carys barges into the infirmary. Her disposition is far more uncontrolled than the Carys I've met. Alys starts to introduce her to Tiernan and Maura, but Tiernan's mind is pulled from the conversation, his empathy senses reaching out to somewhere beyond the infirmary. The door pelts open with a loud bang, and the pounding of footsteps fills the space. Royal Brigade soldiers storm in, weapons ready.

A roughhewn band of blue fabric is tied around each of their biceps—a subtle but loud demonstration of revolt. Tiernan draws his sword and shoves Maura behind him, but she bats him away, struggling to pull something from the pocket of her livery. Panic and guilt pulse from her rather than surprise or fear.

"Stand down!" Tiernan commands the soldiers he outranks. Archers aim their arrows at Carys. She barely has a chance to yelp before Tiernan leaps in front of her.

The arrow meant for the princess barely misses his heart. Red-hot pain sparks to life as another arrow sails by.

The next spike of pain spears into Tiernan's abdomen. He looks down only to find no other injury. Fear and agony slam into him. His eyes land on Carys crouched on the floor with her hands over her head and Maura on her knees, a soundless gasp on her lips. Blood pools through her fingers pressed against her middle. It flows from her mouth. She collapses to the floor, gasping for air, blood gurgling in the back of her throat.

Shouts echo all around them as Alys attends to Maura and Carys cowers on the floor. Tiernan's eyes dart between the future of Erleya and *his* future. The love of his life. Pain far greater than the arrow in his chest weighs on him even as he jumps in front of Carys yet again.

His sword slices one of the traitorous soldiers across the arm.

Blood spurts and the woman clutches at the wound. "Don't move!" Tiernan shouts to Carys. He fights to shut his senses off, her terror nearly rendering him powerless. Another arrow strikes his thigh as he charges at the archer. Tiernan thrusts his sword through the stocky man's middle and yanks the blade free in time to block another attack from the left. Anger and grief fuel his movements, his strikes and stabs hard and ruthless.

The soldiers lay either dead or incapacitated around him. Tiernan scrambles to Maura's side, falling to his knees opposite Alys as the Royal Guards rush in. As the life drains from Maura's eyes along with the anticipation of the child she'd been carrying.

"Alys," Tiernan chokes out over the calamity. "Can you—?"

Alys shakes her head. "You however ..." Her eyes assess Tiernan's injuries. The arrow jutting from his chest, the steady flow of blood from where he'd yanked the other shaft from his thigh.

He strokes Maura's lifeless face.

The memory dissolves, the infirmary disappearing only to be replaced by a cold, dark room with a single oil lamp flickering behind Tiernan.

He's strapped to a chair, ropes securing his wrists, his torso bare to reveal his arrow scar. A brawny man with dark hair looms over him with a wickedly sharp dagger.

"Who organized the attack on Princess Carys?" the man asks. He wears a Royal Brigade uniform with too many badges and patches to count. A domineering aura surrounds him.

"I've told you," Tiernan says. "I don't know. Commander Rheon, I had nothing to do with it."

The commander demands incessantly, and Tiernan repeatedly denies it. Rheon strikes him with such force that the sound echoes through the room. Tiernan's lip splits, his face swells. Yet not one tear slips free from his eyes.

"You are the greatest soldier I have trained in recent years, Kilkenny. It's a damn shame. You remind me of myself as a lad."

Tiernan's jaw twitches, the heat of his anger surpassing the numbness from his grief.

"You had so much ahead of you, but then you sided with the radicals. I'll give you one more chance. Who else identifies with the rebel cause? Give me one name and I will end this. You can serve out the rest of the days with the Veilguards. If not, you will be flogged in the square tomorrow, then hanged for treason."

Tiernan's heart stings like a fresh wound. His coarse voice wavers as he says, "Maura McKenzie."

Ire flares in Commander Rheon's eyes. He presses the tip of the dagger over the scabbed wound of Tiernan's previous arrow injury, then draws it slowly up. It leaves a trail of blood in its wake, carving over his collarbone and up his neck. Tiernan's muffled grunts turn into groans and then cries of pain. He tries his hardest not to thrash but tugs against his bindings, causing even greater pain.

I don't want to see any more.

I can't do this.

I can't see him in this pain.

Falling back into my own body, I sever the connection, the anguish of Tiernan's memories mirrored in my body. I want to comfort him, but I'm still reeling. I wrap my arms around myself, feeling the squeeze of my hands, and I inhale the mossy dampness of the forest until I'm able to peel my eyes open.

I find Tiernan's still shut, a single tear streaking down his face. "Oh, Tiernan." I feel my voice break. As I embrace him, the echo of physical pain in my body dies down, replaced with his grief and fear. I keep my arms around him, never wanting to let go. Never wanting him to experience that again, not even in his memories.

I'm not sure how long we remain like that before I pull back slightly, pressing my forehead to his. "I'm so sorry," I whisper to him. "I'm so, so sorry." I can only imagine how terrifying everything must be for him. His own commander did that to him, and now ... Now he's the bloody sovereign of this land. I tuck some of Tiernan's silver strands behind his ear, my fingers lingering on his face.

He nods, pain still etched into his features, his eyes still brimming. "There's more I want to tell you, but *please* be patient with me."

I nod. "Thank you for even being willing to share with me."

Chapter 34

DURVLA

WE LET the moment simmer and settle, remaining in silence for a while after Tiernan reveals his memories of Maura and of his torture. When he's ready, we stand among the bushes near the river and he says, "Try to replicate what you did to Ava." He walks backward several paces from me and stands there almost as if in surrender. My stomach quivers—I don't want to repeat what I did to Ava. Not with anyone, but especially not with Tiernan. "It's alright," Tiernan says.

I nod and take a deep breath, getting into a stance with my feet shoulder width apart and my hands at the ready. I extend my arms toward Tiernan, and shadows snake up his body. They hold him in place as I try to force myself into his memories. His mental shield is as solid as a fortified wall, and as much as I push, I can't seem to get through it.

I grunt in frustration. "I can't do it."

"Yes, you can," he says.

Stepping back, I release the darkness and shake my hands out. I inhale slowly and hold my breath before exhaling as Tiernan waits with the utmost patience. Finally, I lift my hands, sending ribbons of dark vapor toward Tiernan, envisioning myself breaking through a wall. The tiniest crack appears in the fortification of his mind.

Yes!

Quickly, I grab whatever I can—an opposing soldier slicing him through a weak spot in his armor. War? I don't dwell on the specifics. I tug on the memory, forcing the pain on him. As soon as he winces, however, my hold on him fails.

I run toward him. "Tiernan! I'm so sorry!"

He grimaces, a hand on his upper arm. "Durvla, don't be. That was great." He shakes out his arms. "Do you have it in you to try again?"

"I don't want to hurt you."

"It's not permanent. I'll be fine." He steps away from me, preparing for an attack.

I sigh and step back as well. This time as soon as my shadows have a hold on him, rather than search his mind for a memory, I draw from my own. The last vertigo episode I had months ago in Moicriach. It isn't hard for me to remember the piercing headache, the nausea, the dizziness—I gather it all and shove it through the barrier of Tiernan's mind.

He drops to his knees, the heels of his hands pressed to his temples. I release my hold. Weakness courses through me. I stagger back, pressing my hands against the trunk of a tree and forcing my uneven breaths to stabilize.

Tiernan sits back on his ankles. His face is a little green, and he swallows hard as he wraps an arm around his stomach. It takes him a moment before he pushes to stand, and even then, he sways on his feet. He blinks a few times before approaching me. "Bloody hells, woman." His shaky hands rest on my shoulders. "You. Are. Brilliant." Then concern flickers in his eyes, coexisting with pride. "Are you alright?"

"I don't like doing that. I *hate* inflicting pain."

"That's what differentiates you from other Basduunai." He smiles. "You only need to use this when absolutely necessary. And now you know that you *can*—"

A firm tug comes from within me. A longing to be elsewhere. Light brown hair and a beautiful face twisted by pain floods my mind. As usual, she's standing in the middle of a forest, staring at an enormous tree. There's an ethereal mist around her and a winding river through the trees. I see it as if I'm hovering in the air, staring down at the land. The vision disappears and I sway on my feet as I recall the map that we've stared at so often.

It feels like the air has been knocked out of me. *Winnie*. Oh my gods ... "Oh my gods!" I shout.

"Durvla, what is it?" Tiernan's eyes are wide with concern.

My hand moves to my pocket, the moonstone suddenly heavy against my thigh. It's been in my pack for most of the journey, but I wanted to meditate with it after training with Tiernan. The last time I'd kept this stone near me, I'd also felt this strange *tugging*, I'd seen the tree, I'd seen Winnie. My mouth falls open. *Oh no ...*

"I have a theory that no one will like," I gesture.

"What is it?"

"It's about Siad Nahar. I don't think we can get in on our own. Remember how Carys mentioned that it only welcomes certain people? I think it also calls to them ... and I know someone it calls to. That woman I dreamt of back in the Verge? Winnie? I think I need to daywalk to her to get answers. And—" I pull the moonstone from my pocket, still wrapped in the kerchief. "I have a theory about this ... I may be grasping at straws but ... Will you stay with me while I try to daywalk to her?"

"Of course!" Tiernan signs.

I sit down, crossing my legs, and he sits in front of me. I remove the stone from the handkerchief and clasp it between my hands. My eyes lift from the stone to Tiernan's face, and he gestures, "Go on. I'll be right here."

I close my eyes and count each inhalation and exhalation until my pulse slows and my surroundings fade. I think of Winnie and, very slowly, her presence filters into my mind.

The feel of her fragmented aura crawls against my skin, but I hold on to the recurrent image of the forest.

She isn't there, but I call to her. "Winnie?"

Slowly, she materializes, confusion painted on her face. Her light brown hair is swept up into a messy bun with wavy strands falling over her forehead. Paint smears her dark skin across her neck and cheek. She glances down at her hand where she still clutches her paintbrush, her bewilderment tangible. "Realms, I don't think I'll ever get used to this."

I smile, trying not to appear as nervous as I feel. "Me neither, honestly." I glance toward the tree. "Have you always had dreams of this tree? Where is it located?"

She tucks her paintbrush behind her ear and slides her hands over the front of her dress. "Since ... a year ago. And I'm not sure."

"Do you ever have the urge to leave your home? To follow some ... invisible force?"

She nods, her caramel eyes wide. "How did you—?"

"Have you had that feeling lately?"

She doesn't respond.

My teeth sink into my lower lip as I try to think of a casual way to ask one last question. "Do you have a special stone? I have a moonstone. It's not until after it was in my possession that I began sharing your dreams."

She steps closer again, nodding. "Actually, I do. It's—" Her hand moves to the pocket of her dress, pressing against it. "I've anchored it to something dear to me, but yes, I do have a stone. I don't know anything about it. I don't even know how I got it. I just ... woke up one day and it was in my hand."

I feel my brows pucker. "That's odd."

"There is no shortage of odd things happening to me, quite frankly."

I laugh softly. "I can relate." I mull over my thoughts for a moment. "I've never accidentally dreamwalked to someone I didn't know until this stone. And only when I see you in my mind's eye do I get images of a tree, of a strange place. My guess is that it's a land called Siad Nahar. Have you heard of it?"

Her entire body stiffens as her face goes ashen.

"Winnie?"

I don't miss the tremor in her hands as she clutches the part of her skirt where I'm guessing she keeps this item dear to her. The ground beneath me begins to quake. I plant my feet firmly, having nothing to grasp. Winnie's fists are clenched as she takes a step back, then another. Fissures split the soil of the dreamscape, traveling between us and creating a rift that widens.

"Winnie?" I call out as she squeezes her eyes shut. "I'm sorry if I've upset you!"

I step away from the rift, but the whole dream is rumbling, debris falling from above. I beg Winnie to calm down, but she doesn't seem to be listening. Uncertain of how this will end if I keep holding on, I breathe out and release my hold on the dream.

I wake with a gasp, immediately pushing backward on my bottom to escape the threat.

"*Durvla! You're alright!*" Tiernan's voice shouts in my mind, making me wince.

I blink rapidly and adjust to the sights around me. No debris, no fissure, no Winnie.

There are mountains and slender trees all around us. I tune in to the feel of the ground beneath me, of Tiernan's arm around me, and the crisp mountain air. I turn my face toward the blue sky, the fluffy clouds floating by without a care in the world.

When I feel less shaky, I look at Tiernan again. "She's a Terraforger."

Tiernan's eyes widen.

"I think she's how we can get into Siad Nahar. It explains why we can't get to it when, according to the map, we're *right here*." I gesture to the mountains in the general vicinity.

"You're telling me we need her to literally move a mountain?"

I shrug. "Or perhaps make a path through it?"

Tiernan seems lost in thought, his eyes looking past me. "Well fuck, Ava is going to *love* this," he says.

I grimace. "Well, no point in stalling, right?" I wrap the stone and slip it back into my pocket. Together, we head back to the others.

Ava rises from where she was sitting as soon as she spots us and makes her way toward me. Her face is expectant, and I'm already terrified to break the news to her.

I wrap my arms around myself, and before I lose my courage, I spit the words out. "We can't get into Siad Nahar on our own."

Ava frowns. "What the fuck is that supposed to mean?"

Everyone looks our way, and I fight the urge to sink into myself, to retreat. Instead, I stand my ground and pull the kerchief from my pocket, slowly unwrapping it to reveal the stone. "Your father gave this to me." *Our father.* "And since then, I've had these dreams of a woman named Winnie. At first, I thought it was just my own subconscious, but she's a real person. A Terraforger."

I must speak loud enough, because it draws everyone's attention.

"That's ... unlikely." Ava says, crossing her arms. "There's not been a documented Terraforger for gods know how long."

"Not long ago, I thought all Mages were extinct."

"This is different. Terraforgers were the main Mages wiped out in the original Purge. When the floor and shit starts moving indoors, people get suspicious quickly. It's difficult for a Terraforger to conceal their powers without proper control."

I let her words sink in for a moment. "Well ... Given that she just set off an earthquake and nearly tore apart my entire dreamscape from the ground up, I'd say she's a Terraforger. When I mentioned Siad Nahar to her, she panicked. I'm certain she knows *something*, and it terrifies her. And I'm certain that we're right where it should be, but we can't get in because these mountains are impenetrable. It explains so much. Why no one has heard about Terraforgers for years. Maybe they were the only ones who could get in."

Ava taps her hand against her elbow with agitation, her arms crossed even tighter. She mutters what I'm sure is a series of swear words then heaves a sigh.

"What does this all mean?" Isobel asks.

"It means we've wasted time and resources," Ava snaps.

Guilt heats my cheeks and neck. I resist the urge to retreat, but tears sting my eyes. It means that I've led everyone on a pointless mission.

"Perhaps we haven't wasted anything," says Sloan. Their calculating blue-grey eyes settle on me. "This was a quest for knowledge. We've not only learned a lot about the Purists and the state of things, but now we know more than we did before about Siad Nahar. If Durvla's right about this, we also know there's a living, breathing Terraforger in Mainland. And we know that the moonstone can work as a sort of ... connection to her."

Osheen says something, and when I look his way, he says, "Like the vanishing stones."

All eyes snap to him.

"What are *you* talking about now?" Ava asks.

Osheen turns to Sloan and asks, "You took a couple of rings off the Purists back outside of Diadun, right? They're vanishing stones."

Sloan reaches into their pocket and pulls out two black onyx stones.

"It doesn't have magical properties by itself, but apparently it takes imbuement very well. In this case, it amplifies powers. But not in the way you'd expect, I guess. Those who already have an affinity to mind magic use it as a way to pass messages through a mental network. I'm not sure how that works, but—"

"Why is it called a vanishing stone?" Ava asks, too impatient to listen for much longer.

"So, Dispellers can transport themselves from one point to another, right? The same goes for the power of the vanishing ring. It's how the Purists of higher station travel through Erleya—it's like moving through shadows. But the rings have limits. They only last for as long as the magic imbued in them lasts. I'm not sure if that moonstone works the same way, but the connection seems similar. Except, instead of having any mind magic, it works for you because you have dream magic."

Ava turns and stalks off with steps that appear thunderous, both hands atop her head. Chiyo glances toward her, then back to me and Tiernan.

"Do you know where this Terraforger is?" Chiyo asks.

I nod. "Barr na Cahar." Everyone's face drops. Even Ava stops marching off and spins to face me. She clenches her jaw so tightly that I'm almost certain it hurts.

"Grab the map," she says to no one in particular.

A while later, we're all crowded around the map atop a fallen tree trunk. We are in a series of mountain ranges toward the east.

"The closer we get to Mainland, the greater the chance of danger," Sloan says.

Ava and Tiernan exchange a look—something I cannot quite decipher. Then Ava says, "We'll do what we have to. You're not afraid of danger, are you Sloan?" She pins an intense glower on the warrior.

"No, Warden." Their single hand runs through scarlet hair,

making it stick out awkwardly. "I would gladly run headfirst into danger if needed."

Isobel lifts an eager hand. "I second that!"

Chiyo laughs. "We know you're fearless, Isobel."

The redhead beams, but Ava's face only grows more sullen as she turns to me again. "Are you certain about all of this?" she signs. "That this is our ticket to Siad Nahar?"

"I'm not certain of that, but it's the only heading we have."

Ava closes her eyes as if paying for patience. "But you're certain she's in Barr na Cahar."

"Yes. Unfortunately." I'm aware that the city is right in the heart of Mainland, the closest to Paramount and, therefore, the most dangerous.

Ava sighs and points to the map at the mountain range that we're nearest to. "There seems to be a pathway that leads straight to Dubh Carrig. We don't have the supplies to scale this damn mountain range, so everyone better start praying that this pathway hasn't been eroded or something. If it has, we'll have to backtrack into Diadun and start again."

If anything, Chiyo looks more excited. "At least we know we'll have a place to stop in Dubh Carrig," she says. She looks to Tiernan and smiles, a warmth flooding her eyes.

But I groan inwardly. I've led us here, indeed wasted precious time—*three weeks*—and resources, plus set everyone on edge. Perhaps I should've insisted on gathering even more information before leaving the Verge. We could've had more time in comfort. I could've had more training.

"I'm sorry," I say, tears clinging to my eyelashes. I get to my feet quickly before the tears can fall. The throb in my head intensifies.

Between the dreamwalking, training, and this travel, my body is sick and tired of me. I just want to be back home in the Verge with Taig and the others.

As I walk away, pain stabs through my head and my vision swims. Tiernan appears in front of me, scaring me half to death. I press my hand against my stomach as nausea threatens to empty it. As much as I want to hide it—to pretend that I'm well—it wouldn't do anyone any favors if my ailment flares and I collapse or decline into a full episode.

I open my eyes when I feel Tiernan's gentle grasp on my upper arms. "You should sit down," he says as my body goes warm and clammy at the same time.

He helps me to the ground. I press my head between my knees and remain sitting there with his arm around my upper back. Slowly, I breathe in and out as the ground seems to move beneath me, as my head throbs, and my mouth waters unpleasantly. I have only a few more tinctures left. I've been using them sparingly, but in the constant activity of today, I forgot to take one.

A gentle squeeze and a prod of Tiernan's power against my mind has me lifting my head, but instead of Tiernan's face, I find Alys's. My eyes burn from the overwhelming headache rapidly intensifying. I squint and swallow the bitterness that rises in my throat.

"May I?" Alys asks, holding up her hand. Light already shimmers on her thick fingers.

"Please," I sign silently.

Alys's fingertips gently rest on my temples and my eyes close. The cool sensation morphs into warmth, the piercing ache in my skull fading to a dull throb. The nausea slowly dissipates and the dizziness settles. I release a deep breath of relief and reopen my eyes. Alys sits back on her ankles, looking absolutely worn. She blinks, sluggishly at first, then a little more alert as she asks, "Better?"

I nod, though guilt gnaws at me. "Thank you."

She smiles. "No thanks needed, sweetling."

Tiernan helps her up as she starts to get unsteadily to her feet, then he helps me up. I study Alys, noting her weariness.

Again, I feel awful. This could ruin everything, and suddenly, all the answers about the prophecy and every chance that we should have to help the state of Erleya seem farther away than ever.

Chapter 35

MY HANDS WON'T STOP SHAKING as I stare at the canvas. What started off as a painting of that damn tree is now a series of incoherent brush strokes. The moment my brush touched the canvas, my mind fell into a dreamscape. At least it seems that I didn't actually terraforge anything given that everything is still intact around me. My heart races as I replay the Dreamwalker's words.

Siad Nahar. I've heard the name a few times from the Purists. The fools are obsessed with this mysterious place—and I'm convinced it's purely myth. Even though Nimue claims she's been there. That the main ingredient of the Cleanse is straight from the River Daehan.

Again, nothing but folklore.

I set the ruined canvas aside and pick up a fresh one, placing it on the easel. I lift my paintbrush again and try to envision what I want to draw. Time ticks by, and the next thing I know, grey paint is smeared across my canvas in the likeness of a figure with a tattered cloak. Eyes like shards of ice peer out from beneath a hood, white hair spilling out. In angry, grey strokes the word *Beware* is written—though I don't remember writing it.

A flash of an image fills my mind—a black-cloaked figure with glowing red eyes and a flaming axe. With a gasp, I reel back and nearly fall off my chair—my knee hits the canvas instead and, with a loud crash, the easel and canvas fall to the ground.

I leap to my feet just as there's a knock on the door. Snatching the canvas from the floor, I flip it, holding it so that the image is hidden.

A concerned servant peeks into the room. "Lady Gwyneth, is everything alright?"

"Yes," I say around the boulder in my throat. "Just a clumsy moment. Everything is fine."

"She's a liar, you know," a voice calls from outside. The door is pushed open wider, and Neris stands in the doorway, twirling some of her blond hair around her finger.

The servant curtsies and dismisses herself, rushing off while I do nothing but clutch the canvas to my dress. I'm certain by now I've smeared paint all over my clothing.

Neris's brows furrow. "Are you having those visions again?"

"I—Well, I was drawing. Then suddenly, I'm staring at ..." I turn the canvas to face her, wincing in advance. I'm prepared for Neris to ask me what horrors I've committed to canvas, but instead, she simply stares at it, puzzled.

"Winnie, it's blank."

"No, it's not. There's—"

She snatches the canvas from my hands and holds it up so it's facing me.

There's not even one brushstroke.

"But—" My eyes dip down to my dress. There's no paint smeared on the violet silk. Squinting at the canvas, I try to make sense of how it's a white ground rather than the horrifying image of the icy-eyed old hag.

Neris sets the canvas aside as I scrub my hand down my face. "Come on," she says. "Our carriage awaits. We have a delivery to make to Lord Owen."

Owen is our oldest and most loyal book collector. The old man always appreciates personal deliveries from Neris and I rather than having us send it via a delivery service. Normally, I look forward to witnessing the old man's excitement for a new book, but right now I cannot get my mind away from the images I swore were on the canvas. Hopefully this trip will distract me enough to collect my sanity.

The fresh air is a welcome distraction as Neris and I walk through the city after our delivery. It's a tad warmer today, allowing us to leave our coats in the carriage, but the gentle breeze that blows through our hair every now and then is on the chilly side. So strange for midsummer.

The atmosphere in Barr na Cahar is austere. Peacekeepers are posted on almost every corner, black uniforms standing out against the grey and red stone of the buildings around us. Their swords and crossbows are a loud warning. Nervous energy runs through me, making my palms sweat and my legs shake.

"I hate this," Neris whispers beside me. "Walking in the city used to be fun. Now ..." She glances around, her hands firmly clasped in front of her as though she's some demure highborn. Perhaps I should do the same.

I grip the strap of my satchel with both hands as we walk. "Do you think things will ever return to normal?"

Neris scoffs. "Winnie, things weren't normal in the first place." She's quiet for a moment before speaking again, her voice a mere whisper. "Are you going to answer the sovereign's call for Mages?"

My head whips to her. "Of course not."

If she notices the quiver in my voice, she doesn't say anything. "What if Sovereign Rheon truly does give you immunity?" she asks. "You could be rid of this lifestyle. Rid of your Gruff husband for more than just a few nights." She smirks at her own *Gruff* joke again, and my gut clenches with a mixture of revulsion and uneasiness.

"I don't know if it would be much better than Gruffud."

"Exactly. You *don't* know, Winnie. When are you going to stop being afraid to step out of your comfort zone?"

I halt in the middle of the pedestrian walk, but I wait to speak again as a couple of women in long gowns walk past us. "When are you going to stop lecturing me? Living with the Pendrys is not a comfort zone, it is a safe zone."

She purses her lips, skepticism painting her features. "You're telling me you feel *safe* with Gruffud." Her tone is more sardonic and definitive than it is a question.

"Safer than walking into an unknown situation beneath the damn *sovereign*. Did you forget the mass floggings five years ago by his hand, Reneris?"

"No, but—"

"*But* nothing." I start walking again, though Neris doesn't follow. Eventually, I hear the pounding of her shoes against the stones as she catches up with me. We walk in silence, stopping to look in a few shop windows as if we didn't nearly get into a big argument.

In one window, a gaudy necklace with square-cut emeralds set in gold rests in a velvet box interior. It's either brave or foolish of the shop owners to leave such a worthy piece of jewelry temptingly visible for thieves. Or perhaps they're willing to take the risk in hopes of luring in more affluent customers.

Another window displays pottery that looks no different from the dishware I've seen in other households around here. Unimaginative, like everything else in this godsforsaken city. Not like the beautiful vase Murtagh once brought as a gift, a piece he acquired from traveling tradesmen.

As we walk past a small alley between two shops, a cry of pain meets my ears. Neris glances around and another cry twists my gut like a knife. I peer into the alley where a plump man is slumped against the wall, clutching his chest with one hand and his head with the other.

Before I can say anything to Neris, she peels off, running into the space between the two buildings and dropping in front of the man. His skin is nearly as pale as the cloudy sky. Sweat sticks his dark hair to his forehead and a stream of ruby red flows from his nose, down his neck. His eyes are bloodshot ... or bloodied?

Breathing becomes a challenge for me, and Neris's words only make it harder. "Winnie, I think he's had the Cleanse."

I cannot stop my mind from skidding into the past. I grapple with myself to stay in the present, but I'm pulled away by the memories, and it's as if I'm the one lying there on the cold ground, bleeding out, bleeding within.

"Winnie!" Neris's voice snaps me back to our surroundings. I drop down beside her.

"Please," the man says, his breath rattling in his chest, blood dribbling from his lips. "Kill me."

Neris looks at me with tears swimming in her eyes. "What can we do?"

I shake my head. My body was healing itself by the time Neris found me in the same state as this man. I'm certain that someone else had been there. Otherwise, there's no way I would've survived the Cleanse.

"Winnie!"

"I don't know, Neris!" I shout back.

The man claws at his chest, his head, his eyes—only deep, sobbing breaths leave his lips as he rocks back and forth, writhing endlessly. I know just how he feels; like there's glass in his lungs and fire in his veins. Like his brain is boiling and his heart being wrung. It's unbearable. Unfathomable. Enough to drive a person to madness if it doesn't kill them first.

Neris shakes my shoulder as the man starts to scream. If he draws more attention, we could be blamed for this. "I know it hurts, but the Peacekeepers will hear you."

He swallows down another cry with a whimper, his bloodshot eyes bulging.

"Did you drink something?" I ask him.

The man is unable to respond. He coughs and sputters, and I close my eyes as blood splatters against my skin.

It's a feat not to draw back in repulsion. I focus on his face, on his body language. He continues to writhe, his eyes closed, nothing but groans and incoherent words leaving his lips.

His breathing remains erratic for a while longer before stillness settles in. His breaths become labored, wet and rasping, until his chest stops moving altogether. His head drops to his chest, his shoulders slumping forward.

Neris releases a small sob, but no other sound escapes her. She yanks a handkerchief from her pocket to scrub her face before standing. "Get up, Winnie," she says. There's a low, definitive tone to her voice. Beneath the underlying quiver is more strength than I have.

I just sit there, staring at the man, at the blood crusted on his face and clothes. That could've been me. If someone hadn't saved my life, if Neris hadn't found me. "We couldn't help him." The words slip out. Flat. Numb.

"Get up."

My entire body is numb.

A vise-like grip wraps around my bicep. Somehow, she tugs me to my feet. "Listen to me," Neris says. "You did all you could. Now ..." She stuffs the handkerchief into my fist. "Let's get out of here before we're pinned with his murder."

Chapter 36

IT TAKES ABOUT twenty minutes for us to arrive at the Pendry household. A carriage waits outside, but it isn't the one that we took to get into the city. Strange.

"Come inside and clean up," I tell Neris. "I'll loan you one of my dresses."

Her lips tug up in a halfhearted, crooked smile. "Lovely, a too-short hem and too-roomy bodice," she says, but the joke falls flat. Even to her.

We rush inside, closing the door behind us and heaving a sigh of relief when no one greets us. "Come on," I whisper as we speedwalk into the dining room, past servants, and up the stairs. My heart is racing by the time I'm standing in front of Gruffud's bedchamber. "Hopefully he's not home yet," I whisper. "Wait here. I'll just quickly check."

I open the door and step into the room to find that Gruffud is indeed there. He's in bed, but not alone. His hands grip a woman's voluptuous hips, urging her on. Her breathy moans fill the chamber, tight coils of ebony hair bouncing against her bare back with each motion.

My world halts.

The air leaves my lungs. My blood heats and my stomach churns. A familiar plum-colored dress is discarded on the floor. I drag my eyes from the garment and back up to Arionna riding my husband in my marital bed.

They're so caught up in the throes of passion that they don't notice me standing here. When Gruffud's eyes open to behold his paramour, he does a doubletake. His cold gaze snaps to me, flaring wide with alarm.

"Gwyneth," he growls.

Arionna stops moving and throws a glance over her bare shoulder. Her gasp cuts through my disbelief as she dives off Gruffud and drags the bedcovers over her body. Gruffud has no such modesty; he leaps off the bed naked as he storms toward me. I dash into the corridor where Neris waits. She barely has a chance to look confused before Gruffud grabs me by the wrist, wrenching me back against his lanky frame.

"Unhand me!" I shout as he spins me to face him. His slap comes with such speed that I don't have a chance to block it. Pain bursts in my cheek and lip.

"Winnie!" Neris shouts.

Before my head even clears, I'm shoved back against the wall, Gruffud's forearm pressed against my windpipe. I *should* be able to get out of his grasp easily. But the edges of my vision blur, logic lost amid the panic. I struggle against him, tugging on his arm, trying to get out from his grip.

I need to calm down.

I drop my hands, allowing my powers to manipulate the bracelets on my wrist until I'm holding the smooth handle of a sharpened blade in my hand. But just as I'm about to drive the dagger home, Gruffud's crushing weight diminishes.

He's dragged off me, allowing precious air to pour back into my lungs. The dagger practically melts out of shape as I shove it into my pocket. My vision wanes but I can hear a kerfuffle—grunts of pain and dull strikes against flesh.

Guzzling air, my hand to my throbbing neck, I stare down at the scene unfolding before me. Neris is sitting on Gruffud's bare stomach, firing punches at him while he defends his pretty face.

My heart clenches, driving my pulse up. She cannot do this. Not without repercussions. "Neris, get off him!" Panic bubbles in my chest as I clench my fists and root my feet to the floor. My legs begin to quake, and Neris leaps off the naked Gruffud. They both look startled, and I realize it's not my legs shaking but the whole house.

Shite.

Neris cuts me a sharp look that says *control yourself*, as if she wasn't just pummeling Gruffud like a feral cat. I quickly tamp down on the involuntary flow of my terraforging, and the house stops shaking. "Neris, get out of here," I tell her. I mouth the next word: *run.*

She looks at me with wild eyes, a bloodied scratch on her cheek. She nods and runs faster than I knew she was even capable of. Hopefully she'll go to that spot in the forest where I often go to release pent-up magical energy. I could meet her there. We could figure out the next steps together.

Gruffud is still lying on his back, and a groan escapes him as he runs his hand over his face. He'll definitely have bruises. Plenty of them. Perhaps Father taught Neris to defend herself a little *too* well.

Arionna steps out into the corridor, fully dressed, as Gruffud gets to his feet. "She won't get away with this," he says, his long fingers pressed to his face.

My heart begins to pound again, and without further thought, I set off *running*. Down the stairs, out of the house.

My legs don't stop moving. It's though they've developed their own intellect. As though they're not even connected to me. Hot tears sting my face only to be immediately dried as the breeze blows against my skin.

I wrench the door open and tear into the house with heat in my veins and sweat streaming down my face. Mother leaps to her feet, a cup clattering onto the saucer on the tea table. "Gwyneth!" she exclaims.

My breaths come in ragged pants as I rush past her and up the stairs. I don't stop until I make it to my old room, where Neris has kept my belongings even after moving into it. Mother's footfalls trail me. "What has—" She stops abruptly, her eyes taking in my appearance as I turn to her. My name leaves her lips with a pained, breathless sound.

I turn away and step into the closet to grab a large bag. I throw a couple pairs of trousers and several tunics into the bag and move to my dresser to look for a spare comb and brush.

"What on earth happened? And what in the gods' names are you doing?"

I ignore her as I throw all the jewelry that I'd given Neris into the bag. We can sell them for coin.

"Gwyneth!"

"I'm leaving!" I shout back. My lip burns, the taste of blood on my tongue. "I will not remain married to an adulterous, abusive man!"

Mother goes silent and leans against the wall of my bedchamber as if she needs support. "What happened?" she enunciates, impatience flowing through her measured tone.

I consider telling her the truth, but a voice calls me from just beyond my door. "Gwyn! You cannot tell Moth—" Arionna stops abruptly and reels back, the whites of her eyes showing.

Mother turns her gaze to me instead. "Cannot tell me what?" she demands.

Arionna bites her lip and I meet her pleading gaze with cold fervor as I respond to Mother. "Ask *her*."

Mother's focus flicks to Arionna. "Speak."

My sister's dark complexion may hide her flushed cheeks, but her hair is atypically disheveled, her makeup smudged, her shoulders caving in beneath Mother's scrutiny. With my bag gripped tightly in my hand, I shoulder past Arionna.

As I rush down the stairs, Mother's voice trails after me. "I cannot allow you to leave!"

I arch my brows. "If you plan to bodily block me, you know I can easily get past you."

"They'll come after you," she says, as I step into the sitting room.

"I'd like to see them try."

"Gwyneth, you cannot do this. Not after all the sacrifices we've made—harboring you rather than turning you in."

I spin on my heel to face her. "My *sincerest apologies* for being born the way I was!" The words fly from my mouth far louder than I intend. They taste bitter rolling off my tongue.

Mother flinches, stepping back, and I almost feel bad. Quickly, she gathers her composure, but she looks frailer than ever.

"As for sacrifices, did *you* get married off like some prized cow? Did you endure nonstop insults from your husband while your mother asked you if you were satisfying him? Were you forced to bed someone because it was your marital duty, only to find him bedding another woman?"

For a moment, she struggles to find her words. But when she does, her voice is thick with emotion. "I protected you. Your whole life. I've done what's best for you. I—I covered for you when you couldn't control yourself. I lived in fear rather than allow them to take you away from me."

My throat swells, tears burning my eyes. I continue toward the door when a voice calls, "Wait!"

Arionna steps up beside Mother. "Neris is going to be flogged in the plaza," she says quietly.

My body turns cold, and Mother's head snaps to Arionna. "What?"

"They've already caught her." A plea shines in her dark eyes. My body feels numb, my heart pounding as though it would soon expel itself from my chest cavity.

"The carriage is still outside," Arionna continues. "The disciplinary display will be happening immediately."

Acid tries to crawl up my throat. I swallow forcefully, grimacing. Mother steps forward, but she doesn't say anything. Her throat bobs and tears fill her eyes.

I turn to Arionna, hardly able to see past the woman who I'd caught bedding my husband. The woman who's become more and more of a stranger to me over the years. She may have wronged me, but I still love her despite it all. I hate myself for that.

"Don't fall for his charade," I softly warn her. "He's going to hurt you."

She only pushes back her shoulders stubbornly, schooling her expression into nonchalance. Our mother's child. I scoff; why did I ever allow myself to feel even the slightest sympathy for her? She isn't the victim here.

I step out of the house and run toward the carriage, my satchel bumping against my hip. I'm not sure what my next step will be, but *somehow* I have to save Neris.

She's all I have left.

Chapter 37

GWYNETH

"PULL OVER HERE," I call out the window to the footman. He brings the horses to a halt, and before the carriage fully stops, I hop out. The air buzzes with anticipation, sounds of muddled conversations from every which way as people gather in the town square. I have to push my way through the crowd to get closer to the platform where the flogging will occur—where the sovereign announced his ascension two months ago.

My heart hiccups in my chest as a deep voice rings out, reading a list of misdeeds for a man handcuffed to the whipping pole. The sharp crack of the whip fills the air, the nauseating sound of leather meeting flesh and cries of pain following.

I don't look. I can't.

The cries die down and the limp victim is dragged away. The Peacekeeper announces a name that makes my heart come to a staggering halt. "Reneris Carlile."

I squint against the orange glare of the setting sun. Neris already sports several bruises on her body, evident on her arm through her torn sleeve and her once-unblemished face.

Heat flushes my entire body while the misdemeanors being read from a list barely infiltrate my mind. A soldier uses a knife to slice through part of the back of Neris's dress, then tears through the rest of it with her bare hands.

Neris presses her face against the whipping pole, as though she's embracing it. She squeezes her eyes shut, her entire face pinching tight. My heart pounds, nausea and heat percolating in my stomach.

The whip cracks again, and Neris cries out as the leather strap connects with her bare flesh. Then there's another whip. And another. And another, pulling a louder cry from her.

Neris has been my rock, yet I've failed to stand up for her when I needed to keep up appearances. I let Gruffud talk down to her and allowed Mother to treat her like a servant. Even after that, she still jumped in to save me from an ill-tempered Gruffud a head taller than her. She always chooses bravery when cowardice would be the safer alternative.

Heat seems to singe my skin as a dark figure walks across the dais. The murmurs from the crowd fade to unnatural silence as the figure drags her flaming axe along the platform, dark hair billowing out behind her in slow motion as if moving through water.

Do something, she hisses.

From somewhere behind me, a chill whispers across my neck along with another voice. *Violence is not the way*.

They will kill your friend, the armed figure says.

Mainland doesn't give a damn about half the people in this entire kingdom. Not Undesirables. Not lowborns. Hells, not even highborns.

I clench my fists, seeing red for the injustice of it all.

Neris is the kindest, most loyal person I know. I can't stand by and watch her be flogged to death.

The ground beneath me rumbles, and shrieks of terror break out all around me. Townspeople flee as the Peacekeepers' hold their weapons at the ready. I drop my bag and stomp, bringing up a portion of paved ground larger than my head. More screams resound as people dodge and cower. I send the chunk of earth into a Peace-keeper's stomach, propelling him backward. He doesn't get up again.

Another draws a crossbow, aiming at me until a chunk of earth crashes into her sneering face.

The town square clears with surprising speed as I send hunks of cobblestone flying at any official who tries to approach me. Until someone cloaked in red materializes on the dais seemingly out of nowhere, a limp body in a tattered pink dress as their shield. My eyes snap toward the whipping pole where blood stains the wood.

Neris is no longer there.

Instead, she's slumped against someone, a large dagger pressed to her neck from behind. I halt, hands raised, my terraforging keeping varying pieces of stone suspended in midair.

Golden details of the black mask over the figure's eyes almost glow in the sunset. A black veil covers the rest of their face. This is the same person who'd stood beside Sovereign Rheon on the day of his ascension. The person who now holds a dagger to Neris's throat. When the person speaks, it's with a woman's voice.

"I won't hesitate to slit her throat if you keep up this overpowered tantrum," she says.

I blink at her, furious, and release the hold on my magic. The stones drop. The ground of the square is destroyed—pulverized paving where there aren't craters. People cower, injured and terrified. I shake out my trembling arms and drag in a slow breath, pushing away the guilt that slowly seeps in along with fatigue.

"Come with us, peacefully, and your friend won't be hurt." The woman pauses. "Well ... more hurt."

Neris's breaths appear ragged and uneven, her eyes closed. Her hands are white knuckled on the cloaked woman's arm.

Palms up and out, I surrender. "Please, release her. We won't cause more trouble. If you just let us—"

"No," she interjects. I cannot see her face to know for sure if she's smiling, but I can *hear* it. "Come a little closer, Terraforger."

I step up onto the platform, each stair making my legs quiver more than the last. Another soldier approaches and my muscles tense, prepared for a fight.

"Ah, ah, ah," says the masked woman. "*Without* a fight, Terraforger."

I huff out a breath. "If you hurt her more, I *will* fight," I say tightly, even as my arms tremble with exhaustion.

Neris's eyelids flutter, and a small whimper escapes her swollen lip.

"Oh, I'm so very afraid," the woman says, boredom lacing her words. She glances at the soldiers but takes her dagger away from

Neris's throat. A small trickle of blood slides over Neris's skin. "Shackle the Terraforger," the woman orders.

Are they daft? They're going to shackle me knowing that I can likely bend metal? I almost want to laugh. But as the manacles encircle my wrists, an unbearable pressure pushes into my head, into my entire body. Everything goes still around me. The earth feels dead. The stones, cold. It's suffocating.

What in all the realms ...? I cast a frantic look at the figure, my breaths coming quickly now. "What did you—"

"Dampening runes. Not even *you* can get through those."

I swallow the acid creeping up my throat. "What's going to happen to us?"

"You're both coming to Paramount Castle, sweetheart," says the masked woman. The soldiers start pulling me away. "The sovereign has been waiting for you, you lucky, lucky thing." She clicks her tongue behind her veil. "I expected more, quite frankly. Someone ... taller, at least. Ah well, you can never judge a book by its cover, I suppose."

She grabs my arm and darkness presses in all around me. I'm suddenly tumbling, spinning, unsure of which way is up or down as my stomach twists and jolts. My body feels displaced in time—simultaneously heavy and light, but then the world stops spinning. I steel myself against the assault of queasiness as I'm now facing a large desk piled high with books and a wall of bookshelves behind it.

The room is illuminated with a mellow light, but there aren't any candles or oil lamps in sight. A bearded man sits behind the massive desk. He has dark hair, which is combed back away from his face, and deep blue eyes beneath thick scrunched eyebrows. He rises from behind the desk, brawny arms defined even beneath his livery. He doesn't look much different from the others who hold me captive, so it takes me a moment before I recognize him.

Sovereign Rheon Odhran.

My blood runs cold. Beside me, Neris drops to the floor like a ragdoll, the breath leaving her body before she goes completely rigid.

No ...

Before I can say anything, the unrestrained spasms begin. Her arms and legs jerk haphazardly. Violent quakes rack her body. The blood drains from her face, tiny whimpers forcing their way past blue-tinged lips as her eyes roll back in her head.

I step toward her only to receive a sharp jab to my stomach.

A cough is forced out of me as I double over while Neris continues to seize. "I have to help her!" I choke out. "She's not breathing!" The blue tinge is spreading from her lips to the rest of her face, her neck straining. My fists clench, but my powers don't answer me. It's a stillness—a level of control—that I've always craved, but now ... Realms, I feel powerless.

"Take that one to the infirmary," says the sovereign. His voice is cool, as if nothing out of the ordinary is occurring

He takes another step so he's towering over me. He nods to one of the soldiers who grabs Neris's body from the floor. The soldier disappears from the spot, leaving me with Sovereign Rheon, the masked woman, and the other soldier at my side.

"What is your name?" the sovereign asks.

My shoulders slump even as I try to push them back. "Gwyneth fa Eurig." The words slip out automatically, and I wince, shaking my head. My heart thrums faster. "*Pendry*," I correct. "Gwyneth Pendry of Barr na Cahar."

Recognition sparks in the sovereign's eyes. "fa Eurig. Any relation to Eurig Davies? Royal Guard?"

"Yes, Your ..."

"Excellency," he says with a smile that could curdle milk.

My hand starts to move to my pocket before I remember that my wrists are bound. "Yes, Your Excellency."

"Your family's name is renowned. So, I will give you the benefit of the doubt. I expect you can handle coming to an accord in a civilized fashion. This castle has been through enough; I doubt you want to reduce it to rubble. Especially with your father within its walls, yes?"

The threat rings loud and clear. "I can be civilized, Your Excellency."

"Outstanding. So, let's state the terms of our agreement before I have my enforcer release you from your bonds." He glances up, looking past me at someone. "Ah, Jac, just in time," he says.

I dare to turn my head as a young man with skin a shade darker than mine and red robes walks into the room. A stack of books and a couple scrolls are balanced in his arms.

Is this his enforcer?

"I need you to draft an agreement for me," says the sovereign.

"No problem, Your Excellency." The man hurries to the desk, preparing a quill and inkwell and laying out a fresh parchment, pinned down at the top and bottom with paperweights.

"I, Sovereign Rheon Odhran hereby declare that Gwyneth ... Pendry, is it?" He looks at me.

"Yes, Excellency."

"—be exempt from penalty provided that she joins the Zenith in its quest to restore balance to the realm and provide safety for Magekind."

My eyes bulge. Am I hearing correctly?

His gaze focuses on me again. "What are your conditions should I allow you to join our cause, Lady Gwyneth?"

Taking a breath and straightening my posture at the expense of more pain at my wrists, I say, "Safety for my friend. She was only trying to protect me from a threat in my own home. She is brave, clever, and has excellent baking and cooking skills. She can do anything asked of her with impeccable proficiency." I *hate* to paint her as a servant, but I'm desperate. "She also is a quick learner. She would make a fine scholar." She'll kill me.

Realms, I hope she's alive. Anxiety wraps its hateful fingers around my throat and squeezes.

At the same time, the sovereign grips my chin lightly, and my blood runs cold. My heart thuds wildly in my chest. He tips my face up to his, and I hold my breath. "Is this what she was protecting you from?" Rheon asks.

My brows pinch. With everything that occurred after catching Arionna and Gruffud, I'd long forgotten about Gruffud's impassioned blow. The sovereign's touch suddenly feels less daunting. "Yes, Your Excellency. My husband struck me, and Reneris stepped in to defend me."

"For what reason did your husband strike you?"

I try not to gape at him openly. There should be no reason that would justify anyone striking their partner, but alas. "I caught him bedding another woman."

Silence fills the space as the sovereign releases me. He steps back and addresses the man with the red robe. "Provided that Lady Gwyneth joins the Zenith—" His brow lifts. "What is your friend's full name?"

I lick my lips, feeling it split again. My mouth is horribly dry. "Reneris Carlile." The scratch of the assistant's pen follows.

"—Reneris Carlile is exempt from penalty," Rheon finishes. "You and Reneris will remain here at Paramount Castle until we can ensure your safety outside of these walls."

My legs go weak with relief. With a few more scratches of Jac's quill, he finishes drafting the agreement. The masked woman tugs me over to the desk by my manacle chains. Awkwardly, I take the quill the man offers me, chains clanging and shackles digging into the metal around my wrists. The quill hovers above the space where my signature will seal our fates.

I'm not the naive girl I used to be. I've already signed my soul away once before—for the chance at a cure, for normalcy—but in this instance, I'm hoping to buy myself some time to figure things out.

Perhaps I can find Father. Then I can get both him and Neris out of the castle. Hells, perhaps *he* could get us out of the castle. The quill feels heavy between my fingers. All I need to do is sign—an action that seems so harmless but holds so much power.

I look to the sovereign. "What exactly is expected of me if I join the Zenith?"

An odd smile stretches across his face. "We have a special mission for you. To find and bring more Wielders to safety."

I don't want to believe him. Not when I've seen the Erleya he's already created. I've seen the Peacekeepers at work, but could it be that he isn't aware of their doings? The Forayers have been known to go rogue.

Someone clears their throat—Jac—and I apologize quickly before taking a deep breath and slowly exhaling. Then, with my heart in my throat, I sign my soul away for the second time in my life.

Except this time, it's with the intention to get away.

Huddled in a corner, I wrap my arms around myself and rock back and forth as the memories infiltrate again and again. I've already joined a fanatic group out of desperation before; what makes the Zenith different?

Pulling myself together proves to be impossible as I sob into my knees until the muscles in my stomach are sore. This time, there's no Neris to comfort me. This time, I'm in the most luxurious place in all of Erleya, with two people who I love within the walls. Neris and Father.

My *father* is here.

With that sobering thought, I pluck my watch from my pocket and slide my thumb over the smooth surface.

I will find you, I think as I give the watch a little squeeze for luck and tuck it back into my pocket. I pick myself up from the floor and take a few calming breaths. There's plush carpet beneath my bare feet, sandstone-colored wall, and the floor is tiled with copper and blue. The bed is enormous, with delicate fabric draping across the posts. I head to the bathing chamber to splash tepid water on my face and hopefully stop myself from descending further into despair. I need to see Neris.

And I have to find Father.

Chapter 38

CARYS

I STARE out across the vast ocean beneath an intermittently cloudy sky for what feels like the thousandth time. A few paces from me, Seth and Valdis are lip-locked, practically devouring each other. I could leave, I could go below deck, but I'd rather not be alone with my own thoughts. Or worse, with a devastatingly attractive warrior prince.

Valdis's giggle is cut off by a small gasp. I swivel my head toward them as Seth drags his lips down her neck.

"By the gods, you two!" I exclaim.

Valdis turns to me, her eyes bright with amusement, a grin on her lips. Seth drops one last kiss onto her collarbone before slinging both arms around her waist and smiling at me. "Apologies, we'll behave," he says with a chuckle.

"Thank you."

But when I turn back to the ocean, Valdis giggles again.

I swear colorfully, but I don't even look at them this time. "You have a cabin below deck, don't you? I'd suggest going there."

"Sounds like you should take your own suggestion," Valdis says, and my gaze flicks to her as she winks at me. "Maybe you'll be less cranky if you ... release some of that tension. Alone or otherwise. No judgment."

"Val, leave her alone," Seth says, lacing their fingers as I glower at her. "Come on." He tugs her away.

If there's one thing I've learned about Valdis and Seth, it's that six years of marriage have done nothing to diminish their love for each other. They seem as passionate as forbidden lovers, as insatiable as newlyweds. It's not only their annoying public displays of affection, but the subtle, tender glances between them. Whether in the heat of battle or the banality of supper. They love each other with unwavering devotion and uncanny force.

It takes me a while to decipher the unpleasant heat that builds inside me each time I'm in the vicinity of their suffocating hunger for each other. But it's startlingly clear today.

It's *jealousy*. Ugly, unjustified jealousy.

"Gods, this journey is never-ending," I groan aloud, even though it's only been two weeks on the ocean.

"Take it as a quest for the virtue of patience." Briony's saccharine voice reaches my ears before she appears in my periphery.

Naturally, I startle.

"The ocean can be serene as easily as it can be tumultuous," she says, as if I hadn't nearly jumped out of my skin. "Beneath its surface is an entire unseen world—filled with both danger and beauty."

I turn toward her, my brows cinched. "What in hells are you rambling about, Briony?"

To my surprise, she laughs. It's lighthearted, like a bird's song way too early in the morning. "You tell me."

My eyes are in danger of falling out of my head for how hard I roll them. "You truly are *such* a priestess at times, you know?"

She shrugs and pushes her sandy brown hair over her shoulder.

"Briony, you never explained to me how you're a high priestess of Lugda *and* a Healer. The two don't seem compatible."

"I know. You'd be surprised how many things in life that seem incompatible are actually interconnected."

"Gods, please stop speaking in riddles. I don't have the ... virtue for this."

She smiles. "Alright, fair enough." She folds her arms atop the rail and gazes out at the blue-green water as though it holds all the answers. "Most know Lugda as the god of death but forget that he's also the god of fate. The Underworld has been portrayed as an awful place where the ill-hearted are punished in the afterlife, but Lugda is merciful and grants benevolent souls a place of rest in paradise. As a Healer, part of my role was making a person's last days, last moments, as peaceful as possible. I consider it ushering suffering souls into the waiting arms of Lugda. Or as some believe, into the arms of Rhianu, the Mother, who then escorts them to Lugda's realm."

I let her words sink in. She says it with such conviction, I want to believe her. "What do you think of the Seer's talk of the death of the gods? Since you're best friends with Lugda, where in hells are these bloody gods anyway?"

Briony makes a tiny sound like a half laugh, half sigh. "It's been quite the mystery, but believe it or not, I've been visited on more than one occasion by the god of death."

A chill runs along my spine.

"I've felt his presence when patients have passed on. I've heard his voice guiding me, I've seen him in dreams, seen other restless souls wandering the realm of the living."

"Is that … normal for a priestess? One of Lugda, at least?"

"No."

"I suppose that's what makes you *high* Priestess."

She nods, though she doesn't seem at all prideful about it.

Sighing, I rub my hand over the short-cropped parts of my hair. Everything about the gods is bewildering. Larger waves lap against the boat, making it lurch and my stomach roil. I distract myself with another question for Briony. "I understand what you mean when you speak of ushering souls to the Underworld and all of that—eerie, by the way—but how do you have healing powers? Aren't those typically granted by Ehlach? Moon magic and all of that? I'd have expected Lugda's gifts to be shadow wielding."

"Isn't Durvla the daughter of Dusk? Dusk refers to Ehlach, yet, as far as we know, she possesses no healing powers, only dreamwalking and dreamweaving."

My brain hurts.

"The Veil between the Underworld and the Realm of Dreams is thin. Ehlach, Sunlagh, and Lugda—Moon, Dreams, and Death— were once thick as thieves. The lines are blurred in many ways.

Things aren't just black and white when it comes to the gods or to magic."

"Obviously." My shoulders slump. It would be wonderful if *something* could be clear.

"No need to look so forlorn," a deep voice says from behind me.

My heart leaps and I inwardly curse myself for the response.

"I'm here now. You can smile again."

"Gods, you're insufferable ..." I mumble, refusing to turn to Odgar.

"Insufferably handsome? Insufferably charming?"

I face him. He leans against the mast, his arms crossed, tunic sleeves pulling taught and straining. He's not wearing his leather armor, and his tunic clings to him in places. I swear his muscles have muscles. My mouth goes a bit dry.

"What's truly insufferable is my sister and best mate," he says. "They're like animals in heat. *Loud* animals in heat."

That pulls a small laugh from me.

Odgar's lips curl into a smile as he keeps his eyes on me. I hold his gaze as chatter among the ship's crew continues around us, as waves lap steadily against the boat and birds occasionally call out from above. The steadiness in his gaze tempts me to look away, but I stand my ground, confronting the pull between us.

I'm unable to discern between the desire for quick gratification and something more meaningful. I can't trust my emotions or my intuition—they've never been the most reliable.

"What are you thinking about so hard?" Odgar asks. "I can almost see smoke coming out of your ears."

"The way you're looking at me," I admit.

"What of it?"

"I don't like it."

He laughs, and the deep rumble resonates in my chest, spreading through my insides as if fueled by my own flamewielding. "Why not?" He steps a little closer, one hand on the taffrail, and I step back.

Briony makes a swift escape somewhere to my left and I'm tempted to follow her, but Odgar's persistent gaze pins me in place. "Because ... it's complicated."

"What's complicated?"

"I am." I step back.

"I don't mind." He steps forward.

I step back again and his eyes sparkle, like flecks of gold swimming in the purest sapphire gemstone as he pursues me. His lips are firmly together, but a smile fights hard to break through and eventually wins. He's *enjoying* this.

With another step away, my back hits the rails again, this time in the corner of the stern. I let out a disgruntled huff.

Odgar grins, his teeth gleaming in the sunshine a moment before a cloud passes overhead and hides the sun. "Looks like you have nowhere to run."

I glance over my shoulder at the water starting to lap more fiercely below. The sails flap loudly in the winds that pick up. "I could go overboard," I say, fighting to keep my face neutral.

He tilts his head down to me, his braid slipping onto his shoulder. "I'll follow you even into the depths of the sea," he says.

I'll love you even in death—oh, Callum. My heart hiccups and my throat swells. "Don't say that." The wind picks up even more, carrying my voice away as it whistles across the ocean. The sails crack like a whip and Odgar's gaze diverts from me to the sky.

I follow his line of sight to the dark clouds billowing toward us. The waves grow choppier, higher. The first drop of rain falls right into my eye, and I blink rapidly just before the sky opens to unleash a torrent.

Shouts carry across the boat, everyone scrambling to close the sails and do ... whatever else needs to be done on a ship in the midst of a storm.

Odgar shouts something at me that I can't make out over the din.

"What?" I yell back.

He wraps his hand around my bicep and pulls me, swinging me away from the rail, away from the water that splashes into the vessel. Not that it would make a difference with the sudden downpour. "Get below deck!" Odgar shouts. "And hold on!"

I nod and run for the stairs, my boots slipping on the slick wood. My chest tightens as I turn back to lay eyes on Odgar. He's still standing there in the downpour, watching to ensure I make it below deck. "Be safe," I shout over the commotion.

I rush below and into my cabin as the boat rocks violently. Begging my guts not to upend themselves, I swallow again and again. Crates and barrels slide. Something clatters to the floor as it falls. I pitch forward with the next rock of the ship and land on the cot. My heart hammers wildly as I sit up and hold on to the underside of the mattress.

The howl of the wind and the shouts grow louder above deck, but all I can think of is that Odgar could die out there. Hells, we could *all* die—even us taking shelter below. Perhaps there's something I could do. Anything.

I push myself off the bed and rush for the door, but as I reach toward the latch, the door flies open, making me jump.

Odgar barrels into the cabin and shuts the door behind him. "Where did you think you were going?" His voice cuts with surprising sharpness.

"I was coming to help!"

"To help do *what*?" He looks at me as though I've lost my mind.

"I don't know. Anything but sitting down here, waiting for death?"

He laughs, though he—astoundingly—seems nervous. "Unless you can command the winds and the waves, there's not a thing you can do, *revna*."

My lips part. I intend to say something more to him—like why does he keep calling me *revna*?—but the boat tosses me forward into Odgar's hard chest. He wraps his arms around me, balancing me, but the boat rocks once more, tossing us both to the side. His back slams hard into the wall as he turns at the last moment. It could've been me.

He grunts and I wrench myself from his arms. "Gods, are you alright?"

Rubbing the back of his head, he winces but nods. "Yes, I'm fine."

The boat is still being tossed about, and my heart refuses to calm down over the sounds of water pelting against the ship, of waves crashing, of the shouting of the crew above and perhaps even down here. "Have you been in a storm this bad before? Could we die out here?"

He wraps his arms around me again, pulling my face against his chest so that I feel his words as much as I hear them. "If we are going to die, do you really want to spend our last moments talking about the possibility?"

"No." A tremor rises in me. Even the dark flames at my core shudder. As if even Enidwen's spirit inside of me fears for her life. I can't stop the quaking, but Odgar holds me tighter, his back still pressed against the wall.

"Let's sit," he says over the cacophony of the storm. I sink down to the floor with him, sitting between his legs with my thighs draped over one of his. I press my face to his leathers, taking in the scent of pine oil and perspiration. Normally, I'd be disgusted, but right now it's a comfort.

His chest rises with each intake of breath, and I bask in the warmth of his arms encircling me, even as the boat rocks, creaks, and groans. Even as I fear our impending death.

The ship tilts so hard we begin to slide. My heart leaps, and Odgar tightens his grip on me with one hand while the other anchors us against the floor. I hold my ground as well, my heart pounding in my throat. Water pours under our door, streaming across the floor. Panicked cries seem to bleed from the walls.

This is it. We're going to die.

But the ship stops tilting, and I relax slightly, even though we continue to rock back and forth in the tempest. Odgar's heart thuds steadily against my ear, and as I start to disentangle from his embrace, there's the slightest increase in the pressure of his arms around me.

I lick my dry lips, and though I make no further attempts to shift, I murmur, "You don't have to hold on to me anymore."

"I know." His voice rumbles through his chest, against my cheek. He presses a kiss to the top of my head, and I inadvertently sink deeper into his hold. I find myself desperate to commit this feeling to memory.

If this is the last experience I'll have in this life, it wouldn't be a bad way to go.

Chapter 39

CARYS

STOCKY BRANCHES of a tree stretch toward the inky black sky. Fire rages across the land. Cries of terror and pain tear through the abysmal darkness as the ground fissures and molten rock glowing an angry orange spills from within. The bloodred moon casts eerie shadows into the endless night, and with a howl heard in every hollow of the world, the last orb of light ceases to exist. As if swallowed whole.

As if it had never been.

The next afternoon, I'm drenched in sweat as my body hits the floor. I've barely gotten much sleep in the two weeks since we've been on the sea. But every time I do drift off, it's this fucking dream again.

During the days, I've been working with Briony on strengthening my mind against Enidwen—though the enchantress still slips into my consciousness far too often. The mind strengthening does seem to keep Durvla out of my dreams, however. Thank Sunlagh. As much as I miss Durvla, I don't want her to watch me slip away.

With a groan, I roll onto my back and rub my bleary eyes. As I reach out from the floor to grab the mattress for leverage, I find Odgar sitting on the bed staring down at me. I shriek and clap my hand over my mouth.

Odgar winces, an apologetic look on his face as he lowers a large wooden needle threaded with wool. "I didn't mean to scare you," he says. His eyes drift down as he weaves the blue wool through the needle eye into the knitted fabric.

My tongue feels a tad too large for my mouth as I watch his precise motions. I swallow and stand to sink back onto the bed, leaving a gap between us.

"I still can't believe you knit," I say.

"*Nalbinding*," he corrects gently. "Knitting requires two needles —one holding the wool, and the other weaving it. The nalbinding needle is like a sewing needle but instead of connecting two pieces of fabric—" He lifts his face to me, and I must look as utterly bored as I feel because he huffs out a quiet laugh. His smile wavers as he sticks the needle into the fabric and sets the work in progress between us.

He unstraps a bulbous leather bottle from his waist and hands it to me.

Slowly, I sip the lukewarm liquid and try to remember ... something. What had I been doing last? I don't even remember going to bed. I vaguely recall a conversation of some sort with Briony. Or Valdis?

That strange, shrouded sensation begins to cloak me again. Until a sharp pinch just beneath my inner elbow releases me from the impending daze. My fingernails are digging into my forearm, and I stare at my hand as if it doesn't belong to me. It takes a moment for me to release my own grip. My skin is speckled with scratches and black, blue, and yellow bruises. I pull back the dress sleeve from my other arm, and it's the same.

Have I been doing this to myself? Why don't I remember?

I close my eyes and see myself screaming at one of the ship crew members. Throwing a bowl of mush. Drinking ale. Shouting at Valdis, Odgar, and Briony at different times.

Groaning, I drop my face into my hands. "Gods, I'm dreadful," I mumble against my palms.

"Tell me what I can do to help you through these moments," comes Odgar's voice.

The laughter that comes from me isn't the least bit humorous; it's bitter, nearly deranged. I lift my head and stare across the room toward the door. "These aren't *moments*. I've been like this since childhood. Imagine every emotion in existence being siphoned into one thunderstorm and shoved down your throat." My voice comes out raw. "Sometimes it's so overwhelming I forget who I am. I lose control, and it's like looking at myself from somewhere else and not being able to do a fucking thing about it."

Tears cling to my lashes, but I stubbornly clench my jaw. "The fact that it's happening more often, and these ... episodes ... of not remembering." Fear walks down my spine. I breathe out heavily through my nostrils. "Sometimes I think it'll be best if I ... stopped existing."

"Carys—"

"Nothing you can say will change who I am." The words catch in my throat. "And now with the curse on top of everything? I'm beyond mortal help."

"You are not beyond help," he says. "... If you would only *let someone help.*"

"Once I get to the Serpent's Hollow—Siad Nahar—I can find the cure the Seer spoke of. I can get rid of this curse."

He presses his lips together, his eyes filled with sorrow.

"You don't believe the Seer." The realization sinks my hope.

"It's not that; it's just that prophecies are often misunderstood."

"I'm so glad you think I'm beyond help." I shove off the bed and stride toward the door, embarrassingly unsteady on my feet.

Odgar's rapid footsteps sound behind me and I reel on him, anger bringing flames to my raised fist. But Odgar doesn't bat an eye. He simply takes my fist in his hand, puffs of steam rising as his water-weaving cancels my fire. I raise my other fist, and he repeats the action. I grunt at him and tug away—I should leave. I should head above deck and breathe in the fresh sea breeze, clear my mind, calm down.

But his serenity in the face of my temper is infuriating. I want him to be as angry as I am. I want him to show something other than amusement or happiness or tranquility. I want to drag him down with me so that he understands why the cure is important. So that he knows what it's like to live with a fire breathing dragon inside.

I aim another punch at him, then another. But unlike last time when he was so willing to let me pummel him, he dodges all my blows. As I raise my leg to knee him in the groin, he holds both hands over his crotch, his brows shooting up toward his hairline.

"Alright, now you're playing dirty."

I lift my hand to strike him, and he grabs both my wrists and forces me back against the door with two rapid steps. He pins them above my head and leans against me, his hips immobilizing me. "Stop it," he says softly, close enough for us to share a breath.

My pulse quickens as I remember being bound back in the brig. And as my stomach jumps, Odgar releases my hands. He doesn't step back, however. I drop my own hands, pressing them against the door. Teeth bared, I try to bite back the temptation to snarl at him. I meet his gaze even as my entire body feels dangerously close to bursting into flames.

Something in his own gaze seems to falter, but he still stares down at me, his hands now bracketed against the door on either side of my head. When he speaks, it's steady and irritatingly soothing. "You harbor so much anger, and it has nothing to do with the curse. Pretending to be someone you're not for as long as you've had to would drive even an immortal to fits of rage."

Heat pulses in my hands—I clench them into fists, hoping the door doesn't catch on fire.

"It doesn't make you broken," Odgar continues. "It doesn't make you worthless. You just need to find an effective release without harming others ... or *yourself*."

I grunt and try to wriggle free from his hips that still pin me; I refuse to let him know his words are slowly extinguishing the flames I'd almost wanted to unleash on him. Enidwen's spirit within me is coiled like an adder, ready to lash out. I let the snarl loose to remind him that there's something inhuman within me. That he cannot forget what I truly am.

"You don't scare me, Carys Meredyth." He leaves out my father's name as if I have a right to control my own life, my own fate.

The fury slowly dissipates, leaving me with an uncomfortably warm feeling as my pulse builds. A jumble of emotions swirls around in my body. I become hyper aware of where our hips are still connected, of the weight of him, of his arms trapping me here. There is so much sincerity in his stupid, beautiful eyes. And he's. So. Close. Close enough to kiss. Part of me wants to do it.

But if I keep pushing him away, he'll surely give up. Our arrangement will remain exactly that: an *arrangement*. Marriage for the purpose of an alliance.

Slowly, he steps away, dropping his hands, but my pulse still races. Do I ... miss his weight against me?

"You should try to get some rest," he says.

"No." My defiance is as frightening as a toddler's.

Odgar smiles. "Well, if you're looking for me, *I* am going to get some rest." He drops a kiss onto my forehead, and I step aside, scrubbing my forehead with my palm. Odgar's warm laughter follows him through the door and down the hallway.

I rush from my cabin and head above deck for some much-needed fresh air. Blond hair blows freely in the breeze where Valdis stands, staring out at the sky now darkening with the impending nightfall.

I clear my throat. "Valdis?"

She glances over her shoulder at me, a smirk on her lips as though she has a teasing remark prepared for me. But her amusement immediately fizzles out. I stand beside her, my focus also on the ocean.

"Good to see that clarity in your eyes again," she says.

My stomach sinks. "I'm sorry for whatever I said or did."

Valdis waves her hand dismissively. "You weren't in control at the time. We're all aware."

Somehow this doesn't comfort me; my stomach sinks farther. I turn to her, and there is no unkindness on her face whatsoever. Not even pity. Concern, perhaps. She drums her fingers against the taffrail.

"Whatever you're holding on to—whatever you don't want to talk about—it's festering like a wound inside you. Sometimes, I write things down when they're bothering me. Or take a sword to a tree. Odgar does nalbinding. You ought to find your thing."

"I want to learn how to fight," I blurt.

She tilts her head, one side of her lips lifting before a full smile takes over her face, puckering her birthmark. "Alright," she says. She steps back from the banister. "We start tonight."

Chapter 40

MY CONCERN OVER NERIS—AND the fact that I've not heard a word about her—eats away at me as I get dressed. I've barely finished wrestling with the ties of my bodice when the door swings open with a loud *bang*, sending my heart flying into my throat. I spin toward it, my hand clutching my chest as the masked woman marches into my room. Her crimson cape billows out behind her like a villain straight from a fairytale.

Except, she's very real.

A moment ago, I'd been staring at my puffy-faced, haggard reflection in the mirror. The pink, floral dress I'm wearing fits awfully, and my bust is practically spilling out over the top. It screams *Arionna*, and I despise it. I cross my arms over my torso, and the masked woman cackles beneath her veil.

"It seems you are in need of better fitting garments," she says. "Shall I send for some?"

My brows rise. I'm not certain if she's to be trusted, but I nod regardless. "May I request trousers and a tunic?" I ask.

"There are riding garments in one of the drawers." She makes a *well, go on* gesture toward an upright dresser. I pad across the room and slide a couple of drawers open, indeed finding trousers and tunics neatly folded inside one. Part of me wants to smile at this discovery, but my face doesn't cooperate.

"You're welcome," the woman says in a singsong voice that seems to counter her terrifying appearance.

I clear my throat and hug the clothing to my chest. "Thank you."

The door clicks shut behind her as she leaves. Removing the corset is a relief, but I band my chest tightly for support before tossing on the tunic and trousers. They require rolling at the wrists and waist, and the arms of the tunic are just a tad tight around my biceps. It's a far better fit than the dress, at least. The door flies open as I slip into some thin woolen socks and shove my feet back into my boots.

The masked woman stands in the doorway, her face aimed toward me. She clicks her tongue beneath her veil. "I personally preferred your last outfit, but suit yourself, darling. Come along." She steps through the door, expecting me to follow her.

So, I do.

Our footsteps echo in the corridors. I take the time to admire the ornate columns and high ceilings. For an old castle, the walls and floors look newly installed or, at least, freshly painted. Which is likely since there had evidently been a destructive fire. As we round a corner, I let the words I've been holding back go loose. "Is my friend Reneris alright?"

We step into an immense dining hall with a massive table down the center. The masked woman points to one of the dining chairs, completely ignoring me. "Sit," she says before disappearing behind a door. I'm barely in the seat when she steps out just a few heartbeats later with a bowl and practically drops it onto the table. "Eat up. Then we visit your scrappy friend."

Hope fills my chest. She's alive then, I assume. My eyes dip down to the food—which looks like gruel. I'd expected a feast at the castle.

"The kitchen staff is on break. Eat it or leave it," says the woman.

Trying not to make a face, I scoop a spoonful of the lumpy white mush out of the bowl, and even when I tilt the spoon upside down, the food clings to it. I taste a bit of the gruel off the tip of my spoon. To my surprise, it isn't unpleasant. Cinnamon and cloves cut through the startling, creamy sweetness. I take another spoonful forcing myself to eat though my stomach is knotted up with worry for Neris and with anxiety at the possibility of finding out about Father.

"We don't have all the time in the world; don't make me shovel it into your mouth for you," says the woman.

I eat faster, even though I'm not hungry, even though my arm is beginning to protest each movement. I'm not sure if it was the adrenaline last night that kept away the worst of my pains, but I'm not sure I'll survive much longer without the elixirs. My heart thuds, my appetite receding further.

The masked woman perches on the end of the table, her legs crossed, regarding me. I can just imagine a scowl underneath her veil. "Enough!" she suddenly says, slamming her hand down on the table and rattling the bowl and my resolve. "Let's go." She hops off the table and heads toward the door. I propel myself from the chair and jog to catch up with her.

In silence, I follow her down the corridors, passing a Royal Brigade soldier every now and then. I glance sidelong at each one, hoping to see a Royal Guard, hoping to catch a glimpse of Father. But the masked woman doesn't interact with anyone; she keeps her focus forward until she arrives in front of a door where a couple guards stand. They nod to her, and she shoves the door open, storming in as if she owns the place. A man with wispy dark hair and a soft build jumps hard, his face going white.

He exhales noticeably, blood coloring his peachy face again. On the cot near where he stands is Neris. She's on her stomach, unmoving, a white sheet covering up to her neck. There isn't anyone else in the infirmary. Faint disappointment settles over me; Father isn't here.

The masked woman makes a flourishing gesture in the direction of the bed. "You have ten minutes," she says, then she steps outside and slams the door behind her.

I force my wobbly legs to move, my chest caving in as I hurry to Neris's side. "Are you the healer?" I ask the man.

He nods, a shaky smile stretching his lips. "I'm Vaughn."

"Gwyneth," I respond before turning back to Neris. "Is she going to be alright?" I step around the bed.

"She has a bit of a recovery ahead of her, but I believe so. Occasionally we have a Mage Healer here. I'll be sure to have her take a look at Reneris when she shows up."

My gaze settles on Neris's face. Her usually tan complexion is drained of color, deep purple bruises and scratches crossing her cheek. Her hair is pulled back away from her face, curls tangled, and blood encrusted. The back of my eyes sting, and I blink away tears, swallowing around my constricting throat. On impulse, I grasp the sheet and begin drawing it away.

Vaughn speaks up urgently. "Wait, you ought to know—"

My gasp cuts him off as I drop the sheet at Neris's waist. Thick white bandages intersect across her back, blood seeping through them. Tears pool in my eyes as I sink down to the ground beside Neris, placing my hands on the bed beside her face.

"Neris, I am so sorry," I whisper. She wouldn't be here if she hadn't stepped in to defend me against Gruffud after I saw him with Arionna. We should've run away the dozens of times Neris tried to convince me to.

"I've given her valbane," Vaughn says. "It will allow her to sleep. She isn't in any pain right now. She just needs time to heal."

I nod and slowly stand, my joints and muscles creaking like rusty hinges on a door. Blood doesn't bother me, but seeing the red seep through Neris's bandages turns my stomach.

"She'll have fresh bandages momentarily. I'm taking every precaution to prevent festering. Lady Alys has taught me well." He says it as if I know who Alys is, but he does seem to be capable and comforting.

After some hesitation, I find enough courage to ask, "Have you looked after Sir Eurig Davies of Barr na Cahar? He was a Queen's Guard."

Something ghosts over Vaughn's face. He quickly looks away from me. "Briefly." He pulls the covers gently back over Neris and smooths out the sides. "He was transferred."

I frown. "Transferred?" That doesn't even make sense. "Transferred *where*?"

"Apologies. That is outside of my knowledge."

My heart sinks and I try to push away my confusion and focus on Neris. Again, I kneel beside her, watching her too-pale face.

"You'll be alright," I whisper. "You'll be back on your feet in no time."

For a while longer, I talk to unconscious Neris about everything and nothing, then the masked woman barges back into the room. "Terraforger!" she calls out. "The sovereign has summoned you."

Now I wish I hadn't eaten that porridge, because it's far too eager to make an appearance again. But I swallow hard and follow the masked woman out of the room, leaving my only friend behind. Dashing my hopes of seeing Father again.

I keep my head held high and follow the masked woman, off to face whatever the sovereign has to say to me.

His Excellency is in his study again, his hands steepled on his desk as his young assistant prattles off various laws from books that seem old enough to fall apart. The sovereign holds his hand up, and the assistant closes the book and bows, leaving the book behind before excusing himself from the room.

With my back stiff and my heart racing, I face the sovereign. He smiles and rises to his feet, though he keeps his large hands pressed against the dark wood surface. "Welcome, Lady Pendry. Thank you for joining me today."

Not that I had a choice.

"And thank you, Lynx for escorting her."

The masked woman, *Lynx* apparently, nods slowly and steps aside, keeping an eye on the sovereign.

"Tomorrow, you are to begin training with the other Zenith members. Your first mission will be to procure a Shadow Wielder."

Gooseflesh prickles my skin, and I'm certain my face blanches.

"Fear not, you will be among many other Mages with developed abilities. Your task will be to apprehend the target from a distance. You can manipulate metal, can't you?"

I nod.

"Then you won't even have to get close to the Shadow Wielder. You just need to bind their wrists with the dampening shackles. It will cut off their ability to manipulate and make the transfer back to Paramount safe for everyone."

My throat goes dry. Why does he want a Shadow Wielder, specifically? That's dark magic—one of the most forbidden.

"After this mission," the sovereign continues. "I have another for you to prepare for. As you may or may not know, the Wastelands are surrounded entirely by impenetrable mountains. There are many mysteries about the Wastelands—how did it come to be? In a land filled with lush forests and a wet climate, how did the Wastelands come about? What has caused such an uncharacteristic habitat in the midst of otherwise mundane conditions? It's something many people have attempted to solve yet have failed. The problem lies in a very simple fact: we've been sending the wrong people. That's where your terraforging will come in handy."

My lips part again, but no words come to me. He expects me to be different from anyone else who's gone to the Wastelands? Wait ... I thought people were banished there. How is that possible if it's impenetrable?

Again, I'm at a loss for words.

The sovereign smiles. "For now, get all the training you can, eat well, and rest up. The Zenith is happy to have you among our ranks."

Chapter 41

DURVLA

THE SUN SHINES BRIGHTLY off the black peaks all around us, speckles of dust floating in the beams of light. Sweat beads on my forehead and nose, gathering along the divot of my spine as I cling to Tiernan's hand. Unhurriedly, I step sideways down the steep mountain. There are small bushes and shrubs along the worn dirt path, trodden mostly by mountain goats. My stomach is tangled up in knots, and my throat spasms in response to the threat of vomiting from the lightheadedness. Each time small pebbles crumble out from beneath my boots, I cling harder to Tiernan's hand and squeeze my eyes shut.

When I open my eyes this time, he's staring into them. "Almost there," he says. "Just keep looking at me."

So, I do. It's much better than looking down at the jagged rocks lining the ravine below. Even if it doesn't necessarily ease the dizziness. Already, the horses have descended and, according to Tiernan, are happily hydrating in the small stream below. I breathe slowly, my lips pursed, tears gathering—embarrassingly—in my eyes.

This is an absolute nightmare.

Tiernan keeps my mind occupied with constant chatter of just about anything as we descend. Until my thighs aren't burning as much, and the peaks that surrounded us are farther away and higher up. The ground is leveling out, and we're very close to the stream.

The others have already stopped, Alys sitting on the ground near the stream, Ava and Sloan kneeling to fill their waterskins, and Osheen stretching. Chiyo and Isobel have gone to tend to the horses.

I turn a smiling gaze to Tiernan. "We didn't die," I say aloud, and he laughs.

"And you conquered your fear of heights," he signs.

I hadn't realized how much I missed easily seeing the words on his hands. His mind whispering is intimate in a wonderful way that I never imagined, but his signing feels like a welcoming hug. Like home.

"I wouldn't say I *conquered* my fears," I gesture back.

"Alright, well you've faced it and lived to tell the tale."

I laugh and motion, "Fine. Now I need to conquer my thirst."

We head to the stream, and I kneel beside it, fighting the urge to dump my head directly into the water to cool this infernal headache. That's when Tiernan does exactly what I'm thinking, and it surprises me so much that I snort. Everyone looks our way as Tiernan sits back on his heels again, his dark hair sopping wet, dripping down his face and onto his tunic. He shakes his head like a hound, and I lean away to avoid getting splashed. Water gets all over my face anyway.

Chiyo approaches, presenting me with a handful of strawberries. "The pair of you are sickeningly sweet," she says with a smirk. "I'm glad I don't have to slap anyone." She winks at me and walks away, leaving Tiernan looking puzzled.

I shrug, the picture of innocence, while I cup the strawberries in my hands.

We linger for a while longer, regaining our strength. Then Tiernan looks to me and signs, "I'd like to move ahead and scout for a place we can all rest tonight. Are you up for a small adventure? We can get some time to finish talking."

My heart sputters a little. I look into his eyes—they don't seem guarded, but there's something that looks an awful lot like anxiety in them.

I nod, and he smiles shakily before getting up. "Alright, I'll go talk to Ava about it. Tell Ghendor to get ready." There's the smallest hint of playfulness in his eyes before he turns to walk away.

I refill my waterskin once more and head to Ghendor. I offer him a few berries, which he takes gratefully, then I hook my waterskin back onto the saddle with our packs before climbing atop the stallion. Tiernan returns with a smile and a thumbs up before mounting Ghendor behind me.

As Tiernan maneuvers Ghendor through the group, I catch Chiyo's beaming smile. She waves to me, Isobel hopping into view to join in the sendoff. I can't help but grin back at them. "I will be right back!" I sign to them. "Not going away forever."

"Don't hurry," she signs back while Isobel looks at her with confusion. Her signing isn't very fluent yet, but her grin widens even more when Chiyo says something to her.

Still riding alongside the river, Tiernan and I get some distance from the group. As usual, his arms bracket my body, settling over my thighs, but he lifts a hand to place just above my knee, rubbing gently as if soothing me.

I crane my neck to get a better look at him as that hand comes up to cup my cheek. He only strokes tenderly across my face before lowering his hand again. "*You know I care for you, right?*" he asks into my mind.

"*Yes, of course,*" I respond.

"*Good, I know I've been a bit of an ass, but please never mistake that for me not caring about you. This journey has been far more difficult for me than I thought it would be. Mentally, I suppose. I just cannot fathom anything happening to you when we've only just found each other.*"

My heart clenches, a mixture of fear and warmth fighting within. "*I feel the same way,*" I admit. I face forward again as we happen upon the gaping mouth of a cave. Tiernan dismounts and practically lifts me down from Ghendor. His hands linger on my waist as my body adjusts to being on my feet again. But the heat of his fingers seeping into my tunic makes me feel a bit dizzy nonetheless.

We stare at each other for a while, a hand's width of space between us and the desire to close that gap so strong.

But Tiernan steps back. "I need to tell you something," he signs. "And I'm afraid you'll think differently of me when you know the whole truth ..."

A cold sensation tickles the back of my neck, but all I can do is nod.

There's so much pain in his features, in the way his brows are cinched and his lips are pressed tightly together. "You know all about Maura, and you know that I was in the Royal Brigade," he motions. "I was only sixteen years old when I was conscripted for the Royal Brigade. Back when Erleya was still very much at war with Ardall. Rheon was like a father to me while I was away from my own; I looked up to him. Until he morphed into a monster before my eyes. Until, in the midst of my grief, he chose to inflict such pain. He was willing to take me to the gallows if I didn't speak up. After my years of loyalty, of serving this kingdom."

He exhales heavily and glances toward the cave. "Durvla, I did unimaginable things under Rheon's command." He faces me again. "I murdered innocents. I helped enforce the horrible laws of Erleya; I was an active part of shipping Undesirables off to Paramount—to their deaths." His hands are shaking so hard that he stops and clenches them tightly.

Sweat breaks out along my neck, my heart pounding through the heat in my chest.

"I didn't understand at first," he signs without looking at me. "I was following orders. I was … I didn't … I was a fool. And the moment I started to realize the injustice of it all—the threat was turned on me. I wanted to live. I wanted—"

I step forward and clasp his hands between mine as his chest rises and falls rapidly. His hands are still shaking, vibrating through my palms. He tips his head up to the sky, and when he drags his gaze back to me, his eyes glisten with tears.

"If I could go back in time—"

I watch the words on his lips, the way he presses them together, and his jaw quivers.

"How could you feel all that you do for someone who's committed such atrocities? You should hate me."

The heat of anger and pity feels misplaced among the heaviness in my heart. It hurts to know that he played a part in the disposal of Undesirables, but also … I release his hand, cupping his cheek, and more images flood my mind. I see a man charging toward Tiernan with a dagger, and Tiernan drawing his sword and running him through. And I see his brokenness afterward as he holds the dying man. Another image materializes—Tiernan on horseback, watching Forayers load people into a wagon, just as it had been done to me.

He pulls away, and steps back, leaving my hand hovering in midair, the taste of revulsion on my tongue. Tiernan's revulsion at *himself.*

"They say you never get the first kill out of your mind," he signs. "I remember them all. I regret every last one of them."

"That was self-defense," I sign shakily.

"It was an innocent life. He was only trying to protect his family."

I swallow the knot in my throat.

"That's why when you look at me the way you do ... I know I'm not deserving. You should hate me for what I've done."

I watch the words on his lips, and I can feel the regret and the overwhelming guilt. It sears hotter than the scar on his neck. It hasn't only been Rheon slicing into him haunting his memories, but his own actions toward others.

"Ever since hearing about Rheon as the sovereign, I've been reliving every moment and it's been eating me up inside."

"And you've been afraid to tell me."

He nods.

"Tiernan ..." My heart aches. "I wish you hadn't felt that way, but I understand." I take his hand, giving it a firm squeeze. Ghendor nudges Tiernan's side as if to complain about standing still for so long. Tiernan scrubs his hand down his face and then Ghendor's mane. When he looks at me again there's still that shame lingering in his eyes. I suppose it may be something he'll have to gradually work through, but I don't plan to shut him out while he does.

"I suppose we should commence this little adventure now that I've dragged down the entire mood," says Tiernan.

I smile through the tears still stinging my eyes. "You didn't ruin anything. You told me the biggest thing you feared telling me, and I'm so grateful for it."

He gives my hand a squeeze and grabs a mage lantern from the saddle. I take Ghendor's reins, and we move toward the cave. Cool air surrounds us, stalactites hanging down from the rocky ceiling. The ground is slightly damp and slick, so I tread carefully, hypervigilant as I observe the different rock formations and critters that scurry in corners. Tiernan releases my hand to sign "Looks like a good place to take shelter."

"It does," I say.

Moving deeper into the cave, we reach what seems to be a dead end, though the walls turn and narrow to the left. There's a strange stillness within the cave, but it doesn't feel eerie; it's peaceful.

Tiernan pauses for a moment, a look of concentration on his face, his head slightly tilted toward the direction we're walking in.

"What is it?" I ask.

"Running water." His eyes light up. "I suppose the river continues through the cavern. With enthusiasm, he takes my hand and tugs me onward. The cave begins to widen, a subtle glow emitting from somewhere ahead of us.

"Do you think it's a tunnel that goes out to the other side?" I ask Tiernan.

"Perhaps ..."

But as the light grows brighter, it's not the other side of the tunnel that we find but a large chamber within the grotto. Large rocks encircle a clear body of water, which is dappled in sunlight from an apparent opening somewhere above. Moss and foliage twine up the sides of the cave from the water, and flowering vines dangle from above. It nearly forms a curtain of sorts on one side of the pool. A thin mist radiates off the water, the air around us no longer cool but ...

"Well shit," Tiernan signs. "A *heated* spring."

"No ..." I nearly burst into laughter from the unlikelihood. "This is far too good to be true."

We move closer to the water, careful not to slip on the rocks. The air is denser with the heat radiating from the spring. Tiernan squats, tentatively reaching out until the tips of his fingers set off a ripple across the surface of the water. He grins up at me before he stands again, beginning to unfasten the buckles that keep his swords strapped to his back.

My brows cinch. "What are you—"

"I'm getting my ass in that water!" he says as he lowers his swords to the ground. One corner of his lips quirks up. "The better question is: are you going to join me?"

Chapter 42

DURVLA

My gaze slips from Tiernan's hands to the ink on his forearm as he slips his tunic off over his head and signs *something* to me. Flutters fill my stomach as I find his amused gaze again before he takes a knee to start removing his boots.

I clear my throat. "Are you sure this is a good idea? Shouldn't we be getting back to the others?"

He stands to toe his boots off while he signs. "We probably should but ..." He gestures to the water again. "This one can't overflow like the tub back in the Verge."

I bite my lip around a grin. My cheeks heat up from the memory of what'd occurred back in the Verge. I'd have expected to feel less coy about either of us being undressed in each other's presence after that moment, and yet, as he's down to his breeches, hooking his thumbs into the waistband, I turn my attention to the water.

Tiernan wades into my view, waist-deep in the pool with a grin splitting his face. "You're missing out," he signs above the water. He sinks down until his head is submerged then resurfaces, pushing wet hair back from his face.

"Alright, I'll come in," I say. "But only for a moment. Let me just get some blankets." I approach Ghendor to retrieve our packs then leave him to wander while I return to the side of the spring and set the packs down. Setting two blankets aside, I glance up to find Tiernan watching me, now chest-deep, from the water.

"I feel like you're procrastinating," he gestures.

Painstakingly, I begin removing my own clothing, folding each layer and placing it beside Tiernan's. "Maybe I am," I say, slipping off my breeches. I take a deep breath before I unwrap the band of fabric from around my breasts and place it atop the rest of my clothes.

Removing the ribbon at the end of my hair, I unbraid and let the curls fall over my shoulders. There's adoration in Tiernan's gaze as I hug my torso, my legs firmly together even as my toes grip the very edge of the pool. He wades closer, his body emerging until he's only waist-deep again.

I take his extended hand and slip down into the spring. A sigh of relief comes over me as the water envelops my aching muscles. Tiernan pulls me farther out until the water reaches just below my breasts and I sink down so that it laps across my collarbones.

I hold my breath, pinching my nose shut to dip under for a quick moment before resurfacing. When I turn my gaze back to Tiernan, he's staring intently at me.

Self-conscious, I smooth my drenched ringlets away from my face and ask, "What is it?"

His eyes seem to stare right into my soul. "I don't deserve you. I'm sorry I've been keeping my past from you."

"Tiernan—"

"But never forget that you have my trust as much as you have my heart."

My chest fills with warmth as Tiernan slips his arms around me, pulling me against him. All words flee from me as my arms settle on his shoulders, as I gaze into his dark eyes. With no secrets left between us, with the old wounds opened and our hearts vulnerable to each other, I feel everything all at once. I kiss him with an intensity fueled by all the time we've wasted. His lips roam my jaw, along the side of my neck, and down to my collarbone. My body comes alive beneath his hands that seem desperate to explore every part of me.

Molten heat fills me at the feel of his hard length against my thigh. His fingers knot in my hair, my head falling back as his lips skim over the pulse bounding in the hollow of my neck. I squeeze my thighs together, unable to keep myself from seeking the wonderful friction I crave.

"*Let's get out of this water,*" he whispers into my mind.

I nod, and we rush for the edge of the spring. Tiernan pulls himself out of the water, whipping a blanket open with one flick of his wrists before helping me out of the steaming pool. I wrap my arms around myself, shivering from the change in temperature. Tiernan sits atop the blanket first and gently tugs me beside him before he picks up where he left off, trailing kisses from my collarbone downward. My coldness is immediately forgotten.

I'm unprepared for the jolt that moves through me as he sucks the peak of my breast into his mouth. My back arches, my stomach clenching with surprising intensity. I can't even *think* as his lips and tongue tease my nipples and awareness floods every part of me.

I'm not sure when I end up lying flat, but the blanket's not much of a barrier between my back and the hard ground. The liquefied heat and pulsing need between my legs demand attention.

Tiernan draws in a breath and light pleasure flutters over my skin like thousands of butterflies.

His pleasure.

Gods, what a strange, compelling sensation—feeling what he does. He lifts his head, partially hovering over me. The subtle redness in his cheeks is a sight to behold. "You'll let me know if you want me to stop, right?"

I nod. "Yes. But is it … is it alright if we don't … I …"

He patiently waits for me to get my words out, one brow lifted, no judgment on his face.

"I don't want my very first time to be in a cave."

His laughter ripples through me, but he smiles and twirls a loose curl of my hair around his finger. "I understand. Are you alright with me pleasuring you until you climax?"

Flustered and speechless, I sputter, completely forgetting every word and every sign.

Tiernan's grin widens. "I'm not sure I've mentioned this before, but I'm also very skilled with my tongue."

It takes my inexperienced mind a moment to catch up, but I watch the amusement play across his handsome features as a heat rushes over me. "You don't have to do that," I sign quickly. Embarrassed heat continues to hold me captive until he kisses me languidly. His palm drifts over my breasts, down to the needy ache at the apex of my thighs. A gasp slips from my lips before I press my hand over my mouth to stifle a moan.

"*Don't silence yourself,*" he says into my mind as his finger strokes in a tight circle over *that* spot.

I let my hand fall away from my mouth, and he kisses down my body, his hands gently spreading my thighs. There's a smoldering glimmer in his eyes when he peers up at me from between my legs. "Tiernan ..." I say, my voice wavering. I'm still embarrassed at the mere thought of his mouth being so close to ...

Oh gods ...

My senses scatter as he flicks his tongue against my clit. A slew of pleasurable sensations flow through me. I gasp, my back leaving the blanket for a moment as my hands fist in his wet hair. As he drags that *skilled* tongue up my very core and delves in.

It becomes impossible not to writhe beneath him. My eyes flutter closed as I bite back a moan.

Tiernan lifts his head momentarily, his finger taking over where his tongue had been. "*Don't rob me of those beautiful sounds,*" he says. "*Let me hear you.*"

Then his mouth is on me again, *devouring* me while cool vapors begin to flood my hands. I let my hand slip from his hair, my legs over his back as I grip the damp blanket beneath me. I fight against the powers so eager to unleash themselves. I'm already lost in the pleasure, but I become utterly mind-numbed as he coaxes a finger inside me. His tongue starts to move in tandem with his determined strokes, and my shadows *come alive*. Unbidden, they twine down my arms and stretch toward him. I draw in a breath, tensing.

"*Tiernan. I can't hold—*"

He peers up at me, his voice clear in my mind as his finger continues to move. "*I trust you, love.*" he says. "*You can let go.*"

Love.

My heart swells and pressure builds until I fear it'll shatter me. Until ropes of shadows wrap around Tiernan's arms. I lose the battle to keep from squirming. I'm unable to stop the gasps and moans of pleasure, unable to keep my hips from lifting off the ground when my control snaps. The pleasure ripples through my body, my thighs quivering through the intense, rhythmic pulses around his finger.

Then it's all too much, one wave cresting over into another, leaving me shuddering as shadows dance over his back and across my skin. I shove at Tiernan's head. "Too much," I whisper aloud. "Too much, too much."

He retracts his finger and my shadows scatter. Tiernan lifts his face to me, a triumphant grin on his swollen lips. He kisses up my body again to my mouth, and I eagerly meet his tongue stroke for stroke. The tiniest hint of embarrassment is triggered by the taste on his lips, but satisfaction relaxes my body in a way it's not felt in ... I actually don't recall ever feeling quite this way.

I curl into the crook of his arm as we lay sidelong. For a moment, I just breathe, letting my pulse settle, letting the mindless satiation melt away. He's given me this pure bliss and I— "Do you want me to ..." My hand is already moving down toward his erection when he captures my wrist.

"It's alright," he says. "Tasting you is already more than I dreamt of today."

I smile sheepishly at him, hardly able to meet his eyes. "Are you sure? I don't know what I'm doing, but you can—"

"Durvla ..." He chuckles, tucking back frizzy curls from my face. They bounce right back in front of my eyes. "I think your shadows like me."

My lips part, a question on the tip of my tongue. But Tiernan's eyes flick down then back up to me.

"Oh ... oh gods." I cover my face while I *feel* his amusement tickle my skin. I lower my hands to find him staring at me with such adoration again. He sits up, tucking his own hair behind his ears. "Do you want to clean up before we head back to tell the others? About this cave, I mean."

Right ... I sigh as reality sets in again. We slip back into the pool to wash up, then get dressed as quickly as we can. When Ghendor is loaded up with our packs and we're ready to mount up and head back to the river, Tiernan turns to me with urgency in his eyes.

"What's wrong?" I ask him.

He shakes his head, smiling softly. "I know I've given you a hard time on this journey, but if only you knew how much I wanted a moment like this with you. If I could stop time just to watch you come undone again, I would."

The cave suddenly feels several degrees hotter.

"I love every part of you, Durvla. Your heart, your strength, the darkness that you control with the elegance of a goddess. I will never take you for granted. I'll spend every waking moment trying to remind you of how much you mean to me. Because even though the world is falling apart, you are the one I want to fall with."

My throat spasms, a knot cinching tighter as tears spill over from my eyes and trickle down my cheeks. My mind fixates on one word in particular. On the thing I never thought I'd be capable of feeling —not in this way. But now there's no doubt in my mind about it, and there's no part of me that wants to hide from this. I stare into his eyes and sign, "I love you too, Tiernan."

Relief flows from him.

"But I'm afraid I cannot outdo that speech."

He laughs and swipes away a tear of his own before wrapping me in a tight hug. He kisses the crown of my head then my cheeks and my lips. And when we're out of tears and laughter, we mount Ghendor and head back to the group and back to the journey that could make or break the kingdom.

Chapter 43

GWYNETH

THE TRAINING GROUND beneath the plateau where the castle sits is daunting, to say the least. Around me are the constant clangs of swords and occasional shouts of pain. It's a mild, overcast day, but the cool breeze that blows through my hair every now and then is much appreciated. My eyes constantly wander, my attention being pulled toward the far west where the supposed Veil between worlds resides. Where the Veilguards train to defend Erleya against Otherworldly attack.

I see no evidence of such Veilguards.

There are, however, other Zenith trainees. Each of us has a silver pin on our chest to identify our power. Mine is a cross within a circle, the old symbol for earth. The symbol's also affiliated with a few gods—knowledge that I don't care to brush up on. I find myself in a small group with various Wielders. A willowy girl with three swirls on her chest denoting the water element, a white-haired young man with a lightning bolt on his chest, and a Flamewielder, a triquetra on his chest. Unsurprisingly, there are no other Terraforgers.

I'm an oddity even among other Wielders. I should be used to it; I was an oddity within my own family even apart from my powers. I wonder how many of the others have had similar experiences. The other two trainees in our group are Grounders, and the willowy girl is from a noble family like mine.

My stomach flips as I try to imagine what life is like for my family back home. What has become of Arionna? Is she with Gruffud now that I am out of the frame? What about Mother? I try to force my focus back to the Zenith and Royal Brigade members nearby. I've never actually been trained to Wield by anyone. It was something I figured out all on my own.

All eyes are on me when I pull myself out of my wandering thoughts. Our trainer, a Zenith member clad in the typical midnight blue with black trimming on the uniform, stares into my soul. "Am I boring you, Pendry?" he asks.

Pendry. The name seems so unfitting, but so does fa Eurig. "No, sir," I respond, my cheeks heating.

I rein in my focus and absorb all the training I can. My Wielding capabilities are surprisingly stronger than the others. Perhaps because I have used it in sneaky ways over the years. Still, the training session drags on for hours, with a quick break for repast. By the time we're finally released to our rooms, the sun is beginning to sink.

My entire body aches, for once, not from the curse of my Cleanse but from actual physical exertion. It feels ... not unpleasant. It *makes sense*. I find myself almost blissfully tired as I return to my room.

I start peeling off my disgusting training gear, leaving a trail on the floor as I rush toward the bathing chamber. But as I dip a cloth into the basin of too-cold water and scrub dirt from my face and arms, I'm struck with the sinking realization that this is my life now. Not as Gwyneth fa Eurig, the highborn noble. Not as Gwyneth Pendry, the wife of Gruffud. But as Gwyneth ... the Zenith member?

Who am I?

I nearly lose my footing—as if someone has kicked me behind the knees—as the overwhelming desire to get away from Mainland and head northeast tugs at me. That damn tree resurfaces in my mind, and I mentally blot it out like throwing black paint over a finished portrait. I don't have time for such dreams; I need to focus on training so I can gain Rheon's trust. So I can hopefully find Father and somehow get Neris out of here.

Breathing in through my nose and out through my mouth, I

finish cleaning up. The water in the basin is a nauseating murky brown by the time I'm finished.

In silence, I get dressed and soon I'm rushing through the corridors, heading toward the infirmary.

As I push the door open, my eyes immediately fall on Neris. She's sitting up in bed, slightly hunched over in a loose-fitting white nightgown. Her gaze snaps to me, and a smile lights up her significantly less bruised face. Vaughn glances up from Neris's bedside, a bowl in hand, but before I can further assess the situation, I'm running toward Neris. I halt at her bedside, unsure of what to do with myself.

Vaughn places the bowl on the small table beside the bed. "I'll let you two talk," he says with a smile.

I nod appreciatively as he saunters off. I meet Neris's tired emerald eyes as I sink down to my knees at her bedside. "Neris ..." My voice comes out as a mere whisper. "You imbecile."

Her laughter sounds almost fractured—like she's forgotten how to laugh. It's more likely that it simply hurts too much.

"Guilty," she says, shakily lifting a hand.

I reach out to take her hand, giving it the gentlest of squeezes as I hold back tears.

"Don't look at me like that, Winnie. I'm fine."

"You're—" My voice catches, and I inhale deeply before clearing my throat. "This is my fault."

"Did you shove me into Gruffud? Did you force me to attack him?"

"No, but—"

"But what? There was nothing you could've done. Gruffud is a prick. He's always been a prick. No one can change him. He would've slaughtered you to save his own ass."

"I could've handled him myself. I wouldn't have let him slaughter me." Except he had been close to at least throttling me until unconscious.

Neris studies me somberly. Then she sighs gently and says, "It feels like my back is one giant wound. It's healed now, miraculously. But I've been told it'll scar." A playful glint appears in her eyes. "Maybe it'll make me look like a force to be reckoned with."

"Only if you walk around topless," I say, swiping away a stray tear.

Neris gives that odd little laugh again, and it physically hurts me.

I ignore the tug from within me that resurfaces and force my mind away from the searing heat of a flaming axe swinging through darkness. The image comes unbidden far too easily for my liking, and I'm sick of it.

Blinking, I find Neris staring at me as if I've been in my mind for far longer than I've realized.

"Care to share?" Neris asks, her brow cocked.

"Just exhausted. Training."

Her jaw drops. "Training? Like a soldier?"

"As a Zenith member." My heart hiccups uncomfortably.

"Oh, Winnie," she says with what looks like pity in her eyes. How can she pity *me* from where she sits?

I stand, craving silence now that I see Neris is on the mend. "You should get some rest, Neris. It's so nice to see you awake again. Keep healing, alright?"

"Winnie, wait. Are you sure—" She stops talking abruptly and glances around, checking if Vaughn is listening. She doesn't say much else; she only stares at me with that calculating look.

"I'm fine. I'm working on things." I can't say much else aloud.

Neris nods very slightly. "I've been told that as soon as I'm mended, I can reside in a guest room here. At least temporarily. Is this because of your new role?"

"Perhaps," I say with a forced smile, walking backward to the door. At least that's one good thing that's come from this arrangement.

The night brings feverish sweats and more agony than I think I can survive. Come morning, the inside of my cheek has been gnawed raw, my lip is swollen and split from holding back screams, and my throat is burning from retching for hours. The pain has subsided, but my body is drained of energy.

I'm noticeably shaking by the time I make it to the infirmary. Neris is asleep when I ask Vaughn for a few small doses of valbane to keep in my bedchamber. He hesitates at first, but then obliges when I explain the severity of my pain episodes. He gives me a draft of replenishing herbal tea and tells me to get some rest. As much as I want to look for Father and find out more information about this organization, I drag myself back to bed and sleep for the rest of the day.

Days of training go by, but I never return to the infirmary to visit Neris. It's too painful to see her in a place where I might as well have personally escorted her. I don't have much freedom in the castle as a trainee, but whenever I move through the hallways between the dining room and the training yard, I hope to catch a glimpse of my father. I stare desperately at every guard. I strain my senses to hopefully hear his name uttered. But no such thing happens and the pit in my stomach grows deeper with grief.

By the end of the week, I find myself preparing for my first mission.

I don't recognize the woman staring back at me in the mirror. The deep brown of my skin seems dulled, the waves in my ash brown hair limper than ever. I ache almost constantly, the nightly flareups from the aftereffects of the Cleanse barely manageable even with high doses of valbane. Nights are hellish, and mornings are muddled with overwhelming exhaustion. I cannot tell if this version of my life is better than the last—it feels equally miserable at times, but more bearable at others.

The leather armor over the midnight blue uniform and black cloak should look out of place on my body. But somehow, it feels more like me than the dresses I've worn my whole life. I don't have time to dissect that sentiment because, as I stare in the mirror, red eyes appear behind me, peering out from beneath a black hood.

I jump, but I don't cower. This time, I'm tired—of having no answers, of being in pain, of missing Neris and Father. "Who are you?" I ask aloud.

The eyes blink once, twice, then an ethereal voice fills my mind: *I am the Forge. I am Fury. My patience grows thin.*

"What do you want from me?"

I want you to assist the Heirs of Dusk and Embers. I want you to smite the oppressors.

"Who are the oppressors?"

The red eyes morph into slits like shards of ice. The voice that fills my mind is hollow and feels like spiders walking down my spine. *The gods cannot rise if the Heirs remain.*

An infuriated growl makes the hair stand on the back of my neck as the harsher voice speaks up again. *The gods must die!*

There's a conflict of ice and lava within me. I speak directly to the eyes like ice, my voice shaking as much as my hands. "And who are you?"

I am Winter.

The younger, flaming voice laughs. *You are nothing.* Then to me: *Stop the oppressors who seek to return the gods to their former glory. It will destroy the mortal realm.*

It will refresh the mortal realm, says the icy voice. *Balance will be restored.*

Save the Heirs. The fiery voice reverberates, and I swear heat singes my skin.

I wrap my arms around my body as the fingers of Winter caresses my face before heat streaks across it. *When the time comes, Winter cannot save you, mortal. It is Fury that will give you strength. And when the time comes, call to me.*

"Stop!" I shout, turning to face the ever-changing figure. But there's nothing there. *No one* there.

I stumble over to my desk and open the drawer, grabbing a vial of clear valbane with shaky hands. As it slips down my throat, I try to forget the voices. I have a mission to carry out.

Bring back the Shadow Wielder.

My heart catches in my throat as I remember the curly-haired woman from my dreams. She doesn't seem evil, but she terrifies me nevertheless. She knows about the stone. She knows about the calling that I constantly push away.

The guards in the hallway ignore me as I hurry through the corridors. I don't stop until I'm standing outside a door with gold lettering that spells *Library*. I push the door open and stand there, staring. I've seen many luxurious private libraries, but this one is far grander than any of those. My eyes roam over the floor-to-ceiling shelves and the foliage painted high up, close to the domed ceiling. Once I'm able to snap myself out of the awe, I move farther into the library. I browse the shelves, looking for a book about the pantheon. Until, at last, I find one and pull it from the shelf.

I flip through the pages with the book braced against my forearm until I land on an illustration of a figure in armor, a fiery axe, and eyes that seem to blaze despite it being drawn only in black ink. Below the image is a word written in bold lettering.

Damarlach. The goddess of war and blacksmithing. Of revenge and fury.

I flip through a few more pages and come upon the image of a cloaked figure.

Magdin. Goddess of winter; the veiled one.

What do the gods want with me? Cold terror wraps around my throat, squeezing, and it's as though I cannot breathe. I drop the book and run out of the library, needing to get outside, needing the grass beneath my feet to ground me. Two damn *goddesses* have been speaking to me? Fighting over me? I'm stopped as I make it to a door that leads outside.

The guard stares down at me. "Sorry, Miss, we cannot let you out of the fortress."

I can't seem to calm my breathing as I turn away. I'm not even sure where I'm going until I'm nearing the infirmary. Neris. I just need to talk to Neris. But as I barge into that room, I nearly run into an older woman with dark eyes and greying hair. She steps back, and my knees weaken, forcing me to press my hand against the wall to remain upright.

"Radika?" I whisper.

She holds a finger to her lips, then studies me for a moment before she says, "Ah, Gwyneth. I see you've joined the Zenith."

"What are you doing here?"

She winks at me and steps toward the door. "I gave Neris one last healing before she was discharged from the infirmary."

I glance around her and notice the empty bed. No other patients are in sight. "Where is she?"

"Settling into her new room, I'd imagine."

My heart picks up speed. "Do the gods still speak directly to mortals?" I blurt out.

A smile tugs her lips upward as she faces me again. "I think you already know the answer. They may not be strong enough to walk among us in the flesh, but they find ways to communicate."

My stomach flips uncomfortably. I have so many questions I want to ask about the gods, but I cannot push past the shock of this woman standing here in Paramount Castle. Why is she here? *How* is she here? Given that the Zenith also uses vanishing rings, was she a member of the Zenith? All this time?

She reaches into her pocket and pulls out something, which she slips into my hand. "Neris has her own now. These are for you."

"How—?" I start to ask. But what question do I even begin with? How is she always in the right place at the right time? She'd been there when Neris collapsed years ago. She'd been there when I'd just *barely* survived the Cleanse. And now here she is again as I'm desperate for my elixirs.

She swiftly makes an exit before I can ask anything. The door is still swinging when I slowly open my fingers and stare at the small drawstring satchel in my palm. I open it, several vials of purple elixir clanging against each other.

Did she know this would happen? I try to wrap my brain around everything I know about Radika. I once thought her to be a simple potion maker. A healer of sorts. But she's already revealed her identity as a Sorceress. Perhaps she has the gift of divination? Something used for scrying? My head aches and my pulse refuses to slow down. I need to head back to my room and just breathe for a moment.

I'm halfway across the castle when Lynx steps in front of me, forcing me to come to a halt and tripling my pulse again. "The sovereign has summoned you and the others," she says. "It's time."

Chapter 44

DURVLA

ICY RAIN BEATS down on us barely one hour after we leave the cave. The timing is abhorrent, but we ride on. We desperately seek someplace for shelter, but the wide valley with its smattering of short trees and little else leaves us open to the elements

I cling to the pommel of the saddle as Tiernan urges Ghendor forward. All our horses gallop madly as though riding into battle.

When the rain dies down at last, we dismount in a pasture of shaggy, drenched cows grazing in the wet grass. I'm soaked straight through my tunic and leather vest, even down to the band of fabric underneath. My trousers cling to me, making my thighs rub together. Even my socks are wet, my boots squelching with every step. The others look as miserable as I feel.

The mountains are in the distance now, and there seems to be nothing ahead of us but endless pasture. My hope sinks.

I wrap my arms around myself, trying to stop my teeth from chattering and my body from shivering.

Tiernan strokes Ghendor's soggy mane. The stallion tosses his head and huffs, clearly as annoyed as the rest of us.

Ava waves us over to her, but pinpricks race across my skin. It stops me dead in my tracks, terror slamming into me along with an image of a surprise attack.

"Ambush!" I shout.

Several figures in dark blue with black hooded cloaks materialize around us before anyone can react.

It's eerily reminiscent of the attack outside the Verge months ago. Except this time, there are no assailants in white among them. We all draw our weapons, though I fumble for my dagger, my fingers numb. My hands shake. I might have to take a life in order to save ours.

We position ourselves in a circle, facing outward. Tiernan is on my left and Ava squeezes in on my right. One of the attackers steps forward, a black mask covering their eyes beneath the hood. My pulse skitters, and I grip my dagger tighter.

"Stay close and do not *shadow wield,"* Tiernan says into my mind.

I don't have time to respond before he pushes me behind him to fight against a man with a large, curved blade. He drives the man back as combat erupts all around. The attackers vanish and reappear in a dizzying, chaotic pattern.

A familiar, fractured presence presses into me. I *know* that aura. Like eroded stone. Like a dam with a crack in it, just waiting to break. My eyes lock on to a cloaked figure of short stature and subtle curves beneath her muscular frame. She stands farther away from the other attackers. I can't see her face, but her posture seems stilted, nervous.

Somewhere to my right, Alys is lying in the wet grass. Chiyo doubles over at the waist, one hand still gripping one of her throwing knives. Pain distorts her normally fierce features.

Beside me, Ava is bleeding through her white tunic, a cut on her upper arm. My heart hammers erratically, and as one of the attackers charges me, I breathe in and let my dagger loose. It rotates through the air and finds its home in his shoulder. At the same moment, pain rips across my side. I don't have time to look down, as my dagger doesn't stop the assailant. But the knife now embedded in his chest does.

I glance over at Chiyo, who drops to her knees, her hands pressed firmly against her stomach. Isobel steps in front of her with her sword held in both hands.

My ribcage feels too tight; my friends are getting taken down one by one.

The appearance of a large attacker somehow halts the fighting. He says something while confusion claws at me. Tiernan grabs me by my shoulders, his face wrought with pain, tears glistening in his dark eyes.

"*Durvla,*" he says into my mind. "*Please forgive me.*"

My head reels. Why is he choosing this moment to beg for forgiveness? Before I can ask, he kisses me with a bittersweet fervor that steals my breath away and crushes my heart. I'm steered into someone, strong hands restraining me from behind, draining me as though a dampener has been clasped around my wrist again.

I watch helplessly as the scene unfolds with uncanny sluggishness.

Tiernan turns from me, stepping toward the attackers. Darkness scatters around him as he swings his arm out in a wide arc.

In the distance, the figure lifts her hand. The shadows clear, and an object flies from her hand through the air. Closer and closer until it locks around Tiernan's wrists.

Shackles.

His knees buckle. He glances over his shoulder at me, lips firmly sealed and bound hands unmoving. But I don't feel the nudge of his magic in my mind, or the whisper of his voice in my head.

I feel nothing. As if my body has shut down. As if all magic has ceased to exist.

The large man steps in front of Tiernan, a dark stone ring on his finger. A scream builds in my throat a heartbeat before the man presses his hand against Tiernan's shoulder and vanishes them both from the spot.

All the others wink out of existence one after the other, leaving behind only the shaking ground from the stampeding cows in the field. The grip on my arms loosens, allowing me to wrench myself free and spin to face my captor. The sense of my magic flows back into my body as tear-filled eyes stare back at me. Ava steps away, wrapping her arms around herself. Rage bubbles up inside of me, mingling with the sob that breaks free.

"What did you do?" I shout at her. "*What did you do?!*"

She takes a limping step back and closes her eyes, shaking her head as a solitary tear rolls down her cheek. "I did what I had to," she signs firmly. "I did what Tiernan asked me to do. To save you. At all costs."

I fall to my knees as if the numbness of whatever Ava did to me still lingers. Hurt and anger pours from me, channeled into a scream as I press my hands over my face to muffle it. Tiernan is gone.

He's *gone*.

That shadow show was to divert the attention from me. To take the blame for me. It feels like the ground has crumbled out from beneath me, and I'm falling with no end in sight.

We spent so much time avoiding discussions that needed to be had. I spent precious energy being cross with him. Ruined every moment we had. Moments that could've been our last. And now, just when things were good between us—just when I thought we could conquer anything thrown at us together ...

A hand rests on my back, but I don't bother to glance up. I don't bother to even shove them away. I take one breath, then another, and another, until I no longer have to remind myself to breathe. Until someone hauls me to my feet.

I'm surprised by the bright blue eyes that stare back at me. Osheen's. His gaze is steady, firm. "We have to go," he signs, releasing me. "Chiyo and Alys are hurt."

A couple of dead bodies of Zenith members were left behind. It seems more damage was done to our little clan. Chiyo's horse is without a rider, but Ava sits atop her horse with Chiyo slumped in front of her. Chiyo is paler than ever, her hand clutching her stomach. My heart falls.

Osheen taps me on the shoulder and signs, "We're going back to the cave. Need help mounting up?"

I shake my head and move on my own toward Ghendor. The stallion seems to lower himself for me as I slip my boot into the stirrup and swing my leg over his broad back. Pain flares in my side, doing nothing to help the dizziness that swoops in. It feels incredibly lonely atop the steed by myself—exposed to everything, vulnerable. My hands are slick, shaking as I grasp the reins.

What if they kill Tiernan?

A fresh sob catches in my chest, hurting so badly that it summons more dizziness. Everyone else mounts their horses, and we follow Ava, riding back toward the cave. Each gallop of Ghendor's hooves causes a fresh blaze of pain to ignite in my side, but I bite back the cries and keep my focus on the road ahead. Osheen leads Chiyo's horse, the mare following along obediently.

As we dismount in the cave, Alys summons magelights, letting them float up to the cave ceiling. She seems alright aside from a slight limp as she carries her bag of supplies across the cave to plop it down. With some effort, Ava helps Chiyo off the horse and carries her over to her mother.

Alys gets to work on her, glowing hands pressing against Chiyo's stomach while Chiyo writhes in pain.

As much as I want to go to her, my legs are leaden, incapable of moving.

I see Tiernan in my mind's eye again. Stepping in front of us like a martyr. He'd shoved me into Ava ... and she'd done *something* to temporarily suppress my powers. I briefly recall her referring to herself as an *Obstructor* back in the Verge. Why hadn't I asked what that meant? Why hadn't I known this?

They'd planned this.

Pain ripples through me again. I double over, dry heaving. As the world spins around me again, Isobel appears in front of me, peering into my face. "Are you hurt?" she asks.

I don't respond. I straighten my posture, trying to take a deep breath, but a stabbing sensation lances through my left side again. I cry out and hunker over, my hands tightly over my side.

"Let me see," Ava signs, suddenly replacing Isobel.

I step back from her, one hand desperately trying to suppress the pain, the other stretched toward her. Subtle shadows thread unbidden through my fingers, but I don't bother to rein in my control. "You let him take the fall for me. You *knew*." Tears spill down my cheeks.

"Durvla, we can discuss that later."

I want to scream at her. She let Tiernan take the fall. She let him be snatched from us. From *me*. Sardonic laughter claws out of my throat, but another stabbing sensation cuts it off. I lift my hand from my side and my palm comes away bloody. There's a slash through my leather armor.

"I know you hate me right now," Ava signs. "But we need to see how injured you are." This time I don't resist. She unfastens my armor from over my shoulder and lets it drop to the cave floor. She tugs my tunic up to reveal a bloody gash against my side. Ava waves her hand to draw my attention from it. "You're losing a lot of blood. You need to sit down before you faint."

So, I do, since it would be better than cracking my head on the stone floor if I collapse. It isn't a moment too soon either. I'm no outsider to darkness or its tendency to forcefully close its arms around me.

But I'm too overcome to fight, so I surrender to nothingness.

Chapter 45

TIERNAN

As I'm hurtled through the shadows, I can't stop thinking about the wounded look on Durvla's face. I'd bet my ass that whatever these people do to me, nothing could ever hurt more than seeing that look in her eye. When my feet hit solid ground again, I blink a couple of times until I can make sense of what I see. My wrists are still shackled, and the man who apprehended me still grips my shoulder as though he intends to break it.

Beneath my feet is a red carpet.

Marble statues of the gods and goddesses all around.

I know exactly where I am, even before I drag my eyes up the carpet-covered stone steps to the throne. And there's the bastard in all his newly crowned glory. He doesn't need an actual crown on his head to exude terrorizing dominance. Arrogance practically leaks from his pores, surprise, confusion, and intrigue in tow. Someone stands beside him, dressed in all black save for a red cape and the golden accents on a bizarre face mask. There is something dizzyingly familiar about them, but I can't quite put my finger on it.

I don't have much time to dwell on the masked person before Lord fucking Commander Rheon, the *sovereign*, stands and steps toward me. My entire godsdamned body shudders against my will, and from the gleam in his eyes, I know he notices.

"*You* are the Shadow Wielder?" he asks.

"Why does that surprise you?" My words fly out, unbidden.

He's close enough to practically share a breath, his eyes raking over the side of my neck with a sickening sort of satisfaction. At the scar that *he* inflicted. Pride pulses from him in overwhelming waves. Sick fuck. As much as I want to appear unaffected, my knees are quaking and sweat beads on my palms. My chest expands only after he takes a step back.

These shackles may dampen my Wielding mimicry, but my Empath powers seem intact. I have yet to decide whether that's a good thing. I need to keep my wits about me.

"Remove his weapons," Rheon says to the man at my side.

My eyes flick to the man. There's a flowy, luminous air to him— Waterweaver. A short Zenith member who I hadn't noticed before, is the exact opposite, an unyielding, ponderous ambience within her. Damarlach be damned, she's a Terraforger. I've never encountered such an aura, but I'm certain of it. Somehow.

The Waterweaver tugs my swords from the sheaths on my back. They clatter against each other on the carpet. He pulls the visible dagger from my hip next.

Rheon, the leech, sets hard eyes on me. "Do you have any hidden weapons?" he asks.

"Didn't you train me, sir?"

The corner of his lips twitches up into a sneer. "Where?"

I clench my jaw to keep from telling him that he also taught me not to reveal any hidden weapons to the enemy. It's hard to believe I once considered this asshole to be a decent human—my gods-damned mentor. And now I consider him my greatest enemy.

"Pendry," says Rheon, and the woman hesitates before she exhales audibly, her anxiety and remorse worming their way under my skin. She lifts her hand, palm up, and I suck in a sharp breath as the dagger in my boot slices through my sock and grazes my ankle. The other two hidden within my vest, luckily, do no harm.

All three daggers hover in the air in front of the woman before she lets them clatter to the floor just beyond the carpet.

I've never seen a Terraforger at work before, and I hate to admit it, but her abilities are impressive. I try not to think how easily she could transform any metal into a weapon. How easily she could probably slit a man's throat without even being in close range. She'd sent these manacles onto my wrists from quite a distance.

Yet she seems unwilling. Grudgingly doing Rheon's bidding. I know that feeling.

"Lynx, confiscate the weapons," Rheon says, though he never takes his eyes off me.

Who in hells is Lynx?

The figure in the red cape quickly descends the steps from the throne. I cautiously lower my mental shields just enough to hopefully find a crack in her mind. But I'm met with a frustratingly imposing blockade not unlike Ava's. Not necessarily Ordinary, but I sense no Wielding either ... There is, however, something oddly unstable about her. Unable to get a better read on her, I give up for now.

"Kilkenny!" Rheon's authoritative voice hauls my wandering mind back to him, but it's as if I've been catapulted into the past. I stomp to attention, but my salute is stopped by the damned shackles.

Rheon's amusement tickles my nose. I scrunch my face to keep from sneezing. As much as I want to reel my Empath powers in, as much as it exhausts me to keep using them, I need all the information I can get.

"When I sent my men out to find the rumored Shadow Wielder, the last person I expected to show up in my castle was you."

His castle. I bristle, wanting to put my fist through his face. I've spent five years in this castle. Five years of literal blood, sweat, and tears, secrets, pain, and love. The people here were like family to me. Though only ghosts of the past walk this castle now, it will never be his. I would pluck his sorry ass off the throne myself if it was within my power.

"My apologies if the revelation that *I* am the Shadow Wielder you sought is a disappointment to you, sir."

"Excellency," he corrects, and I damn near scowl at him. "Not a disappointment, but a surprise. I don't suppose you would willingly join the Zenith? We seek to make Erleya a safe place for everyone to be who they are. Where Mages are not feared but revered."

Rheon is not a Mage as far as I can tell. Why would he go to such lengths to make things safe for Magekind? "Not feared?" I ask. "Somehow, I highly doubt that, *sir*."

His eye twitches and I suffocate a grin.

"Fear is your middle name, if I recall." Gods, is this what it feels like to be Carys? To not be able to hold my tongue?

Rheon smiles, something deranged flashing in his eyes. The heat of his anger stings my skin, but he speaks with unnerving calm. "Fear is only necessary if reverence is not upheld."

I clench my teeth to keep from speaking, but then again, this egotistical bastard seems more than willing to give up information. Even if he doesn't realize it. "What drives your interest in Magekind, if I may ask, sir? Do you possess magic?"

A muscle twitches in his jaw, and I know I've struck a nerve. "We shall chat again tomorrow. For now, you're dismissed."

I stare down at my shackles. I have a feeling this dismissal is—

"Take him to the brig," Rheon tells the Waterweaver.

"Yes, Excellency." The Waterweaver grips my shoulder, and we go tumbling into the shadows again. I'm still not used to it, and when we land in a dark cell, my stomach clenches and my throat constricts. I close my eyes and fight the nausea. The Waterweaver says nothing to me; he simply steps out of the cell and a guard just outside of it slides the gate shut with a *clang*.

My eyes roam the small space as the click of the lock reverberates. The cell is about twice my arm span in width and perhaps a little deeper. A chamber pot sits in one corner and there is no mattress in sight. On either side of me are roughly hewn stone walls. Only the front is gated, but it doesn't allow me to see much aside from darkness and oil lamps. No ... not oil lamps, magelights.

Magelights in Paramount. Oh, I could find the humor in this. I *could*.

Cries and pleas echo somewhere outside of my stony cell. There are other prisoners here. A surplus of emotions and powers that makes my head spin and crawls through my blood. Voices echo in my head—a steady stream of incoherent words muddling in my mind until bile rises into my throat. I swallow forcefully and reel in my Empath powers, blocking everyone else around me. Only my surroundings fling me into the memory of Rheon towering over me, of the blade that scarred my skin and my dreams.

How long before he figures out that I'm a Mimic and not a Shadow Wielder? How long before they go in search of Durvla? Until she's here in this horrific place?

No one pays me any attention, but I know how these things work. They'll let me sit here, let the anxiety take hold of me. Maybe someone will eventually bring me water. Maybe food. Then the real threats will begin.

I sit down on the cold ground and tip my head back against the wall, closing my eyes. I can't let fear control me. Keeping it together is the only option I have. What did I always tell Durvla? Be brave? Don't break?

My stomach sinks at the thought of her. Shortly before leaving the Verge, Ava took me aside to explain the extent of her Obstructor power. It was at that moment that I asked her if she could block Durvla's shadow wielding if ever there was danger of her being exposed.

"Ava, please do this for me," I begged. "She might never forgive us, but we'll deal with that later. She has to get to Siad Nahar."

"I'll ask you again, Kilkenny. Could you go on living, knowing that you broke her heart *and* her trust?" Her words were a knife to the heart.

"I could go on knowing she's alive," I said. "And let's face it, Ava, if they take me into custody and discover I'm not who they're looking for, I won't have to *go on living* for very long."

Ava remained silent for a while longer. I thought she would just walk away or say something snide. Instead she twisted the dagger already in my heart. "Maybe so, but *she* would have to live without *you*."

Boots echo on the stony ground as someone approaches my cell. I allow my shields down, but I still feel *nothing*.

"Open the gate," a hoarse, feminine voice says.

I'm met with an impenetrable mental shield again as the masked woman steps into my cell. If she's Ordinary, she must have magical blood to enable her to keep her defenses up this way. She chucks something at me, and I reflexively catch it. The shackles dig into the skin around my wrists. The soft bread is surprisingly still warm, but why would they give fresh bread to a prisoner?

"Thank you," I dare to say, awkwardly holding the bread in my shackled hands.

The masked woman stands there in uncomfortable silence, observing me. Refusing to be rattled, I munch on the bread slowly.

"Bizarre," says the woman, her voice laced with amusement. "Seeing the great Major Tiernan Kilkenny diminished to a groveling prisoner."

My hackles rise. It takes longer than it should for me to get the bread down my throat.

"For now, anyway," she adds. "Oh, I do hope you don't make things too easy."

She takes a waterskin off the belt hidden underneath her red cape and tosses it toward me. It hits the stone ground with a sloshing sound. I know she expects me to rush for it right away, but I don't dare take my eyes off her.

"Who are you?" I ask.

"A nightmare," she says. A surge of sensations momentarily flows out over her fiercely erected wall—cold sweat, searing pain, and white-hot fear. In a heartbeat, she mentally smothers it all again. I shudder.

Interesting.

She sweeps out of the cell with excessive flare before I can pick up on any more emotion.

I miss Durvla's presence—I miss the way her thoughts are launched at me. I miss the sound of her sweet, melodic voice, her laughter, her body against mine.

If these miscreants end my life, there will be so many things left unsaid. But maybe it's for the best. At least when all is said and done, I will have given the woman I love a chance to live. She'll one day be able to move on without me.

Chapter 46

TIERNAN

THE NEXT TIME I hear footsteps, I perk up and give my visitor my full attention. Lynx peers at me through her mask from the cell entrance. The guards open the gate, and she gestures impatiently to me. "Well, come on."

Stiffly, I get to my feet, and as soon as I am beside her, she lays a hand on my shoulder and jumps us out of the brig and into ... somewhere else. I slowly breathe through my nose, trying to ward off the sick feeling in my gut. We're standing in a passageway before a door, with two guards plus the Terraforger already there. This time, the Terraforger is unmasked, light brown eyes teeming with so much emotion that I'm inclined to keep my mental shields firmly up.

"We don't have all day, Pendry," Lynx bites.

The Terraforger seems to hesitate, but then she snaps her fingers and the chain between my shackles disconnects with a rattle. The cuff on my right hand breaks apart next, and all the pieces float into Pendry's waiting hands. I'm left with a simple manacle on my left arm and the continued dampening effects pressing into me.

Lynx steps forward, close enough for me to be overwhelmed by the scent of roses and bitter herbs. As if she's attempted to cover up something more medicinal with far too much perfume. I stand still as she grasps my arm and lifts it, checking the shackle. Satisfied, she drops my arm.

344

"Tidy up, get dressed, and be ready for your summons from the sovereign. All your clothes were left untouched."

She takes a couple of steps, then vanishes as if *walking* is beneath her. Pendry seems inclined to say something to me, but her pouty lips pucker even tighter, and she turns on her heel to hurry off. I dare to peek at her emotions; her guilt barrels into me with such strength that I nearly lose my balance.

The guard opens the door to the bedchamber for me, and I step inside. There's a familiar, massive bed, black curtains drawn over the large bay window, and multiple swords hanging against one wall. Lynx's words suddenly make sense. *My clothing* ... Because this is my chamber. The last time I was here, I'd come to change out of my knight's armor and into a suit for the Feast.

To dance with Durvla.

The ache in my chest becomes unbearable, and I rub at it as I force myself to push past the sentiments. A bath and fresh clothing should do me well. Then I'll figure out what in hells my next step will be.

There are no servants to fill my bath, nor do I have the freedom to fetch the water myself, so I scrub the filth off my body with a washcloth and tepid water from the basin in the bathing chamber. I trim my beard close to my face and stare at my scraggly reflection in the mirror. I've seen better days.

But I've seen even worse days.

My hair is in need of a trim as well, but time isn't on my side. I pull it back into a bun at the nape of my neck and slip into a fresh shirt and lightweight trousers. My maroon uniform stares at me from the wardrobe. I run my fingers over the material. Five years in Carys's service and just as many in the Royal Brigade.

Just when I'd gotten used to being my own man ... here I am again.

A sigh drops from me as my door swings open. I'm fully clothed, but I feel naked without weapons. No swords, no daggers, no Wielding. Only my mind.

"Let's go," says Lynx.

My steps appear sure, but my legs feel shaky as I follow her out of the room and down the hallway. We walk past several doors, making our way swiftly toward what I'm certain is Iywan's study. Or Rheon's now.

The burly man sits behind the desk. I'm reminded of the many times I've been summoned to his office or tent during my active duty with the Royal Brigade. How many times have I stood before this man and received orders I was reluctant to carry out? How many horrendous laws have I enforced in the name of *justice*? How many Forayers did I train? How many Grounders were hanged or banished because I felt obligated to follow Erleya's twisted laws?

"Welcome," Rheon says, standing from the desk and dismissing a man with dark brown skin and flowing robes.

Jac! I glare at the youngest Master Historian Erleya has known as he bows to Rheon. That pretentious shit can irritate me by mere proximity. He'd always sided with Iywan, and now Rheon? He averts his gaze before sweeping out of the room. I've never trusted him and neither did Carys.

I turn back to Rheon. "You've retained the Council, I see."

Rheon smiles with a coolness that I'm too familiar with. "Jac is the only survivor, evidently."

My back straightens. I feel my nose wrinkle before I school my features into disinterest.

"Ah!" Rheon says lightheartedly as a clanging sound comes from somewhere behind me. I glance over my shoulder as a couple members of the kitchen staff file into the room with dome-covered silver chargers. A savory aroma reaches my nose as they walk past me and into the adjoining dining chamber.

Rheon holds his hand out toward the chamber, smiling courteously. I give him a nod and make my way into the next room. He follows me. "I hope you enjoy lamb and leek pie. We also have fresh mussels and seasonal vegetables."

It's an odd combination of foods, but the golden crust of the meat pie does look tempting. "I do," I say to Rheon, though it feels like there is a rock in my throat.

"Sit." He gestures to a chair.

I highly doubt he's cursed the chair or anything, but it still takes me a moment to sit down. A tan young woman with curly blond hair glances askew at me as she fills Rheon's goblet. As she moves to fill mine, I gently hold my hand up. "No, thank you."

Surprise and intrigue lifts her brow.

"You mistrust me," Rheon says, and the young woman straightens, glancing between us. Unease rolls off the other servants, a crawling sensation down my spine.

"I don't generally consume alcohol."

"You're not on duty."

"I'm always prepared." A smirk twitches at the corner of the blond woman's lips, amusement lighting up her green eyes.

"You can leave the bottle," says Rheon. "You're free of duty now, thank you."

The blond dips a gentle curtsy and leaves the room silently while one of the other servants cuts the pie, dishing out slices for Rheon and me. The other servant piles vegetables and mussels onto our plates.

"Enjoy," Rheon says after dismissing the servants with a wave of his hand.

I lift my fork to dig into the pie, but that rock in my throat slips down farther with the first bite I take. For a while, there's only the sounds of the metal against porcelain and quiet chewing. Even as the rock descends farther and settles into my stomach. I place my knife and fork down, folding my hands atop the table.

Rheon's eyes land on the manacle enclosing my left wrist and I keep my gaze unfaltering when he meets it again. "That must be uncomfortable," he says.

"I've been in worse discomfort." The scar along my neck itches, and I resist the temptation to scratch. "Why have I been brought here?"

"It seems your patience has dwindled over the years, soldier."

I shrug. "I'm no soldier."

"Ah, see that's where you're wrong, lad." He waves his fork in the air before unceremoniously popping more pie into his mouth and chewing. "Once a soldier, always a soldier. We're brothers—bound beyond blood. Ties that cannot be broken."

Bullshit. Needing something to do with my hands, I pick my fork up again. "Commander, if you could be straightforward with me, I would appreciate it." *Before this fork* accidentally *ends up in your neck*.

"Join the Zenith. That's all. Join our cause, fight for the winning side, and you will be pardoned of all misdeeds."

"Misdeeds?" My knuckles go white on my fork before it drops onto my plate with a clang. "Do enlighten me."

Rheon gently places his utensil down and leans back in his chair, his dark blue eyes narrowed on my face. "Your involvement with the rebels and their attempted slaughter of the princess five years ago. You never served your sentence."

My stomach plummets. The sentence was fifty lashes prior to being hanged. "Are you threatening to hang me, Commander?"

He forces his jaw to unclench as he smiles through the annoyance jabbing at him. It takes great control not to grin knowing that not calling him Excellency is getting under his skin.

"Not if you join our cause."

"Queen Morwenna pardoned me years ago," I say.

"The queen is dead."

The words feel like a physical blow, even knowing what I do. Silence fills the space between us, and long gone is my appetite. As risky as it is to fully open my mind, I gently do so, prodding at his. The man radiates a strange energy I can't place—it feels dissonant and unnatural. Yet I can't sense any Wielding within him, and his emotions come to me so scarcely. I'm almost certain he has something that protects his mind. Everything about him feels *wrong*.

"Your beloved princess nearly burned down the castle. The entire council room was ash by the time I arrived. Councilors included. Jac survived because he hadn't been present at the final meeting."

My heart lurches. "How fortunate for him." *The bastard*. "What is expected of Zenith members?" I inquire, shifting my focus so as to not dissolve under my hatred for Jac and Rheon.

"Support in our endeavor to create the strongest army Erleya has ever seen. The strongest army the *world* has ever seen."

Queasiness stirs in my gut. "A Mage army?"

"Indeed."

My jaw nearly unhinges. "How do you intend to do that when, for years, we have enforced anti-magic laws?"

A wicked glint appears in his eyes. "Perhaps it appeared that way on the outside, but I have been recruiting Mage soldiers for years now. Slowly. Surely. Patiently." He grins at me then lifts his fork to resume eating. Mince falls from the tines as he shovels more pie into his mouth.

"You have no powers, though. Why do you think you're the right person to lead a Mage army?"

He takes another mouthful of food and chews with a strange, closed-mouth smile. He drinks a few sips of wine and says, "Because I've given them sanctuary in a kingdom that has sought to and succeeded in killing their ancestors. Because *I* am the hope of Erleya."

Damarlach smite me ... With an argument like that ... We are in for a world of trouble.

Chapter 47

DURVLA

I'VE BEEN reluctant to leave the comfort of unconsciousness. Even unprepared to face reality, I peel my eyes open to find Chiyo lying on blankets on the cavern floor beside me. Her head is angled toward me as I blink and rub my eyes. I roll onto my side with a movement that makes my bones ache and my side sting. Chiyo tries to muster a smile, but her eyes are weary and dull, her face paler than I've ever seen it before.

"You're alive." I'm certain that my voice croaks for how dry it is.

She rolls onto her side, propping her head up on a shaky hand and nodding. "*You're* alive," she signs one-handedly.

Slowly, I sit up and lean against the cave wall. I lift my tunic to get a look at my wound, but there's nothing there save for a thin white scar against the light brown of my skin. Isobel brings me a waterskin, and when my head begins to clear, I spot Ava sitting a short distance away, whetting her sword with focused precision.

Anger rises up in me, rivaling the grief in my heart. But I don't get the chance to dwell on it before Sloan crouches down in front of me. "How are you feeling?" they ask.

I watch the words on their lips and shrug an achy shoulder.

"Alys is sleeping to regain her energy. She lost quite a lot of blood herself. As did Chiyo. Then there's you. We almost lost three of you."

We lost one. My chest hurts as my heart constricts, and suddenly

350

I cannot breathe. My pulse spikes as I think of Tiernan. Is he alive? Is he being tortured like Carys said she'd been months ago?

Sloan places their stump on my shoulder. "Deep breaths."

I listen, but it's easier said than done.

With another pat on my shoulder, they leave. I lean back and close my eyes, hoping that sleep takes me, because it's easier than confronting reality right now.

Chapter 48

CARYS

"You call that a punch? Come on, Princess." Valdis blows her golden hair out of her eyes and ducks beneath my flying fist yet *again*.

Three weeks on this ship and it's felt like three months. I have plenty of steam to work off. I growl in frustration and immediately swing wildly when she's upright again.

"I didn't take you for a slow learner," Valdis taunts. "Come—*oof*!"

Sharp pain cuts through my knuckles as the sound of my fist connecting with her face draws Seth's attention.

"Fuck!" Valdis says under her breath. She holds a palm over the unmarked side of her face.

Seth is staring up at Valdis from where he has a map rolled out on the deck. If I didn't know better, I would say that he looks worried. But that can't be it. I've seen Valdis fight.

I shake out my hand, knuckles still throbbing as a couple of crew members playfully jeer at Valdis. "How's that for slow learning?" I ask her.

"How's your hand?" she teases. She shifts her jaw side to side, making sure it's intact.

"How's your *face*?" I grin at the red spot my fist left on her cheek now, rivaling her birthmark.

"Lucky hit," she says. She dodges to the side as my fist flies at her face again. "Alright! Aim for something other than my face."

"Val," Seth calmly calls from the side.

Valdis ignores him, but as I narrow my eyes in his direction, her foot comes at me. I manage to dodge, though I lose my balance and fall onto the deck. My hands take the brunt of my fall, pain spreading up to my wrists. Valdis's raucous laughter travels on the sea breeze that chills my sweaty neck and face.

She extends her hand to help me up, but I swat her hand away and jump to my feet. She straightens, raising her fists again with a proud smile pulled across her lips. "Well, what are you waiting for?" she asks.

Using what she's taught me, I execute a series of jabs and kicks, evading when I can, my heart rate rising in an exhilarating way. I try to predict her movements, managing to block blow after blow, earning encouraging words and corrections from her every now and then. *Good one. Faster. Follow through.*

Her fist catches my shoulder, and I wince, though it isn't hard enough to truly hurt. "You should've seen that coming, Princess. Do better!"

"You're going easy on me!" I complain.

She smirks. "And you're still losing. Again, aim for something other than my face."

I aim lower and hear Seth draw a breath while Valdis blocks my strike with her forearm. Before I can attempt another strike, the back of her hand whacks me across my face so hard that I stumble back, my cheek stinging.

Valdis straightens, white teeth flashing. "Payback," she says.

"Seth distracted me," I protest.

Valdis glances at him as he leans against the mast, an odd look on his face. "Could I interrupt the two of you for a brief consultation?" he asks in that clipped Ardallan accent. "Val?" He eyes his wife, and she huffs out a breath.

Glancing at me, she says, "Good session. Let's resume with swords next time."

"Excellent," I respond, slightly winded.

Valdis claps me on the shoulder, and I wince from the soreness.

Odgar has been busy conferring with the crew. My eyes wander toward where he's locked in conversation with the man currently steering the ship. As if he senses me, Odgar looks my way, and even from this distance, I can see the smile that lights up his face.

My heart gives an annoying little jolt, and as I look away, I find Briony approaching. I wipe sweat off my brow as she beams at me, though I groan inwardly. I'm also supposed to train with her today.

It's easier to block Enidwen out when my mind is occupied—especially during fight training with Valdis. However, once that distraction ends, Enidwen's voice blows through my mind like an incessant wind. It rattles against my barriers as she loudly reminds me of her presence. As if I could forget.

I've been reluctant to use my firewielding as it seems to only strengthen the connection between us—her shadowfire readily melds into my flames if tumultuous emotions are involved. Which ... given my history, is very likely at any given moment. When I'm not keeping myself busy, my powers call out to me. They beg to be released, leaving me feeling jittery, unsettled, and even overheated at times.

"Ready?" Briony asks me.

"No," I admit. "I'm exhausted."

"Well, what better time to practice shielding your mind against the enchantress than when your body is exhausted. It's a great opportunity, in fact." Her hair is braided over her shoulder today, and there's some color in her cheeks. Ship life seems to have done her well.

We step away from all the chatter and make our way toward the back of the ship, where it's a little quieter. Gripping the taffrail, I stare out across the water. "Do you think I could ever learn to *completely* block her out?" I ask Briony.

She leans her back against the rail, one hand wrapped around it to keep herself steady. "Perhaps," she says. "It would be hard to do, however, given that her strength is tied to yours. The stronger you get—" She stops when I wince. "But keep in mind that the stronger you get at *shielding*, the easier it will be to block her out. Perhaps not permanently, but enough that it doesn't completely disrupt you."

I inhale deeply. "Alright," I say. "Let's do this."

Chapter 49

GWYNETH

AFTER RETURNING with the Shadow Wielder, I was rewarded with trust. After meeting with the sovereign, I returned to my room to find Neris sitting there, beaming at me as though she'd never been flogged in the square. I hugged her for as long as she allowed me, then apologized profusely for getting her into this situation until she threatened to slap me.

And now I can wander the castle as I see fit, so long as I show up to training and report to the sovereign whenever summoned.

Large archways and columns with beautiful carvings usher us through the never-ending corridors of the castle. My heavy boots drown out the *click clack* of Neris's shoes as we wander the passages, exploring beyond where I've been allowed before. There are no appearances of aristocracy to keep up, no husband to please, no suffocating family members to get under my skin. Yet I have never felt so burdened.

I cannot get the look of pain in the captive's eyes out of my mind. Something about his face and even his name reminds me of someone I've met before, but I cannot put my finger on it.

I haven't given up on looking for Father but it's certainly starting to feel futile.

Neris is prattling my head off as we round a corner and wind up in a more secluded area of the castle. My heart grows heavier and heavier with the thoughts of Father and the thoughts of the Shadow

Wielder I helped capture a week ago. In the field where we ambushed those travelers, I felt the pulse of my pocket watch. It prompted me to look across the field to a woman with curls escaping her braid.

I'm certain that *she* is the Shadow Wielder the sovereign seeks; I'm sure she's the one I've seen walk through shadows in my dreams.

Then again, we all saw the man wield darkness when our troop leader demanded that the Shadow Wielder reveal themselves. What are the odds there were two Shadow Wielders reluctant to use their powers to smite us right away? It goes against everything I've ever learned about Dark Mages. What's worse is that, even though I was halfway across the field, I saw the man's interactions with the woman. I saw the way he protected her, the way he took her into his arms and kissed her before ensuring that she was held back. He surrendered to us, seemingly to protect the rest of his friends. To protect *her*.

He seems to be a good man. But he also seems to have a less-than-pleasant history with the sovereign. Their encounter in the throne room leaves a gnawing feeling in the pit of my stomach. I wouldn't put anything past the sovereign; I've seen his brand of cruelty enforced in the square. I've heard stories from Father. He'd once told me that as long as a person stays in Commander Rheon's good graces, they would be fine.

A sharp jab in my rib forces a whoosh of air from me, and I jump, startled. "Realms, Winnie, lost in thought?" Neris asks, stepping in front of me with a worried look in her eyes.

I rub my ribs. "Yes, apologies."

She huffs an exasperated sigh. "Did you hear a word I said?"

"I—" The thought of lying to her crosses my mind, but I know she'll just ask me to repeat what she said. I don't think I could repeat even one word.

Today she's in a green silk dress with tiny white flowers throughout. Her blond curls are pulled up into a ponytail with a large bow that droops down the back of her head. Her cheeks are a healthy, rosy color. Two weeks in the castle have surely done her well, even with her occasional shift in the kitchen.

"I want to get us out of here," I say in hushed tones. "But ... you seem to be doing so well."

She looks at me as though I have mud splattered all over my face. "You're kidding me, right? Winnie, this place is disturbing. If you can figure out a way for us to get out of here, I wouldn't be too disappointed. The luxury is wonderful, but this is not the freedom I want. And I'm sure it's not what you want."

My stomach squirms.

"Where are we going anyway?"

"This corridor is rarely guarded, and if you look closely ..." I move toward one of the columns bracketing an archway. Running my fingers along the marble, I feel for cracks. My fingertips brush against a disruption in the stone and, indeed, there are tiny fractures within it. The faintest sign of discoloration becomes more obvious. I hold my open palm up to the column, reaching out with my terraforging. Black specks float onto my fingertips.

"What in the hells is that?" Neris asks.

"Ash." I let the particles float away and turn my gaze down to the floor. "I can sense it along this entire corridor ... sort of ... in the tiles. They've done a great job cleaning, but this must be closer to the source of the fire perhaps? Or maybe just a spot they never expected anyone else to reside in. Not yet, at least, so ..." I start to move again and Neris follows until we happen upon a door that's very slightly ajar.

My forehead creases as I stare at the door.

"Winnie ..."

I push the door open and peek inside. The room looks like it's been ransacked, papers and books strewn all over the floor, sheets hanging off the bed, and drawers open. I push it open farther to find a large four-poster bed adorned with wispy white canopies. A stately oak desk on one side is stacked with books, a diadem sitting atop them. I gasp, and Neris clamps her hand over my mouth. "Shh." She practically shoves me into the bedchamber, and the door quietly clicks shut behind us.

A tense silence fills the room.

"What do you think happened?" Neris asks, gesturing to the surroundings.

"I don't know, but I think this is—*was*—the princess's room."

Awed, she begins to carefully step over the items strewn on the floor, making her way farther into the immense chamber. She doesn't touch anything, but she removes her spectacles from her pocket and sets them on her small nose before crouching to get a look at each of the books. "These are all romances," she says.

At last, she picks one up and flips through the pages. Her eyes drink in a passage and she giggles. "Let's see ..." I watch her eyes roam over the page, her finger tracing the lines. Then she reads aloud in a theatrical tone, "Lust burned in Eideard's loins—"

"Realms ..."

"—as he feasted his eyes upon Finella's ample bosom." She glances up at me with a smirk. "Oh look, Winnie, she's like you. Or how did you say Lady Mari put it?"

I make a face and groan. "Neris, by the realms, it really is time to grow up. We're not children anymore."

The smile is wiped off her face instantly. She doesn't drop the book, but she snaps it shut and carefully steps her way back through the sea of objects. Her eyes hold no amusement. "I think you need to grow *down*, Winnie. You've forgotten how to have fun."

Heat floods my head. "Well pardon me. Getting married off to an abusive prick and watching my friend be nearly killed because of it took the fun out of life. As did being arrested and forced into the service of a dodgy organization."

Neris stops moving, staring down at the book in her hands. To my embarrassment, my tears break loose when she looks at me again. I scrub the tears away and confront the mixture of resistance and sympathy on Neris's face.

"Life isn't fair," she says steadily. "In fact, it fucking *stinks*. My father abandoned my mother when I was a wee babe, and my mother is forever gone from my life. I don't want to lose my best friend too. So ..." She grabs my hand and slaps the book into my palm. I grip it in both hands before it can fall. "I'd love it if you could do me a huge favor and find my best friend. My chosen sister." Her voice catches and it breaks my heart.

The last time I saw Neris truly cry was after her mother died. When her emerald eyes brim and overflow now, she doesn't bother to wipe them away. She doesn't hide her emotions but rather embraces them as if they give her strength.

"Listen," she continues. "I don't know what the fates, or the stones, or the gods—or *whoever*—has in store for you. But it's up to *you* what steps you take. There's no one forcing you to make the wrong decisions. Every time you had the opportunity to change your life, you made an excuse not to. You never take matters into your own hands because you're afraid to stir the pot. And that's what's holding you back."

I can only stare at her. No words come to mind. No thoughts even. I just stand there, in the princess's room, staring at Neris with tears slowly trickling down my face.

Neris releases a breath and wraps her arms around me, hugging me far too tightly, the book trapped between us. Yet my shoulders relax for the first time in days, and that overwhelming buzzing under my skin settles. She continues to hug me, and it does nothing to stop the flow of my tears. "It's time you lived, Winnie. I know you're looking for your father, but ..." She gives a watery smile and shakes her head.

"I know," I say, my voice thick with choked back tears.

"We'll figure it out. But in the meantime, I want to know what happened with Finella and Eideard."

"What ...?"

She casts a pointed glance down to the book in my hands, a smirk on her face despite her still-glistening eyes.

"You're ridiculous," I say, thrusting the book at her. It opens slightly as she grapples for it, and a piece of folded parchment falls from between the pages and flitters a small distance away.

"What's that?" Neris asks.

I step over a few hair accessories and makeup brushes, retrieving the paper from the floor. Beautiful penmanship fills the page, the ink smudged here and there, the paper wavy and deformed as though it had been previously wet.

Born of the moon and hewn from the stars,
You are shrouded in starlight, in shadows and dreams,
The darkness within you is yours to command
You will long for solace, but fear holds your hand

Born of the sun and cursed by the fates,
You are gilded in sunlight and forged from the flames,
The darkness within you you're certain to blame,
You'll long for life's pleasures but sorrow's lain claim

United in shadows, in a blaze of reveries
You will thwart the hand of Chaos
In the depths of memories

United in fire, in light and in dreams
You will foil the wiles of Chaos,
You will spur Death's victory

The words seem to float in the air in a visible wave of iridescent colors, the melody playing through my mind as clearly as if there were a bard singing into my ear, backed by melodic strings and percussion. With a gasp, I drop the parchment and watch it flutter to the ground.

"Winnie, what is it?"

I stare down at the parchment for a while before squatting to pick it up again. Neris willingly takes it, curiosity etched into her expression as she pushes her spectacles up her nose and reads the lines. She takes a while with it, then glances up at me. "Alright, please enlighten my Ordinary mind."

"I heard music in my mind. I even saw it."

Neris swears under her breath. "You know, sometimes I do not envy you, but other times ... Music? Is it pleasant?"

"It is." I smooth my hair back before my hand moves to the pocket of my dress.

"I hate you." Her voice holds no edge, and she giggles. "Who do you think wrote it? The princess?"

I shrug. "I think you should keep it."

The skin between Neris's brows pinches tight. "Why?"

"I'm not sure. It feels important and I don't want it confiscated or ruined. Keep it close."

Realms bless her, she doesn't question me further. She folds up the note and tucks it into the top of her bodice. After looking around for a while, she asks, "What do you think happened in here?"

"Someone was looking for something."

"No shit."

I huff a laugh before it's snuffed out. "Everything about this castle is strange. Something feels off about it. This room, especially. There is something devious at play here, and I'm not sure what it is."

A grin slowly spreads across her face, her eyes expectant.

"And I'm going to figure it out," I say. "I may have to play into the Zenith's mission for a while longer, but I'll get us out of here somehow."

Neris cheers. "There's the Winnie I know!"

Chapter 50

DURVLA

I'M OUT OF TINCTURES, so I'm left with herbal tea to take the edge off my headaches. It doesn't do much to help with the usual dizziness, but Alys exhausted a lot of her healing magic after the ambush, so I'd rather give her time to recover.

I imagine that the cavern is rather silent right now. Chiyo and Ava are on opposite sides, Sloan is nowhere in sight—patrolling, perhaps—and Osheen, surprisingly, is chatting with Isobel.

"How do you feel?" Alys signs as she passes me a small copper cup wrapped in cloth, so I don't burn my hand.

I shrug a shoulder. My chest feels overstuffed, and my jaw aches from keeping it clenched to suppress more silent tears. I've already shed so many.

"Any pain?"

I swallow thickly and blink away more tears that brim.

"Oh, sweetling. I wish I could heal your heart right now more than anything else. We'll figure something out. You know Tiernan is tough. I'm certain they already regret having him in their custody." She winks, but I cannot find it in myself to indulge in the mild light-heartedness. "It will be alright."

Alys, bless her, seems to understand that I want to be left alone. She cannot be sure that he'll be alright. We don't know what the Zenith is capable of or why exactly they want me, but Iywan had told Carys back when she was being tortured in Paramount that they wanted to open the Veil. If that is the circumstance, perhaps it's the same reason they want me, given that I share Carys's bloodline. What will happen when they realize Tiernan isn't the person they seek? Will they kill him?

My chest grows tighter, my stomach roils. I close my eyes as darkness begins to infiltrate my vision. *Breathe.* I force myself to draw in a breath, to hope with everything I have that if he left this world, I would feel it. The same way he had faith that I would feel if Carys had been killed.

But right now, I don't have the same faith in myself that he did in me.

We set off again under the cover of night, this time taking a path north of the Wastelands, heading toward Dubh Carrig. With us all so worn out from travel, the major setback with Siad Nahar, and Tiernan being captured, we agree that it would be far too risky to cross over into Mainland right now. That with the Zenith and the Purists at large, we wouldn't stand a chance.

It still feels unnatural being atop Ghendor by myself, but mercifully, the horse seems to sense my grief and takes on an uncharacteristic gentleness. By sunrise, we stop in an area secluded by trees to rest and eat something. Chiyo converses with Isobel and Sloan, but very obviously avoids even looking at Ava or Osheen.

Ava stands as I bite into a too-acidic bilberry. I track her steps across the small space. She walks not with her usual grace or ease but clearly favoring one leg, and her face is pinched as if she's the one who ate the berry.

Alys is snoozing against the trunk of a tree, and the others aren't paying attention. In fact, Chiyo is *intentionally* not looking Ava's way. I pop another terrible bilberry into my mouth and set the rest aside on a cloth before standing slowly. My body feels battered; my head takes longer than usual to adjust, dizziness lingering. But as soon as I can move without a huge risk of collapsing, I hurry to Ava.

"You're hurt," I say just before she can disappear behind the thick shrubs.

Surprise sparks in her eyes, but she denies it. "I'm fine. Just going to piss, if you don't mind."

With a sigh, I turn away from her, but I don't leave. There aren't many trodden paths near us; I suppose many don't frequent this area. At this point, I wish we'd never left the Verge. None of us would be hurt, and Tiernan would still be here.

My throat is just starting to close when Ava steps out from the bushes again, tightening her sword belt around her waist over her leather vest. Her lips are pinched tight with what I'm certain is pain, but she faces me with her usual bravado.

"Has Alys healed you?" I sign to her.

"I'm fine," she signs back. She takes one step and winces, glancing sidelong at me.

"Oh, clearly." I fix her with a look of cynicism.

She waves me off and walks back toward the group again, trying her hardest not to hobble. And I thought *I* hated accepting help from others. She might be stubborn, but I also know that she never turns down a challenge. "Ava!" I call, pulling a dagger from my waist in front of everyone. She turns and I point the dagger toward her.

She rolls her eyes, laughing dryly. "You cannot be serious."

All eyes fall on us. My own gaze falters, meeting Chiyo's as she rises with a brow quirked.

"I challenge you," I say, hoping I sound sure of myself as I tuck my dagger back into the holster and stride toward Ava.

She gets into a fighting stance. *Of course* she does.

My weary muscles quiver as I do the same. Without giving her any time or announcing the start, I throw a punch. Ava moves to dodge and sets her left foot down. I barely weave from her strike and throw another punch her way. But as she ducks, I summon my shadows, a ribbon of darkness wrapping around her right foot and forcing her to set it down to regain her balance. She cries out in pain and goes down, catching herself on her hands. Chiyo rushes toward her, followed by Alys who's wide awake by now.

I take a knee in front of Ava as she sits on her bum. Both hands cling to her right shin. I move aside to give Alys room as she kneels beside Ava. "Let me see," she says.

Anger flares in Ava's eyes. "No," she says as she releases her shin and scoots back away from her mother. "I'm *fine*."

The hurt is clear on Alys's face, but she doesn't back off. She doesn't move forward either, but she says, "Remove your boot."

"I don't have to do anything you say."

I look back and forth between them.

Alys mumbles something—I'm certain it's not the Common Tongue—and it's clear that Ava understands it. But she doesn't relent; she only frowns harder.

"Ava," Alys says, her face set.

"I don't want you to touch me, and you have no right to command me. I'm not a child. You already missed those years."

Chiyo's eyes soften for the briefest moment, but then she says, "Lugda's hells, Ava. We need you in fighting condition, and you can't do a thing on that foot. Now take the damn boot off!"

Ava meets Chiyo's gaze, many unspoken words between them. At last, Ava huffs and turns to look at her mother again, nodding her head subtly. Chiyo's shoulders slump with relief.

Carefully, Ava unlaces her boot, gritting her teeth as she very slowly removes it from her foot.

"Socks too," Alys says.

Ava seems to hold her breath as she slowly pulls her sock off, revealing an ankle triple the size and deep angry purple against her warm brown skin.

Chiyo flinches noticeably, and Isobel appears out of nowhere to look on. Her face crumples as Ava closes her eyes.

"Ava!" Chiyo exclaims. "You were just going to keep your mouth shut about this?"

"It's broken," Alys says. "And ... more complex than that. Do you feel any burning or numbness above or below the injury?"

"Burning," Ava says, looking more annoyed than anything by now.

"I'm going to have to reset the bone. It's not going to be pleasant."

"Just get it over with."

Alys nods. She places her palm over the top of Ava's foot, and the other above her ankle. Her hands glow with her healing powers, a warm blue, and Ava's hand shoots out to grab something, anything. Chiyo catches Ava's hand, and her face contorts as Ava squeezes.

It's over an instant later, and Ava's body relaxes.

Alys gives her an apologetic look. "Now, I'm going to heal as much of the internal damage as I can."

"No!" Ava says.

Alys's large chest expands before she releases a breath. "Listen—"

"I just mean, don't use up all your energy on me."

A pained smile blooms on Alys's round face. "It's the least I can do," she says. Her gentle gaze remains on her daughter.

"Bare minimum then," Ava says at last. She manages a small smile before seeming to realize she's still holding Chiyo's hand. She quickly releases her grip as Chiyo's cheeks redden.

She pats Ava's shoulder and says, "I'll fetch you some water."

Ava nods while Alys finishes patching her up. Alys wraps her ankle firmly with bandages for continued support, and once we've all eaten something, we take two brief shifts napping, ensure that our horses seem ready, then we set off on our journey again.

Overnight, I try again and again to dreamwalk to Tiernan, but each time, I fail. As I curl up in blankets that faintly smell of him, I cannot stop the tears that fall. *Please, Tiernan. Please be alive.*

We're underneath dense trees, pure darkness around us, but I sit up and pull the moonstone from my pocket. I run my finger over the smooth surface and close my eyes. It hums and warms against my skin. I close my eyes and focus on one particular person.

I envision her face—I reach out for steel and stone and defiance. Rather than conjuring a certain image, I try to envision *her* surroundings, and I'm surprised to be staring at a very familiar room.

Textured burnt sienna paint, dark blue and copper tiles, a hearth, and a large desk fill the space around me. This is the room that had been mine in Paramount almost four months ago.

I'm suddenly peering over a shoulder, watching a drawing materialize. That tree. The one from the dreams I shared with Winnie.

I speak her name, and she jumps to her feet, spinning to face me. Her caramel eyes widen, and as soon as her hands clench into fists, I unleash ribbons of shadows to bind her. I close my eyes and picture us elsewhere.

We rematerialize in the garden of the castle with flourishing roses and thick, thriving bushes. Winnie looks around, baffled, as I release the hold on my shadows. She points, and of all things, she says, "Flowers haven't looked this good in ages."

"Anything is possible in dreams, I suppose," I say.

Her fingers brush lightly over the deep red petals of a rose. She's suddenly calm, as if she's simply given up being afraid. "Are you going to kill me?"

I startle. "What? Why would I kill you?"

She doesn't lift her gaze from the rose, but she slowly walks along the bushes, her hands sliding over the leaves before she plucks a rose free. She winces, a thorn cutting into her hand. As she sticks her bleeding finger into her mouth, I smile wryly.

"I suppose I should create dream flowers without thorns." I muster an awkward smile, but she drags her reluctant gaze to me and pulls her finger from her mouth with a grim look on her face.

"I know you saw me back in that pasture. When I captured your … whoever he is to you."

My heart begins to race, my palms slickening. "Is he alright?"

"Yes. He's with the Zenith now. The sovereign wants him alive."

As hard as it is, I fight to keep my breath steady. I'm unsure whether to allow myself to feel relief just yet.

"What do you want from me?" Her voice hardens, her patience running out. But beneath the stony exterior, she seems anxious.

"I want to know if you're alright."

"I'm fine." She folds her arms across her chest, her muscles straining against her sleeves, one hand still clutching a rose.

"Do you still feel called to that land?"

She uncrosses her arms and silently admires the rose in her fist for a while. Then she begins gently plucking petals from it, tossing them one by one and watching them flitter to the ground. "You have the wrong person," she says.

"I'm certain that I don't."

There is fire in her eyes now. "Look, I'm not the one who will save anyone. I don't want to have some strange, twisted destiny tied to the gods. All I want to do is survive. If only everyone would leave me alone and let me do just that. Let me survive."

I blink at her. I've been there. On the way to the Verge, all I wanted to do was find Taig and live a safe, mundane life.

Winnie watches the last petal float to the ground. I take a deep breath and begin to conjure a new image. I summon open fields, the bog, the Hatchling's Nest, the different citizens of the Verge. Those considered Undesirable, those able-bodied. Those with magic, those without.

"What is this?" Winnie asks, her eyes wide as she turns slowly in a circle, taking in the new surroundings.

My body outside of the dreamscape starts to feel heavier, fatigue setting in. "This is what all of Erleya can be if we fight to make it that way. This is what the rebels want. Freedom for everyone to be themselves." I funnel in visions of Oksana with her beautiful lightweaving, and Isobel and Sloan with their galemaking.

"The sovereign has promised safety for all Undesirables and Mages," Winnie says, her eyes trained on the wavering images of my friends. "Elemental Wielders included."

I'm silent for a moment. Her words are clear, but the emotions that the dreamscape brings me are murky. She doesn't believe what she's saying. "What exactly is the mission of the Zenith?" I ask.

"To allow all Magekind to live openly without fear."

Tempting. But I don't believe a word, and I don't believe that she does either. "Do you truly believe the sovereign can do that?"

She falters for a moment, but then says, "Yes."

"Why are you lying to me?"

She doesn't respond.

"Alright ... A different question then. Can the sovereign prevent *this*?" I cast my memory of my recurring dream out to her. The frozen land, the fires raging, the sky turning black.

Winnie clasps her hands over her temples and squeezes her eyes shut. Tears stream down her face.

I hate doing this to her, but I don't have a choice. "I believe that is what we are meant to prevent," I say, the words effortful. She doesn't open her eyes. I let the image fall away, returning us to the garden. Pain pulses at the back of my head, and my muscles strain, my hands beginning to shake.

Winnie opens her eyes and sighs with relief.

"We have to get to Siad Nahar. We have to find out more about this vision. I know you feel called to that place. We need you to guide us, and we need a Terraforger to get us in."

Her fear threads through the dreamscape. Fear of the unknown. Fear of letting go. It's so uncannily relatable, but before I can tell her I understand how daunting it feels, she turns and snatches another flower from the bush. She crushes the thorny stems intentionally in her hand, pain cutting across her flesh.

"Winnie!"

"Release me, Basduun," she says.

The intended insult has no real sting. It's an act. I pity her attempt to hurt me—to make me balk. I pity her attempt to convince herself of the Zenith's mission.

"I may be a Basduun, but I know what's right and what's wrong. And so do you. I don't understand why you're being stubborn right now when I know you want to get out of the situation you're in!"

"I am doing the best I can to make the right choices! I'm tired of people telling me how I'm supposed to live!"

"Winnie, listen to me, please. I'm not trying to tell you how you're supposed to live. I'm trying to tell you that you are needed for something bigger than all of us. I know it feels unfair. I know it's terrifying. But we need you. And we need Tiernan." My eyes well, my voice breaks. "I need him."

Winnie snatches another rose and crumbles it. The thorns tear at her skin, and blood begins to leak from her hands. "I suspect you can't keep me here forever. If you don't release me now, then once your energy is spent, I will tell the sovereign we haven't caught the real Shadow Wielder. I'll expose you."

My pulse quickens. "Winnie—"

"Your secret is safe with me if you let me go."

As much as I want to hold her here until she agrees to follow her calling to Siad Nahar, I can tell she isn't bluffing. "Alright. I'll release you."

"Then you have my word that I will keep my mouth shut."

I nod. She drops the flowers to the ground and meets my eyes, tears in hers. "I am sorry. But I'm no hero. I just want to get my friend out of here. It's too risky to travel across Erleya for some place that may or may not truly exist."

I don't dignify her words with a response. I simply release my hold on the dreamscape and let it crumble.

When I fall back into myself, my own hands sting as though I was the one crushing roses, and a hammer pounds against the back of my head. My body breaks into uncontrollable shivers as I slip the stone back into my pocket and curl in on myself. I lie there, my eyes clenched shut, my body revolting. Until the shivers subside, until I can breathe evenly again.

If we don't have Winnie, we're going to have to find another way to get to Siad Nahar. One way or another.

But at least I know one thing: Tiernan is alive. For now.

Chapter 51

DURVLA

ISOBEL'S FIST slams so hard into my forearm as I block, I'm certain she bruises my bone. I bite back a cry of pain and step back, clutching my throbbing arm to my chest.

"I'm sorry!" she exclaims. The trees around us waver in the breeze. "That was a perfect block, but ducking would've been better." She smiles, her nose scrunching up in a way that would've been endearing if annoyance didn't have me in such a tight grip.

I'm not fast enough, not strong enough. My headaches persist even through the tinctures, and I'm tired of Alys having to heal me. On top of it all, I've trained nearly every day, yet I don't seem to be getting much stronger.

"Bugger, did I hurt you that badly?" Isobel asks, a shadow falling across her face as the sun momentarily disappears behind dense clouds. "Here, let me see." She reaches out, but I step back.

"I'm fine."

Her sibling steps closer and says something to her. She nods and steps aside as Sloan faces me. Sloan holds up their right hand, splaying all five fingers, then the other arm that stops at the elbow, the sleeve rolled back from the smooth stump. "What do you see?" Sloan asks.

I fumble to find words, my eyes roam the wild grass, the mountain peaks all around, the dimming and brightening sky. Forcing my focus on Sloan's face again, I find them seemingly apathetic, but there's something oddly comforting about it.

"Don't think about hurting my feelings, just answer the question," they say.

I brace myself to see hurt on their face. "A missing limb," I say.

Sloan nods. "Right. When I started fighting, that's all I could see as well. That's all *anyone* could see." Sloan pulls their sword from its scabbard with such swiftness that I flinch and step back. "So, I trained harder and harder. I pushed myself, and I strove to be no different, to look no different." They step back, putting enough space between us and waving Ava toward them.

Ava steps forward, grabbing her own sword from her waist. I watch as Sloan and Ava strike and parry in a rapid series of exchanges that makes me hold my breath. They stop when Ava's sword is at Sloan's neck, then she sheaths her blade again. Sloan returns to me, mopping their forehead with a sleeve. "Watching me fight just now, did my missing arm make a reappearance?"

I hesitate. "No."

"Was I equally matched against Ava, even with only one hand?"

I nod.

Sloan tilts their head at me, face stony, but something like intrigue shines in their blue-grey eyes. "Were we truly *equally* matched?"

My eyes dart to Ava and then back to Sloan. "Well ... Ava ... strikes sharper and more precisely. But you strike faster and block more readily."

Something that *almost* looks like pride casts over Ava's face, and Sloan nods. "We all have our strengths and our weaknesses. If we choose to focus on the negative things that make us different, we miss the opportunity to see the positive."

They raise their sword, swinging it at me, and I throw up my forearm, summoning a shield. The sword bounces right off it.

"See?" says Sloan. "I cannot do that. Nor can Issy." They sheathe their sword again. "I think you're doing a great job. We've had a few setbacks, but not even an Oracle can predict *everything*. In the end, we're all human. We're all just doing the best we can." They hold up their stump again, rolling back the fabric of the sleeve once more as it starts to loosen. "People look at our differences and underestimate us. But if there's one thing I've learned, it's this: *let* them underestimate you. Then prove them wrong."

I watch Sloan walk away, my forearm still throbbing from Isobel's fist. I wish I knew how to fight without magic, but I suppose I do need to stop focusing on the negative things that make me different.

Perhaps *I* am the one doing the underestimating; I am the one who needs to prove myself wrong. Tiernan always believed in me, and yet I find it so hard to believe in myself. My heart sinks. As I turn, I nearly run head-on into Osheen. He starts to sign, but I can't deal with more reminders of heartache right now, so I turn away.

Ava gives me a look as I move past her. I don't stop until I reach the small pond where Ghendor is drinking. He lifts his head, and water droplets splash onto my face. Ghendor snuffs at me, nudging my shoulder. "I know, boy, I miss him too," I say as I stroke his muzzle.

I reach into the pack against his flank and remove a small cheese-cloth with a few berries, offering them to him. As Ghendor nibbles the berries, a hand settles on my shoulder and I startle. I turn to face Chiyo. No kohl lines her lower lashes today, making the purple half-moons beneath her eyes more obvious. Her hair is pulled back into a simple ponytail—no accessories, no special attention to detail—and the blue is fading to a lustrous silver.

For once, she seems utterly drained, grief in her eyes. "Are you alright?" she gestures to me.

My first instinct is to smile and nod, but the smile never comes. I remain absolutely still, hoping not to lose the grip on my emotions. The subtle shake of my head has Chiyo reaching out to give my hand a small squeeze. She takes a deep breath, then glances backward to where Ava is fussing with her braids.

When Chiyo looks at me again, she seems slightly more pulled together. "It seems foolish to hold on to anger and grudges when ..." She pauses, hesitating. "You never know what could happen."

My heart spasms. I hate how easily the physical pain of being apart from Tiernan resurfaces.

"There's no going back in time," Chiyo continues. "But ... talk to Osheen. I told Ava she should talk to Alys. And you should also talk to Ava." Her eyes are pleading. "The Zenith is bloody strong. And the Purists are mental."

She's right. Unfortunately.

"Isobel and Sloan argue all the time. But they love each other. People who love each other fight. It's just part of life, I suppose. I know what Osheen did was inexcusable. But life is so short."

I smile faintly. "When did you get so wise?"

She makes a disgusted face. "Blame it on the sword that tried to claim my life." Her grin lets me know she's more than alright with joking about it.

"Speaking of blades, can you help me with the no-spin throw? I cannot seem to get it."

"That's because you were always distracted by a certain some-one," she teases. She looks immediately remorseful of her words. "Come. Before we set up, we can do a few throws. The tree over there is a willing participant."

Each step toward Dubh Carrig makes me feel sicker with grief. Even with the exhaustion weighing on me, even with logic glaring at me, each step feels more and more like giving up on Tiernan.

About four months ago, Tiernan gave up everything to get Alys and I to safety. Yet, here I am, walking away from him instead of running toward him. Every so often I swear I feel a sliver of his pres-ence. Then it's gone. A taunting reminder that he's alive, but out of reach.

My breaths grow shallow as the horses canter through the winding pass within the valley. Ghendor has been docile; I know he senses my grief. He comes to a stop as soon as my chest grows painfully tight, as I struggle to gulp down any air. My vision blurs, tunneling as I think of Tiernan taking the fall for me.

This cannot be the end of us, but what can I do when grief and exhaustion weigh on me?

Ghendor tosses his head as I battle within myself to keep up the appearance of being unbothered. To be alright with heading to Dubh Carrig instead of toward Mainland. Of wasting *yet more time.*

Suddenly, Chiyo is beside Ghendor, looking up at me, one hand soothingly stroking the horse's mane. We're on a forest path with nothing much to look at, but everyone has stopped, and all eyes are on me. I hadn't even realized. The mortifying awareness causes my chest to grow even tighter. I squeeze my eyes shut, and Chiyo rests her hand on my knee.

When I open my eyes again, Ava is there beside her. "Dismount," she says.

Getting off Ghendor is quite the task. I stumble off to the side, my head spinning, and sit down clumsily on the ground just off the trail. With my head tucked between my knees, I force down breath after breath. A hand gently rests on my back, and I don't know whose, but I don't budge.

The old fairytales that always made me feel better have no place here anymore. Not when I know there's truth to them. Not when Enidwen was real, her spirit apparently living within Carys ... through *my* bloodline. Not when the prophecy has two different powers coming after Carys and me. Not when the entire kingdom, maybe even the whole realm is in danger.

The hand on my back moves in slow, soothing circles, and eventually my head clears. Slowly, breathing becomes easier. I glance up to find Alys sitting beside me. She shifts, getting into my line of sight to sign, "Tell me what you see, feel ...? You know the routine, sweetling."

I close my eyes again. "There's not much to see," I say, given that it's been much of the same—hills, mountains, fields and the occasional herds of goats or sheep.

When I open my eyes, the look in hers almost pains me.

"I feel hollow," I whisper, knowing very well that's not the kind of feelings she's referring to. "I'm constantly forced to part with those I care most about. Taig. Osheen. Tiernan. And I'm so tired of it."

Behind Alys, Osheen looks my way. It's clear he's heard me, but he turns his attention back to his horse, stroking her flank.

"I know," Alys says. "I *know.*"

She glances at Ava who's pacing back and forth, clearly annoyed about yet another stop.

"We should get going." I scramble to my feet and my head swims, my entire body teetering. Alys jumps up to steady me.

We take a quick break, then get back on the road. No one speaks as we ride. We pick up the pace as night begins to fall. Every now and then, we stop for the horses to graze. We nap and rehydrate. Then we do it all over again. Until all my aches begin to feel like a second skin, until my mind has turned over so many possibilities of Tiernan's end that it's purely numb. *I* feel numb.

Two weeks after Tiernan was captured, the familiar black mountains of Dubh Carrig come into view along with thatched rooftops and the scent of metal and smoke clinging to the air. My heart hammers as I remember leaving here months ago with the town going up in flames. There are many houses now in charred ruins, but otherwise, it seems the village has been rebuilt from the ashes.

We stop in front of a house, the bull knocker forged from iron still on the door. Chiyo's face is awash with so many emotions that my heart cracks. Tears stream down her face as she practically leaps off her horse and dashes toward the door.

Somehow, before she even lifts her hand to the knocker, the door flies open and Haruka, her neck-length grey hair shimmering from the interior candlelight, throws her arms around her daughter. We all dismount as the two remain locked in a tearful embrace. Haruka finally relinquishes Chiyo and looks at the rest of us, a dejected crew.

I'm close enough to her to read her lips when the dreaded words are aimed at Alys. "Where is my son?"

And just like that, the numbness that settled into me disappears, ignited once more by grief, guilt, and anger.

I think I prefer feeling nothing.

Chapter 52

DURVLA

AFTER A DREAMLESS SLEEP, I wake to minimal sunlight flitting into the room through slightly parted curtains. I rub my hand across my cheek where saliva has crusted over—*embarrassing*—and glance around with bleary eyes. It seems my blankets are the only ones remaining in the seating area, but Alys is fast asleep in the threadbare armchair and Osheen is barely awake on the couch. Even Isobel looks half asleep as she polishes the sword resting across her lap.

As her gaze connects with mine, she grins. She makes sure her weapon is balanced before signing, "Good morning."

It tugs a genuine smile from me. "Good morning."

A dull ache persists between my eyes and at my temples, but it's nothing I cannot handle. My body is sore and heavy, but I feel somewhat refreshed, and sleeping on a carpet is far more comfortable than sleeping on the ground, open to the elements.

Chiyo steps in, her hair loose, her feet bare, and a dressing gown tied around her waist. She holds a cup of steaming tea and a saucer in her hands. With a soft smile, she says, "Oh, thank Rhianu. I felt awful that I was going to have to wake you."

I rub sleep from my puffy eyes, then I slide my hand over my hair. It feels simultaneously dry and oily, and I don't even want to think about the tangles that exist within the messy braid. I'd only sponged off with a wet cloth last night before going to sleep—I crave a proper bath.

Thanking Chiyo, I sip the hot tea as others file in and out of the room, doing various things. It's impossible for me to keep my mind off Tiernan; I keep expecting him to walk out of the bathing chamber as he did the last time we were here. The sinking reminder that he's not with us makes the tea churn in my stomach.

When I get the chance, I bathe and wash my hair, remembering how he twined my curls around his finger back at the hot spring, how he revered my body. I didn't reciprocate. I told him I didn't want to go further. My gut clenches with regret—what if those were our last moments together?

It takes me a while to regain my composure, and by the time I return to the sitting room, my chest aches from holding back tears.

The house soon fills with the aroma of breakfast. Haruka lays out rice, eggs, potatoes, and soft steamed buns. I remember this breakfast from the last time we stayed here, and it feels oddly comforting even though it's so different from what I'm used to. It seems my stomach has grown accustomed to not eating much, but I take my fill.

As everyone clears the table, Haruka looks at me and signs, "May I speak with you, alone?"

My breath catches slightly. Does she blame me for her son's abduction? It is my fault that he's gone, but—

"*Stop that,*" she says into my mind. I jump so hard that my knee hits under the table, the dishes shaking atop it. She gives me an apologetic smile, and I watch the next words form on her lips. "My son wasn't wrong when he said your thoughts were loud."

Laughter escapes me and I nod, tears prickling at the back of my eyes. "He constantly reminds me."

I stand and follow her out of the kitchen, into a small room with a simple bed. The room is immaculate, the bed perfectly made. A few crude weapons hang on the walls, and there's a beautiful view through the window of the rolling black hills.

Haruka stands in front of me. She's the same height as Chiyo, and I look down very slightly at her, but gods she is intimidating. I'm certain that her eyes could slice me in half. They remind me even more of Tiernan's than Chiyo's do.

"I wanted to apologize for putting pressure on you to join the rebellion when I first met you," she says.

I blink. That was not what I was expecting. "It's alright."

"It's not alright. It was unfair of me. As you know by now, there are a lot of powers at play, and to know that there was a Dreamwalker in our midst—it is an incredibly strong gift. But that doesn't excuse me for trying to take away your choice."

I nod. "It's fine."

"You ... are so sweet." My brows furrow as she chuckles and adds, "Just don't let people walk all over you. Especially when you can give them nightmares." She winks before grinning at me in a way that makes it impossible for me to keep from giggling.

"I've not fully figured out the extent of my dreamwalking."

"It takes time. When my mind whispering manifested, I couldn't turn off anyone's thoughts. It was torture constantly hearing what everyone was thinking. Tiernan is a little different—he couldn't turn off the emotions he felt from others. I made sure he learned from a young age how to shield his mind. And clearly ... you've also learned that very well."

"I've gotten a lot of chances to practice."

She smiles, but it slowly fades away. She picks at her cuticles for a moment before sadness fills her angular eyes. "My son has always been one to follow rules. It's ironic, being the son of rebels. Yet he never took much of an interest in joining the rebellion in any aspect. Elviera—Alys—told me he'd been speaking with her about it every now and then. But more as a way of keeping in touch with what was happening on the outside rather than joining. I don't think he ever intended to leave Paramount. I'm certain he would've remained there for his lifetime and gladly died for the Crown. Then he met you."

My heart skips a beat. I'm not sure how to feel about that.

"He cares for you in a way I never thought possible. And I have to thank you for that."

My throat swells with tears. "It's because of me that he's been captured."

"No." Haruka shakes her head. "He made that decision. You didn't hold a knife to his throat. Your guilt is misplaced."

I swallow around the rock in my throat and take a few steadying breaths. He broke rules for me. For the first time in his life. It hits me that I would gladly break every rule for him. I cannot let his sacrifices be in vain. I cannot go to Siad Nahar without him. He's as much a part of this journey as I am. As much a part of the journey as Winnie, who thinks she isn't.

Breaking the rules is terrifying, but I'm beginning to learn that sometimes it has to be done. Even if it seems wrong or too risky.

Was that how Osheen felt when he lied to me and put *Taig's* life at risk? He was trying to protect his family.

But he should've told me the truth.

At least this time it seems he's been honest about everything. He's given us valuable information about the Purists—their plans, the Cleanse, their vanishing rings ... Wait! Their *vanishing rings*!

I forget to breathe for a few heartbeats as my thoughts trip over themselves repeatedly.

Haruka's presence weighs heavily in my mind before I remember to pull my shields up from the emotion wearing on it.

When I focus on Haruka's face again, there's a knowing smile on her lips. "You have an idea," she says.

Nausea roils in my stomach. "It's not a good one."

Haruka smiles. "Sometimes a bad idea is just what you need to get the job done. I would love to hear it."

Chapter 53

DURVLA

"No. Fucking. Way!" Ava exclaims, lurching to her feet from where she'd been sitting on the couch in the Kilkenny household's sitting room. "Absolutely not."

Sloan looks unperturbed, as always. Isobel, Chiyo, and Osheen are wide-eyed. Alys's face is fixed, her full lips pursed as if she's trying to restrain herself. She's the very opposite of Ava, who stands in front of me with her fists on her hips. Haruka is unsurprised, having already heard my idea earlier.

Ava looks around. "No one else has anything to say about this?"

Alys scoots to the edge of the chair, her ankles crossed beneath one of her flowy multicolored skirts and not the trousers she's been traveling in. "I'm with Ava," she says. "It's too dangerous."

"It's dangerous simply existing," I say. "Last time we were here, remember how that ended? We're in danger *everywhere*."

Ava pulls one of her freshly twisted plaits through her fists over and over—as if she just needs something to do with her hands. "Jumping right into the castle is foolish, regardless. You'll be killed on sight."

I straighten my back, putting my brave face on. "I'm a Basduun." The smile that twitches on my lips feels forced and unnatural—I don't doubt it looks that way too. "I'm of value to the Zenith for whatever reason."

"And what, *pray tell*, do you plan to do once you're in the damn castle?"

The blood drains from my face. Admittedly, I'm not certain.

"You can't do it alone," Chiyo says. "We can come up with a solid strategy. I'll go with you."

Ava's head snaps to her. "You cannot be serious!" She signs as she speaks, ensuring that I get every word.

"We could create some kind of diversion and allow Durvla to get into the castle. Vanish in and vanish Tiernan out."

"Oh, it's that simple, is it?" Ava asks with a sardonic laugh. "And how the fuck do you propose doing that without knowing exactly where Tiernan is in the castle? What if there are wards to prevent people from vanishing in? If it was that simple, don't you think the Purists would've stormed the castle by now?"

Chiyo shrugs. "Perhaps they've tried."

"They would've needed an object from Paramount or to have physically been there before," Osheen chimes in.

"I have physically been there before," I say.

Ava seems lost for words for a moment, her mouth opening and closing before she finally finds something sensible to say. "Have you all forgotten who the sovereign is? He owns the entire Royal Brigade, the Zenith, the Veilguards ... He owns every force in Erleya. He owns *Erleya!*"

"What if someone from the inside—someone working with him —can help us?"

All eyes turn to me.

"Winnie, the Terraforger, is *in* the castle right now. I *know* she isn't fully on the sovereign's side. I just need to convince her to help us."

Isobel waves her hand to get my attention. "Do you think you can?"

"Yes." My hands shake. I know very well just how stubborn Winnie has been about not helping.

Standing beside the couch where Isobel sits, Sloan runs a hand through their hair—the only indicator of anxiety. "The *possibility* of getting her to help is not good enough," they say. "We need something more solid. We need her word." Ava gestures dramatically to them, her head bobbing in agreement.

I gnaw on my lower lip. I know Sloan and Ava are right, but this is the best idea we have.

Ava looks between me and the others. Out of desperation, she even looks to Osheen. "How do *you* feel about this, Sulky? Do you think any of this makes sense?"

He swallows noticeably and picks invisible lint off his trousers. When he glances up, he looks directly at me. "Tiernan did everything to save us," he signs. "We should at least *try* to get him out."

I can imagine steam coming out of Ava's ears. She looks at Haruka as the woman enters the room with a tray bearing a teakettle, and then to Alys. "Mam, tell them this is a terrible idea."

Alys hesitates but doesn't say anything.

Ava huffs and storms out of the house, the couch quivering slightly as she slams the door. Haruka sets the tray down on the low table, then steps out of the way.

No one speaks for some time until Alys breaks the tension. "It is an immense risk. You could die. We all could."

"I know," I admit. "But I *have* to try. We cannot afford to wait for a rebel army to storm the castle. Tiernan could be dead by then." I fight the tears that threaten to come. "If you can all help me train a bit more in the next couple of days, I'd appreciate that. Then one day to rest."

"Sweetling, you must also consider all the factors logically."

"All I've done my whole life is think logically about everything, Alys. And still, I was taken from my home, arrested *twice*, and I've been running from mercenaries and now two different organizations."

She nods. "I understand but still, think about it."

I shift my gaze from Alys to Osheen and find him looking back at me. It's time I spoke to the man. It's long overdue. "Whether I receive help or not, I'm going to do this. I'd rather die trying than live with the knowledge that I didn't."

As I step out of the house for fresh air in the evening, I find Osheen sitting on the grass, turning a rock over in his hands again and again. As he hears me, he glances my way and my breath catches unpleasantly. I close my eyes and pray for courage, for patience, for the strength to forgive him. Without a word, I sit down on the grass in front of him, and moisture immediately seeps into my trousers.

I grimace. "Why are you sitting in the wet grass?"

He smirks, his face more ruggedly handsome than I remember it. "It's not that bad," he signs after setting the rock down. His smile fades when I don't reciprocate. He smooths his hands over his trousers repeatedly.

At last, he voices the words it seems he's been fighting not to say. "I miss you, Durvla."

I clench my fists only to loosen them again. Perhaps it would be polite to say that I miss him too, but the words sound wrong in my mind. "I'm having a hard time forgiving you."

His jaw tightens. He scratches at his beard, which has grown thick again. "I deserve that," he gestures.

"You do," I gesture back. "I understand you wanted to protect your mam and Granny. You know I love them. But I trusted you to look after Taig. I trusted you more than I trusted anyone else in this world. You were my best friend. You could've told me the truth. We could've figured something out together. Maybe we could've destroyed the scrying tether. You didn't give us the chance to defend ourselves. You took the coward's way out."

Surprise crosses his face, deep grooves in his forehead. But then his frown slowly curves upward into a smile, his forehead smoothing out.

"Why on Rhianu's earth are you smiling?" I sign sharply.

"You've changed," he says.

My brows knit together firmly.

"You would've never spoken your mind like that. Although your face always showed more emotions than you intended, you kept your thoughts to yourself. Even when you should've spoken up."

My lips tug down—I don't know what to say.

"It's a good thing. And you're right. I had no excuse. I'll spend a lifetime trying to make it up to you. Whether you forgive me or not,

I'm glad you're talking to me now. I think you should go to Paramount. I've seen you and Tiernan together. I understand why you need to do this."

I press my fingertips lightly against my eyelids as though it can keep the tears away. Osheen's hand rests on my arm, and when I open my eyes, he's looking at me with a familiar warmth I don't want to remember. I can't fully let my guard down.

"I don't want you to come to Paramount," I say. He frowns and starts to say something, but I interject. "You know too much about the Purists and about everything we've encountered. Important information that should be passed on to Dayfyd and Chief Badeaux. If all fails, get back to the Verge ... Tell Taig about me. Don't let him forget about me."

Tears swiftly leak from Osheen's eyes, and he bats them away. He takes my hand and gives it a squeeze before letting go to sign, "Just stay alive and you can tell Taig yourself."

I laugh through my tears and nod. "I'll try my best. For now, I still need to figure things out."

"I'm sure you will. I believe in you."

I approach Alys and Haruka where they sit in the kitchen chatting over tea and honey cake. They both glance up at me, weary smiles on their faces. "Everything alright, sweetling?" Alys asks.

"This may be an odd question, but do you know anything about amplifiers?"

Alys looks slightly startled, but Haruka seems intrigued.

"The Lightweaver who trained me back in the Verge mentioned something about them," I explain.

"Ah," says Haruka. "I know that usually it requires an elemental or celestial gemstone or something—old magic, but they're good natural amplifiers. They can even be used to imbue potions."

Alys's eyes go wide. "Where did you hear such a thing?"

"Niall. It seems the Purists have a plethora of loopholes for magical use."

I pull the handkerchief-wrapped moonstone from my pocket and slowly open it in the palm of my hand.

"Gods above and below, that's ..." Haruka's eyes go wide.

"Dayfyd gave it to me. He said it belonged to my birth mother."

Haruka doesn't even bat an eye at that. Of course, she knows the woman who raised me wasn't the one who gave birth to me.

"Unfortunately, you'd need a Sorcerer to turn it into an amplifier. I'm sorry I cannot be of better help."

I look to Alys desperately. "Are you able to conjure something?"

She shakes her head. "I've focused on healing my whole life. Runes are tricky, abstracting and imbuing is even trickier. The tinctures I make are the extent of my potion making abilities. Your birth mother—Morwenna—was brilliant with runes and potions. It's how both your and Carys's powers were so securely dampened for decades."

I sigh, my shoulders slumping. That's unfortunately unhelpful at the moment. I do know some runes, but not for amplifying. "Alright, thank you." I start to get up, but Alys reaches across the table to place her hand on mine.

"You know, perhaps it runs in the family. You may be able to learn. We'll look into it as soon as we can, alright, sweetling?"

As soon as we can is not soon enough, but I smile and nod. "Wait ..." I wet my lips. "Can you tell me more about Morwenna's powers? How did she get away with honing them when she was the queen? Without anyone knowing?"

"Ah." Alys drums her fingers on the table, and I clasp my hands together to keep from fidgeting with nervous energy. "Morwenna used to unleash her shadows in a wooded area close to her home. She'd actually been doing exactly that the first time I met her." Her smile is wistful. "She'd also meditate frequently to strengthen her mind. It helped her learn to better control her dreamwalking.

"She was a prodigy—and a powerful one at that. She was also an Oracle, though unlike her other powers, she had no control over her visions. As Dayfyd mentioned, she was plagued by prophetic nightmares. Mainly about her children." Alys's throat works as she swallows hard. "Her abilities extended beyond creating dreamscapes—she could manipulate memories by infiltrating people's subconscious. It's how, when Carys accidentally killed Aneirin, Morwenna was able to make it so that no one remembered."

My gut twists. "Terrifying," I breathe.

"Indeed. But, like you, she never wanted to be a Basduun. She only practiced to remain in control; she only used the darker aspects when it was absolutely necessary."

I let her words sink in for a while longer. Could I be like Morwenna since her blood flows through me? Could I learn to control my powers to such an extent?

At last, I thank them both for taking the time to talk to me before stepping outside to get some time to myself. Somehow, I'll have to embody Morwenna's control, because I'll need it to enact the first part of my plan.

Chapter 54

TIERNAN

OF COURSE I don't agree to join the shithole's sect, so I wind up back in the brig. For hours, I sit there, time ticking by. I pace the cell until I realize no food or water is being brought to me. Then I sit down to conserve my energy. As soon as my ass hits the floor, Lynx appears beyond the bars. She angles her masked face toward me and says, "Sovereign Rheon asks if you are ready to cooperate and join the Zenith."

I know where this is going. "I believe he already knows my answer."

Lynx makes a pleased sound in the back of her throat, something partially like a giggle, partially like a hum. Then she vanishes from the brig.

As time crawls by, more and more cries and occasional screams fill the darkness of the cells beyond mine. Voices plead for mercy, for death. Whispers of power and torture, threats and the like echo through the passageways. At first, I try to take in any information, but then I choose my own sanity and block out as much of the cacophony as I can for as long as possible.

The next time Lynx appears, I'm not sure how much time has passed, but it's much of the same. She asks if I'm ready to join the Zenith, I say no, and she jumps away.

All the while, no food or water is brought to me. By the time my throat feels like the Wastelands and the pangs in my stomach become unbearable, Lynx makes another reappearance. "Last chance," she says.

This time, I don't even bother to respond.

"Alright then." There's sickening glee in her voice as she looks to the two guards who stand outside my cell and says, "You know the next step."

One guard unlocks the gate and lets it swing open. As the other guard steps into my cell, I jump to my feet and ignore the dizziness that sweeps in. "I can walk," I say. I'm uncertain where they're taking me, but I will not be dragged along like a common criminal. Even if my legs are a bit shaky. We travel through tunnels, up a set of stony steps, and out into the encampment where the harsh sun hurts my eyes. I stare across the encampment at the barracks, at the entrance to Fiada Purlieu, the lush forest unassuming as always.

A jail wagon awaits me, and a guard nudges my back, pushing me forward. The jail wagon contains three other people. One is a man who has clearly committed theft; his right hand has been severed, and bloody bandages wrap around his wrist. Another bounces his knee up and down, jostling the wagon. The third man glowers at me with such unsettling steadiness that I look away, but his thoughts slam into me: *I hope he goes last.* I can't stop my forehead from creasing.

Five years ago, I escaped the brunt of Rheon's punishment. And now, it's as if none of the time between even mattered. Anxiety squirms in my stomach as the creaky jail wagon makes its way through the gates of Paramount and into the city. The wheels jostle over the cobblestone street as we pass small groups of soldiers in black uniforms—Forayers? But no, Forayer uniforms aren't so detailed. These aren't Zenith uniforms either, or even Royal Brigade or brig guard uniforms. Gods, how many different regiments does Rheon command by now?

It isn't Rheon this time, however, who awaits the prisoners at the whipping post. Instead, there's Lynx and a couple of those guards in black. We're hauled out of the wagon one by one. First is the thief who pleads with his whole heart as they drag him up the steps to the whipping post.

Each sound of the leather lashing against his bare skin causes me to flinch, even as I fight to keep my Empath powers under control. His screams die down to whimpers and silence follows. He's thrown back into the wagon, completely unconscious, and I refuse to look beyond his face. The nervous prisoner is next, followed by the glaring man. I'm once again forced to listen to his cries, my empathy slipping into the foreground of my mind, the pain and fear of the man dizzying me.

I'm sure it was Rheon's idea to leave me for last. So I can hear what's coming—as if I wasn't there when he held the mass flogging years ago. Fifty victims had been brought out one at a time, their *crimes* read aloud before they were publicly and brutally punished.

They were whipped until they lost either consciousness or their lives. Whichever came first. Each prisoner was accused of having committed treason—by the use of magic, by speaking ill of the queen, by harboring an Undesirable. All for the purpose of nailing fear into the heart of every Erleyan and Outer Islander. Rheon claimed he had been given the command by Morwenna, but the rumors that spread through the castle at the time said she had no idea. By the time she realized what was happening, the floggings were already in progress, and to have the queen admit she was not in control of the Royal Brigade's commander would've been an admittance to weakness.

The victims' screams of pain are forever branded in my mind. And now, if I survive everything, I'm sure it's a feeling I will never forget either.

I'm strangely detached from my body as I'm hauled up the steps. As my name and past stations are announced. Lynx declares me a coward and a deserter, and the crowd jeers at me and calls out for my blood. My boots slip on the bloodied ground as I'm tugged toward the whipping pole. I'm forced to my knees, the magic dampener still shackled around my wrist, the ropes digging into my skin as I'm bound to the pole. I press my face against the wood, closing my eyes and preparing myself for the first strike.

The cool air hits my back, a chill sliding down my spine as my tunic is torn away.

The first lash sends an arc of pain through my back and down my thighs. My spine arches, my head flinging back as if my body tries to get away from the whip. With the next strike, I clench my jaw and force myself to keep breathing through my nostrils. The smell of blood fills my nose, but my throat barely spasms before the next stripe nearly steals my breath away. From my constant clenching, my jaw begins to ache more and more with each strike, but I refuse to cry out; I refuse to give the sadistic bastards what they want.

I pull up my mental barriers as much as I can, this time to lock myself away from the torment. From the sound of the whip. From the feel of my skin being slit open and blood coursing down my back, seeping into the waistband of my trousers. I never cry out, but my throat feels raw as though I've been screaming, and my body grows heavier and heavier. Until I silently *beg* my consciousness to flee.

I'm not sure how many lashes I take, but my body eventually gives in to the overwhelming anguish and I black out at last.

The first scream builds in my chest and rips free from my throat before I even open my eyes. I'm on my stomach, but as I move my hands to grapple for my searing back, something digs into my skin. My eyes are too bleary to make out anything, but it's clear that my wrists are still bound. The pungent scent of herbs fills my nostrils, pulling nausea from my gut. I dry heave, and the pain nearly tips me back into unconsciousness. A voice I don't recognize says, "Deep breath. In through your nose. I'm almost done here."

Obeying, I take a deep breath through my nose. Again, and again until the nausea subsides, but the pain in my back comes and goes in waves. Icy cold undulates across my skin, causing first more pain, then relief.

The surface beneath me is soft. I curl my fingers, and they bunch in crisp sheets. When I open my eyes again, there's only white fabric. I lift my head as best as I can and vaguely make out bright white curtains and other cots in a line.

The infirmary.

I'd expected to wake up in the brig.

"Almost there," says that voice again. I strain my neck to get a better look at her. Dark eyes focus on my back, her face reflecting the glow from her hands. A Mage Healer openly practicing. In Paramount.

Well, I've seen everything now.

At last, the woman shifts to stand behind me, grey hair falling onto her shoulder. "There," she says.

My body is exhausted, but I allow my senses to reach out for her magic. I'm met with something that reminds me of Alys's powers, but far darker. A Dark Mage Healer? Is it possible? My mind must still be shrouded from the pain.

"Ah, he's awake," says a voice that causes my heart to lurch painfully.

My head snaps to the other side as Rheon marches into the infirmary, Lynx in tow. My healing back protests my sudden movement, and I grit back a groan.

"I've been told you didn't even cry out once," says Rheon. "Very impressive. Next time, I will ensure that they don't stop until you scream for mercy. Or the next time. Or the next."

My throat spasms, but my stomach is completely empty. My body is too spent for me to even come up with something witty to say. Especially when it's frighteningly clear why Rheon ordered that I be healed.

"You're going to do this until I break," I say with certainty.

"You've always been a brilliant soldier. I've seen many talented fighters in my day, but not everyone is as intelligent as you are, Major Kilkenny." He smiles, squatting so that he's face-to-face with me. "Do you remember when you received that title? Major? I can still remember the pride on your face. You could've been commander someday." He tsks and stands upright again. "How would you like to regain your title as major to start? The Zenith really could use a brilliant fighter such as yourself."

"No," I grit out.

"Suit yourself." He looks to the Healer woman. "Is he able to return to the brig now?"

"Yes, I'm finished with him," she responds, and I almost want to beg her to let me stay longer.

"Perfect. Lynx, have some broth brought to him. Nothing more."

"Yes, Excellency."

He turns on his heel and marches out of the infirmary. Lynx, however, struts toward me. "Come along, pretty boy. The brig is getting lonely without your presence." She begins to work at the ropes around my wrists and forces me to sit up.

My skin feels stiff, pulling unpleasantly and sending small ripples of discomfort through my back. But I sit up, swinging my legs over the side of the cot. My vision sways and I close my eyes.

Lynx yanks my arm up and I open my eyes to see her staring at the sword tattoo inked into my forearm. She doesn't say anything, however. She only pulls me to my feet and vanishes us back to the brig.

I land rather hard on my ass and bite back a small cry. I place my hands flat against the cool floor beneath me and struggle to remain upright. Lynx crouches down in front of me, holding an almost black, double-edged blade before my face. "Do you like my new toy?" She asks, her husky voice filled with amusement.

As best as I can, I remain absolutely still. There's no way in hells that I want that blade to touch my skin.

"You won't believe how much effort went into forging such a blade. Mind-boggling, really." She makes a small humming sound of satisfaction then says, "Not that I forged it myself, of course." With a giggle, she stands upright and sheaths her dagger. "Have you heard the screams? In the night? Reminds me of the horror stories my parents read to me as a child. You know, to scare me into behaving like a lady, no doubt."

My brows pinch together.

"Do they give you nightmares, pretty boy? The screams?"

My mouth remains tightly shut.

Anger flares brightly around Lynx, and before I can think of what to do to prepare myself, her mask takes up my whole field of vision again. I take a breath and hesitantly allow my magic to reach out to her, but there's a strange blockage. She doesn't draw her dagger this time, but she runs her finger along the side of my face, drawing an invisible line. Her hand feels surprisingly unsteady, however, and I can feel pain writhing within her, mixed with annoyance and frustration.

"The rugged look suits you," she says. "Do you have a lover by now who appreciates it?"

A sort of sadistic lust emanates from her like a purr as she continues drawing that unsteady, invisible line down the side of my neck, over my scar. I shudder.

"Are you disgusted by me?" There's a sudden bite to her voice that makes me wince. "I wouldn't have taken you for a superficial man." The hysteria filling her tone tempts me to scoot away from her, but I remain in place though my arms shake from the continued support against my palms.

I don't take the bait, and her finger lingers on my scar. Somehow, I manage not to move.

Lynx huffs. "My, aren't we a bore." Her tone is back to being light and aloof. "Well, pretty boy, keep being stubborn and"—she splays her hand over my bare chest—"you'll *wish* the only punishment you receive is subsequent flogging."

I'm busy staring at her bright green eyes through her mask when something pierces my flesh. I grit back a groan of pain, and Lynx takes her hand away, claw-like nails retracting. I blink, certain I'm hallucinating.

She laughs gleefully. "That's more like it." A satisfied sigh leaves her lips, and she stands, her crimson cape swishing around her. "That's all for now. Enjoy the screams."

I watch her retreating form until she vanishes from sight outside the cell, and it's only when I'm certain she's not coming back that I look down at my chest. I'd hoped the claws were just a figment of my imagination, but sure enough, small droplets of blood trickle down my chest from five shallow cuts in an arc.

Chapter 55

DURVLA

Chiyo sits on her bed across from me, staring at me as though I've lost my mind. "What do you mean you're going to hold her hostage?"

Having the words said back to me chisels away my courage. "Last time, she threatened to destroy the dreamscape. I've relived that moment again and again and I realize, while the dreamers do have a say in what happens, *I* rule that realm. I weave the dreams, I control the imagery ... I can hold Winnie until she gives in."

Chiyo's face grows increasingly whiter the more I speak. The words sound awful even to me.

"I'm aware how that sounds."

"Lugda's scalding balls, Durvla," she says. She doesn't speak for a while, but then she asks, "Can't you dreamwalk to Tiernan?"

"I've tried, but I suppose the distance does play a part. With Carys, we're connected by our bloodlines. With Winnie, we have the stones. With Tiernan ..." My throat closes as I speak his name. He's Chiyo's brother; I cannot fall apart over him when she's probably hurting even more than I am. "It's odd," I say, pausing again to clear my throat. "When we're together, when I practiced my dreamwalking with him ... something *different* happened. I felt his emotions, heard his thoughts. It's like—"

"Your powers merged."

I nod. "Yet, when we're apart ... I hardly feel anything."

She frowns, reaching out to place her hand on my knee. "You two are disgustingly adorable together. Have I mentioned?" she says with a tearful smile.

I sniffle, even as I smile. "Once or twice."

The brief moment of lightheartedness fades as reality sets in again. "Now," Chiyo says. "We need that information from Winnie."

I nod and take the opalescent stone into my hands. It warms against my skin as I close my eyes and slow my breathing. I recall the royal library, building the shelves in my mind, layering in books, the floor, the velvet couches, the table, and the candlelight fixtures. Once I'm happy with the dreamscape I've created, I ensure the doors are locked, and I call out to Winnie with my mind, my powers reaching out to latch on to her subconscious.

She doesn't come willingly—not even close. If they've been training her to shield her mind, they've been doing a great job. She fights, her consciousness slipping from me several times. Nonetheless, she finds herself within my dreamscape.

Her hair is pulled back into a bun, and she's in her Zenith uniform, a deep frown on her face. She looks bewildered for a moment before fear takes over her features.

"I just want to talk," I say quickly. As I've done many times before in dreams, I step through my own shadows and land in front of her, scaring her witless. "I'm sorry; I don't want to scare you."

"Then stop entering my dreams!"

"I will leave you alone if you help me with one last task."

She only lifts her chin with defiance, her lips sealed.

"Can you tell me with a clear conscience that you truly believe in the Zenith?"

She marches toward the door and begins tugging on it, to no avail. "Let me out."

"Just talk to me. Please."

The door rattles as she yanks on it repeatedly. My instinct has me sending shadows skittering across the floor toward her. They turn to mist, surrounding her, and she steps back, frightened. I close my eyes and exhale slowly, trying to find a memory.

One of *her* memories.

In rapid flashes, I see a curly-haired blond—they're laughing together, crying together—I see a woman hand her a vial of a strange purple liquid—a man pressing his forearm against her throat—the commander asking her to find the Shadow Wielder—two cloaked figures: one with blazing red eyes and the other with blue. At last, there's an image of people clad in white, chanting, offering her a drink in some sort of cavern, and overwhelming pain shatters my connection.

I release my hold on her memories, feeling as though I've had the wind knocked out of me. "Forgive me ..." I recall the last image and realize that she'd also been in white. "You were a Purist?"

Her deep brown skin blanches and she steps back, leaning heavily against the door.

"I'm not putting any blame on you. I'm just trying to figure out your motivations."

"You are prying into my innermost thoughts."

Her words cut through me worse than any knife could. "And you were part of a group known for slaughtering anyone with magic."

"I was desperate!" she shouts, a hiccuping sob tearing through her. "I wanted to believe that *something* could change my life for the better. That I could cure myself of this horrible thing that made my mother loathe me and made my life a living hell. I gave in to their ideals because I *wanted* to believe it. I wanted to have hope instead of only desperation."

With all my heart, I want to release her, to hug her, to apologize. "I understand desperation," I say. "Desperation is why I am holding you here. I don't want to do this. I don't want to hurt you. But we *need* your help. Do this one thing and I will leave you alone for good. If that is what you want, I will respect your wishes."

She hiccups again, letting the tears fall. For a while, only her sobs fill the dreamscape.

I sigh and unlock the library doors with an audible click. "You can walk out right now and never look back. Block me out of your mind. Destroy the stone." I release the hold of my shadows and her back straightens slightly. "Or ... you can keep in mind everything I've shown you, and all the times I've pleaded with you. I can't force you to believe me or to be a hero, as you put it. Trust me, all I ever wanted to do was to be safe and sound at home. But personally, I can't continue to sit back and allow bad things to happen when there's *something* I can do about it. Can you?"

Her hand moves to her pocket, and she stands unmoving for a while. She turns, and for a moment, I think she's going to walk away. To take the only hope we have left. To sever the connection.

But she pauses, her hand on the door as she glances over her shoulder at me. "You're right; I don't believe in the Zenith. I want more than anything to get out of here, but I'm afraid. I may be the one with magic, but my best friend is braver than I have ever been. I've lied to myself for so long. And I hate who I've become. I hate that I've allowed people to make me complacent. But it's so hard to stop running away, to stop pretending ... when I'm terrified *all the time.*" She closes her eyes, more tears rolling down her cheeks.

My heart aches for her. I wait patiently for her to find her words again. It feels as though a long time passes before she releases the handle of the door and turns to face me. "Alright," she says. "What do you need me to do?"

Chapter 56

GWYNETH

MY HEART FLUTTERS erratically as I'm escorted to the sovereign's study and into the small dining area. I'm barely over the Dreamwalker trapping me in that dreamscape, and her words have burrowed into my heart and eaten away at my conscience. She's right. Neris is right. Every time I try to take a step forward, my own cowardly nature slams me right back into a place of indecision. It's been just over three weeks since my arrival at Paramount, and I feel no closer to getting out of here. I need to try harder to push through the fear.

As I enter the room, Lynx turns her masked face to me. To my surprise, Neris is seated there, a picture of beauty in her flowy cerulean gown and her golden curls tumbling over her shoulders.

"Welcome, Lady Gwyneth," the sovereign says lightly. I nervously smooth my hands over my own dress, feeling surprisingly even more out of place now than I do in Zenith uniforms. I curtsy and ease myself into the seat next to Neris. She glances askew at me before her eyes flick forward to the sovereign again.

"You must be wondering why I've invited you and Miss Reneris to dinner," he says.

"Yes, Excellency."

"I like to get to know my recruits, and I haven't had the chance to properly converse with you."

Servants bring food in, metal domes and plates clanging and clattering lightly as they set down a variety of foods: mutton, cabbage in a parsley sauce, and thick slabs of crusty bread. Once they leave and our plates are piled high, the sovereign's deep blue eyes settle on me again. "When did you learn about your terraforging?"

Neris and I glance at each other briefly. "I was very young."

With a thoughtful look, Neris adds, "Maybe five or six years old?"

I nod, and the sovereign places food in his mouth and chews slowly.

I glance across the table at Lynx, who sits there, her hood still up, her eyes peering out from her mask. A few strands of honey blond hair peek out from under her hood as she slowly twirls a fork between her fingers. Her sleeve slips back slightly, something like white fabric visible underneath. When she catches me staring, she tugs her sleeve down and stops twirling her fork.

"I'm told that Wielders who do not use their powers after they manifest—unless they wore a dampener—are slowly driven mad," says Rheon. "How did you manage to avoid that, living in Erleya under the late Queen Morwenna's reign? And especially in a renowned household such as yours, where privacy is a rarity."

I think back to the visions, the delusions perhaps—have I, indeed, gone mad? It would make sense in the grand scheme of things. But I respond as casually as I can. "I used small amounts of my powers daily. Gardening, fixing small cracks in walls, chopping wood simply by controlling the axe with magic, repairing jewelry, etcetera. Whenever I could, I moved rocks and boulders in the forest on the outskirts of the city."

"Clever," the sovereign says.

"Thank you, Excellency."

He's silent for a while, and there's only the sound of scraping forks and sawing knives. After a while, he says, "You don't seem to be fond of your powers."

Something between a cough and a gasp catches in my throat, and I clear it forcefully. "I ... Sometimes I wish I were Ordinary, admittedly."

Neris gives me an odd look.

"And you, Miss Reneris?"

Her eyes dart to the sovereign's.

"Have you ever desired having powers?"

"Perhaps ..." She smiles with a natural casualness that I envy.

"What if I told both of you that I've been working with a Mage on a ritual of power transference? It doesn't work with mind magic or sorcery, but using Skinchanger blood lends to the possibility of transferring powers from a Wielder to an Ordinary."

My pulse skitters, my blood running cold as I shudder. I open my mouth to say something, but my voice refuses to come out. Most people don't know this, but powers are more than just an accessory that a person has; powers are a part of the person's *soul*. Unfortunately, I'm living proof of that; trying to carve my terraforging from me nearly killed me.

"That ..." My voice comes out squeaky, so I take a hefty sip of wine from my goblet before speaking again. "That sounds dangerous, Excellency."

He smiles, unbothered. "Every novelty is dangerous at first, Lady Gwyneth. It is a work in progress."

What does that mean? I refuse to look away from him, not wanting to raise any suspicions. He smiles, and I swear something changes in his gaze. I cannot quite wrap my mind around it, but this man makes my flesh creep.

"The Shadow Wielder continues to defy me. If he does not agree to join the cause, I will relieve him of his powers and give them to someone else who does care to make this kingdom a better place for all."

I'm barely over his last comment, but this one makes me feel even more uncomfortable in my own skin. I fidget in my seat.

"As much as I loathe the Purists and their mad attempt to rid Erleya of Magekind, they have had success in removing a person's powers. I seek to simply ... redirect it. Why waste a gift, right?"

Neris places her hand over mine as it begins to tremble in my lap. If my heart beats any faster, it'll burst out of my chest.

"Have the pair of you noticed the blight worsening?" The abrupt change of subject makes my head spin.

In silence, Neris and I nod.

A strange darkness seems to shift into Rheon's eyes, but when I blink, it's gone. I need to get a grip on my emotions.

"The land is dying," Rheon says. "I've heard the Purists are gathering sympathizers to overthrow Paramount so they can open the Veil at Fiada Purlieu. Ironically, we once thought that was the right course of action. That we could unleash Enidwen and use her power for the betterment of Erleya. What we didn't know at the time was that not only has Enidwen's spirit been in this realm for ages, but the Veil has never been fully closed. Like a crack in a foundation, it's been *slowly* reopening, draining our land, causing the blight. It will get worse if left open—completely destroying all our crops and livestock."

My brows furrow. Enidwen as in the enchantress of the Basduunai? Why would anyone want to summon *her*? And if the Veil is cracked, wouldn't *monsters* and Otherworlders be upon us? Not just our plants dying? "Apologies, Excellency. I am not following."

"Ah." He smiles and dives into a story about a mortal Grounder named Enidwen, who was taken to the Otherworld by an immortal. She forged a weapon in the Otherworld and used it to slaughter her lover, throwing off the balance of the realm before escaping back to ours. She went on to claim more powers for herself before summoning the Underling Prince. He was supposed to grant her unlimited power, but his spirit corrupted hers and she lost control. A group of Wielders and Mages called the Heirs of Dusk and Embers ended up defeating her. They banished her to the realm where the Underling Prince came from. She was thought to be gone, trapped forever along with the Underling Prince, but it turns out she's been trapped in our realm somehow.

We've heard the tale before, but somehow, the way Rheon says it ...

"If she summoned the Underling Prince," Neris says quietly, "then that couldn't have been the Veil to the Otherworld. Wouldn't that be ... the *Underworld*? As in Lugda's realm?"

"Oh, another clever woman," says the sovereign. "But that is a detail we have been trying to figure out. If indeed it is the Underworld, we're not quite sure what difference that makes. What we do know is that the Veil needs to be closed to stop the other realm from draining ours. And the Purists—"

"—they want it open," Neris interrupts. "Wouldn't that let more magic in?"

"Not necessarily. But it may restore the full power of all the gods —good and evil."

Cold rushes down my spine. I recall Magdin and Damarlach in my mind, two different sides of one coin, both asking me to smite the oppressors. But who are the true oppressors? Will closing the Veil truly end the blight? Would opening it really unleash the gods?

Despite Rheon's words, he's nonchalant about it. He only smiles, that murky shadow creeping into his eyes again, as he pops more food into his mouth. This time, I feel myself flinch, but he doesn't seem to notice.

"To close the Veil, we believe it requires a Shadow Wielder," says Rheon.

My pulse jumps.

"Why?" Neris asks.

"Enidwen was the first Basduun. After her demise, her followers —the other Basduunai—continued to wreak havoc on the realm. And because Basduunai no longer exist in our modern era, a Shadow Wielder is the closest we will find. However, if the Shadow Wielder does not cooperate, the Veil will continue to open. And it isn't just Erleya that will be doomed but the rest of the world. If the Purists somehow get to Fiada Purlieu, they won't hesitate to open the Veil by whatever means. They have their ways."

Oh, I know. Just as much as I know that Basduunai very much exist. Just as the *Purists* are aware. They are after the Heirs. I am certain they're after that Dreamwalker. I suppose it is because, if the sovereign is right, she can destroy the only hope they have of opening the Veil.

But what exactly do the Purists gain from opening the Veil to the Underworld? Unless they also think it's the Otherworld?

My brain itches to know. Something is not adding up. Something is off with this whole situation. It seems both the Zenith and the Purists want extreme versions of balance. Neither of them is right.

The Dreamwalker says that I play a role in this grand scheme. I want to believe that I don't, but I have flipped both sides of the coin; I have lived two different lives. I have seen things I never wanted to see, experienced things I never wanted to experience.

I know what it feels like to have nearly had my powers cleaved from me, to live with a fractured soul.

Neither of these factions can be allowed to reign.

"This is why a Mage army is important," the sovereign says, snapping me out of my thoughts. "We can protect Erleya in case it does happen."

I don't say a word.

"Lady Gwyneth. I require your assistance to convince the Shadow Wielder. Tiernan Kilkenny is stubborn. I know because he was one of my soldiers years ago. He is exceptional and an undefeatable fighter, even at a young age, but he is dangerous. And for that reason, he is the perfect ally. Convince him with the truth. Tell him what you've been through and the world you and the Zenith envision for this kingdom. But whether he agrees or not, you will be helping me close the Veil. Are you in agreement?"

My throat goes dry, but I nod. Because I have to pretend for as long as I can so I can help the Dreamwalker with her plan.

"What a madman," Neris says with a giggle as soon as we step into our room and close the door behind us.

I turn to her, my face drawn. "It's no laughing matter."

She sobers rather quickly. "You don't believe all of that, do you?"

I wring my hands together and bite the inside of my cheek before releasing a breath. "Every word." My throat feels too tight. "You know about my visions. You know what the Purists believe."

"The Purists are—"

"Neris, please listen to me."

Her mouth snaps shut. I finally tell her about the Dreamwalker and details of the visions I've been having.

By the time I'm finished, she's sitting on the bed with her eyes wide as saucers. "Did you see the sovereign's eyes when he was talking to us?" she whispers. "They seemed darker at times. Shadowy."

"I did see that. I just wasn't sure if I was imagining it."

"No. And that Lynx woman is like something out of a nightmare."

I nod. "I think she had bandages on her arms today." I rub my hands over my arms, suddenly cold as a chill runs down my spine. "If I can't get out of here, I need to somehow get *you* out of here, Neris. I don't know how, but I don't like the way the sovereign was looking at you, or how he spoke of transferring powers after asking you if you ever wished for them yourself."

Neris's eyes widen again. "I didn't even consider what he might've been implying."

We talk for a while longer before a knock sounds on my door. "Bring that gorgeous face of yours out here," Lynx's voice calls from the hall. "Time to convince the Shadow Wielder."

My stomach turns over.

Neris frowns at me. "Good luck," she whispers.

I leave her in my room and answer the door to Lynx. She tilts her head at me for a moment, and without any discussion, she grabs my shoulder and vanishes us away.

We touch down in the cold cells below where urine and other pungent odors flood my nose, and I hold my breath. Behind the metal bars ahead of me sits the man they all think is the Shadow Wielder. He's huddled near the wall, his body trembling, but he glances up at us with weary eyes.

"Well, get on with it," Lynx says to a guard, gesturing toward the cell. The guard steps forward to unlock the gate, and the bars swing inward, allowing us entry. Anxiously, I follow Lynx into the cell.

Confusion marks the man's sickly pale face, his brows scrunched above bloodshot eyes. Lynx nudges me forward roughly. I gather my skirts about me and crouch a small distance from the man—Tiernan, the Dreamwalker and the sovereign had called him. There's a small cut on his right eyebrow, a trickle of dried blood down the side of his face. His lips are pressed together so firmly that they turn white.

Lynx clears her throat, and I recall the sovereign's words. *Convince him with the truth. Tell him what you've been through and the world you and the Zenith envision for this kingdom.*

I inhale deeply. "I've spent my whole life hiding who I am," I say. "My powers, my desire to paint the world rather than rule it through affluence. My mother rarely allowed me to wear dresses with short sleeves lest others see the muscles *unbecoming of a docile highborn*. My only fate was to be married to another notable lord. I want nothing more than to live in a kingdom where people are allowed to be who they truly are. Where a person does not have to go to great lengths to rid themselves of their power only to live half a life for the rest of their existence."

I pause, fighting to hold back tears.

Tiernan's eyes narrow, his lips turned down. Despite his silence, I can tell he's listening attentively, so I continue.

"The sovereign says he aims to create a world where Magekind and Ordinaries can live in harmony. Where people like you and me don't have to hide. Where people like my friend, who has an ailment, don't have to be afraid of being taken away from their loved ones. Or being persecuted or killed."

Something softens in his expression, his uninjured brow raising slightly.

"Don't you want a world like that? A world of balance?" I ask him.

He licks his lips and clears his throat. Then, with a scratchy voice that sounds like he's not had anything to drink in ages, he says, "Yes. But Rheon is not the one who's going to create such a world. He can burn in Lugda's fires."

I stare at him.

"He's stringing you along like a puppet. He'll make you forget who you are."

The truth of his words stings.

Laughter rips through the tension. I stand upright again and glance at Lynx as she continues to cackle. "Predictable," she spits out behind her veil. "Give up, little Terraforger. Tiernan is hopeless."

I keep my eyes on him. "Would you prefer that they keep

maiming you—that they take away your powers and likely destroy you in the process—rather than just joining the Zenith?"

His dark eyes do not even falter. "I will never relinquish my values for some delusional tyrant. I know who I am, and I refuse to play any part in his twisted schemes."

I swallow, shame scraping my throat raw. I wish I had his strength. I wish I had the Dreamwalker's strength. Oh, how I hope I can prove it's not too late to grow a backbone, because soon, I will hopefully be getting Tiernan, Neris, and myself out of here.

When I turn and hurry out of the cell, Lynx begins to cackle again. "Oh, gods, this is top-notch entertainment. Who needs theater?"

I don't turn to look at either her or Tiernan. I simply wait until she joins me outside the cell to jump me back to my room.

And give me time to think and prepare for the escape.

Once I'm back in my room, I change into my midnight blue Zenith uniform again and take to exploring the castle. As I'm walking past a corridor I've never dared to enter before, I hear voices whispering. I stop, pressing close to the wall to listen.

"Unpleasant effects are bound to happen, Sire." The feminine voice sounds familiar, but before I can try to place it, the sovereign responds.

"Unpleasant effects, yes, but otherwise mundane. They are burning out too readily; it isn't working."

"Patience, Sire."

The sovereign huffs. "I'm not sure how much more Lynx can take. If only we can find more with her skillset. Before I arrived here, the damn fools had Kenna Gallagher right in their grasp. How in hells did they let rebels break her out?" He makes a scoffing sound.

Kenna Gallagher? As in Murtagh's daughter?

"I could've skinned every last one of them," the sovereign continues. "If Carys hadn't broiled them all like the dragon she was. Do we need to find her again? Or more like her?"

My mind tumbles endlessly, trying to process and pry details apart.

"Sire," the feminine voice responds. "It's a rare power. Lynx is enough for now. I've just healed her once more; she's taking strengthening elixirs to replenish the lost blood. It's similar to elixirs I've made for victims of the Cleanse."

The puzzle pieces fall into place. Elixirs. The Cleanse. Realms ... A knot forms in my throat.

"We are on the right path," she continues. "A magical talisman, like an amplifier stone, would help shorten the process. But it has to be given *willingly* by the person who owns it."

"What do you mean?"

"Amplifier stones are elusive. They choose their Wielders and mysteriously appear in their possession. Some people believe it's a gift from the gods. But they don't necessarily work for everyone, and they have to be imbued and runed before they *can* work."

There's a pause before the sovereign says rather than asks, "You know where I can find one of these."

"I do. But as I've said, it must be given willingly. Or else it is futile."

My hand flies to the pocket watch in my trousers, and I back away as quietly as I can. When I'm far away enough, I turn and run back toward my room, not stopping until I'm behind closed doors. It's only then that I let the panic consume me. Sinking down to the floor, I try to grapple for all I have learned.

There must be a reason for all of this. There *must* be.

When I finally get up, I take half of my last elixir—made by Radika who has been working with the sovereign all along. Too distraught to care, I climb into bed, still in my uniform. Tomorrow, I'm supposed to witness the sovereign's attempt to cleave Tiernan's powers from him. Powers that I'm sure he doesn't even have.

I hope the Shadow Wielder and I will succeed with this risky plan.

Chapter 57

GWYNETH

Loud pounding on the door rouses me from my sleep. I jump straight out of bed, my entire body aching. Before I can even say anything, Lynx bursts through the door. "Get dressed and meet us at the sovereign's study," she says. Then she slams the door again, and the room plunges into darkness.

I do as she says, and as I step into the study about ten minutes later, the sovereign stands there with an enthusiastic grin.

"I won't keep you long. I just wanted to brief you. The Shadow Wielder will be made an example of in the square. Then afterward, I need you to restrain him at Fiada Purlieu. Tonight, we will close the Veil, and we will be one step closer to making Erleya the safest and greatest kingdom. Report to the infirmary. There, you will meet the Sorceress I have been working with. She is a key player in tonight's ritual."

My stomach bottoms out, but I smile and nod. "Yes, Your Excellency. Thank you for entrusting me with this task."

He lowers his head and dismissively waves the back of his hand toward me.

I leave the room and pull in a breath before forcing myself to take step after step toward the infirmary.

My pulse quickens more with each step until I'm standing in front of the door with my heart racing in my throat. I somehow find the courage to push the door open and step into the infirmary. To my surprise, there is no one in there except for Radika. She turns from where she's pouring a purple liquid into a bulbous glass vial and smiles at me.

Anger rises within me so fiercely that tears embarrassingly well in my eyes. Realms, I hate being an angry crier. "How long have you worked with the Zenith?" I demand.

Her smile doesn't falter. "I told you, I work for no one but myself." She moves closer to me, the glass bottle still in her hand. The purple liquid sloshes within it. Slowly, the liquid begins to darken. My gaze darts up from the bottle to Radika's face.

"I heard you speaking to the sovereign last night."

"Ah," she says with a smile on her weathered face. "I thought I sensed you nearby." She's close enough that it's uncomfortable, but I don't step away.

"How can you *sense* me?" I ask, looking at her like the madwoman she is.

"The same way I sensed you over a year ago when the Purists nearly destroyed your lovely soul. Your lovely, yet loud, soul." She laughs deeply in her chest.

Now, I do step away from her.

"I've always been different. A Sorceress with the ability to mimic what a Healer can do, but also with an aptitude for dark magic. The dark forces always call to me. Hence why your poor, tainted soul cried out to be rescued."

Spiders scuttle down my spine. "What are you saying?"

"You're not the first I've tried to save from the Cleanse. But you are the first I've successfully saved. When I found you ... well, you saw the blood. You had no heartbeat. No breath in your lungs."

My stomach churns, ice filling my veins. My heart hammers so hard that my head spins.

"You were dead. *I* brought you back. Some might say your existence is an abomination, but I say we rightfully defeated destiny."

Her eyes flash with something sinister, and I nearly trip over my own feet as I take another step back. She advances on me as my chest heaves with panicked breaths. I always thought I'd been close to death and survived, not that I'd actually been *dead*.

"I saved you because you were meant for more than meeting

your untimely end at the hands of those ridiculous fanatics. Because you deserved the chance to choose where you stand in this war of the gods. You deserved to control your own fate."

I swallow thickly as vomit crawls up my throat. I'm barely able to catch my breath through my bounding pulse as I say, "How is that possible? No one can bring someone back from death! I had to have been—There's no—*How*?"

Radika looks at the bottle where the liquid within has turned a murky black-green color. Lifting it, she nods with satisfaction and walks to the counter to cork it. It's as if she hasn't even heard me.

"*Radika!*"

With her back still to me, she says, "There are only a handful of people with the gift to bring the soul back from Lugda's clutches." She turns back to me, swirling the liquid around in the bottle again.

"Necromancy is *forbidden*," I whisper.

"As is terraforging. And divination. And magical healing." She gestures with her arms wide, the bottle still clutched in her hand. "Yet here we are. Our people have been killed for too long. It's time to fight back."

"You're mad." I retreat another step, shaking my head.

"Tonight," Radika says without missing a beat. She slips the bottle into the pocket of her cloak and returns to me. "You'll have to make a choice." I brace myself for her to say something even more terrifying, but she only smiles at me and sweeps out of the room.

My knees quiver as I stand there, unable to move until I finally rush toward a receptacle to retch until my stomach is empty.

Radika truly brought me back *from the dead* over a year ago. I shouldn't be here.

Given that the gods do exist, I'm sure Lugda must want my soul.

Chapter 58

CARYS

I AWAKE to the sensation of metal cuffs around my wrists. The sear of tearing flesh as Eefa's knife cleaves into me again and again. Flames break out along my palms and crawl up my arms as my heart threatens to burst and my lungs fight for air. Stumbling out of bed, I try to steady my breathing. I struggle to recall all the ways Alys taught me to ground myself over the years.

But how do I ground myself when the whole bloody boat is rocking? Why did I think going back to Erleya would be a good idea?

Gods, I've made a mistake. What if I'm captured again? What if they lock a conduit onto my wrist once more and wield my soul like Eefa said Iywan would have. They might be dead, but more monsters prowl the kingdom.

I try to push the flames back into my body, but no matter how hard I will the fire away, it remains. The small cabin grows hotter, my breathing harsher.

There seems to be only one way to stop this. Before I burn the ship down and kill us all. I don't want any more blood on my hands. Especially not these wonderful people who left their *homeland* to ensure my safe return to Erleya. To aid me in a completely impossible task.

Still breathing harshly, I rush toward the water cask in the corner of my cabin, struggling to get it open without setting it on fire. As I yank the cover free, it drops with a loud *thud*. I wince but waste no more time before I plunge my arms elbow deep into the lukewarm water.

To my dismay, the water simmers, then begins to bubble and boil. More heat surges through me, becoming almost overwhelming. I yank my arms free, and tiny sparks flicker along my fingers and the backs of my hands, as though fighting to find a way out.

My powers howl within me, darkness warring with flames. Cold battling heat. Enidwen's glee bleeds through the fortifications of my mind, light cackling filling the spaces where I've managed to keep her out.

Embrace it, she whispers.

"Stop."

You cannot keep fighting.

I somehow keep my voice low, though it trembles from the effort. "Make it stop. Please."

Drip, drip, drip.

The water from my hands drops onto the floor and my mind is thrown back into the tunnels below Paramount. To the incessant dripping that spanned the days I was tortured. I clutch my hands to my body and stumble, falling to my knees.

The door creaks open and Odgar peeks in, a lantern casting a shadow on his face. "Carys," he says, shock lacing his voice. He sounds distant over the roar in my ears.

"Don't come in!" I shout.

The infuriating man steps into the room, closing the door behind him and hanging his lantern on a hook on the wall.

"I said stay away! Water's not helping. I tried. I tried ..." I nod toward the cask as sobs quake in my chest. I squeeze my eyes shut and try to swallow the tears, to pull myself together. "Leave! *Please*."

I keep my eyes shut until I feel him close by. He's on his knees in front of me, his hand reaching out to my face. Lurching to my feet, I quickly back myself against the wall and press into it. I concentrate on keeping the heat within me. But it's burning. Blistering. It's not supposed to be this way. I wish I could phase through the wood and into the ocean. Perhaps that's the solution. Perhaps I should submerge my entire body—to sink to the bottom of the sea. I'd never be able to use my powers again. Everyone will be spared.

"Carys, if you keep trying to hold it in, you're going to implode," Odgar says as he rises from the floor to approach me.

"If I release it, I'll burn down the whole fucking ship!"

"I won't let you do that. Just trust me." He holds his hands out to me. "Place your hands in mine. I can take it."

"You're mental!"

He chuckles. "So I've been told." His large hands are still held out, palms up, waiting patiently.

"I'm going to hurt you." I sound like a whining child, but I'm desperate to get away from him while he insists on only getting closer. I'm helpless! My brother's screams echo in my memories. The blast of fire is so vivid in my mind, as is the guilt, the agony, and grief.

"Dammit, Carys. Give me your hands before you detonate."

Closing my eyes again, I slam my palms against Odgar's. I expect him to go up in flames, for *everything* to go up in flames. Instead, a cool sensation streams through me. The fire doesn't immediately dissipate, but it dies down to embers. I open my eyes to a pained expression across Odgar's face—his teeth are clenched and sweat beads on his skin. Steam rises from our hands, wavering in the air.

"Odgar—"

He pulls me against him and wraps his arms around my body, holding me tight as the coolness of his magic surrounds me. Slowly, the overwhelming burning begins to wane. I press my face to his chest and relax in his embrace, tuning into the strong beat of his heart, and each steady breath he takes. I remain there in his arms until my teeth begin to chatter and I start to shiver.

It's only when I lift my head from his chest that his arms relax and he releases me. He steps back and takes my face in his freezing cold hands. "Better?"

I nod against his hands and swallow, my mouth as dry as parchment. His nightshirt is charred in places, holes large enough to peek through to the tattoos along his torso and arms. His cheeks are red, eyes watering. My breath seizes in my lungs.

When I speak, my voice sounds arid. "You are either brave or foolish."

He smiles wearily. "Why not both?" He lets his hands fall as his eyes drop from my face to the rest of me. I dare to glance down at myself. The hem of my nightgown is singed, charred holes scattered over the rest of the garment, just like Odgar's. "When we get to Erleya, we should see if there's a Mage who can charm some of your clothing," Odgar says. "So, they don't constantly burn right off you."

My heart pounds at the thought of being back in Erleya.

"You need to release some of that pent-up magical energy, immediately. Get dressed. Just a light gown and some boots. I'll be right back."

A while later, I'm climbing down a rope ladder against the side of the ship. "This is ridiculous!" I call down to Odgar who awaits me in a rowboat below.

"Well, do you have any better ideas, *revna*?"

I huff with annoyance. Above, Seth is stabilizing the rope. "If you're afraid of heights," he calls down, "just keep your sight level, or up here. I'll let you know when you're almost at the bottom."

"No, I'm not afraid of heights. I'm afraid of—" My gaze sweeps behind me, over the water. I can still remember the burn of it in my lungs. My heart races, but I keep moving.

Until my feet hit solid ground ... or well, the swaying bottom of the boat. Gods, this may be even worse than the bloody ship. I plop down nonetheless, and the boat rocks furiously, causing Odgar to grab on to the sides.

"Careful," he says with a smirk. "I'd hate for you to fall in after taking an eon to get down here."

"Shut up."

He grins and grabs the oars, beginning to row away from the ship. I watch in silence as the ship grows smaller and starts to disappear into the dark of night. The thought of water filling my lungs and stinging my eyes returns to my mind and the panic ratchets up.. "Why in hells are you sailing so far away?"

"I'm attached to that ship. I'd rather not see it go up in flames."

My heart lurches. I take a deep breath, and when we're far away enough, Odgar throws an anchor tied to a chain overboard. We sit there, the boat bobbing up and down in the serene waves. At least the ocean seems fairly calm tonight.

"Alright, raven warrior. Do your worst. Or your best."

"I ... don't know what to do?"

He gestures with a grand sweep of his arm, and I huff a sigh at him. "Just blast fire out there ..."

I frown but scoot toward the front of the boat, awkwardly fixing my skirt around me, bracing my feet against the bottom. I extend my hands, but nothing happens. Then again, and again, with still nothing. Even though the magic bubbles beneath my skin.

"It's probably just performance anxiety," says Odgar. "Maybe you need to stand up."

"And fall in?" My voice is shrilly, panicked.

Odgar chuckles. "I won't let you."

"You are awfully cocky, you know that?"

He sidles closer with a mischievous smirk. "*Cocky*, eh?"

I slap the back of my hand against his arm.

In turn, he waves his hand over my head. What in hells is he—? But cold water splashes over me before I can finish the thought, drenching my hair and my dress.

I gasp, my muscles seizing up. "What the fuck, Odgar?" I shout, clearing wet strands of hair from my eyes and blinking the water from my lashes.

His resonant laughter is truly irritating. Immediately, sparks rise in my palms, drying them. I turn my glower to Odgar.

"You're welcome," he says with a shrug, and I mumble more swearwords than perhaps are necessary.

I hold on to his muscular shoulder and get to my feet, water dripping from my hair. "You're fortunate that worked," I grumble.

Grinning, he sidles closer and wraps his hands around the place just above my knees to hold me steady.

I ignore the tiniest jolt of lightning from his touch and the warmth gathering in my belly. Drawing in a breath, I focus on the energy growing in my hands. With an exhalation, I push my hands forward, propelling a stream of fire out into the ocean.

Shades of radiant orange dance over the dark water, an oddly soothing sight, turning the night air balmy and my skin slick with sweat. When my magic stops pulsing like an erratic heartbeat and my muscles begin to tire, I stop and plop back down into the boat.

Odgar stares at me in awe as I take steady breaths.

"How do you feel?" he asks.

"Better."

"Good."

As I stare across the water, bright flames flare to life on the surface. I startle, but when I blink, there's nothing there. Still, I can smell the acrid smoke and feel the singe of heat—I can see the bushes beneath Paramount burning all around me. My hands begin to shake, and I clasp them together. The pent-up magic may be soothed for now, but the memories will never be.

"Are you alright?" Odgar asks, something heavy and warm settling around my shoulders. His cloak.

I exhale shakily. "No." Closing my eyes, I search for balance within myself. "I told you that everyone thinks I'm dead, but I never truly explained ..." When I look to Odgar again, his head is tilted slightly, his eyes intent.

"You don't have to."

"I want to." I blow out a loud breath through my lips and shake out my arms, the mere memory tensing my muscles. I pin my gaze on the dark water as I tell Odgar my story. "My royal advisor Iywan, Briony, and one of my servants, Eefa, had been working with the Zenith. When they discovered that I could read ancient texts, they held me captive in hopes of getting me to tell them about the prophecy. I don't even know how long they tortured me for, but—"

I pause to breathe through the panic hurtling toward me. Odgar's hand on my back steadies me, comforts me. "Eefa took pleasure in every cut, every sordid word about me. She stuck her dagger into me, over and over. Until I didn't think I could take it anymore. Until I wanted to die. But Briony kept healing me."

The words pour out of me like wine from a broken cask. I bite my lip, wanting to hold back the words, but they just keep flowing. I tell Odgar how Briony turned against the Zenith, and how she and Angharad arranged my fake death. I let myself relive the fear of drowning, of my own powers burning through me, of the difficult recovery.

It takes all my courage to turn to Odgar, to face his glistening eyes and pained expression. I swallow and feel the trickle of tears on my face.

Water laps against the side of the boat, the soft whoosh of the waves keeping me calm. It's a while before Odgar says, "You are so much stronger than you realize."

I let out a shaky breath.

"I'm glad that you made it to Uldarvik."

"Me too," I say tearfully.

He wraps an arm around my shoulder, tugging me close. I feel tons lighter, though I know it won't last. After a while, the wind has me trembling even under Odgar's warm embrace and his heavy cloak.

Odgar leans away and lifts the oars again. "Let's get you warmed up," he says. He rows us back to the main ship in silence. I look at my hands, surprised that so much power can willingly be Wielded, but at least this time, no one was hurt.

When we're almost back at the ship, I glance at Odgar again. "Thank you," I say.

He smiles at me, and my stomach somersaults. "Any time."

Chapter 59

CARYS

As I CHANGE into my nightgown and comb out my hair, I no longer feel the pulse of my powers demanding my attention. There's no sense of overheating, no itch, yet I'm bereft and unsettled. Diminished. So annoyingly lonely. How often had I confined myself to my bedchamber back in Paramount and allowed myself to simmer in my despair? Those were the moments when the cauldron of emotion soup boiled over and consumed me. When I lost control of my actions.

Not tonight. Tonight, I want to maintain control. I'm not ready to face those darker parts of me again.

I hurry out of my cabin and down through the tight corridor to Odgar's door. Quietly, I rap three times, and only a heartbeat later, it opens, revealing Odgar's perplexed face.

"Are you al—?"

Not giving him a chance to finish his sentence, I throw myself at him. He starts to protest, but then his lips soften against mine and his muscles relax. I press my hands against his tattooed chest, pushing him into his cabin and nudging the door closed with my heel. Odgar's hands slide into my hair as his tongue glides against mine.

The kiss is heady, fervent. Too many sensations and emotions fill me at once. All impossible to pry apart. As Odgar's mouth explores my neck, he drags me against his hard body. Damp heat gathers low in my belly, between my thighs, as I reach down to fumble with the laces of his trousers before palming his growing cock through the fabric.

His intake of breath against my skin makes me grin.

"Carys," he whispers. "Are—"

I slip my hand into his trousers and wrap my fingers around his thick length. He groans my name and the sound thrums through me.

"Are you sure you want to—"

My gaze is fixated on the arousal dominating his features as I stroke and he fails to finish his sentence again, his eyelids heavy, his breaths uneven.

Satisfaction curves my lips as my hand moves steadily.

"Carys ..." He stills my hand with his. "Are you sure you want this?"

"If *you* don't want this then—"

"I've wanted this—I've wanted *you*—for far longer than I should admit," he says breathlessly. "But you've had a rough night, and I don't want to take advantage of that."

I've had many rough days and nights. It's been nothing but a dark cloud of constant misery. I want to feel something else. I want to feel powerful in a way that has nothing to do with the flames I've inherited.

"I *need* this." Desperation laces my words. I need *him*. "Don't make me beg."

His large hand cups my face, his thumb lightly tracing my lips. "You never have to beg me for anything, *mineh kelsska*."

I nip at his thumb, and he pulls his hand away, surprised. "Then take your trousers off and get on the bed," I say.

A spark of something lights up his face. Admiration? Amusement? The corner of his lips twitch, his eyes crinkling. "Yes, Your Majesty."

I huff, starting to unlace the top of my nightgown. "I'm not queen yet."

His hand hovers over his chest. "In here you are," he says.

My fingers pause on the ties of my nightgown, my eyes roaming the symbols that span his chest, save for one spot over his heart. The spot where his hand now rests. I expect him to look away, but his gaze latches onto mine, totally unabashed. He removes his trousers, letting them slip to the floor. An eager ache clenches in my core at the sight of him.

I remind myself to pull in a breath as I step closer and tug my nightgown over my head, casting it aside. "Didn't I tell you to get on the bed?" I ask.

He smirks. "I don't think that bed is large enough for the two of us."

My eyes flick to the mattress then to Odgar's impressive height and girth ... I whip the furs off the cot, spreading them on the ground and gesturing to it.

Grinning, Odgar sprawls out on the furs, leaning back against his hands. As he stares up at me, I'm painfully reminded of my gauntness and the scars that Briony couldn't fully heal. Yet Odgar looks at me as though I'm the most beautiful sight he's ever beheld. Perhaps I have the dim candlelight to thank for that.

I push my hair backward over my shoulders and sink to the floor, shoving Odgar onto his back as I straddle his broad waist. His chest undulates with a ragged breath, laughter seeping through. His hands move to my face, then lightly trail down my neck and over the small swell of my breasts.

"Carys ..." My name on his lips is a plea.

I position myself over him, reaching between our bodies to press his tip against my entrance.

"Are you absolutely—" His breathless question is cut off by a pleasant sigh as I ease him into me.

I push past the doubt and fears, through the momentary discomfort as my body stretches, bit by bit, accommodating him. *Gods* ... The blissful look on his face puts another small crack in the icy exterior of my heart. Flutters skitter across my stomach as it tightens. I brace my hands on his sturdy chest, trying to breathe through the overwhelming fullness of him.

His eyes slide reverently down my body before he reaches between us to stroke his thumb over my clit. My muscles relax and I roll my hips forward, eliciting a small moan that rumbles in his chest. I snatch his hand from between my legs and pin it against the floor.

A heartbeat later, I have both his wrists restrained. His eyes widen, his hips rising in a way that drives him even deeper inside me. A shuddery moan escapes me, drawing a slow grin across Odgar's face. He surrenders to me, practically boneless.

Those sunburst eyes stare into my soul as I rock lazily against him, adjusting, finding a rhythm.

He bites back a curse as I lift myself only to sink down again. Slowly at first, savoring the sweet buildup, then with more reckless abandon. Releasing his wrists, I press my hands against his chest for more leverage. My nails dig into his flesh, raking down his chest. His back arches off the furs, a moan threaded with a mixture of pain and desire rushing past his lips. I drive my hips down against him with fervor, until he wraps his arms around my back and tugs me down onto his chest. As he thrusts up into me, I let out a gasp. My head falls onto the curve of his shoulder, my blood singing for more.

Odgar is still somewhat controlled. Until he isn't. His arm tightens around my waist and a yelp of surprise slips from me as he flips us. Our connection breaks as he hovers over me, his hands braced on either side of my body. Lips parted and face flushed, he dips his head to kiss along my neck and down to my tits.

My chest heaves, my body bereft and wanting, *aching* for him. My inner muscles clench around nothing. "Odgar, for fuck's sake," I groan, tilting my hips with impatience.

He laughs and repositions himself, pushing into me so *slowly*. I lock my ankles around his back and yank. He lets out a string of Uldaran words, his forehead lowered against mine as sparks of pleasure thread through me. But then he remains still. I squirm beneath him. "Odgar, I swear to the gods if you don't move—"

He pulls back, then eases into me again. "You'll what?" he dares. His voice is smooth as honey as he pulls out even more this time. When he slowly eases back inside me, I intentionally clench around his cock.

He hisses out an Uldaran curse, but his movements remain so intentionally, achingly, *frustratingly* slow. My heart is hammering as I wrap my arms around him, my inner muscles tightening needily, desperately. "More," I moan against his shoulder.

Yet he keeps this slow pace, Uldaran words mixed with incoherent Common Tongue whispered across my flesh.

My breath catches, pressure building in my core as he shifts and sets my ankles on his shoulders. The angle is agonizingly sweet, deeper, as he thrusts into me with increasing urgency. Bliss graces every angle of his beautiful face as his fingers grip my thighs. Deep groans resound with each movement of his hips.

Those sounds ... Gods ...

And the reverence in his eyes even as he pounds into me. This man was supposed to be my *political* gain.

And yet ...

My heart may just implode.

I shut my eyes to avoid the longing in his, while my hips undulate of their own accord. I clench my fists in the furs beneath me, unable to breathe, unable to think. My focus breaks from the warring feelings in me, chasing euphoria as each crash of Odgar's hips against me obliterates every torturous thought. The harmony of our sighs and moans fills the cabin, Odgar's pace picking up as he calls my name like a prayer. Like it's the only word that matters.

Like *I'm* all that matters.

"Carys ... Look at me, *mineh kelsska*."

I open my eyes, not expecting the enamored smile on his lips. Not expecting his gaze to draw me in and fill me with a greater surge of emotions than I can handle.

"Let me see those eyes when you come," he says.

They stay open for mere seconds before my head falls back, a shattered cry on my lips as the trace of smoke fills my nostrils. Pleasure pulses deep and strong within my belly, leaving me quaking and whimpering beneath Odgar. Tiny jolts of bliss continue to flow through me almost endlessly. I'm breathless and buoyant and utterly spent.

In the afterglow of my release, I resurface to full awareness with Odgar's lips against my neck. He pulls out of me with a blissful sigh, and I immediately find myself missing the weight and the fullness of him. Rolling onto his back, he tugs me toward him so that my head is nestled in the crook of his neck.

We both lay still, our chests heaving as our breathing gradually levels out.

I refuse to think of anything other than the utter satisfaction. I know too well how temporary such gratification can be, but I want this to last.

Gods, how I want this to last.

I want to hoard this memory, to replay it when life no doubt goes to shit again. When I've forgotten what it feels like to experience something other than brokenness.

The cool air within the sleeping quarters settles onto my sweaty skin, but my body feels too heavy—comfortable drowsiness setting in—for me to care.

But when Odgar runs his fingers through my hair, the act is so tender—so outside of mere indulgence—that I jolt upright as though lightning shoots from his fingers. Odgar looks at me with a mixture of concern and adoration, and I beg my icy heart not to thaw. It's just sex, I remind myself. A much-needed distraction. An outlet.

Even if this felt so different from any encounter I've had before.

I can't afford to form attachments. He may claim he isn't afraid of me, but he hasn't seen the worst of me. We barely know each other. We were supposed to be wed for convenience, not for love, not for ... whatever this is.

Clumsily, I grapple for my nightgown, throwing it over my head as I head for the door.

"Carys," Odgar calls, his low voice firm but not hostile.

I keep my hand against the knob though I don't turn, even as my skin, my whole body, continues to hum. Like his touch has left a lasting song, an imprint on my skin.

"Did I do something wrong?"

No, you big oaf, you did everything right. Tears sting my eyes as I press my forehead against the door. Odgar's footsteps pad toward me. "Odgar." My voice is quiet as I refuse to turn away from the door. "I'm *begging* you ... Do not touch me or ask me to stay."

He sighs, and I make the mistake of glancing over my shoulder at him. At the pain in his eyes and the confusion playing over his rugged features. His hands are clenched at his sides, as if it's taking every bit of his control not to reach for me.

As soon as I open the door to step out of his cabin, a whisper of that voice within me stirs, bringing an odd feeling of impending doom along with it. I step backward and close the door, pressing my forehead against the wood again.

"Carys ..." His voice is quiet, and I feel him close to me, but he doesn't touch me. Because I bloody asked him *not* to.

"Fuck me," I mumble under my breath.

"Again?" he says. "Well, if you insist ..." Amusement permeates his tone.

Laughter sputters out of me, followed by the most unattractive, wet hiccup. I turn and step right into his arms. He doesn't hesitate before folding them around me.

"Stay," he says as my tears begin to flow.

"You don't understand." I hiccup again. "You can't ... fall for me." It physically hurts to unleash the words. I push away from him, and my back hits the door.

Whatever you don't want to talk about—it's festering like a wound inside you, Valdis had told me.

My chest feels too tight, but I need to speak up before I lose my nerve. "I slaughtered my brother," I whisper. "I was five. I lost control of my magic. And I—" Not wanting to see Odgar's reaction, I squeeze my eyes shut. Tears gather beneath my lids. "Ellynne was killed, right beside me while I *slept*. Then Callum, right in front of me. Eefa slit his throat because I wouldn't give them the information they wanted." My voice breaks.

Silence expands for a while before warm hands rest on my shoulders. "The one who scarred you." Odgar's voice is steady, tight.

I nod, my lashes holding back the dam of tears while I keep my eyes shut.

"Callum and Ellynne are dead because they were loyal to me. My brother. My mother." The words taste like bile as they rush out.

"It's not your fault," Odgar says.

"Everyone I care about dies. Or leaves. I don't want to lose you too."

"Carys, my *revna, mineh kelsska,* I'm right here. Life can be cruel. I know. But right now, I'm here and I'm not going anywhere."

More unattractive sobs come from me, and I bury my face in his chest. He strokes his hands over my back while I properly drench his chest with tears and snot. Yet he doesn't recoil in disgust.

"Stay," he says, still holding on to me as if he's afraid that *I'll* leave.

"Alright," I concede through tears. "Alright, I'll stay."

He slowly unwraps his arms from me, then takes my hand to guide me to the too-small bed. Odgar climbs in, patting the spot beside him as he edges back against the wall. I climb in, curling onto my side so my back presses against his front. It's a tight squeeze, but somehow comforting.

I'm certain it'll take me ages to fall asleep, but as soon as his arms circle my waist, I slip off into a dreamless oblivion.

I wake up feeling overheated, something nearly pinning me to the bed. Panic spears through me before the familiar scent of pine and perspiration floods my nostrils.

Shit.

So last night was not a dream. Not only did I fuck Odgar, but I poured my heart out to him. I *remained* with him. I expect the shame to set in as it often has—with Wynn, Eefa, Callum, and the others whose names I hardly remember. This time, however, there's no shame. There's only disappointment. Not because of the sex, but because I'd come to him for pleasure. For power. And in an ironic plot twist, it ended up feeling like so much more.

Odgar stirs, and his erection presses against my arse. My stomach clenches eagerly, my body immediately coming alive and begging for more, but I shift, putting some distance between our lower halves.

"*Solni risgur,*" he murmurs. Then, as if remembering himself, he repeats it in the Common Tongue. "Good morning."

"*Solni risgur,*" I respond. I feel his smile against my shoulder. "I want to learn more of your language. Will you teach me?" I roll toward him, the bed creaking as I face him, and he smiles.

"I would love to."

He leans close to kiss me, but I place my fingers lightly over his lips. "I have to go train with Valdis, and I doubt that kissing me is going to deflate your eager cock."

He barks out a laugh that startles me before it warms my heart. His free expression of emotion is refreshing.

"May I ask you something?" I say.

"Of course."

"Why do you call me *revna*?"

He grins. "Well, *revna* means raven." He reaches out and lifts my hair, catching a streak of gold instead. "Your hair has more golden bits than before, but it's still raven black."

I roll my eyes, thinking there had been some more enlightened reason behind the nickname. Especially since even the ends of my hair are starting to fade to a lustrous gold.

"*But,*" Odgar continues, and my brows rise. "Ravens represent divine justice, wisdom, magic and prophecy. Because Hofadr—the father of the gods—uses ravens as his messengers. They often bring visions and open our eyes. Like you opened mine."

My brows furrow. "I ..." The words slip away, and I clear my throat, averting my gaze. "You think far too highly of me."

"Maybe you think far too little of yourself. I call you raven warrior and huntress because I want to remind you of the strength inside of you. And I'm not talking about your flamewielding. You'd be powerful even without it."

My chest feels too heavy. "And ..." I swallow around the sudden knot in my throat. "You called me something ... *Mineh* ...?"

Confusion crosses his face for a moment before recognition sinks in. "*Mineh kelsska* ... My ... beloved." The hesitation is evident in his eyes, but his words feel pure, genuine.

I smile, tears brimming, and catch myself as I'm about to caress his beard, to slide my finger over the antler tattoo on his cheek. I need to get out of this space. I have no intention of crying again today. Or sleeping with Odgar again—not until I have my bearings about me and I can be sure I'm not using him only for pleasure or to feel powerful.

"I'll ... have to ask Briony about a fertility suppressant," I say, grimacing as I sit up.

"I take a powder," Odgar says with a smile. "You don't have to worry about the suppressant."

His words give me pause for a moment. Then I slip out of bed and adjust my nightgown. "I'd better get ready for the day."

"Wait," Odgar says. The bed creaks as he gets up and crosses to a cabinet on the other side of the room. He's nude, as he'd been last night, and I can't help but stare at the flexing muscles in his arse as he stalks off. I fight to keep my wits about me despite the desire building all over again. He collects something from a cabinet and strides toward me again. Draping a dusky blue material over my neck, he says, "I finally finished it."

I frown, confused. The fabric is soft and fuzzy—woven. It's warm—far too warm—against my neck. It takes me a moment to recognize that this is what he's been working on since he first visited Paramount. "You knitted me a scarf?" My voice comes out as a whisper.

"Nalbound, not knitted." He winks. "Remember? One needle versus—"

"*Odgar.*"

He laughs. "But yes, I made this for you. I know the winters aren't as harsh in Erleya, and I wish I'd finished this earlier but—"

"Thank you," I say, cutting him off. I inhale, my chest feeling crowded. This scarf is *definitely* too warm. The flush takes over my whole body, forcing me to step away from Odgar. I feel a tug toward him, my gaze settling on his lips, avoiding those eyes that I know can melt me. His muscular, tattooed chest isn't any less inviting. I turn and briskly walk away. "And thank you for last night. Not the sex, but ... you know." I rush out of the cabin before I can hear whatever heartfelt thing he no doubt has to say.

Chapter 60

AFTER I MANAGED to convince Winnie to help me get Tiernan, as well as herself and her loved ones, out of Paramount, we all practice using the vanishing ring to jump from one place to another. Chiyo, Ava, and I jump from her house to the bathhouse. From the bathhouse to the forge. The first few times we vanish, I vomit as soon as my feet touch solid ground again. The others practice the same.

Practicing daywalking and dreamweaving, however, turns out to be easier on me than vanishing, but Alys still has to replenish my energy every now and then. Sloan is more than willing to let me practice on them as much as needed. With uncanny bravery, they let me turn their fears against them, inducing terrible images—like their sister being taken away—or replaying a memory that leaves them heartbroken that I haven't dared to look too deeply into.

Haruka allows me to do the same, as does Chiyo and even Osheen. Isobel is reluctant to let me into her mind, and Ava wants nothing to do with any of this. I respect them both. But on the second day, Ava approaches me as I stand outside, hugging myself against the chill and watching the sun slowly sink behind the black mountains.

"You're even madder than I thought if you believe I'm going to let you jump into the damn castle without me," she says.

I open my mouth to respond, but she cuts me off.

"You need to choose who's coming along wisely. You need a

429

balance of strengths and weaknesses. Your dreamweaving is impressive, you have a heart of gold, but you don't have the head for combat. And Koko may be the most talented and versatile weapon wielder we have among us, but she can be impulsive."

"Koko?"

Ava winces but continues as if she didn't hear me. "I still think this is a *terrible* idea. Don't get me wrong. But I'm not going to let you and Chiyo do it alone. You're my blood. You're going to need the lot of us to assist. Not to mention Isobel and Sloan should be backup."

For a few heartbeats, I'm unsure how to react. Ava's lips twitch, a smile fighting to get through.

"Alright," I say. "So, what are you suggesting?"

Haruka sends word to her husband via enchanted parchment, asking him to connect us with a rebel safehouse. It takes only a day before a rolled notice appears on her table, with a single name on it and directions to use the parchment as a tether to jump to the correct location.

Holding the note, I take Ava's hand while she takes Chiyo's. It requires a lot of focus—not helped at all by Ava's increasing impatience and my growing doubt—before we finally find ourselves tumbling through the abyss.

I expect us to land in a home somewhere in the Grounds, but instead we touch down in an empty room with shiny wooden floors and ivory walls filled with framed paintings. Chiyo and Ava draw their weapons, and I spin, following the line of their gazes.

A young woman stands with her hands over her mouth and a now-broken wooden frame on the floor in front of her. She runs through the doorway behind her, strawberry blond hair billowing.

Not a moment later, an older man with thick grey hair and cunning cerulean eyes appears. He smiles and holds his hands up innocently, saying something that makes Chiyo sheath her dagger and Ava lower her sword.

"This is my da's contact," Chiyo signs. She slowly fingerspells *Murtagh*. "We're in a jewelry shop in Barr na Cahar. The safehouse."

The man approaches us, and I struggle slightly to read the words on his lips. They're slightly obstructed by his thick beard and mustache, and he has a thick accent, though it seems similar to Isobel's and Sloan's. "Apologies," he says. "I never learned to sign. But welcome. I was expecting more of you."

Ava explains that we left the others behind so we could gather information first. Murtagh leads us out of the gallery, bringing an oil lantern along with him. We follow him into the corridor where he opens a trapdoor that drops down to a narrow staircase. It grows darker as we descend, but Murtagh's lamp does a well enough job until he's able to light the sconces against the walls.

A common area becomes visible, a large couch, area rug, and brick fireplace making the space cozier. There are a couple other doors that Ava insists on checking, leading to several bedchambers and a bath chamber.

Once satisfied, Ava takes the vanishing ring and goes to fetch the others two by two.

We're all gathered in the sitting room before long, discussing the mission over tea. We're joined by Murtagh's daughters Siobhan, the strawberry blond who we'd scared earlier, and her older sister, Kenna, a tall, silver-haired woman with eyes that shift from blue to bright green as she regards us. They couldn't be more different. Siobhan is reserved, but clever and conversational, while Kenna is animated, her excessive gestures confusing my senses as she speaks.

She bears tiny white scars on her face and the backs of her hands. A dark bruise stands out on her otherwise smooth pink face and more across the knuckles of her right hand. She continuously refills everyone's teacups and fetches more pastries from the kitchen, courtesy of Siobhan.

By the end of the night, we all retire to our rooms. I still feel bereft without Tiernan, but hopefully soon, I'll be reunited with him.

Chapter 61

TIERNAN

HEAVY FOOTSTEPS GROW LOUDER, and I lift my head weakly from where I'm slumped on my cell floor. I expect to see Lynx's masked face, but instead, it's Rheon. Without a word, the guards unlock the gate and Rheon steps in, though he moves no farther. He levels a steely gaze on me and says with cold detachment, "Last chance, soldier."

I straighten slightly, but my back protests, the newly made and half-healed flogging wounds stinging. "I'm not your soldier," I grit out.

So far, I've survived two trips to the whipping post. I'll endure one hundred trips if it means Durvla remains safe—if it means Rheon never finds out I'm not the Shadow Wielder he seeks.

A smile stretches his face and his pupils dilate, inky darkness swirling in his eyes, melding with his irises for a moment. My heart jolts. His eyes return to the usual dark blue, but I swear shadows creep across his skin. The veins standing out in his neck appear darker than they should, and his skin is paler than his usual complexion.

Lowering my mental shields slightly, my senses immediately catch the vile, murky aura that surrounds him. It feels tainted, *wrong*, causing my skin to itch and crawl and my stomach to twist with queasiness. I pull my shields up and scuffle back on my ass, away from whatever beast Rheon is turning into.

His smile turns into a sneer as he steps closer. "I know you aren't the Shadow Wielder," he says.

My stomach drops like a damn rock.

"Either you surrender the information of *who* is, or I will continue to send you to the whipping pole until you submit."

I keep my lips firmly sealed.

"Whatever your power is, I will have it. Whether you are willing or not."

I breathe slowly. "What have you done, Rheon?"

"What needs to be done, boy."

"It's dangerous to fuck around with forces you don't understand. Whatever shit you're mixed up with could destroy the whole kingdom."

Rheon only laughs, a rumbling, unnatural sound in his chest. My blood crawls. I shudder, wincing as pain ripples across my back. My body feels too worn—the lack of sufficient food and water weakening me with each passing hour. It makes it harder for me to keep my shields up and block out the discordance of emotions around me.

"Will you give me the information I seek?" he asks.

I keep my mouth shut. I'll be damned if I give in to this monster and whatever twisted plan he has.

"Very well," he says with a sigh. "Come tonight, I won't have to deal with you, *and* I will have your powers at my disposal." He gives no further explanation, but leaves my cell, the gate clanging shut behind him.

I've overheard Carys reading countless stories about dark magic corruption. Rheon has all the classic signs: the darkening eyes, the shadows, the murky aura. Whatever plans he has for me tonight ... I cannot even fathom it.

Chapter 62

DURVLA

ALREADY, my palms are slick with sweat, my clothes sticking to my skin. Sitting in the common room of Murtagh's safehouse, I close my eyes and try to center myself, blocking out the rest of the team waiting for the moment we have to jump into Paramount. Our plan is beyond risky, but there doesn't seem to be another way to do it outside of gathering an entire rebel army to storm the castle. Arguably, that would be even riskier.

The moonstone is in the pocket of my trousers, feeling heavier than ever as if it, too, understands the weight of this situation. There's an overwhelming feeling of urgency that overtakes me, causing nausea to gather in my throat. We have a set time we're supposed to jump into Paramount, but something is practically shouting at me that the time is now.

"We have to go!" I announce. Everyone turns to me. Chiyo's eyes are more kohl-lined than usual, her hair pulled back from her face, her vest adorned with a multitude of blades. There's a bow and quiver of arrows at her feet where she rises from the couch. Ava's equally armed though most of her hair still hangs down. She also jumps to her feet.

"Now?" she asks. "How—"

"*Now*," I repeat as Isobel enters the room nonchalantly, as though we've not been waiting for such a scary plan. Even more

434

sweat breaks out around my neckband and trickles down my sternum. "I know we had a time, but something's telling me—"

"Then we go," Ava interrupts, glancing at the others. Chiyo grabs the quiver of arrows, slinging it across her back. I spin the vanishing ring on my finger as Isobel holds her hand up and grabs her sibling, pulling them close. We gather at the center of the room, Chiyo and Ava grasping hands before Chiyo grabs mine and I grab Isobel's. Sloan closes the circle, and I quickly take in everyone's determined expressions.

"If all fails," I blurt. "I love you all like you're family."

"Beautiful heartfelt words," Ava says dismissively. "But let's go!"

I close my eyes and all I can somehow picture in the moment is my old bedroom in the castle. Now Winnie's bedroom. We're pulled through darkness and space, an endless somersault until our feet touch solid ground again. We take a few seconds to get the dizziness under control before Ava says, "You know where you are?"

I nod and swallow back the nausea. "When we get out of here, we head right and keep going." Everyone nods and we rush out of the bedroom, only to run straight into a group of soldiers dressed in midnight blue. Zenith members.

Weapons are drawn from both sides, but I contain my shadows, afraid to reveal myself. As a woman produces daggers of ice from thin air, Isobel blasts a gust of air into her face.

My head is still reeling from the transfer between locations, but Chiyo grabs my arm. "Run," she signs. She gestures over her shoulder to where Isobel and Sloan are fighting the Zenith members. Ava joins us in running through the immense corridors, toward where I know we can find an exit from the castle.

My lungs already burn from running. We careen around a corner, and Ava yanks me back to jump in front of me, her sword raised to block another blade. Chiyo flings a dagger into someone's eye, and I resist the urge to close my own. I turn as I sense a presence behind me. A man almost double my height comes at me with a long sword. There's no point in holding back, so I let loose a ripple of my shadows. It's enough to stall him before Ava's sword slices across his stomach.

Then we're running again. I try desperately to *feel* for Tiernan's aura. For Winnie's. It isn't until we round another corner, so close to the exit, that an overwhelming sense of both Winnie and Tiernan rushes into me. It's strong enough that I'm certain I can jump right to them.

"Grab Ava!" I shout to Chiyo as I snatch her hand back just as she's about to throw a dagger at a new attacker. Chiyo grabs Ava's hand, and we go tumbling into the abyss.

Chapter 63

THE MOMENT I'm taken across the encampment beneath the Paramount plateau, an entire hour before planned, I know that the sovereign has lied about my part in this so-called ritual. And, of course, the time I told the Dreamwalker when she appeared to me last night is now incorrect. The searing realization that the entire escape plan may be out the window squeezes my lungs as I continue across the land beneath the castle plateau.

The dark sky is streaked with purple, the low sun glowing weakly on the horizon. But already, the stars are visible, and the encampment is shrouded in darkness save for speckles of magelight.

The closer we get to the entrance of the forest, to Fiada Purlieu, the faster my heart beats. I've been cynical about the existence of the Veil, especially given that there is nothing out of the ordinary about the appearance of the forest, but something feels off.

My mind screams at me to flee as we get closer. A large bonfire illuminates the area, including several guards and a few other figures up ahead. One is obviously the sovereign. He's flanked by Lynx and Radika, Lynx's mask more ominous in the wavering flames nearby. Two thick, wooden posts have been erected before the forest entrance, a body bound to each of them, their hands secured behind their backs.

A book that looks old enough to fall apart, bottles of potions, and other artifacts sit on a stony table—an altar of sorts. My eyes trail

437

from the table to the two bound figures. Tiernan's head is slumped forward as if he's unconscious, but the other captive looks at me with pleading emerald eyes and tears streaming down her face.

Neris.

The breath whooshes out of my lungs and my knees buckle, but I stand my ground. A soldier nudges me, and I stumble forward to face the sovereign, whose lips stretch into that oily smile. His eyes are darker than usual, as are the veins standing out on his neck.

"I'm glad you could make it, Lady Gwyneth," he says lightheartedly, as though we're taking a morning stroll through the castle grounds. "Get ready to witness the sacrifice of the Shadow Wielder, and the opening of the Veil!" His eyes seem demented tonight; too wide, too dark. His grin is unsteady, wild.

My heart stills for a moment. *Opening?* He'd said he was going to *close* the Veil! To end the blight. I shouldn't be surprised that a man like Rheon would blatantly lie this way.

"Not only will there be a sacrifice, but a transference of power," Rheon continues. "Your Ordinary friend is about to become a Wielder, if all goes according to plan."

Two Zenith members step out from among the rest of the soldiers, a large knife in each of their hands. Neris draws an audible breath as a blade is held to her throat. The other soldier grabs Tiernan by his hair, forcing his head back, and the man's eyes fly open, consciousness crashing into him. He immediately stiffens as he realizes his predicament, remaining statue still as the soldier also holds a knife to his throat.

"Winnie," Neris whimpers.

I look frantically at the sovereign.

"Balance requires sacrifice," he says.

It's a phrase I've heard from the Purists as well.

"Once the Shadow Wielder's soul exits, his powers will transfer from him and cling to Reneris."

My eyebrows furrow. That doesn't even make sense.

Yet Radika pulls a silver stiletto from her robes and strides toward Neris, who doesn't dare to move and risk the soldier ending her life. Chanting loudly in a strange language, she holds Neris's arm still. With one hand, Radika begins carving something into the flesh just below the short sleeve of Neris's dress.

Neris cries out in pain, and it takes everything in me not to run to her rescue, but Radika continues, calm as if she's simply drawing on canvas. She then tucks the thin weapon away and snaps her finger.

The potion she'd been mixing that day in the infirmary floats from the makeshift altar and lands smoothly in her waiting palm. As she uncorks the bottle, I grapple for something to do, anything that would stop whatever's about to happen. I cannot let her give Neris that potion; I cannot let Tiernan be *sacrificed,* whatever that entails.

"Stop!" I shout as Radika places the bottle against Neris's tightly sealed lips.

All eyes turn to me.

"I have something you want." My voice cracks, coming out breathless. I pull my pocket watch from my trousers and hold it up for everyone to see. "It's a stone. I heard it's of great value. As an amplifier."

The sovereign perks up, intrigued.

I look at the golden hands of the clock one last time. At the beautiful details nestled within the brass. The milky white stone veined with mossy green is visible beneath the outer glass rim of the clock—where I'd melded it with the watch a year ago to keep it safe for reasons I hadn't even known at the time. Tears sting my eyes as I think of destroying the last keepsake I have from Father. But he wouldn't want me to hold on to sentiments for the sake of it. I close my eyes and call to the stone within.

The glass fragments, the shards digging into my skin, then the entire pocket watch practically melts as the stone is drawn into my palm. I drop the broken pieces and close my bleeding fist around the stone. It hums in my hand, heating up until it's almost unbearable. Like it's begging to be released or warning me not to release it. As usual, I cannot decipher my own intuition.

"Winnie, no!" Neris says. "Don't."

"Is this what you want?" I ask, holding out the stone in the palm of my bloodied hand. I step forward, but the sovereign doesn't budge. I swear his pupils dilate, but he seems afraid to move closer to me. Or afraid to claim the stone.

"Radika." His tone is clipped, uncertain.

"That's the one," Radika says without him even asking the question.

My eyes shift to Tiernan, who is staring into my soul as though he can see my thoughts. Then I hear his voice, though his lips don't move. *"Release me from the dampener so I can Wield."*

I try not to startle, but my heart jumps. He's a Mind Whisperer?

"And a Mimic. Release me, then toss the stone toward Rheon. I'll redirect it."

I hesitate for only a heartbeat. Then I clench my fist, the cuts on my palm stinging. I will the shackles on Tiernan's wrists to break—releasing his magic and his body from the post. If it makes a sound, I don't hear it over the roar of my pulse in my ears.

"Well, Pendry, what are you waiting for?" the sovereign asks. "Give me the stone."

"Yes, Excellency," I say. But instead of moving closer to him, I hold my breath and toss the stone in his direction.

Panic fills his eyes as he realizes he'll have to catch it. He steps forward, but Tiernan holds his hand out and the stone flies into his waiting palm.

No sooner have his fingers closed around the stone than a sizable feline with grey fur hurtles out of nowhere, claws extended, ripped clothing clinging to its body. It pounces on Tiernan, tackling him to the ground. He cries out in pain, and the stone rolls from his hand and into the grass. The wildcat pins his arm with a large, clawed paw, snarling and baring its teeth.

I barely have time to process my own shock when the sovereign shouts, "Seize her!"

As a soldier steps toward me, I pull up a mound of earth and he trips over it. Everyone that comes my way is met with a blast of dirt or rocks in their face. I sink a couple of others waist-deep right into the ground, trapping them.

Between attacks, I look around frantically, seeking Neris. I need to get her out of here. But she's no longer bound to the post.

Not again!

A man comes at me, his fists flaming. I release the bracelet on my wrist, morphing it into a dagger that I fling into his chest. His flames die before he drops to the ground.

Another Zenith member cloaked in midnight blue appears before me. His dark eyes are wild, a mop of unruly black hair plastered to his forehead and temples. I summon my dagger from the Flamewielder's chest as I take in this new attacker. Dark veins cobweb out from the corners of his eyes. My gaze dips down from the painfully familiar face to his fists. To the hands that'd gently held my face when he last bade me farewell. When he'd pressed a loving kiss to my forehead and told me to keep my fighting spirit alive in his absence.

These same hands that are prepared to smite me are the same hands that tended many a childhood wound.

A lightning bolt pin sits on his burly chest, and I blink, forcing my eyes back to his feral gaze. A few heartbeats pass before I finally find my voice—barely.

"Father?" I whisper.

He snarls as if the title provokes something animalistic in him. As he lunges for me, tiny sparks melded with dark mist play on his fingertips. Bitterness creeps into my throat, and my heart squeezes agonizingly. As I leap to the side, the hair rises on my neck as the tiniest zap of lightning illuminates the space where I'd just stood.

He has *powers*?

"Father! It's—"

He shoves his hand toward me, and more sparks laced with darkness form. A breath later, they die on his palms. He looks partly bewildered, partly panicked. Darkness moves beneath his ashen brown skin—as if ink flows through his veins. His eyes seem too large, blackness bleeding into where it should be white. My heart hammers so rapidly that my body goes numb.

"Father!" I call. "Please. *Eurig*?" I send a chunk of earth into someone in my periphery. I don't even look to see what's become of them as Father closes in on me. Weak sparks sputter at his fingertips.

Another chunk of earth hovers at my side, prepared to be brought down upon the head of the man who'd been my greatest role model. Who'd disrupted societal norms to teach his daughter how to defend herself. Who'd believed in her. In *me*.

Something flickers in his eyes, the darkness receding and a familiar, tender gaze locks onto my face.

"Father. It's me. Winnie." My voice comes out breathless. "*Please.*"

But my father, or whoever this man—this creature—is, shakes his head. The recognition disappears from his eyes. I step back, raising the chunk of earth, but he closes his eyes and vanishes from the spot. More Zenith members begin to jump away.

They're ... fleeing?

The sovereign is nowhere in sight, and the big cat is still grappling with Tiernan. The animal's head whips toward me, its face riddled with bald patches within the fur. Then suddenly, the cat morphs into human form with tattered clothing hanging off her body. She knocks Tiernan out with a swift cuff to the temple, then grabs the discarded red cloak before vanishing along with Tiernan.

There's no one left, save for Radika, the stiletto held to Neris's neck from behind.

My knees quiver as I root my feet. "Radika, it's over!" I shout. "Everyone's gone. What do you want?"

"The stone," Radika says simply.

My lips tug down. I'd thought it lost but, sure enough, there in the grass lies the stone. My memory of the discussion I'd overheard returns; the stone is needed to be given willingly for it to work. I pluck it from the grass. The white bits are still red from the cuts in my palm. From the pocket watch that I melted.

"Winnie," Neris's voice sounds far away with my pulse still pounding in my ears. "Don't give it to her. Let her kill me. You're more important. The world needs you."

I look at her with exasperation while she remains still, her head pressed back against Radika's shoulder, her chest rising and falling rapidly.

"The world needs *you*. Ordinary doesn't make you unimportant!"

"Oh, for the gods' sake," says Radika, impatience lacing her voice. "Give me the stone or I will pierce her thro—"

Her words are cut off as darkness surrounds her legs like fog, vines of shadows looping around and around her body. She drops the blade, shuddering. Then she claps her hands over her head and falls to her knees.

Neris clutches her throat, shock filling her eyes as she backs away from Radika. I glance around as a woman with hair pulled back into two thick braids approaches, shadows clearly swirling around her hands even in the darkness. On her left side is a shorter woman holding a bow, a quiver strapped across her back, and on her right is a taller woman with several long braids down her back and a sword in hand. The Shadow Wielder drops her hand and the vapors dissipate.

It's *her*. I'm not sure whether to be afraid or relieved, but Neris runs to stand beside me. "Are you alright?" I ask, not taking my eyes off the three women approaching.

I should know better than to turn away from the enemy, but I suddenly hear Radika's voice, speaking in that language I've heard her utter in the past. I turn to her as her hands start to glow purple from where she's kneeling on the ground. But she stops abruptly, clutching at the arrow shaft that appears in her chest.

A sick feeling overcomes me, bile searing my throat, pain stabbing through me so fiercely that I break out in a cold sweat. A *shing* fills the air as the taller woman pulls a sword from her belt while the shortest of them grabs a fresh arrow from the quiver strapped across her back.

Radika coughs, then closes her eyes and disappears from the spot. When the women are close enough, wide brown eyes meet my gaze. *The Dreamwalker.*

I nearly laugh with relief, but I can hardly breathe—my chest is on fire.

"Winnie?" The Dreamwalker's soothing voice pulls my attention.

I nod and Neris links her elbow with mine, holding me close. She's shaking like a leaf, truly scared.

The Dreamwalker takes in our surroundings, then swallows so hard that it's noticeable. "Where is he?" she asks. "Where is Tiernan?"

Chapter 64

DURVLA

We arrive to absolute chaos and no sign of Tiernan anywhere. "Where is Tiernan?" I ask Winnie. I hate for it to be my first words to her after everything, but I'm certain more Zenith members will be after us soon. We need to get Tiernan and get out of here before it's too late.

Winnie mutters something, but she's looking away while she says it.

I tilt my head to try and catch the movement of her lips, but she's lost in her thoughts. "Please, look at me," I say. She turns back to me, her brows furrowed. I point to my ears. "I can't hear, but I can read lips."

Surprise washes over her face through evident pain and exhaustion. "Apologies," she says. "He's been taken by the sovereign's enforcer. I don't know where to."

"Where was he last?"

"The brig." Her eyes dart down to my hand that's trembling from the use of my powers. Ava sheaths her sword and glares at Winnie and her friend. Winnie glances around, her eyes homing in on a dead body in a uniform like hers. She holds her hand out and something flies through the darkness and into her hand. "I can take you to the brig," she says to me. She opens her palm, a vanishing ring resting atop it. "But I need one of your friends to get *my* friend out of here."

The blond begins to speak, but Winnie shushes her.

Ava squints at the duo. I don't know what exactly happened here, but I'm sure reinforcements are coming. We need to *move*. "Alright," I say. "Your friend can go with Ava and Chiyo."

"No!" Ava says firmly.

"Ava, please. Take her friend to safety, get the others, and we'll meet up with you."

"I cannot just leave you."

"I'll stay," Chiyo signs. "We'll be fine." She gives Ava's shoulder a reassuring squeeze.

I remove the ring from my finger and hand it to Chiyo who slips it into Ava's palm. As she closes Ava's fingers around it, so much emotion fills Ava's eyes that I'm not sure if she'll cry or rage. Instead, she yanks Chiyo close, her lips practically crashing against Chiyo's. As quickly as she kisses her, she releases her.

"I hate this," Ava says, her face contorting. Her jaw clenches as she shoves the ring onto her finger. "I hate every bit of this. You all *better* make it out of here alive, or I'll find you in the Underworld just to kill you again."

She grabs the blond's arm and they disappear.

Winnie dries her face on her upper arm before offering me her hand. "Ready?" she asks.

Chiyo blinks, still stunned, but I grab her hand. "Ready." As soon as I clasp Winnie's hand, we hurtle through the shadows and touch down inside a cold, damp place. Guards rush at us, but Winnie stomps and they stumble over a newly made fissure in the ground. One guard draws a sword, slashing wildly, and I summon a shield of darkness before I send out a whip of shadows. I grab on to whatever memories I can find. A cut of a blade, a death in the family, and I force all the feelings upon them, pulling them down until they're overcome with grief and pain. Until they're lying on the ground, writhing, useless, then unconscious.

Pain arcs through my head. I squint through my spotting vision as Winnie steps forward. Her fists close around the bars of the cell, muscular arms quivering as she slowly pulls the bars apart.

Within the cell, a figure cloaked in red holds Tiernan firmly against their front. There isn't a weapon of any kind visible, but one arm is wrapped around his neck. The other is somewhere behind him. Winnie looks at me and says, "She has a dagger against his back."

My heart is ready to split in two as I look at Tiernan's ghostly face. Beneath copious amounts of blood and dirt are deep gashes. One of his eyes is swollen shut, and his teeth glisten red as he grits them against the pain. His shirt is in tatters, the grey fabric darkening from the blood seeping around his midsection. Tears streak down Chiyo's face as she levels an arrow in her brother's direction.

The figure behind him has a crimson cape drawn over her body, but her legs and feet are bare. Frizzy blond hair spills over her shoulders and across a face marred with angry red welts and puckered skin. The damage is concentrated to both her cheeks and her disfigured nose, but burn scars continue over her chin and down her neck.

"Take one more step and he becomes one with my pretty new dagger," she says. Her bright green eyes are wild and frantic, her pupils tiny—animalistic.

My breath catches as recognition sinks into me. *"Eefa?"*

She tilts her head then smiles crookedly, her warped skin pulling taut as her pupils expand again. "Well, hello, Miss Durvla. You have missed quite a lot since you left Paramount. Let's see, where do I start?"

Anger bubbles in my veins. "You can start by releasing Tiernan."

If Eefa had eyebrows, they would've risen. Surprise blooms on her face. "Oooh, how bold you've gotten." Her eyes flick to Chiyo. "Tell your friend to lower her weapon."

"You first."

She pulls Tiernan tighter, and his heavy-lidded eyes settle on me. He isn't fighting her and his breathing is too rapid. I'm certain he can feel the dagger against his back.

She has the upper hand; if I strike, she can still stab him. Unleashing my shadows would be too obvious and give her a chance to make a move. My pulse thunders, my breath growing short. "Lower your arrow," I say to Chiyo, feeling my voice crack.

I wish Winnie knew sign language. I wish I was the Mimic right now. But there's no magic to fall back on, and my wits seem scattered. Maybe Ava was right. I have no mind for combat. How am I going to get us all out of this in one piece?

"Do you have the stone, gorgeous?" Eefa asks, looking at Winnie.

Winnie's lips remain sealed, but her eyes dart to me. I nod very subtly to her, and she reaches into her pocket.

Eefa repositions the dagger, pulling it out from behind Tiernan's back and pressing it against his side. The blade is black as obsidian, a vein of glowing purple running through it. It's a very loud threat although Eefa doesn't say a word. Chiyo's hand flies to her mouth.

I have to think *fast*. "Eefa," I say, gently. "Tiernan has done nothing to you. If you can just ... release him, we'll be out of your hair."

A scornful grin crawls across her lips before she says, "So, so very clever. But no."

Tiernan's eyes are glassy and unfocused as he tries to settle his gaze on me. He's trembling so much that I fear he'll inadvertently get himself stabbed regardless. The familiar nudge of his powers against me is such a warm welcome—I drop my shields. His voice in my mind is so faint, so distant. *"She'll kill me rather than lose. Get everyone out of here and don't look back."*

I keep my face as stoic as I can though my chest lurches painfully. *"I can't—"*

"Listen to me, love ..." His voice is fading, the sound wavering in and out. Cold sweat coats my skin, my breath growing shorter. *"I'm sorry I didn't tell you ... I'm ... just ... stay alive for me ..."*

I step forward and icy cold races from my scalp down to the soles of my feet. Just outside the cell, a blast of fire fills the space. Winnie jumps, grabbing Chiyo's hand and starting to run toward me. A tall man in a Zenith uniform materializes before my eyes, towering over me, blocking my path to Winnie and Chiyo.

My stomach tumbles out of my body, my heart threatening to do the same. Frozen in place, I gawk up at the man's eyes. They're the deepest blue I've ever seen, but inky black swirls around in them before receding. Gasping, I step back, but his hand whips out, only to rest heavily on my shoulder.

"Where do you think you're going?" he asks, tilting his head.

I don't move a muscle, but my gaze flicks sidelong to where Tiernan and Eefa stood.

They're gone. My pulse hammers in my throat and temples as Chiyo and Winnie are dragged out from behind the strange man into my field of vision.

"I've been looking for you," says the man as Winnie and Chiyo thrash in their captor's grip. Chiyo's jaw is set stubbornly though tears brim in her eyes. Winnie's gaze is almost pensive, her lips pressed tightly together.

"Please let them go," I say.

"Let them go?" He laughs. "Pendry here is one of my own."

Winnie bites her lip, her brows furrowed, and fists clenched.

"She will be tried ... fairly, of course. And this other spitfire would make the perfect candidate for transference."

I frown at him, desperately trying to think of a way to get us out of this. "Transference?" I ask, hoping to buy time.

To my dismay, he doesn't take the bait. My gaze flicks back and forth between my friends and this monster. There has to be *something* I can do. They gave into this plan all because of me. I can't let Winnie go under trial or Chiyo go through whatever *transference* means. I've seen Winnie's strength. Chiyo is intuitive and quick-thinking. I just need to give them the perfect opportunity—the perfect distraction—to get away. After that ... gods, I don't even know.

"Come with me," says the man, extending his open palm to me. "We have much to discuss."

I step back and stare at Chiyo as I sign, "Do *not* wait for me." Then I inhale deeply and sweep my arms outward, releasing as much of my shadows as I can. The cell plunges into darkness. I hold my shadows for as long as possible, dark mist swirling through the room. The ground shakes once, twice, then something latches onto my upper arms, yanking me forward.

My shadows fall away, and inky eyes fill my vision as the room brightens again. A mixture of relief and dread fills me; Chiyo and Winnie are gone. As I try to tug away from the man, a strange force presses in on my head, morphing from pressure into agony. My mind tumbles through darkness, my body weightless—almost nonexistent.

A disembodied voice echoes eerily in my head within the swirling chaos. Agony rushes in, sharper than an attack of my ailment. I clench my jaw, blinking, trying to find where I am in the room. But there's *nothing* to see. Emptiness.

Void.

Darkness calls to Chaos, the dissonant voice booms. The sound is warped, Otherworldly. Searing pain rakes down my back, an icy sensation following. *Balance requires sacrifice. You will run to me sooner than later, Daughter of Dusk.*

The strange man's face surfaces in my mind, wavering as though I'm looking at it in the reflection of a dark loch.

The old gods cannot help you, mortal. The old gods are dead. My vessel is not yet ready, but when he is, my reign will begin. You and the Daughter of Embers will join me. Mark my words.

I shudder.

Tread carefully, Nightmare Maker ...

The presence subsides, leaving behind the whisper of a name: *Caiolair.*

With all the power I have left, I fight to regain my own mind. My lungs burn, as does my throat, and no matter how hard I try, I can't catch my breath. The memory of the disembodied voice continues to rake over my skin like ghostly hands.

Except it's the man's hand that's closed around my throat, squeezing. His eyes fly wide, the darkness receding from them again. He staggers back, disoriented. Pain bursts through my wrists and knees as I drop to the stony floor and cough until tears spring to my eyes. I wheeze, greedily gulping down air.

I need to think. But my thoughts feel sluggish, my body exhausted. I'm being hauled to my feet, passed from the man to one of the Zenith soldiers. What are they going to do with me? Will I be tortured the way Carys was? Can I somehow get to Tiernan? I lower my shields, desperately searching for any sign of him, desperate to feel even a whisper of his presence. But I'm met with silence.

Silence and nothingness.

A sob catches in my throat as the man says, "Get a dampener on her and throw her in a cell until she's ready to talk."

Panic flows through my body, calling my powers to my fingers.

Black mist bursts from me, scattering across the room. One of the men tightens his grip on me, impossible heat sinking into my arm, blistering, *burning*. I shriek and retreat into myself.

Memories come unbidden to me: Tiernan telling me to go on without him, Osheen betraying me, being branded, taken from my home, my most recent wound, the years of headaches and vertigo. I breathe in and unleash every negative feeling, all the pain and anger and grief. The man's grip on me falters, then falls. Through bleary eyes, I watch as the soldiers contort and bow over in pain.

Darkness floods in, and I plead with all the gods to get me out of this. I imagine myself in safety, far away from these soldiers. Away from Paramount, from the disembodied voice. I imagine away all the hurt and betrayal. My body is pulled and twisted, nausea rolling through me.

It seems to go on and on, until I'm certain that I'll lose consciousness. Until I think I'll never regain any semblance of *life* again.

Then everything goes still, dull pain slamming into my hip.

When I open my eyes, I'm on the floor. Bright stars dapple my vision, the world around me a blur of oblivion. My muscles tremble, feeling like water, my stomach churns, and my skull threatens to split open. Dark tendrils of vapor cover my hands, reluctant to withdraw. Shadows creep into the edges of my vision, pressing in on me.

I blink again and again, trying to see *anything*. I don't know where I am. I cannot tell if I'm alive or dead. I don't know if *Tiernan* is alive or dead. Or even Ava, Chiyo, Winnie, her friend. I've failed. We've all failed.

Ice shudders through my body as I keep trying to think warm thoughts. As I fight to retract the shadows. But they persist.

Is this how it ends? Is this how the dark magic is going to over-take me?

Something warm and comforting rests on my shoulder, but I cannot seem to open my eyes. A familiar sensation coaxes into me, over me, and my shadows withdraw. It's swift and abrupt, leaving my body drained. Consciousness is already slipping out from under me. As much as I try to hold on, I can't.

A different kind of darkness swallows me whole before I can grasp anything.

Chapter 65

I'M NOT sure exactly what I expected, but Murtagh's newest *business endeavor*—the building he'd allegedly *stolen* from Gruffud —is a far cry from it. The archer and I are lucky to touch down, fairly unscathed, within the building. Her bow and arrow clatter to the floor before her body follows. I'm left speechless, watching her dissolve into tears as I stand there. Useless.

"Koko!" someone exclaims.

My head whips up, my fists already poised for attack when the woman with the long braids appears. She rushes forward, a few others behind her, then stops abruptly. Her hazel green eyes dart around wildly before she sets a seething glower on me. I nearly wither on the spot.

"What the fuck happened?" she asks. "Where is Durvla?" She looks down at the archer, weeping on the floor. "Chiyoko! Where's Durvla?" Panic laces her voice, and I look up just as someone barrels into me with full force. Arms wrap around my torso, hair that isn't mine tumbling into my eyes as I'm crushed in a smothering embrace.

"Winnie. You're alive. You're alive." Neris practically shakes me. I remain boneless, numb.

The Dreamwalker had come to rescue Tiernan, only to end up rescuing me instead ... and sacrificing herself. I'm overcome with sickening guilt. The woman with the long braids is on the floor, her arms wrapped around the archer—Chiyoko—while the girl continues to sob.

When Neris finally releases me, I take in the other worried faces in the room. A curvaceous woman with a deep brown complexion stands aside, one hand crossed over her chest, the other over the lower half of her face. Beside her is a man with auburn hair, and two other redheads keeping a small distance.

They step aside, letting Murtagh walk through. I pull myself up to my full height, uncertain of how to respond to this familiar person from what feels like a totally different lifetime.

He approaches me, his ordinarily mirthful face drawn in melancholy. His arms clasp mine, and he says, "I'm glad you've made it." He gives my arms a squeeze, but I can only nod.

My face is damp as Neris tugs me away. I follow her, but I'm unable to process much of anything. We got out of the castle.

But now Rheon has the Shadow Wielder he sought.

Shite ...

"Winnie, what happened?" Neris whispers.

"I ..." The words slip out of my grasp, and I shake my head again.

Neris holds my face between her palms. Firmly. "You're all bruised up." It's the least of my worries—in fact, I don't feel any pain. For the first time.

And I almost wish I felt something rather than nothing.

The older woman makes her way across the gallery, getting onto the floor with the other woman and Chiyoko. She whispers soothing words, and they pull Chiyoko to her feet. Her face is a blotchy mess, but as she stares across the room at me, the resemblance to Tiernan is glaringly obvious. His sister? Guilt rushes over me anew.

I need to get away. I wish I could head outside, but that would be dangerous and stupid. Instead, I march toward the doorway at the back of the room, hoping that it will lead me anywhere that isn't here. That isn't this moment.

A whooshing sound fills the room, a chill glossing over my skin seconds before a loud sound and startled shrieks follow. I turn as a small vortex of shadows swirls on the ground from where Chiyoko had just been moved. The shadows recede very slightly, enough to reveal that a body lies within it. A woman. She tries to sit up, but her arm gives way under her and she slips back onto her side.

"It's Durvla!" Chiyoko shouts.

Everyone rushes toward her only for shadows to whip out at them.

"Ava, do something!" Chiyoko says, jabbing the woman with the braids.

Ava faces the shadows, her hands up, but nothing happens. More shadows whip out, sending everyone another step back. Neris mutters a slew of swear words beside me, her elbow linking with mine and squeezing.

"Ma, can your light get through enough to at least soothe her?" Ava asks the older woman.

The woman nods, rubbing her hands together and taking a deep breath. Her hands glow a warm white light as she steps forward, the shadows receding slightly, bending around her like water around a stone. The darkness seems almost reluctant, pulsing, as if it has its own life force. I watch as the mother-daughter duo work together to get close enough to Durvla, to reach through the dark mist, the older woman's hand resting on Durvla's arm before Ava follows.

In the blink of an eye, her powers die out, and Durvla lies still.

"Is she breathing?" Ava asks. Her own breath goes out of her as she leans close, pulling the neckline of Durvla's top away for her mother to see. Tears blur my vision as Durvla is flipped onto her back, as Ava's mother—a Healer, by the looks of it—gets to work, her hands running over Durvla's body from head to toe, healing light emitting.

Ava turns, looking at Chiyoko and then me. "Somebody explain what happened, dammit."

Neris nudges me again. Chiyoko still seems too overcome to speak, so I take a breath and explain to the best of my ability what happened back in Paramount. The auburn-haired man eventually volunteers to take Durvla downstairs to one of the bedrooms. Everything seems to happen too fast and too slow.

Somehow, I get my legs to move. I get cleaned up, my mind turning over a million things at once. Somewhere between washing up and putting on fresh clothing, the sobs begin. It takes me a while to realize that the sound is coming from another room and not from me, though my heart feels heavy. I stand in the corridor, an oil lamp flickering as if it's about to die out, and I listen to the gut-wrenching cries. Durvla *begs* to go back to Paramount. To save Tiernan. Her words are half incoherent, half lucid.

Then there's abrupt silence.

I lean against the wall, my eyes squeezed shut as I sink down to the floor. As I listen to the quiet that seems so much louder than anything else.

Everyone is kind to Neris and I, which feels unnatural given that this is my fault. As with everything, Neris takes this new transition with the utmost grace. The Healer, Alys, suggested that it would be best to keep Durvla in a sleeping state—for the sake of her overtaxed body and her mental state—so things remain almost deathly silent. As if everyone's afraid to wake her.

Neris and I sit side by side on the couch of the common room, my entire body humming with a dull ache that reminds me I have no more elixirs as the adrenaline finally starts to wear off. Neris silently combs through her golden curls.

I cannot get the image of Radika holding that blade to her throat out of my mind. Even now, there's a small cut on her neck. I shake the thoughts from my head, reminding myself that she is safe. She is alive.

Father however ... My throat knots again, and my eyes burn.

"I cannot believe Rheon somehow succeeded in transferring powers," Neris says as if she's read my mind. She peers at me through curls partially covering her eyes. For a moment, there's only silence, then she asks, "Can I tell you something?"

"Of course." My voice comes out raw.

Neris hesitates, averting her gaze to the overly patterned carpet. The swirls and multitude of colors do nothing to help my already aching head, so I turn my focus back to her.

"I'd briefly entertained the idea of having magical abilities," she says.

My spine straightens, my muscles whingeing, and Neris breathes out an embarrassed laugh.

"I know. Ridiculous after everything I've seen you experience. But what if I'd drank that potion? What would've become of me? Would I turn out like how you described—?" She leaves her sentence unfinished, an apologetic look on her face.

My heart sinks again. "It doesn't matter. You didn't drink the potion."

"But I *could've*. And sadly I think, given the chance, there are many who would."

Silence stretches between us for a moment.

"But don't worry, I might not have the magic, but I want to brush up on my fighting skills."

My heart tugs awkwardly as I remember all the times we spent training with Father. His skills are now within the hands of yet another corrupt sect. There was recognition in his eyes for a brief moment. Can whatever was done to him be reversed? My chest feels hollow, but I cannot return to Paramount to find out. We cannot even remain here in Mainland for much longer; it's too dangerous.

As much as I've hated masquerading as someone I'm not—within the Zenith, within my own household and the Pendrys'—the thought of leaving Barr na Cahar feels scarier. The unknown is always scary. But it will never become known if I don't find the courage to face it.

In the middle of the night, I'm ripped out of my sleep by a voice practically shouting in my ear.

I have not forgotten you, Terraforger. And I suggest that you never forget me. I am Fury, and even after my end, I will always remain in the hearts of you fickle mortals.

I frantically search the dark, but I don't need to see the glowing red eyes to know who speaks to me. But why is she always so bloody cryptic?

Do not ignore the Calling any longer. Caiolair's reign will soon be upon us.

I feel the heat of the goddess and, briefly, I see a blazing axe rising in front of me and slashing through the air.

With a shriek, I cover my head, prepared to be smote.

"Winnie!" Neris exclaims, grabbing my arm in the darkness.

My pulse races, outrunning my thoughts, and it takes me a moment to reel in my panic. When I finally do, all I say is, "I'm fine."

The Purists were wrong about many things, but the gods certainly are at work in some capacity. Unfortunately, so is the Zenith—and it's worse than I could've imagined. My father ... Will Mother ever learn the truth of him? Would Arionna? What has become of them? Of the Pendrys? Why do I even care?

Unable to get back to sleep with so many thoughts churning in my mind, I head into the common room as soon as Neris drifts off again. I sit near the fire and close my eyes, enjoying the warmth.

Soft footsteps enter the room, and I jump, but it's only Murtagh. The older man smiles warmly at me.

"Sorry to startle you, lass." His voice is gentle as he crouches so that he's level with me.

"It's alright. I couldn't sleep. I ... just don't understand a lot of this."

"I'm not sure any of us understands. Not fully at least." He rises to sit on the stony platform in front of the hearth, leaving some space between us. "I believe you ken that I was good friends with your da."

I nod.

"He sent word shortly after the incident at the castle, speaking of great atrocities occurring within the walls. He feared for his life."

I keep my mouth shut.

"I dinna ken what happened after, but I ken that while he served the queen, toward the end of her reign, we agreed that the rebels aren't to be feared. In fact, the rebels are the hope of Erleya—they might be a quiet force, but they fight against tyranny and corruption. Against the Purists and the Zenith, the darkness that threatens to destroy our kingdom. Through wee acts. But even the littlest acts matter." He stares into the fire wistfully. "We do what we have to do to survive, and to help those without the means to survive on their own."

Also gazing into the fire, I ask, "Do you think the gods are real?" I turn my head back to Murtagh as a smile slowly spreads across his face.

"Oh, yes. I believe that they choose some of us to carry out tasks we would otherwise not have the courage to carry out on our own."

My ribs constrict my heart. I think of my visions of Fury and of Winter. Damarlach and Magdin. Their confrontation within my head about the oppressors and the destruction of the gods. Even now I'm unsure of what to believe. "But not all the gods are on the right side," I say.

"Aye. That's why we have our own conscience and free will, young Gwyneth." He stands stiffly from the small platform and straightens his nightshirt. "I hope one day you will be reunited with Eurig."

My heart pangs.

"He's always been proud of you. His artistic daughter with a heart of gold and fists of steel."

I laugh through the tears gathering on my lower lashes. "He said that?"

Murtagh laughs. "I ken you've had a lot of people telling you who they think you are or who you should be, but don't forget that you ken yourself better than anyone else." It reminds me of Tiernan's words back in the brig. Murtagh turns and makes for the doorway, pausing before he leaves. "Try to get some sleep. Even warriors need rest."

A heart of gold and fists of steel. I chuckle and shake my head again before sighing. I do hope to see him again someday, but if I never do, I'll try my best to make him proud.

Chapter 66

CARYS

BEING on the ocean feels never-ending. My moods waver from good to bad to worse. Happy to ecstatic to angry with the world. Some days I want to dive off the ship and swim to some other land, and other days I just want to be home in Erleya again. I'm frightened by the unknown of what awaits me.

Just as I'm frightened by what is right in front of me. Odgar and I don't sleep together again. We don't even kiss. To prevent winding up in bed with him again, I avoid being with him alone. I'm just not ready to give my heart away to someone when I barely know how to love myself.

And sadly, I'm not sure if or when that will ever change.

Odgar is almost never without his knitting, or nalbinding, or whatever. Clearly trying to distract himself. I train with Valdis whenever I get the chance. It helps me remain in the present more often than not.

The closer we get to Erleya, the more nauseated and tense I feel, but I try my best to relax.

As I'm dozing off beneath the uncannily hot sunlight, Briony speaks up out of nowhere, and I damn near jump off the boat. I straighten from where I'd fallen asleep leaning against the mast, and Briony's brows rise.

"Apologies," she says. "But you are clearly not getting enough sleep."

"You are as obvious as ever, Briony."

She smiles and I sink down against the mast, leaning my head back. My body craves sleep, but my mind cannot be still. The anxieties eat away at me.

"What's on your mind?" Briony asks.

I open one eye and peer at her. It's sometimes still so odd speaking to her as a friend when she played a role in my torture nearly four months ago. Even now that I know it was for show, sometimes it still triggers me.

"What *isn't* on my mind?" I retort.

"What happened between you and the Uldaran prince?" She sets a knowing gaze on me. For a woman only in her late twenties, her eyes hold the maturity of someone much older.

I sigh and lower my voice, trying to make my language as delicate as possible for the priestess. "We ..." I grapple for a mild word. "Slept together."

Briony titters. "I am not offended by the word *sex* or others you might care to use, but I appreciate your censorship."

"Fine, we had sex. Then we didn't. Nothing really *happened*." I shrug and hug my arms around my frame. If nothing happened, why do I feel so out of sorts about him now? Why do I want to get closer to him as much as I want to get farther away?

Then again, when have any of my thought processes ever made sense?

"Land!" Someone calls out from the distance, and activity bursts on deck.

I swallow and rise, following Briony to where everyone gathers to look at the stretch of dark green on the horizon.

Valdis and Odgar appear on deck, Odgar smiling at me from a distance before stuffing a ball of wool and his work in progress into his trouser pocket. He begins calling out orders and exchanging quiet instructions with other crew members. As we get closer to the land laden with trees, another larger landmass looms behind it. *That* is Erleya.

"Do you think it would be wise to touch down on the Outer Isles and perhaps then sail across under a guise to Erleya?" Odgar asks.

The Royal Brigade was not heavily active in the Outer Isles when my mother was on the throne, but I'm not sure what's become of military affairs since then. "Perhaps," I say at last. "Getting into Erleya in a small boat may not be as easy as you'd think. You lot don't exactly ... *fit in*." I eye his thick leather armor and battle-axe over his shoulder. At least he's shed the fur as we arrived near warmer shores than Uldarvik.

It takes hours still before we are close enough to see the port of the Outer Isles.

As we draw near, a high-pitched sound cuts through the air before an arrow embeds in the ship wall behind me. I shriek and duck as another arrow nearly lodges in my forehead. My heart rate soars, my body immediately growing hot and cold at once.

Everyone scrambles to gather weapons. Guilt rolls through me— I was wrong about the Outer Isles. I was wrong. More arrows rain down, striking some of the crew. Valdis drops beside me on the deck, shoving leather armor onto me, cinching the belts so tight they hurt, then pressing a bow and quiver into my hands. Briony dons leathers as well, but she doesn't take up a weapon. Instead, her hands are glowing, prepared to blast whatever powers she can at the enemies.

Odgar appears at my side, his axe clutched in his hands, while I think of the best solution given the map. "Sail north," I whisper to Odgar beside me.

"What?" he shouts over the clatter of arrows.

"Evade and sail north!"

To my horror, small boats are sailing toward us, and even more terrifying, several men clad in dark blue uniforms and black masks over their eyes *appear* on our deck. Everyone shifts into battle mode as wind, water, and fire whip around our ship.

Fuck, these are all Wielders. How in Lugda's hells ...? I scream as a man appears entirely too close to me. Briony blasts him with blue light, but it never hits him. He disappears only to reappear directly in front of me, and I slice my hand through the air, sending a blade of fire carving through him.

Odgar tugs me away as the man falls hard to his knees, his hands trying and failing to keep his innards where they belong.

One by one, crew members start to fall. My chest aches from the loss all around me. My heart thunders then slows as a terrifyingly familiar power builds hot and dark within me. I want to push away the voice, but more boats are coming, more reinforcement, more Wielders.

After the kindness that these Uldarans have shown me, after everything they've done for me and been willing to do, I cannot let them go down this way. I know what my fire can do if I let it. If I embrace it rather than be afraid of it.

I grab Odgar's hand, squeezing it hard. His sunburst, golden-blue eyes focus frantically on me.

"Don't try to save me," I tell him. He clings to my hand, a protest on his lips, but I pull away and race toward the front of the ship. Breathing in deeply, I reach for all my pent-up magic and rampant emotions. My hands grow blazing hot as I nock an arrow into my bow and call to my powers. As I allow that dark voice within me to unleash herself, to funnel directly into me. I send a flaming arrow forth and reach for another as Enidwen's voice booms in my head: You *are the weapon! Let me in!*

Enidwen's power purrs like a housecat, then roars like a dragon. It blasts through the wall between our minds and fills me to the brim with more exuberant vigor than I know what to do with. I drop the bow and channel the power into my hands, crossing them over my chest before thrusting them outward with a bellow of rage and pain. Orange and black flames fill my vision. Screams assault my ears. I inhale and repeat the motion. Again. And again.

The world around me slows and blurs. I'm nothing but flame and shadow and power.

I burn and burn and burn, until I feel myself burning out.

Until the cries around me die down to whimpers, and the clattering of weapons ceases.

My body feels like a raw conflagration instead of flesh and bones.

At last, my flames flicker out. A distorted voice calls to me, and that power within me winks out in a heartbeat. I drop, but I feel no pain.

I'm overheated.

Perhaps for the last time.

Flames. Pain. Fear. Annoyance. Darkness.

I wake repeatedly, only to fall back under. My body is buoyant, drifting between awareness and oblivion, and I long for the awareness to stop returning. I long to feel nothing. I hope to have saved my friends from a terrible fate, and I don't want to know if I've failed.

I hope they sail to Siad Nahar and meet up with Durvla and the others. That they help put *her* on the throne rather than me.

I hope they save the kingdom.

That Odgar finds true love in someone who can actually grasp the concept.

Perhaps Briony will help raise a magical army to war against the same people she once fought for.

Perhaps everyone will find redemption.

It's too late for me.

My time is over. And with it, Enidwen's reign is at an end. There will be no heir. No continuation of her tainted bloodline.

No more curse of embers.

Chapter 67

DURVLA

EVERY TIME I resurface from the stupor of pain and nausea, invisible hands pull me back under. My body is heavy and buoyant, aching and numb. Heat covers my skin, burning my eyes. Within my bubble of silence, I'm unaware of anything happening around me. I'm tugged from one place to another, rough hands on me, then soft. Cool. Then hot. Damp. Then Dry.

I'm standing on the bow of a ship, looking out over blue-green waters. The air is crisp; I'm in my summer cloak.

"Durvla?" a voice calls.

I spin to find Carys leaning against the mast, regarding me with confusion.

The sight almost makes me laugh because the first time I'd dreamwalked to her after leaving Paramount, I'd been the one at the mast with her gazing off into the ocean. Had she been contemplating death then? Or had she been contemplating life? Freedom?

A land beyond this one.

Could Sunlagh really take me to the land beyond the Veil like it's sung in the songs?

"Gods, you look awful," says Carys.

I press my hands against my face. Wherever my body lies now, it's burning with fever. I can feel the sweat gathering on my skin each time I'm strong enough to temporarily resurface. Or perhaps it isn't *my* body I'm feeling.

No, it's definitely not my body.

I stare at Carys, trying to see past the perfect image of Erleya's princess being projected. Momentarily, I'm met with a flushed face, hair different than I remember it, and eyes almost glowing gold. I jump, startled, and the image of Carys as I know her replaces what I just saw.

"I think ... your body isn't doing so well," I admit. My muscles feel weak, my knees barely able to keep my weight up, even in this dreamscape. "Perhaps, neither is mine, actually." Slowly, I sit on the deck of the ship, and Carys joins me. Except she collapses onto her back, her hair spreading out around her like bedcovers.

Gingerly, I lay beside her. There are sounds around me that I cannot quite make out. Whether it's the sound of the waves or the sound of the sails—I'm not sure I've ever heard them before with my physical ears.

For some time, I'm lost in it, until Carys speaks. "Did you bring me here?"

"I'm not sure. I don't remember anything."

"Hmm," she murmurs thoughtfully.

"Do *you* remember anything?"

She blinks, her brows knitting together. "I think I've burned myself out. Too much power usage. Do you think I'm dead? Are *you* dead?"

A memory resurfaces, filled with darkness, but Tiernan's face takes the foreground. I lurch upright, and Carys sits up right after.

"Durvla?" Her eyes widen with panic, shifting from that bright gold to the ochre I know. "Durvla," she demands.

"I'm thinking ..." Yet everything feels so odd and floaty. I'm not sure if I've ever been so exhausted—especially in a dream.

"Durvla. Should you be dreamwalking right now? You should conserve your energy."

Grief hits me, everything flooding back to my mind all at once. I hold back the tears that threaten. If Carys isn't doing well, then I shouldn't burden her. Maybe I'm here by some divine intervention. To save her since I couldn't save Tiernan. "Carys, I need you to promise me something."

"Alright."

"If anything happens to me, find the others at Siad Nahar. Don't let the Zenith or the Purists take over. We have to stop them somehow."

"Durvla, you're going to be fine. But you really need to stop using your powers. Please wake up." There's a desperate edge to her voice.

I smile. "Only if you wake up first." I reach out and grip her shoulder, and the dream falls away.

I blink as a face materializes above me. Grey eyes peer into mine. Then another face hovers. Blue hair. Her lips move, but I don't make out anything she says.

The tears come hot and fast, blinding pain that isn't physical hitting me. "We have to get Ti—" I'm unable to finish my sentence before I'm consumed by unconsciousness again.

Chapter 68

ALL MY LIFE I've repressed so much. My enthusiasm for life, my free-spirited nature, my joy for things like sweet baked goods and the *perfect* mix of colors on canvas. I've been told who I was supposed to be, married off to someone I hated and who considered me spoiled goods.

For over a year now, I've pushed away the call to flee from my home. The call to a land that I was more willing to believe was a myth than to face the scary unknown of it.

But even with my heart pounding relentlessly and my body on edge as if I'm about to dive off a cliff, I give in to the Call.

I stand behind Murtagh's safehouse, my back against the brick wall, my bare feet in the dirt, eyes closed, and senses open to the land around me. I allow visions of the tree, of beautiful fields of flowers and misty waters to flood my mind. It fills my body with a strange certainty of just where to go.

Perhaps someday soon I can come back to Paramount—to find Father. Perhaps someday I'll be able to face my sister and mother again. But for now ... For now I need to get everyone to this sacred land.

The goddesses have gone quiet in my mind, but coming to terms with the truth of my existence is hard to accept. It's difficult to know that I'd truly been dead before a dark Sorceress who deemed herself a Healer had brought me back to life. I'm not sure exactly what that means for my future; I'm not sure if I'm living on borrowed time because Radika robbed Lugda of a soul.

What I'm certain of is that it's time for me to stop living half a life. It's time for me to lay down my complacency and faint-heartedness.

Time for me to take charge of my life and to embrace who I am without shame.

Chapter 69

DURVLA

WHEN I OPEN MY EYES, I've lost track of how many times it's occurred. Lifting my head feels like a chore, but as I slowly come to and I remember the state in which Tiernan had been in when last I saw him, I bolt upright with his name on my lips. Everything around me jostles, making me reach out to steady myself.

Someone reaches for me instead, and I turn to find a very familiar face staring back at me.

Osheen.

My heart leaps, then sinks. I rub my hand over my face, the movement feeling unnatural and stilted. There are bags of gods know what lying around and a fabric of some sort over us. As if ... are we in a covered wagon? I feel along beneath me, finding straw and a scratchy sheet. "Tell me everything has been a nightmare," I say to Osheen.

He shakes his head, his blue eyes duller than I've ever seen them. "We're on our way to Siad Nahar," he signs, fingerspelling the last two words.

He fills me in on what occurred while I healed from the magical expenditure. We've been traveling already for days. Sloan and Isobel stayed behind to hopefully get more information on Tiernan and keep an eye on the situation at Paramount. We're traveling under the guise of traders and, by some miracle, haven't drawn the attention of Peacekeepers or anyone else.

My heart feels cracked into a million pieces, but no tears come. It seems I've somehow cried myself dry.

Since hearing Caiolair's voice in my head back in Paramount, my body seems reluctant to retain any warmth. I sit huddled in the wagon with two blankets drawn over me as I try to stop my occasional shivering. This time, it's Chiyo beside me; this time, it's been two weeks since the debacle at the castle.

"Who or what do you think Caiolair is?" Chiyo signs after I tell her about my encounter when I faced the sovereign.

"I'm not sure," I say. "But I think he's somehow tied to Rheon."

For a while, Chiyo doesn't speak, then at last, she says, "I didn't want to leave him either, you know. But he would want us to go on. I'm holding on to the hope that Murtagh's people will be able to somehow rescue him."

If he's still alive.

I look away from her welling eyes, determined not to cry anymore. Not when all I want to do is run right back to Paramount and find the man that my heart aches for.

It's another couple of weeks of traveling through pastures and brush—abandoning our wagon off route at some point—before we move into a woodsy area. We settle beside a small brook to rest, but as we're getting ready to set off again, an odd, prickly feeling crawls over my skin. It's similar to that sensation I experienced before we were ambushed last time. I search the trees for any sign of attackers, but I only find Winnie doing the same. We lock eyes and then slowly turn toward a thick set of bushes just beyond where we'd briefly camped.

Towering over the bushes is a massive brown stag, each of its antlers as long as my arm. There seems to be a strange white glow around it, its eyes eerily sentient as it stares at us. The rest of the camp goes still. No one moves. No one dares to. Not when that stag could possibly maul us. Yet it tilts its head almost imperceptibly before it turns and walks away.

Winnie's eyes snap to mine, and I focus on her lips as she says, "I think we need to follow it."

She's been leading us with such calmness and such grace. Neris beams with pride at her friend.

"Alright, let's go then," Ava signs.

Osheen helps me onto the horse we'd been riding in tandem and mounts after me. We take our place beside Winnie as everyone mounts up.

The stag never looks back at us but continues to calmly move through the forest. The woods grow denser and denser until we have to ride in nearly a single line.

Soon the trees give way to a wide clearing with a cave set into the rocky hillside. The stag has disappeared, and Winnie is suddenly tense in her saddle, her horse unmoving. I look over at her, at the way she fidgets with her pocket and gnaws on her lip. Her hands are shaking so hard on the horse's reins that the creature shifts uncomfortably.

"Winnie," I call gently.

She glances over at me, eyes wide. "Sorry," she says. "Just … need a moment. Caves bring back … memories." She blows out a breath and rubs her hands on her trousers.

"It's alright. Take the time you need," I tell her, ignoring Ava's very clear impatience.

It doesn't take long before Winnie dismounts her horse. "Let's do this," she says with a tight smile.

We dismount our horses before stepping into the cave. Alys casts a light, illuminating the space around us and revealing that the cave only goes several paces deep. An almost electrifying sensation exudes from the dead end, the hairs rising on the back of my neck. No one speaks for a while, as if we're all at a loss for words.

Then Winnie says, "This is it." Water seeps from somewhere above, streaking down the cave wall. But otherwise, there's nothing more to it than the strange buzz that, somehow, feels very familiar.

"It feels like the wards outside the Verge," Alys signs.

Winnie steps closer to the wall, pressing her hands against it before looking over her shoulder. "You all might want to step back," she says.

So we do. We retreat to the mouth of the cave as she clenches and unclenches her hand against the cave wall. Her body tenses for a moment, then as all the rigidity seems to flow out from her back and shoulders, a light begins to shine through the wall. The ground shakes beneath us. It takes me a moment to realize that the stone is cracking, splitting. Then it crumbles completely, debris scattering, and sunlight pours into the small grotto.

I swipe my arm in an arch in front of my body, a shadow shield forming in front of us as dust and grit pelts against it. The ground stops shaking, and Winnie turns to face us as I lower the shadows. The strange, uneasy feeling remains—whatever wards that protect this entrance are clearly still in place.

We all approach again as Winnie presses her hand against the now open cave. "There's something ... tangible," she says. Her hand seems to meet an invisible wall. "It reminds me of one of your shadow shields. But invisible.".

Beyond the invisible wall, there seems to be more forest. "What now?" Chiyo asks.

"I think ... I can bring down this ward. It's—"

"A light shield," Alys signs at the same time I do.

Neris pokes at the space with her finger as Osheen steps aside.

"Oksana had me break through hers often. This one probably takes runes much like the ones to get into the Verge. The problem is that it *could* reject us depending on what exactly it's warded to do." My pulse quickens.

"Well, that's just great," says Ava. She gestures toward it as if inviting me to a cup of tea.

I take a deep breath, imagining the light falling away, imagining us on the other side. I remember what Alys and Dayfyd, even Haruka, said about my birth mother. That she had an affinity for runes. Perhaps I do too.

I close my eyes and press my hands against the tangible empty space—symbols come to mind, and I draw them with my finger in the space until the strange feeling begins to dissolve, until my hand passes through nothing but air instead of meeting resistance.

My body grows tired, my head woozy as I step back, blinking. Winnie is the first to move forward again, waving an arm through the archway. Her face is ecstatic. "You did it," she says.

I smile back wearily. "*We* did it."

Gathering our horses again, we step through the now fully open wall to what feels like an entirely different realm. I wave my arm to put up fresh wards that'll likely need more strengthening later, but Alys gives my shoulder a small squeeze and says, "Well done, sweetling. That was impressive."

Green mountains fill the backdrop, a large waterfall cascading in the distance into a wide, winding river that seems to never end. A gentle mist coats the forest, bright unblighted leaves filling out the treetops and colorful fields of wildflowers all around. On the other side of the forest, a tree towers above the rest, its trunk wider than any I've seen before.

The tree from our dreams.

My gaze lingers on it before I turn my attention to the sky. It's the clearest blue, not a cloud in sight. Everything is almost ethereal.

In fact, this place seems unreal, supernatural within its own right. We all look around in stunned silence until Neris asks, "Is this the Otherworld?"

"I don't think so," I say. "But it certainly feels different."

We roam our surroundings, and I numbly walk toward the stream to fill my waterskin. This journey was so much longer and filled with even more obstacles and dangers than any of us imagined. My heart aches with the realization that it may be quite a while yet before I see Taig again. And as much as I try to keep my thoughts off Tiernan, I simply can't. I know Taig's being well taken care of, but I'm uncertain of the state of my Killjoy.

Something tells me he's not dead. Perhaps it's wishful thinking. Perhaps it's my powers. But I hold on to it—a little beacon of hope.

Ava suggests we set up camp and investigate this new land tomorrow. We split up the tasks of setting up camp, Chiyo and Osheen going off to fish in the river, the rest of us setting up the tents Murtagh supplied us. The sun dips low and a warm glow of orange settles over the otherworldly land.

Briefly, I catch Osheen's gaze as he returns with a large catch of fish. He smiles at me, and for a moment, I consider holding on to the anger and resentment. But instead, I tentatively smile back at him. As we gather around the fire, the mouth-watering aroma of broiled fish filling the air, Ava leaps to her feet.

"Someone's here," she signs.

Chapter 70

CARYS

THEY TELL me I slept feverishly for days while they sailed in small fishermen's boats, unperturbed, around the coast of Erleya. How they got them, no one tells me, but I wake up in a strange home that I don't know. In the Grounds, of all places.

I come to with a gasp, and Odgar and Briony rush to my side as pain and exhaustion press in on me. It's not as bad as back in Paramount, but I burst into tears regardless. Odgar holds me in his arms and promises me it'll be alright before Briony's healing light puts me under again.

The next time I wake, my mind is hazy, but we borrow horses from the kind family who'd allowed us to stay with them and travel northward. Odgar and I share a horse, as does Valdis and Seth, while Briony leads, following an apparent *tug* in the right direction that she cannot explain.

My powers slowly return as we travel, a small flicker of my flame, but the rest of me feels exhausted. None of us speak much as we simply ride onward—for as long as our horses can tolerate, for as long as we can keep going.

Every pause in our travels leaves us fearing we'll be discovered and taken to Paramount or killed on sight. And indeed, as we stop for a moment as night falls, torches spark to life around us. It all happens so fast—arrows flying, Briony and Odgar deflecting with their magics before I'm practically thrown onto the horse by Odgar.

The horse is already running, and there's a scream stuck in my throat as Odgar retrieves his axe from a man's chest and sprints to catch up with the steed. He manages to leap onto the horse while it's in motion, while Briony, Valdis, and Seth mount up again and follow along. Arrows continue to pursue us, a few whizzing past my head, tearing a screech from me.

I turn in the saddle, leaning around Odgar to funnel a jet of flames toward the attackers. The trees catch fire as the attackers scream, but Odgar extinguishes them with the wave of his hand as we ride on.

I fear that this entire journey will be for naught. But soon we find ourselves in a dense forest shrouded in mist. A stag that seems to be surrounded with a strange light steps out in front of us, causing our horses to rear back, though we manage to keep them in check. We halt, the thunder of hooves behind us, the impending risk of our doom drawing closer, but there's something about this creature.

It makes its way through our party, seemingly made of nothing but light and shadow. It stands behind us as the attackers draw closer, but their arrows don't touch us. As one man makes to charge past the stag, his horse is thrown back. It tramples him in its escape. The other two pursuing us are similarly thrown from their horses, but as they try to swing at the deer with their weapons, they suddenly drop to their knees, screaming with their hands over their ears.

When their screams are no more and they lie listlessly on the ground, we stare in awe at the creature. It seems to give us a slow nod, a bow almost, before it vanishes from sight.

It takes a while for the shock of the moment to pass before Odgar spurs us forward again. There's a cave not far ahead, and a strange sensation prickles my scalp as we step inside.

"I think we're here," Briony whispers, her voice echoing in the cave as her hand casts a light on our surroundings. Massive stones litter the area around the exit of the tunnel, a buzzing sensation growing stronger the closer we get to it. One of Odgar's arms wraps around my waist, holding me to him, and Briony slides down from her horse and moves to stand in front of the opening.

She barely lifts her hand to the opening of the tunnel before pulling it back. "Wards. But I think I can dismantle them."

I swallow hard, and Odgar's hand slips from around my waist to rest against my thigh. We've not had much physical contact like this since that moment of weakness back on the ship. I ignore the subtle flutter in my stomach and steel myself.

Briony presses her hands against the invisible wards and bright blue light ripples like the surface of water. I squint until the light dissipates, then Briony steps through onto the other side and smiles back at us. We all follow, and for a few heartbeats, it's silent. No one moves as we all wait to be smote for not being worthy of a place that's magically warded. But nothing happens.

It's utterly ...

Anticlimactic.

And, gods, am I grateful for that. A strange mist shrouds this place, and voices reach our ears as we venture further into this land of flowers and waterfalls. In the dark we can't make out much of anything, but there's a fire somewhere in the distance. I grab an arrow, my magic setting the arrowhead aflame as we step closer. Everyone else arms themselves, but another strange sensation—this one not unpleasant—overtakes my body.

It's like a memory. A kinship.

"Hold," I whisper to the others, and they do, though Valdis buzzes with restless energy at my side.

I make out a mane of curly hair and my heart nearly gives out as the realization rushes at me all at once.

Chapter 71

DURVLA

Tension bleeds into the atmosphere as everyone jumps to their feet, weapons at the ready. My hand moves to the dagger at my waist.

I replaced the wards as best as I could. It seemed secure enough, so who else has gotten in here? I sense a flickering flame and stubborn resolve. My powers buzz beneath my skin as if calling to the power of one of our visitors. I find myself stepping forward and Ava immediately follows, close by my side as we walk past the others. I'm surprised she doesn't stop me.

I squint at the massive man a few paces ahead of us. The glow of our fire plays off the terrifying battle-axe raised in his hand. There are four others with him: another man just as tall, a slightly shorter woman with blond hair, and a brunette of average height and slender build.

But the person I'm most drawn to is the statuesque woman beside the axe wielder, her curtain of raven hair down to her hips. There's a newfound rigidity to her narrow shoulders and a commanding stride as she approaches us with a flaming arrow aimed our way.

Her golden eyes are nearly as bright as the campfire, but very quickly, they soften, her flaming arrow snuffing out as her hands drop to her sides.

She says something I can't make out, then she's rushing toward me, her bow and arrow falling to the forest ground. She halts, her eyes brimming with tears, a pink scar slashed across her freckled face.

"Carys," I say at last.

I hesitate at first, but then I step forward and pull her into a hug. Her thin arms remain limp at her side for a moment before they wrap around me. Then suddenly she's crushing me to her. It's a long moment before Carys finally steps back and her eyes dart around as if she's searching for someone. When she looks at me again, there's slight panic in her eyes and a question in the quirk of her brow.

The crushing grief returns to me, and I shake my head slowly. "I'll explain later," I force myself to say.

She nods and inhales deeply. "Looks like we have a lot of catching up to do."

Chapter 72

TIERNAN

My thigh fucking *hurts*.

And my teeth. They've been chattering relentlessly, sounding like hundreds of crabs scurrying across the cave floor. I've been sitting here beside a pitiful excuse for a puddle for gods know how long. I cannot even scoop any of it into my hand to drink, even when my throat feels as though it's been scorched on the inside.

My hands shake as I stare at the strange blade perched atop a rock nearby. There's a sheen of purple within it that glows in the darkness of the cave.

Something just feels off. Not only about the dagger ...

But the searing throb in my thigh.

I stare down at the dirty strip of fabric ripped from my tunic. I've wrapped it around my leg as tightly as I can, but already, blood has seeped into it. I need to go. I need to move. Somehow. But I'm hot all over—sweat drenching my clothing. Each shiver makes my leg hurt even more, my vision filling with white spots that float in the cave.

How in hells did I get here?

My eyes wander to my hand, a black stone ring on my finger.

A flash of bright green eyes fills my memories. A severely burned face and sadistic sneer. I remember. She was taking me somewhere— to a healer? But for some reason, I knew I needed to get away from her.

"What happened to your face?" I'd asked. Just to see how she would respond. Somehow, I don't remember if she answered, but I do remember glowing yellow eyes and fire erupting from another woman's hands. My captor had been burned. Suits her right, probably.

I groan through my teeth as I somehow manage to push myself to my feet. Staring at the ring again, I force myself to think. This ring ... it had been hers. I snapped her wrist to get it. And I'd ended up here. I slip it off my finger and into my pocket.

My first step sends lightning through my thigh. "Fuck," I grit out. I take a few more steps, teetering like a newborn foal.

Newborn foal legs.

An image slams into me. Curly hair and compassionate brown eyes. Warmth pours into my chest. It isn't feverish but ... my heart leaps. A feeling not too unpleasant until it sinks with inexplicable sadness. I try to hold on to the image, to this breathtakingly beautiful face, but it drifts into the back of my mind like a distant memory.

I'm shaking all over as I leave the cave and step into the night with the dagger tucked firmly into my trouser pocket. At this point, I'd probably laugh if it sliced into my leg. But I want to live.

For whatever reason. I need to keep breathing. I need to keep walking.

My ankle gives way as I step into a particularly uneven part of the forest ground. I go down hard, disparaging laughter ripping from my throat as I lie there in the mud. I shift and pain ripples through my ankle, through my bloody thigh again. I scoot back against a tree, leaning my head back before I'm swept into a daze.

Magnificent, rolling black hills stretch out before me, the sun rising from the ocean in the distance. I reach my hand out, basking in the feel of the warm rays against my skin. No pain lingers. There are no Zenith members to taunt me, no Royal Brigade to answer to, no wars to fight, no fear ...

Then I feel her shadows—dark but never frightening. Cool but never frigid. Like refuge from the burning rays of the sun. Like shelter from the striking raindrops of a storm. Her soothing voice is a blanket around me. *"Tiernan ..."*

I reach out, but there's nothing there.

"Keep fighting," the voice says. *"Keep fighting for me. Be brave. Don't break."*

My chest swells painfully. Those words sound familiar. I shield my eyes against the blinding sun and look around, blinking a couple of times. There is nothing else around me. Nothing to ground myself in. Nothing that feels like home.

Keep fighting for her.

Too bad I don't know who she is.

Pain brings me out of my trance, bright spots obscuring my vision as soon as my eyes fly open. Soft hands press my shoulders down as I try to rise. "Don't move. Relax," says the woman.

I swear I'm on fire.

Gods ... I struggle to breathe, but even that hurts. I blink, expecting brown eyes and the faintest dusting of freckles to be looking back at me.

Instead, there's a pale face, a white hood drawn over a mess of platinum blond hair. "I'm so sorry to startle you," the woman says. Her eyes are like pools of translucent blue. "You're severely injured."

A flash of pain fills my mind along with a taloned hand slamming a dagger into my thigh. A second before I'd ended up at the cave ... and then somehow here.

"Sweetheart, can you hear me?" says the woman. "Keep listening to my voice. Try to stay awake."

I blink up at her, my eyes blurry.

"Can you tell me who you are?"

I remember the voice from the dream. She'd called me something. "Tiernan," I say.

A smile stretches across her face. "It's nice to meet you, Tiernan." She holds a wineskin out to me. "This will help. It's a pain tonic. It'll help with the fever too until I can get you to a proper Healer."

I take the wineskin with trembling hands. I don't know her or if I can trust her, but I just want it to end. What could possibly be worse when death seems like it would be a relief?

The liquid goes down my throat smoothly, and the effects slowly start to take place. I breathe out a sigh, straightening against the trunk I've been slumped against.

Slowly my surroundings filter in. Thick trees and bushes all around. I turn back to the woman who helped me, and there's an odd familiarity in those eyes. "What did you say your name was?" I ask her.

The grin that splits her face is *wrong*. A rush of something that feels off drifts over me. There's an eagerness, along with something more sinister that I cannot put my finger on. Her voice whispers something in my mind, but I force myself to keep a straight face, to not respond to the overwhelming desire to run from this woman who clearly does not have good intentions.

"I didn't say," she responds.

"Alright ..."

She rises to her feet with an airy giggle. "But you've told me your name, so it is only fair I tell you mine. My name is Nimue."

Wrong, something inside of me screams. *Wrong, wrong, wrong!*

I struggle to my feet as her lips tilt into an odd smile. Her thoughts are so clear that had her lips not moved, I would've sworn she spoke the words aloud: *His blood will be perfect.*

Shit.

Just as Nimue extends her hand to me, I turn.

And I fucking run.

to be continued

Acknowledgments

Oh boy ... where do I start? This time around, I've had so much more love and support that I just know I'll accidentally leave someone out! *hahasob*. (If I do, I'm so, so sorry!) Let's try to do this without sounding like I'm winning an Oscar Award lol. Time to auctioneer-style rattle off important names! To my biggest fan, my husband. Thank you for reading every version, for putting up with my super late night conspiracy board moments, and encouraging me every step of the way. To my first writing friends as an indie author, you continue to be so much more than I ever imagined. H.E. Bauman and Hayley Turner, you both mean the world to me. The advice, the moral support, the putting up with all my endless questions, the unhinged group chat ... thank you! Hayley, stepping in to read SoD right before emergency beta reading VoF for me on *a one week deadline* was wild. You're magical. (And thank you for all the music that'll go into my audiobooks).

To my tiny but mighty brigade, H.E., Hayley, Sam, Kïrsten, and Lindsey B., I know if I even *hint* at someone hurting my feelings–either in the writing space or personally–you're ready to throw hands. Kïrsten, I guess this time my word was "stasis" hahaha. Thank you for the many heart-to-hearts. Thank you Kaila Desjardins, Jasmine Willis, Mariet Kay, and Amanda Sloothaak for always being so supportive and encouraging.

Sam, thank you for enabling me way too much every step of the way and for somehow ending up as my sounding board. To think you started as a beta reader and ended up as a friend ... who reads almost every version of everything I write (competition with my husband, much? Ha). Ciara Hartford, my way-too-late-night buddy, art mentor, fellow weirdo, thanks for all the things. All the deep conversations and putting up with my spirals, whoops. And sorry for assaulting your eyes with early drawings of my characters. Morgan and Lillie, way to super step up from coworkers to friends and for listening to all my writerly crap at work lol.

Welp the music is here to kick me off stage ...

Alpha readers, beta readers, street team? I can't thank you enough for bringing the hype, being supportive, and reminding me of why I write even when things seem pointless or difficult. Bekah and Jasmine S., thank you for stepping up when I needed emergency beta readers (round two), because working on the late-stage developmental edits just about nearly broke my head.

Last, but not least, THANK YOU readers! Every DM, every wonderful post I've been tagged in, has really kept me going. The messages about readers relating to my characters absolutely make everything worthwhile. Thank you for coming back for more! I hope to see you all again for book three!

VOF Pronunciation Guide

Characters

Aine (AWN-ya): twin sister of Purist leader

Aled (AH-led): father of Gruffud; founder of the clockmaking empire

Alys (AH-lis): ex-royal healer; mother of Ava, wife of Dayfyd

Aneirin (ah-NYE-rin): Carys's deceased brother

Angharad (ang-HA-rad): ex-Brig Guard

Arionna (are-ee-OH-na): older daughter of Isolde and Eurig; older sister to Gwyneth

Ava (AA-vah): daughter of Alys and Dayfyd

Briony (BRY-uh-nee): high priestess of Lugda; Healer

Cahel (CA-hel): older brother of Nuala and daughter of Jacinta

Callum (CAL-uhm): Carys's ex-guard and ex-lover

Carys (KA-ris): fallen Princess of Erleya

Chiyoko (chee-OH-ko): sister of Tiernan; blacksmith, bard wannabe, storyteller

Credia (CREH-dee-ah): Purist Elder

Dayfyd (DAY-fid): husband of Alys; second in command in the Verge

Durvla (DERV-la): older sister of Taig; Shadow Wielder, Basduun, Dreamwalker

Eefa (EE-fa): Skinchanger; sister of Ellynne

Ellynne (EL-in): servant and best friend to Carys

Elviera (el-vee-EH-rah): Alys's birth name

Enidwen (EE-nid-wen): evil enchantress; evil spirit that resides within Carys

Eurig (YOU-rig): former Queen's Guard; father to Gwyneth and Arionna, wife to Rhosyn

Ffion (FEE-on): brown mare originally ridden by Osheen

Ghendor (GEHN-dor): Tiernan's favorite stallion

Gruffud (GRUF-id): son of Aled and Mari; Gwyneth's husband

Gwyneth (GWEN-ith): highborn daughter of Isolde and Eurig; resident of Barr na Cahar; Trraforger

Hamish (HEY-mish): footman to the Davies family

Isobel (IS-oh-bell): Galemaker

Iywan (EYE-wan): ex-royal advisor

Jali (JA-lee): cousin of Alys

Kenna (KEH-nah): daughter of Murtagh Gallager

Kirk (kerk): Uldaran ruffian

Lyon Badeaux: (lee-ON ba-DOH): chief of the Verge

Mari (MAH-ree): wife of Aled, mother of Gruffud

Mirren (MIR-en): Tiernan's favorite mare

Morwenna (mor-WEN-ah): former queen of Erleya

Murtagh (MUR-ta): traveling businessman from Darragh and Bayenbar

Niall (Nile): father to Tiernan and Chiyoko, husband to Haruka; tradesman/craftsman; rebel safehouse coordinator

Nimue (NIM-oo-eh): leader of the Purists

Nuala (NOO-la): 10-year-old from Glinrew, daughter of Jacinta

Odgar (OHD-gar): Prince of Uldarvik

Oksana (uck-SAH-na): Lightweaver; Durvla's shadow wielding trainer

Osheen (Oh-SHEEN): Durvla's childhood friend

Radika (rah-DEE-ka): potions maker

Reneris (aka Neris) (Ren-EAR-is): unofficially adopted daughter of Isolde and Eurig; best friend to Gwyneth

Rheon (REE-on): Lord Commander of all the forces in Erleya

Rhosyn (RO-sin): highborn lady of Barr na Cahar, silent owner of the main bookbinding business
Sage (sage): servant in the Pendry household
Seth (seth): husband to Valdis; originally from Ardall
Sloan (slow-n): brother to Isobel; Verge warrior; Galemaker
Taig (tie-g): 6-year-old brother of Durvla
Tiernan (TEAR-nan): ex-Major of the Royal Brigade and ex-princess's guard; Mimic, Empath, Mind Whisperer
Valdis (VAL-dis): sister to Odgar, wife to Seth

Locations & Other Terms

Ardall (ARD-all): country to the northeast of Erleya
Barr na Cahar (BAR na ca-HAR): capital city in Mainland
Bayenbar (BAY-en-bar): Mainland village
Caldeon (cal-dee-ON): rival country to Ardall
Cluain Baile (CLOO-in bail): village in the Grounds; Durvla's hometown
Daehan (DAY-han): a mythological river
Darragh (DA-rah): Mainland village
Erleya (ear-LAY-ah): the main kingdom, previously ruled by Morwenna the Good
Fiada Purlieu (fee-AH-da pearl-you): entrance to the forest thought to be the Veil to the Otherworld
Moicriach (moy-CREE-ak): village in the cliffs
Siad Nahar (see-AD na-HAR): mysterious sacred land of myth
Uldarvik (OOL-dar-vik): kingdom to the west of Erleya
Basduun (bas-DOON): "death bringer"; a mage of forbidden dark magic; once used to refer to the followers of Enidwen
Basduunai (bas-DOO-nye): plural of *Basduun*

Pantheon (Erleya)

Agryna (Ah-GRIN-ah): goddess of the summer and sun
Aoinlir (awn-LEER): god of the sea and storms; lightning
Bhugearan (byoo-GEAR-ahn): god of Autumn and harvest

VOF Pronunciation Guide

Caiolir (KYE-oh-lair): god of chaos; Underling Prince; Destroyer of Worlds; fallen one
Damarlach (da-MAR-loch): goddess of war, blacksmithing, fire, revenge, terror
Ehlach (EH-loch): moon god; healing and mysticism
Lierwen (LEER-win): the Father; King of the Overworld; the protector; god of justice and honor
Lugda (loog-DA): god of death and the underworld
Magdin (MAG-din): goddess of winter; the veiled one
Ostanha (us-TA-na): god of spring, rebirth, flowers, youth, love
Rhianu (ree-AH-nu): the Mother; fertility and children, life, birth; Queen of the Overworld
Sunlagh (soon-LA): goddess of dreams

Uldaran Pantheon and Phrases

<u>Pantheon</u>
Hofadr (hoh-fah-durr): the Father and ruler of the gods
Amodir (am-oh-deer): the Mother, goddess of fertility, love, beauty
Fyera (fee-eh-ra): goddess of the underworld
Brenjor (bren-jor): god of thunder, protector of humanity

<u>Phrases</u>
Mineh kelsska (min-eh KEL-skah): my beloved
Revna (REV-na): raven
Solni risgur (sol-nee RIS-goo-rr): good morning
Sumarvegr (soo-mar-VAY-grr): Uldaran summer solstice pilgrimage

About

K. V. Meadows is the proud wife and the mother of two young children. With both children on the Autism Spectrum, and one with multiple disabilities, she longed to see more disability inclusion in fantasy.

When K. V. is not poring over words, plotting, or spending hours upon hours making playlists and Pinterest boards for multiple interests, she enjoys spending time with her family, knitting, crocheting, sewing, and playing video games.